"WHO ARE YOU?"

"I'm a man with few choices and fewer joys. Be my joy tonight."

Temptation dragged at Miriam. He was the embodiment of her fantasies. He was a silver-tongued devil. Like the tide raking the beach, his tender words dragged at her will to resist. "I don't trust you."

"Trust doesna come so quickly to people like you and me."

"What do you mean?"

The Border Lord tugged gently on a lock of her hair, pulling her over him again. "You're a fighter, Miriam MacDonald. You wilna stand by and let others wage your battles. The only battle you fight is with yourself. Over your desire for me. You'll win, lassie. I trow you always do."

She hadn't expected praise from this rogue. "You're bold."

"Aye," he said, the warmth of his lips teasingly close. "I'm fair smitten. Kiss me. I need you. . . ."

Books by Arnette Lamb

Border Lord
The Betrothal
Highland Rogue

Published by POCKET BOOKS

BORDER LORD

ARNETTE LAMB

POCKET BOOKS

New York   London   Toronto   Sydney   Tokyo   Singapore

An *Original* Publication of POCKET BOOKS

POCKET BOOKS, a division of Simon & Schuster Inc.
1230 Avenue of the Americas, New York, NY 10020

ISBN: 0-671-77932-X

First Pocket Books printing February 1993

10 9 8 7 6 5 4 3 2 1

POCKET and colophon are registered trademarks of Simon & Schuster Inc.

Cover art by Lina Levy

Printed in the U.S.A.

To Sandra and David,
the Pettystuffers
of Petosky, Michigan

Special thanks to my own pride of literary lions: Susan Wiggs, Joyce Bell, and Barbara Dawson Smith.

Prologue

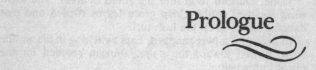

Summer 1713

The stallion burst into a gallop. Duncan threw back his head and inhaled the glorious fragrance of heather. His tartan cape snapped like a loose topsail in a raging wind. His blood coursed with the song of excitement.

Behind him rode a dozen loyal clansmen and one fugitive. Before him lay a quest fit for the bards.

Power seeped into Duncan's bones, and the pounding of hooves deafened him to all sound save the siren of impending danger.

Hadrian's Wall loomed ahead.

In the light of the full moon, the barrier cast a slashing black scar on the fair face of his homeland.

He crouched over the lathered neck of his steed and whispered an ancient word. The mighty crimson bay lunged. Forelegs tucked, the animal sailed over the wall.

And into England.

A battle cry rose in Duncan's throat, but he set his teeth and stifled the motto that would announce his arrival and endanger his mission.

The troop raced across the rolling hills. The land should

look different now, he thought. English demons should crawl from beneath the rocks and peer with evil eyes at the Scottish intruders.

The fanciful image brought Duncan to his senses. He tempered excitement with purpose, and turned southeast to a copse of stunted beech. Once there, he raised a gloved hand to halt his men. Between his tense thighs, the horse's sides fanned like a bellows.

Alone, Duncan rode into the stand of trees. The night wind soughed softly. Crisp green leaves rustled and cast dancing shadows on the lush turf.

To his right, a twig snapped. Ears twitching in alarm, the horse turned toward the noise. Duncan reached for the pistol in his belt.

A small figure, caped from head to forest floor, stepped into the moonlight. The horse snorted. Duncan cocked his pistol. "Who's there?"

The figure gasped and drew back. "'Tis Adrienne Birmingham," she whispered, her voice quivering with fear. "I came alone just as your message said."

Duncan secured the weapon. She'd been his special little friend since the day eight years ago when she'd strewn rose petals in his path and giggled when he'd kissed his new bride.

He leaped from the saddle. "I'm glad you've at last learned obedience."

Putting one hand on her cheek and the other at her waist, Adrienne laughed. "Sir Border Lord. I should have known 'twas you, brother of my heart."

Chuckling, he doffed his cavalier's hat and sketched an elaborate bow. "Your servant, mistress."

"Servant?" She surveyed him, from the black scarf tied pirate fashion over his thick blond hair to his flowing tartan cape and bucket top boots. "Since when," she challenged, "is the infamous Border Lord lackey to any?"

Pride forced him to say, "Since your gullible mother married that greedy, worthless bastard."

"Oh, Duncan." Her hand slipped from her cheek, revealing an ugly bruise. "He beat me!"

Simple loathing turned to fierce hatred. Aubrey Townsend, baron Sinclair, would pay dearly for all his crimes.

2

Duncan Kerr, in the guise of the Border Lord, would mete out justice, but not tonight.

With a familiarity born of friendship and honed by affection, he held out his arms. On a sob, she flew into his embrace. He hugged her close, and as she clung to him, years of treasured memories flashed in his mind. Sprigs of heather tucked into his scabbard. Hunting arrows dressed up with pink ribbons. A merry wedding. Her first dance. A sad funeral.

Her sobs turned to hiccoughs. "When I refused to bed that fat magistrate, the baron had my Charles arrested for treason. Then he hit me and locked me in my room. He said if I didn't do my duty he'd have poor Charles hanged."

Hearing the fear in her voice, Duncan said, "You're certain this Charles is the man you want?"

"Oh, yes. I'd go to the ends of the earth with him."

Duncan held her at arm's length. Had she matured enough to know what she truly wanted? He hoped so. "'Tis no jest, Adrienne, for you'll have to do just that."

She smiled a woman's smile, knowing and resolute. "'Tis my heart's desire."

"Very well. Your adventure awaits." Duncan whistled a signal.

A lone rider guided his horse into the copse and dismounted. "Adrienne?" he called out.

She peered around Duncan. "Charles?"

Then the lovers were in each other's arms. Pledging troths and promising eternity.

Longing pierced Duncan. Would he ever find a woman to pledge away her life and her home for his sake? If not, he prayed for God to cool the need that burned inside him.

He jammed his hat on his head and pulled a bag of coins from his belt. Approaching the lovers, he held out the money to the young man. "I'd not have her come dowerless to you, nor would I have her suffer at your hands."

The young man drew Adrienne to his side and smiled down at her. "My adoration for her has no price."

"Ah, but it does, my young friend," Duncan said sadly, "for you can never return to England."

"That matters not. We'll start a new life across the sea."

"So you shall," said Duncan. "Take this for luck." He

pressed an ancient Roman coin into Charles's hand. "Go quickly now, for the tide won't wait. Get you to Whitley Bay and then to Barbados."

Charles clasped Duncan's arm. "Our first son will bear your name, my lord, and with God's blessing, your kind and good heart."

Duncan smiled and gazed at Adrienne. He thought of his wife, dead these seven years. Would that Roxanne had been more like her sister, Adrienne.

Melancholy stabbed at him. Adrienne stood on tiptoe to kiss his cheek, and whispered, "Please watch out for little Alpin. Don't let the baron break her spirit or . . . worse."

Duncan swallowed hard. "I promise."

He'd never see this spritely lass again. He'd never pluck another thorn from her finger or take a fish from her line. She'd never again call him the brother of her heart. But he would keep his word and protect another wee lassie.

With bittersweet satisfaction he watched them ride away and out of his life.

Angus MacDodd, his second-in-command joined him. At fifty, Angus could still wield his claymore and vanquish opponents two at a time. He could also carve the best toy sailboats in Kildalton. "'Tis Her Majesty's wrath you've gained tonight, my lord. Baron Sinclair will complain again. I'll bet my precious lady crackers on it."

Duncan chuckled. "You can't afford to lose that wager, my friend."

Angus scratched his bushy beard. "She'll send the dragoons this time."

Thoughts of the aging and sickly Stewart monarch swam in Duncan's mind. "Nay, she'll do as she's always done."

"What will you do, my lord?"

"I'll either bribe him or trick him."

As he mounted, Duncan Armstrong Kerr, earl of Kildalton by day, Border Lord by night, conjured a picture of the official emissary Queen Anne would send.

"Sweet Saint Ninian," he swore, "he'll be another gouty minor lord with an empty purse and a mind to match."

4

Fall 1713

"Sweet Saint Margaret," Miriam swore, "he'll be a gout-ridden Scotsman with braids in his hair and beer on his breath."

Her companion, Alexis Southward, laughed. "Does that mean you're finally going to tell me what we're doing here?"

Miriam quelled her anger. "We're going to see a bull-headed Scotsman who can't stay on his side of the wall."

"Let's just pray he's sensible, Miriam. I do so hate it when these bickering men don't take you seriously. 'Tisn't a pretty sight, the way you can strip a stubborn man of his pride."

"Nor do I relish the exercise." Miriam flicked the reins and guided her horse through a gap in Hadrian's Wall. Behind her, the wheels of the luggage wagon creaked under the load. Seated atop the trunks and wig boxes, her twin scribes, Saladin and Salvador chatted in their second language, Español. The carriage, empty but for food and drink, brought up the rear. A dozen cavalrymen, more interested in filling their bellies than performing their duties, guarded the well-stocked conveyance. Where the men stationed themselves mattered little, for the only danger they'd encountered since leaving London had been in the forest near Nottingham.

A pack of hungry wild dogs had crept into camp. Miriam's sleuthhound, a female named Verbatim, had charged the intruders. When faced with a snarling protector that weighed six stone and stood waist high to a man, the trespassers yelped like frightened puppies and scurried into the woods.

Now Verbatim loped ahead, long ears flapping, black nose skimming the ground.

Once clear of the ancient wall, Miriam gazed at the land.

Scotland. Her home. Long buried memories, like the mirages she'd seen in the deserts of Araby, shimmered to life. She shivered. No longer a respected diplomat in the court of Queen Anne, Miriam saw herself as a frightened child of four. Instead of the rolling hills of the Border, gilded by the setting sun and kissed by the chill of fall, she saw a frozen glen, blanketed with snow and splattered with the blood of her clan.

"Miriam?"

She turned. A smile of understanding wreathed Alexis's face. Her pale blue eyes swam with sympathy. She maneuvered her mount close and extended a gloved hand. Miriam took it.

Squeezing gently, Alexis said, "There are no demons here, my friend. Only memories, fond and bad. 'Tis all in the way you choose to see them."

Miriam sighed. Melancholy dragged at her. For twenty years, Alexis had been mother, sister, and consoling aunt, as the situation dictated. She could give advice in nine languages, scold in fourteen. Miriam understood them all. Together they'd traveled from the lavish courts of the czars to the exotic palaces of Persia. Discreet to a fault and as loyal as a true mother, Alexis could be trusted with the most delicate of state secrets. On an hour's notice, she could pack up their household and move them cross country or continent with the skill and speed of the queen's own steward.

"Thank you." Miriam gave the helping hand a last squeeze, then shifted to a more comfortable position in the sidesaddle.

"So," said Alexis, "tell me why Her Majesty would be sending the star of her diplomatic corps to a gouty, drunken Scot?"

"Her Majesty would have sent me to hell, I think, had Lord Shepton not intervened."

In her most motherly voice, Alexis said, "You shouldn't have told her she didn't know what she was doing."

Miriam ground her teeth. "That's not what I said."

"Oh, no? Then the gossips must've been wrong. Let me guess the truth of it. Her Majesty said 'twas time you were wed. You did a merry sett of verbal dancing, but your brilliant effort went for naught, for the queen knows you too well. She commanded you. You grew angry. You must be slipping."

Miriam tensed. Her mount sidestepped. Gathering the reins, she considered telling Alexis the truth about her quarrel with the queen. For years Miriam had asked Anne to bring to justice the Highlanders who'd murdered Miriam's family. For years Anne had refused. This time Miriam had demanded. Anne had become so furious Miriam had feared the sickly monarch might swoon. But Anne had rallied and threatened to betroth Miriam to the minister of Baltic affairs.

Out of loyalty to Alexis, Miriam told a part of the truth. "I had every right to question her. The men in her service do. And if she tried to force one of them to marry a dottering lech, they'd trip over their own tongues in their haste to object."

"True. But losing your temper and arguing with her, not to mention insulting her, no matter how delicately, was foolhardy."

The queen's unfairness gnawed at Miriam. Everyone else on the negotiating team had been excused from court to pursue their private concerns. But not Miriam. "I didn't set out to insult Her Majesty. I only reminded her that negotiating contracts for marriages or peace was my expertise, not hers. She can't have it both ways, Lexie. One moment she orders me to Utrecht to end the War of the Spanish Succession. The next moment she expects me to grovel like a 'tween stairs maid who's grateful that a footman wants to be her beau."

A rueful smile lent a timeless elegance to the older woman's face. "You don't have a beau."

Girlhood dreams shone brightly, then faded. The horses started down another of the rolling hills. Miriam braced herself with a hand on the pommel. "Nor will I ever, it seems."

"There's no disputing that. Five and twenty is a bit long in the tooth for courting."

"Ha! You're eight and forty, and you preened like a virgin when that French count fell off his horse to gain your attention and your favors."

Alexis Southward, onetime duchess of Challenbroke, smoothed the folds of her velvet riding habit. In a throaty voice, she said, "Gervais was a delightful diversion. Need I remind you that his son was . . . shall we say *eager* to divert you as well."

"I'll believe that when the queen conceives her eighteenth child."

"Honte a toi. You should not say such a thing."

"I know. But the cavalier didn't want me, you sly creature. He wanted advance information on the treaty."

"Perhaps," said Alexis, her voice rife with disbelief. "But so long as you pine for a Sir Lancelot who divides his time between defending the poor and domineering his way into your bed, you'll never find a suitable husband."

A gaggle of honking geese flew overhead in a wavering V formation. A lone pair of birds brought up the rear. Mates, thought Miriam. Her girlish dreams might never come true, but she had no intention of wedding a man she couldn't respect. He'd also have to best her at chess and outwit her, but not too often.

"Dreaming of Sir Lancelot again?"

"Oh, bother it, Lexie. It makes no difference anyway."

Alexis chuckled. "Tell me about this gouty Scotsman. It's not like you to be so secretive."

Remembering her disastrous audience with the queen, Miriam upbraided herself again for not choosing her words more carefully. She'd expected gratitude from the queen for the success at Utrecht. An orphan without a dowry, Miriam had earned the queen's generosity. Instead, the angry sovereign had banished Miriam to the Border for another negotiating task.

"And should you fail," the queen had said, "you will forfeit any chance of bringing the Glenlyon Campbells to justice. Although why you're so determined to dredge up the crime, I cannot imagine."

Angry and exhausted, Miriam had replied, "Your parents weren't butchered."

"How dare you!" Seething, Anne threw down her scepter. "Strike a peace on the Border, Miriam, or you'll marry the minister of Baltic affairs."

Even now Miriam cringed at the thought of living in so cold a climate. She breathed deeply of the crisp fall air, ripe with the promise of winter. Perhaps she'd linger awhile in Scotland. The queen wouldn't be the wiser if Miriam dawdled in the Borders. She needed a respite from England's politics. A winter sojourn in Scotland seemed the perfect answer. Could she face the snow?

Aye. The alternative gave her courage. She'd toast her toes before a roaring peat fire, warm her belly with mulled wine, and dream of a hero who could slay dragons and discuss Socrates.

In a nearby vale, a roebuck with a magnificent rack of antlers stalked a flirtatious doe. Verbatim quivered with the need to give chase, but the dog was too well trained. The agile doe dashed away, kicking up fallen leaves in her wake. The prime buck threw back his head and trumpeted his frustration. The doe stopped and twitched her white rump patch. When the male resumed his pursuit, she darted away again.

Verbatim went back to her inspection of Scotland.

"I do so love a courtship, don't you?" said Alexis.

"Courtship? I'm here to settle what might be a war, not to arrange a betrothal."

Alexis rolled her eyes to the heavens and blew out her breath. "I was speaking of the rut going on over there. 'Twas a jest, Miriam."

"Oh."

Humor had always been lost on Miriam. She wanted to join in, to get caught up in the amusing subtilties that others found so entertaining. She could wade through a stream of rhetoric, but couldn't catch an innuendo. She recognized it for the fault it was, but had no idea how one learned how to be jolly.

They were joined by her escort, the leader of Her Majesty's Fifth Regiment of Horse. A gust of wind ruffled the white plume in his cap, and the fading sunlight lent an orange cast to the golden regalia on his uniform.

She nodded. "Captain Higginbotham. Won't you join us?"

He drew himself up in the saddle. Leather creaked. Clean-shaven and as neat as a parson on Sunday, he spent the noon hour polishing his boots and scabbard.

"Almost there, Lady Miriam. I'll send a man ahead to announce you," he said, staring at her breasts.

How common, she thought. How degrading. But she was accustomed to such base behavior. Smiling pleasantly, she said, "That's very thorough of you, Captain. I think, however, that just this once, we shall forego protocol and simply pop in."

When he opened his mouth to protest, she added, "I'll be sure to tell your uncle, Lord Drummond, of your unwavering competence in the field. I have been truly impressed. The czar's personal guard couldn't have done better."

He toyed with the cuff of his gauntlets, and tapped his teeth together. The annoying habits signaled his disapproval.

Alexis said, "You will, of course, want to lead us in, *ma capitaine.*"

"Thank you, my lady." He nodded curtly, fell back, and ordered his men to advance. Amid the rattling of swords and the pounding of hooves, the soldiers began moving.

"Well?" prompted Alexis, eyeing the double column of soldiers as they passed.

Over the jingling of harnesses, Miriam said, "Well what?"

"Why are you being so secretive about this mission?"

Mission? thought Miriam. Predicament seemed a more fitting term. "Oh, Lexie. I'm not. I've told you everything I know about the trouble here. The queen said, in so many words, that I overstepped myself. She thinks I've become too world-wise for a mere woman. Sending me here without telling me what's going on was my punishment."

Alexis spat a curse that she'd learned at her father's knee. "How swiftly my royal cousin forgets that you gained your experience in service to her—mere woman or no."

"I know," said Miriam, thinking of the years she'd served the queen. Miriam's apprenticeship had begun when the then Princess Anne had taken in the orphaned Miriam. At the age of five she'd often ferried the sad message to Prince George that yet another of the queen's children had died. Remembered pity softened her next words. "She also said that since I knew her mind so well, she needn't waste a royal breath explaining the participants or the particulars of the problems here."

A whistle escaped Alexis's lips. "She *was* angry at you."

Miriam studied the horizon. "Indeed. The burr in her voice was as thick as the towels in a Turkish bath."

"'Tis a wonder you still have your head. 'Twould be a pity, though, to let all that glorious red hair go to waste."

The compliment brightened Miriam's black mood. But she still couldn't bring herself to tell Alexis what had truly angered the queen. "When she told me that I could either marry the Baltic minister or earn my keep in the usual way, I told her I would sooner join the harem of King Ahmed."

Alexis made the sign of the cross. "She knows how much you hate the cold."

"Aye, she does. I decided to fall back and regroup. I just didn't think I'd be doing it in the Borders."

"You'll make quick work of this dispute. How will you begin?"

Miriam hated being ignorant, but what she knew about the Scotsman wouldn't fill a thimble. "I'm not sure."

"I have every confidence in you, my dear. Now, tell me. What did Her Majesty say about the Englishman?"

"Little. His name is Aubrey Townsend, Baron Sinclair. He was the one who petitioned for assistance, accusing the Scotsman of kidnapping, thievery, etcetera. Oh, and she commanded me to visit the Scotsman first."

"That's odd, even if the Englishman did bring about a complaint. She's always careful not to show favoritism to

11

her countrymen. Maybe she knows the Scot. Or—" Mischief sparkled in her eyes. "He could be a cousin of sorts."

"I wouldn't think so. He leads a clan of Lowlanders. I don't imagine they have any ties to the Stewarts—on either side of the blanket." Realizing the slight, Miriam rushed to say, "Oh, do forgive me, Lexie."

Alexis waved her hand in dismissal. "'Twas nothing. What's the fellow's name?"

"Duncan Armstrong Kerr, the earl of Kildalton."

"Sounds very Scottish . . . and promising. Has he a countess?"

"Not anymore. He's widowed, according to the innkeeper back in Bothly Green."

"Very promising indeed, my dear."

Miriam had to shield her eyes from the setting sun to see her friend's face. "For you, me, or the negotiations?"

Alexis wagged her finger. "You, of course." Then she gazed at the rolling hills and rocky terrain. "Perhaps Sir Lancelot waits o'er yonder hill. Him or the legendary Border Lord they spoke of in Bothly Green. Then you'd be preoccupied with matters of the heart. A legend could sweep you off your feet, beguile you with poetry, and cart you away to his bower of love."

At the edge of her vision, Miriam saw Verbatim perched on the hill in question, her long tail arched over her back, her nose in the air. The animal had scented something. She whined in fright.

"Wait here." Miriam kicked her horse into a canter and raced up the hill. At the summit, she gasped, and flooded her lungs with the biting odor of stale smoke.

In the glen below stood the charred timbers and hearthstone of what had been a crofter's hut. On the periphery of the blackened field she saw a freshly mounded grave. She slumped, wondering if the destruction had been the result of a carelessly banked fire or a consequence of the trouble she was here to settle.

If the latter was true, she'd need more than diplomatic flummery to bring about a peace. She conjured a picture of Duncan Armstrong Kerr, and saw a gouty, stubborn Scotsman who would challenge her expertise and try to bully her into taking his side.

But the man she encountered an hour later challenged her in a different way.

Standing in the common room of Kildalton Castle, Miriam was reminded of Louis XIV's least gifted fool the day he had once again failed to amuse his sovereign.

Pity and confusion overwhelmed her.

Dressed in a waistcoat and knee breeches of forest green velvet, a crimped and powdered wig aslant on his head, and spectacles thicker than church glass perched on his nose, the man looked more like a disheveled jester than the lord of the keep.

"Have you brought the peacocks?" he said, hope dancing in green eyes that were distorted by the lenses.

"The peacocks," she repeated, stalling for enough time to form a reasonable reply.

Behind her, Alexis coughed to hide a giggle. Saladin and Salvador stood frozen, their mouths open, their eyes as large as the earl's.

To Lexie, she pointedly said, "You'll want to warm yourself by the fire. Take the twins with you."

Alexis nodded and led the boys to the far side of the room.

Turning back, Miriam said, "Where were we?"

"The peacocks. They haven't molted, have they?" he asked in the clipped speech of a scholar. "If so, I hope you brought the creatures anyway." He held up a contraption of orange-brown feathers attached to a hook. "Can't catch a fish with a pheasant. These are as useless as another coal in Newcastle."

For some reason, he laughed. His wig jiggled and shed a handful of gray powder on the rounded shoulders of his waistcoat. Then he took a faltering step toward her.

That's when she noticed his shoes; they were on the wrong feet.

Through a shroud of compassion for the poor fellow, she dredged up her kindest tone. "You've mistaken me for someone else, my lord." Executing a perfect curtsy, she said, "I haven't brought you peacocks."

Frowning, he poked the contraption into his pocket, but when he withdrew his hand, the hook clung to his finger. He shook his hand, but to no avail. Finally, he plucked the hook free. Grunting, he clapped it on his sleeve. "You're travelers.

ARNETTE LAMB

How splendid." He wiped his hand on his breeches, leaving a thin smear of blood on the green velvet. Shuffling toward her and extending his hand, he said, "Allow me to present myself and welcome you properly. I'm Duncan Kerr, eighth earl of Kildalton."

She took his hand and was surprised to find blisters on his palm. Her logical mind stumbled, then settled on the inconsistency. How had he gotten blisters? Plucking feathers? She didn't think so. Why would an absentminded, near-blind nobleman have the hands of a workman?

He released her, then tipped his wigged head to the side, as if waiting. Through a haze of possibilities, she fell back on manners. "Thank you, my lord. I'm Lady Miriam MacDonald."

"Ah, you're a Scot."

She tried, but couldn't pull her gaze from his. Intelligence and something else lurked in his eyes. Instinct told her that he had the upper hand. Necessity demanded she take control. He knew the problems here. She didn't. But she couldn't admit her ignorance.

"Father!" bellowed a childish voice behind her. She turned to see a gangly lad with pitch dark hair dash into the room and to the earl's side.

Over a tartan kilt, the boy wore a man's scabbard and sword buckled around his waist. The heavy weapon scraped the stone flags and the belt dragged at the plaid she recognized as the symbol of the Kerr clan.

"There's soldiers in the stable," he declared, his voice breaking. "English soldiers! We must to arms." He tried to draw the sword, but succeeded in disturbing the pleats of his kilt. The garment slipped beneath the swordbelt, revealing pale buttocks and skinny legs.

As the earl leaned over to right the garment, he whispered to the boy, who froze in rapt attention.

Like fingers drawn to the rough edge of a ragged thumbnail, Miriam's senses toyed with the idea that something was wrong here. How could this bumbling man command the clans of Kerr and Armstrong? He didn't look capable of kidnapping or any of the charges brought against him.

"Lady Miriam," he said, "this rowdy lad and defender of the true faith is my son Mal—"

14

"Father!" snapped the boy. "You're doing it again."

"So, I am." The earl fished in his pockets, retrieved a scrap of paper, and squinted at it. "Ah, yes. My son Rob Roy."

The now-beaming boy bowed from the waist. Miriam stood stupefied, for the earl couldn't even remember his son's name. Another oddity, she thought. Distracted, she managed to say, "A pleasure, Master Rob Roy, I'm sure."

The boy whispered to his father. Miriam's mind hopscotched through the conflicting bits of information, trying to draw a logical conclusion. According to the queen, the Englishman swore this Scotsman was a Border reiver who led an army of thieves.

Again Miriam cursed herself for losing her patience with Anne and gaining her wrath. If only Miriam had held her tongue, she'd know the peculiars of the trouble here. She'd sit down with Duncan Kerr and ask him direct questions. Then she'd do the same with his English neighbor. Then she'd make peace between them. As it was, she didn't even know what questions to ask. Now she'd have to sleuth out the truth.

Like discovering a path out of the wilderness, she found a starting place, a tangible. "Excuse me, my lord," she murmured, and headed for the castleyard to investigate.

2

Bursting at the seams of his self-imposed idiocy, Duncan watched her go. Through the lenses she appeared as a dark red blur. Over the rims of the spectacles she looked like a vision in crimson. He surveyed the tilt of her chin, the set of her shoulders, the sway of her hips, and the purpose in her stride. The impulsive exit of his charming guest spelled trouble.

Why was she going outside? And why hadn't she told him her reasons for coming to Kildalton? No flighty female, the Lady Miriam MacDonald and her diplomatic accomplishments were legend.

Oh, but her mission here was doomed. She'd secure no peace in the Border, for there was none to be had. Her fancy rhetoric would be wasted on a dispute that involved burned-out farms and freshly mounded graves. Duncan Kerr would deal with his English neighbor in his own way. But first, he had to convince her of his innocence in the Border feud. Then he'd send this delectable diplomat and her odd entourage packing.

Quickly, too, for the Border Lord had work to do.

A pity, he thought, that he couldn't have met her under different circumstances. He liked women with brains and experience, and if the rumors were true, she possessed the lion's share of both.

She also had skin with the luster of polished pearls and eyes as gray and intriguing as snow-laden clouds. Perfect poise and a cleavage that made his lips pucker seemed cruel wrappings on a package he couldn't afford to open. She *must* see him as a bumpkin with fishing lures on his mind and cowardice in his heart.

Over the chatter of his son and Lady Miriam's traveling companion, Duncan chose a plan of action that would turn Miriam MacDonald upside down. That decided, he pulled the bellcord to summon his housekeeper, then turned his attention to his only offspring.

The kilt-clad boy stood before the two lads in Lady Miriam's party. An interesting pair, they were: one dark as a Moor and thinly built, with the obsidian eyes and wooly black hair of his African ancestors. The other boy had the noble profile and olive complexion of a Spanish grandee. Yet there were similarities in the lads: identical widow's peaks in their foreheads and spaces between their front teeth.

Why would a diplomat travel with two lads? Duncan stepped forward to greet them.

Before he could accomplish that, Lady Miriam glided back into the room. Curiosity over the young men fled like trout before a pheasant lure.

She moved with the grace of a deer, and smiled with the assurance of a queen. What tidbit had she gleaned in his castleyard that gave her such confidence? His people were loyal; none would betray his disguise.

Assuming the blank expression he'd practiced since the lookout had brought word of her imminent arrival, Duncan shuffled toward her. "Did you forget something? I could have had a servant fetch it."

A winsome smile illuminated her heart-shaped face. "I did indeed, Lord Duncan. I neglected to introduce you to my friends."

He could grow to hate that placating tone, unless, of course, she were lying naked in his bed and whispering

17

endearments in his ear. He almost smiled at the prospect of making love to so fine a lady. But now was not the time for smiling or seducing. If he wasn't careful, he'd give himself away.

"They're twins, Father," declared his son, still tugging at his tartan, which was precariously close to landing in a heap on the floor. "And they're twelve years old."

Lady Miriam stepped between the boys and draped an arm over each of their shoulders, which were almost on a level with hers. "My lord, may I present Salvador and Saladin Cortez, the finest scribes in all of Europe and England. Gentlemen, this is Lord Duncan, the earl of Kildalton."

Each greeted him pleasantly, and why not? They'd learned their manners from the queen of protocol. Duncan shook their hands and noticed other peculiarities: ink stains and modesty.

Blinking like the fool he pretended to be, he said, "Scribes? Well, isn't that a fine occupation. I always have difficulty with numbering pages. Get them all ajumble every time. I suppose age truly has little bearing on some achievements, does it not, gentlemen?"

If expressions were words, Duncan faced disgust in two languages, both foreign. Saladin frowned, his mahogany-hued skin oddly light at the corners of his mouth. Puffing out his chest, Salvador shot Duncan a measuring glare and found him wanting.

Smiling innocuously, Duncan said, "You've met my son, Mal—"

"Rob Roy," Malcolm put in.

Duncan wanted to blister the boy. He could hate his name, refuse to answer to it, but not, by God, in front of the emissary of the queen. Vowing to have another talk with his stubborn son, Duncan breathed a sigh of relief when his housekeeper, Mrs. Elliott, bustled into the room.

She glanced at his disguise, humor twinkling in her eyes. Drawing up the skirt of her apron, she buried her pug nose in the cloth and faked a sneeze.

"Welcome to Kildalton Castle, my lady," said Mrs. Elliott. "I've just prepared rooms for you. If you'll follow me, I'll show you to them."

Thinking of the rooms his guest would occupy, Duncan relaxed. A maze of tunnels in the castle gave him access to every room. The secret passageway outside her chamber would allow him to eavesdrop on her conversations. By pushing aside the panel in the wardrobe, he could enter the room and inspect any correspondence to or from London.

He bowed from the waist. "I'll say goodnight then."

Malcolm cradled the unwieldy sword and bounded up the stairs. The scribes and the other lady with an oddly familiar face followed.

To Duncan's surprise, Lady Miriam slid into a chair by the hearth. "Will you join me, Lord Duncan?"

He glanced at the clock. The need for vengeance thrummed through him. In less than an hour, his men would gather near Hadrian's Wall. He would lead them across the Border, where they would reclaim a herd of stolen sheep. Would that he could avenge the deaths of his crofters. His conscience plagued him, but he could not take the lives of poor English tenants. He wanted a peaceable end to the violence.

He took the seat facing Lady Miriam. "Can we keep this short?" he whined. "I have a batch of owl feathers to clean."

Tracing the grain of the wood on the chair arm, she absently said, "How enterprising. 'Tis wonderful to be off that horse."

He was prepared for rhetoric. "Surely you didn't ride all the way—" He swallowed the words "from London," for he wasn't supposed to know who she was or why she'd come.

Gray eyes fastened on his. "But of course. I simply refused to take another ship so soon. I do love to ride, as does Lady Alexis."

His curiosity about the lady overrode his need for haste and discretion. "Who is she?"

Not batting an eye, she said, "Alexis Southward."

That caught him off guard. Alexis Southward was the most talked about bastard of the late Charles II and cousin to the queen.

"I was wondering," his guest continued in a congenial tone, "why there were no soldiers on the battlements when we arrived, and yet just moments ago, at least fifty armed men manned the walls."

Hell and Hogmanay! That's why she'd gone outside. The wench was as sneaky as a badger on the prowl. But Duncan Kerr could match her. "I'm sure I don't know. I shall have to ask that burly fellow who trains them. Perhaps we always have so many guards. No. We are a peaceable people. I'm certain your safety is at the root of it."

"I see."

An understatement, for she saw too much. His first instinct was to plead exhaustion and flee. His men awaited. But watching her, so sedate and appealing on the surface, yet conniving and clever beneath, Duncan decided he wanted to play. "I wish I could," he said on a sigh.

She blinked and glanced at the portrait of Duncan's father that hung over the hearth. "Could what, my lord?"

He sighed again and adjusted the ridiculous spectacles. "See. I wish I would see even half so well as normal people. I just pray my son's eyes never grow as weak as mine."

Her fingers began to strum on the wood. The tick-ticking of her fingernails filled the room. Duncan applauded himself; she wasn't as composed as she let on.

She caught him staring at her hands. The strumming stopped. "The soldiers who accompanied me will stay the night in your guardhouse. They'll be returning to London on the morrow."

She'd accompany those prissy English soldiers, too, if Duncan had his way. "I'm sorry you'll be leaving so soon."

"Oh, but I'm not leaving."

He gasped and drew his hands to his chest. "But we can't entertain a lady here. That is, we offer shelter to any traveler. 'Tis the Scottish way. But I have my work. You'll interfere with my schedule."

"I promise not to disturb you too much."

The thick glass gave him a magnified view of her cleavage. Flawless, satiny skin rose and fell enticingly. Poor vision, he decided, had its advantages. So did he at the moment. But the instant she confessed her purpose and stated her intentions, he would better know how to deal with her. "Who will escort you home?" he said. "You can't travel alone. 'Tis too dangerous."

"I know." She smiled much too sweetly. "I saw the burned farm . . . and the graves."

What the devil had she been doing so far off the road? If she knew people had died, what else did she know? Those calculating eyes stayed fixed on his, but Duncan wasn't about to reveal the sorrow he felt for the crofters. "The sheep can be replaced." And avenged. "My steward will take care of the matter."

Her fine eyebrows shot up. "You buried sheep in those graves? Ah, I see. And you blistered your hands in the doing."

He felt as if he were picking his way through a bramble bush. One slip, and he'd feel the prick of her thorns. Vowing to outsmart her, he said, "They were good, sturdy animals that never did any harm. Not as smart as fish, though. Now you take a Scottish salmon. You can't fool them with just any lure. But when they take the bait . . ." He showed her his injured palms. "They'll make you pay the price."

Her eyes stayed fixed on his hands. "Do you always plant crosses on the graves of slaughtered sheep?"

She thought she had him. Scratching his wig, he said, "I couldn't say for certain. To hazard a guess, I'd say they were valuable animals. People get attached to them, I suppose. Like I get attached to my fish. Did I tell you about the sunny trout I caught last May Day? Weighed almost two stone. People came from as far away as Carlisle to see it. Mrs. Elliott served it with a cream sauce that was simply divine."

"No. You didn't tell me about the fish. But if you would," she said slowly, concisely, "please tell me who burned out the crofters. For my own safety, of course."

Safety? She persisted and lied with a skill even the duchess of Perth would envy. "'Twas my neighbor to the south. He's responsible. What a bother he is. Why, a fortnight ago he poached my finest peacocks. Stay away from him."

"That would be Aubrey Townsend."

If she knew the name, she knew the particulars. Why didn't she just come out and say why she was here? He wasn't about to ask. Let her think him more interested in fishing than feuding.

"I believe," she went on, "that he's also called baron Sinclair."

Duncan couldn't stop his lip from curling in revulsion.

21

"Baron Sin he's called on this side of the wall. A lady like you shouldn't go anywhere near him. So you see, you're better off departing with the cavalry."

Her gaze didn't falter. "What do they call you?"

He fought the urge to squirm like a guilty schoolboy. Dredging up a sweet smile of his own, he said, "Most often they call me—'my lord.' Unless, of course, they've come for one of my prize fishing lures. Then they've been known to call me a genius. I make the best lures in Scotland."

"I'm certain you do, my lord." She folded her arms at her waist, which pushed her enticing breasts above the square neckline of her stylish riding habit. The single ruby she wore on a thin gold chain disappeared in the folds of her cleavage. "Will you retaliate? Will you punish baron Sinclair?" she asked.

Duncan's skin grew warm. "Me?" he squeaked, his mind on the hidden ruby. "Can you truly see me bounding over the Border, sword in hand? Besides, my son would never part with the family blade."

"Yes, of course," she said, suspicion on her lovely features.

He wanted to pick her apart like a clock and see what made her mind tick. But he couldn't afford so pleasant a challenge. She had to see him as the innocent victim. Then she had to go. Straightaway. So did he.

Faking a yawn, he stretched out his arms and got to his feet. "Pardon me, but it's well past my bedtime. I've had a trying day of sharpening hooks and writing in my journal. There's still my owl feathers."

She rose. "Then forgive me for detaining you, my lord. We do, after all, have plenty of time to chat."

Duncan stopped so fast he almost tripped on his own feet. "I don't understand."

"You will, I assure you."

Shocked, Duncan realized that he'd woefully underestimated his adversary. Sinclair had applied to the queen, and she'd sent her prized settler of international squabbles. The clever red-haired wench had managed to dismiss her guard and entrench herself in his household—indefinitely. "What about the cavalry? You can't wander about without an escort."

"Don't trouble yourself about my safety. 'Tis all arranged, I assure you. You have owl feathers to clean, and I—well, I shan't bore you with my affairs."

When he didn't move, she held out her arm. "We can walk up together and you can show me my room."

He took her arm when he wanted to wring her neck. Surely in all of Christendom there couldn't be a more wily, tenacious female than the incorruptible Miriam MacDonald. Why couldn't she have been open to bribery like the other emissaries? Duncan Kerr would have to deal with her, but tonight his schedule was full. The Border Lord had a pressing engagement with revenge.

Once in her chamber, Miriam leaned against the heavy oaken door. Iron studs and metal bands pressed into her back, yet she was keenly aware of the shuffling footfalls as the earl retreated to his own room.

Conversing for an hour with him had drained her, as if she'd spent an evening mediating an argument between a Jew and a Christian on the validity of Jesus Christ.

"Leave it be for the night, Miriam, else you'll never get to sleep." Alexis had donned her gown and robe. Her dark hair lay in a thick plait over her shoulder. She shook the wrinkles from Miriam's night rail, then laid it over the bed. "Come, I'll help you undress."

After a fortnight of primitive camps and poorly furnished inns, the bed looked inviting. Miriam couldn't resist touching the plump feather mattress or sighing with relief at the thought of sleeping in comfort. "You're right, of course."

She removed her hat, jacket, and blouse. Alexis stepped behind her and started to work on the lacings of her stays.

"Where are the twins?" Miriam asked, pulling the pins from her hair.

"Beyond my room." She pointed to an opened door. "Which is through there."

To the left of the portal stood an enormous vanity in Jacobean mahogany, a lighted, twelve-hour candle on top; to the right of the door, next to the hearth, stood a spotless cheval glass and a native basket overflowing with fragrant dried heather and gorse.

Two massive wardrobes and a washstand, complete with

fancy soap and thick towels, filled the opposite wall. A bank of velvet draped windows lined the outside wall. An assortment of nubby woolen rugs, each bearing a blazing sun, the symbol of the Kerr clan, dotted the stone floor.

Her last mission had entailed months spent amid the pomp and circumstance of European nobility. Miriam embraced the cozy comfort of this Scottish castle.

Once free of her chemise and stockings, she slipped the gown over her head and sat down on the vanity stool. Alexis began her nightly ritual of brushing Miriam's hair.

"That feels wonderful," she said, her scalp tingling from the drag of the boar bristles.

"Hum. A bath would be heaven, but 'tis too late to inconvenience the staff." Yawning, Alexis separated Miriam's hair and began to braid it.

Miriam glanced at the candle. Her fatigue vanished.

"What is it?" said Alexis.

Miriam slid the candle closer. In the mirror, her gaze met Alexis's. "This wick has been burning for two hours. We arrived only an hour ago. Don't you find that intriguing? Look at the room. Lady's soap, the clean linens. He knew we were coming. But how? He left the impression that we were merely travelers."

Alexis squeezed her eyes shut, creating a fine web of wrinkles. On a groan, she said, "I thought you were done for the night. Besides, country castles always offer shelter to travelers. Haven't you heard of Scottish hospitality?"

Miriam stared at the telltale candle. "Of course I have."

"Then who's to say that candle hasn't been lighted before tonight?"

"Me, that's who. The coincidence is too great. Remember the housekeeper said she'd just prepared these rooms."

"Oh, Miriam." Alexis shook the brush. "Given enough time, you could find a flaw in the Ten Commandments."

Undeterred, Miriam said, "I know this—several things about the earl and his household are not what they seem."

"All right." Alexis pitched the brush onto the vanity. "But if we're going to pick apart this poor sod, I insist we do it by the fire."

Contrite, Miriam said, "I'm sorry. Let's just say good-night. You're cold and tired, and I'm—"

"Mistaken." Alexis chuckled without humor. "I'm wide awake, and as anxious as a beggar on Alms Day." She pulled Miriam to her feet. Although shorter than Miriam by half a head, and almost twice her age, Alexis had a grip like steel. "But if I didn't insist that you sleep at least once a day, your head would never touch a pillow. When you do retire, you never sleep the night through." A maternal smile, full of love and understanding, glowed on her face.

Miriam hugged her, bussed her satiny cheek, then pulled her to the hearth. Seated cross-legged on a rug like young girls defying a nanny's curfew, they faced each other. Miriam related the story of the sudden appearance of the armed guards on the walls.

"I wondered why you went outside. I thought you might be fetching Verbatim from the kennel."

"No, but I'll manage to move her in here tomorrow."

Humor sprung from Alexis's lips. "Remember the time in Rouen, when the duke of Burgundy planted a spy under your bed?"

Miriam laughed, too. "Poor fellow. Instead of gleaning information from me on the bride's dowry, he took one look at Verbatim and babbled on for hours about the concessions the duke was willing to make for his son."

"You won a few more from him, as I recall."

Pride infused Miriam. "A woman needs more than pretty promises from a courting swain."

"I have every confidence in you, my dear."

"Good. Now that I've met the earl I think I'll need it."

A horse nickered. Miriam jumped up, ran to the window, and pulled back the drape. A cloud passed over the quarter moon, throwing a blanket of darkness over the yard.

Alexis joined her. "What do you see? 'Tis black as a Cornish cave down there."

Miriam peered into the gloom. Below lay a walled court-yard or garden. She pressed her cheek to the cool glass. A shadow moved. "There," she whispered, pointing to a moving shadow.

"I don't see anything."

Squinting, her foot tapping as she waited for the moon-light to return, Miriam tried to follow the progress of the darkened shape. Was it a person or merely the night breeze rustling the bushes in the courtyard? She strained until her eyes ached but she couldn't see enough to make a decision.

Clouds continued to shroud the moon, but she knew as surely as the sun would rise tomorrow that she'd seen a man slipping from the castle.

"If someone was there, he's gone now," said Alexis, pulling Miriam back to the hearth. "'Twas probably a maid sneaking out for a tryst with a stableboy."

"What time is it?" Miriam asked.

"Just past ten o'clock."

Miriam paced the floor, trying to piece together the information.

"All right," said Alexis. "Tell me everything."

Like an anchor tethered to her thoughts, the contradictions about the earl and his household pulled at Miriam. She relayed each one. By the time she finished, the candle was another hour shorter.

Alexis slapped her thigh. "Well, I agree that your observations are enough to make a saint seem circumspect. But I think you should take your time. You don't want to move too fast."

"True." Miriam turned her palm up. "Tomorrow I must tell him who I am and why I'm here. Now. Honestly, Lexie. Tell me what you think of him."

Propping an elbow on her knee, Alexis rested her chin on her hand. "In spite of what you said, I think he's adorable. Don't squinch your face up like that. You'll wrinkle before you're thirty."

"Heaven forbid I should wrinkle."

"If you weren't so determined to give your heart to a doer of gallant deeds, you might see something appealing in the earl. He's better than a fat ambassador who speaks fluent German."

"I intend to rule my own life and live it in Bath."

"But you'd like it better if Sir Lancelot were there."

Miriam groaned. "Could we please concern ourselves with the earl of Kildalton?"

Alexis laughed. "That boy of his. What's his name? Rob Roy." She rolled her eyes. "Have you ever seen a child who needed a mother so?"

"Never mind the boy. There's something about the earl,

Lexie. He looks like a bumbling idiot, but I see a confidence or power in him."

"Sometimes I wonder," said Alexis, staring into the fire, "how a woman with so little intimate experience with men can be so observant. Alas, I find him intriguing, too."

Immensely flattered, Miriam stretched and fought off a yawn, "I'll talk to him first thing in the morning."

Alexis got to her feet. "First thing?"

"You can sleep until nine."

Smiling, Alexis said, "You'll thank yourself."

Knowing too well how much Alexis hated rising early, Miriam said, "Yes, I will. Let's just hope it all goes as planned tomorrow."

Nothing went as planned. Miriam awoke at dawn to find a mysterious scrap of paper under her door. Scrawled on the parchment in a childish hand was the name Roger.

To her dismay, she learned that the earl never roused himself before noon, so she spent the morning in a leisurely breakfast and bath, then dried her hair and dawdled while Alexis supervised the unpacking of their trunks.

When word reached her that the earl had risen, she donned a simple dress of pearl gray wool, with an over jerkin of red satin. As a further concession to the country atmosphere, she tied back her hair with a ribbon. Then she marched downstairs and knocked on his study door.

"Come."

Miriam let herself in. The earl sat at his desk, which was littered with a brilliant array of feathers, dozens of sharp hooks, and a rusted carpenter's vise. He wore the same green jacket and thick spectacles, but today he sported a full black periwig that draped his shoulders in a waterfall of curls. Miriam was reminded of royal portraits of Alexis's father, Charles II, who introduced the wig into fashion during the last century.

Spying her, the earl tilted his head to the side. "Come in, come in, Lady Miriam." He rose and indicated a wing chair. "Do sit down."

His son, wearing his tartan and a sporran big enough to hold the crown jewels, dropped the book he was reading. The lad wore his pitch dark hair tied at the nape of his neck with a strip of leather. His warm brown eyes glowed with curiosity.

She had hoped to speak alone with the earl. Hiding her disappointment, she said, "Hello, my lord, and Rob Roy."

The lad pursed his mouth. "'Tis Roger. I even wrote it down for you. Didn't you read the note?"

She remembered the scrap of paper, but even her logical mind couldn't make the correlation. Baffled, she turned to the earl.

He smiled indulgently and folded his arms over his chest. "My son doesn't like his given name, which is Malcolm."

The boy made a gagging sound. "Malcolm's a prissy name."

Miriam wondered why the earl didn't pad the shoulders of his jacket in the fashion of the day. Or why he allowed his son to behave so disrespectfully.

Sighing, the earl said, "'Tis also a king's name."

"Malcolm the Maiden," spat the boy, hands on his hips. "I refuse to answer to it."

"My son hasn't settled on a name he likes."

"Yes, I have. 'Tis Roger." He hitched up his plaid. "After Roger Bacon."

The earl raised his gaze to the ceiling. The lenses not only magnified the size of his eyes, but also the length of his lashes. Through the thick glass, they fluttered like dark fans. Beneath the wig, his hair was probably dark, too, the same as his son's. Quite attractive, she thought, then caught herself. Objectivity was her watchword.

"Excuse me." The earl went to his son, clasped him on the shoulder, and whispered in his ear.

Malcolm slapped a hand over his sporran. "No, Papa. Roger Bacon had a mistress and her name was Rainbow. I don't think she was as pretty as your mistress, but she was comely all the same."

Society expected a nobleman to keep a mistress, but when did the earl find the time or the wherewithal to seduce a woman?

"You're mistaken, son."

The boy stomped his foot. "I swear 'tis so, Papa." He snatched up the book from the floor. "I read it here. See for yourself."

The earl turned beet red. He poked his nose in the open book and read. Teeth clenched, he said, "You misunderstood the text. Roger Bacon was a theologian, a Franciscan. He said 'theology is the mistress of all the other sciences.' He was merely studying the rainbow and prisms of light, not bragging about his manly prowess or naming his mistress."

The boy craned his neck to stare at his father. Looking crestfallen, Malcolm said, "You mean he didn't use his 'precious lady crackers'? Never?"

"I hardly think this is the time for such a discussion."

The boy glanced at Miriam. To hide her confusion, she focused her thoughts on King Ahmed III and his cultural revival of the Ottoman Empire.

Malcolm's expression grew mischievous. "You mean I shouldn't mention my precious lady crackers in front of a lady."

The earl's hand tightened on the boy's shoulder. Turkish kings forgotten, Miriam wondered if the earl was angry.

"Precisely, Roger."

"Oh well." The boy slammed the book. "'Tis just for today. I'll take another name tomorrow, and the day after, until I find the one I want. Right?"

"Right. I think you should excuse yourself."

"I'll go this instant if you give me a baby brother."

The earl flushed, but his voice was calm when he said, "Don't you have something dirty to get into?"

"Aye," said the lad, squaring his shoulders. "'Twill be a duel to the death!" He dashed out.

The earl studied the toes of his shoes, which were splayed. "My apologies. He spends too much time with the soldiers."

Miriam's confusion vanished. "The ones who patrol the wall, fifty at a time?"

"You're very observant, my lady, and may I say, that's a beautiful gown. The precise color of cardinal feathers."

Was the bumbling earl resorting to pretty compliments? Or was he trying to distract her? How interesting, and disappointing.

"Thank you." She sat in the chair he'd indicated. "I was hoping we could have a chat about Baron Sinclair."

The earl returned to his seat. "Why ever would you want to talk about that scoundrel? His methods are not the sort of

29

topic one discusses with a lady. We could talk about—" He snapped his fingers. "Fashion!"

Silently Miriam counted to ten. "I wish to discuss baron Sinclair."

His eyes grew as large as his coat buttons. "Why?"

How dare Alexis think him adorable. Slow-witted, perhaps, but definitely not adorable. "Because he's your neighbor and he's been complaining of trouble."

He smiled apologetically, his broad forehead furrowed. "A Border dispute seems a rather harsh subject for a gently bred lady. How did you come to know of it?"

Baffled, Miriam said, "I can't believe you don't know who I am or why I'm here."

"I've offended you." His hands fluttered, disturbing the feathers on his desk. "I'm a country boor and beg your indulgence. Please, enlighten me."

Miriam suspected all the Greek scholars couldn't enlighten Duncan Armstrong Kerr. Speaking slowly and concisely, she said, "My name is Miriam MacDonald. I'm an emissary of—"

"Yes, of course." He slapped his forehead with his palm. "I have the gist of it now. You've come at the insistence of the earl of Mar. Well, I'm sorry to disappoint his lordship, but my answer remains the same: I will not side with the Jacobites. I abhor politics."

While the earl of Kildalton gave her a dissertation on the dissatisfaction among the Highland clans over the Act of Union, Miriam counted to one hundred.

When he finished his speech, she noticed that he was staring at her hand. She looked down and realized she was strumming her fingers. She made a fist and fought the urge to pound his head.

"Let me begin again, my lord. I have been sent by the queen to settle your dispute with baron Sinclair. He's charged you with robbery, vandalism, kidnapping, and bodily injury."

He scratched his forehead, leaving the elaborate wig askew, but not enough to discern the color of his hair. "Bodily injury? Me? Don't believe him. He'll say anything to impugn my character. Don't you agree?"

He assumed she knew the baron. Let him continue to do so. "That's what I'm here to find out."

"Why would Her Majesty send a . . . a woman? No offense, of course. Some of my best feathers come from female birds. Take the moorhen—"

"Because mediation is my job," she said through clenched teeth. "I am a member of Her Majesty's diplomatic corps."

Mouth open, he levered himself up in the chair, then plopped down again. "Well, I'm impressed. I thought you a minion of Mar's here to turn my head and sway me to his cause. You must be horribly embarrassed."

He could think her a Persian harem dancer, for all Miriam cared. She hated losing control of a conversation. "Enough about me. I'm here to listen to your side of the story. Proceed, if you will."

Duncan bit his tongue to keep from howling with laughter. He had the chit exactly where he wanted her. When he was done with his tale of woe, she'd pack up her entourage and report back to the queen. Baron Sinclair would go to jail. Duncan's life would return to normal, his household to his bidding. The first order of business would involve blistering the seat of a certain seven-year-old brat who was playing at being a disobedient son.

"I'm waiting, my lord."

"Of course. But won't you be needing those soldiers you sent away this morning?"

"No. I intend to settle the matter without further bloodshed."

Nearly gagging on his own insincerity, he said, "I can't tell you how grateful I am."

"Please, you needn't waste a noble breath trying."

She needn't waste her time, either. The baron would think twice before ordering his men over the wall again. Once, that is, his men recovered from the trouncing the Border Lord had given them last night. "Would you like to write down his offenses—for posterity?" He remembered the unusual twins. "Or perhaps call in your scribes?"

"That won't be necessary." She gave him that supercilious smile again. "I never forget anything."

He'd like to put a few memories in her mind. He'd also

like to know where she acquired that charming concoction of gray wool and red satin. Splendid indeed, and a perfect foil for all that red hair. Lord, he could pillow his head on that mass of curls.

Thinking of the texture of those silky strands, he felt his fingers relax. Thinking of the price he'd pay for such an indulgence, he got to the business at hand. "Twould take days to list all of the baron's crimes against Kildalton," he warned.

She leveled him a gaze that said she doubted he could list his own titles. "I'm in no hurry."

Duncan cleared his throat, and began speaking in a high-pitched tone that would have set Malcolm to giggling. "His men have burned three farms this year alone. Ghastly, smelly business. Now there are cinders in my best trout stream. All that soot turns my sheets gray—"

"How many deaths?"

Banishing the image of the bodies, he said, "Four. He also encourages his fishermen to net the salmon in the river Tyne. Poor creatures never make it to spawn."

"Poor creatures indeed. Go on."

"He steals cattle at will. The churl even had the gall to take a new herd my agent just purchased from Aberdeen." Rifling through the clutter on his desk, Duncan said, "I have the transfer of ownership here somewhere. Oh, this blasted mess. Things are never where you put them. Most annoying—"

"You can find it for me later."

A feather settled on his nose. Duncan made several attempts to shake it off. He even stuck out his bottom lip and huffed, but to no avail. She started tapping her fingernails again. He plucked off the feather. Pretending to examine it, he held it an inch away from his spectacles. Over the rims, he examined her. How did she manage to compose herself so? He'd trade one of his hideouts in Hadrian's Wall to show her the man he really was.

He chose discretion instead. "I'll save this one for a fat trout," he said, dropping the feather into a drawer.

"What about the kidnapping charge?"

Duncan thought of Adrienne and how happy she'd

sounded in her letter. Charles had purchased a plantation in Barbados. They were expecting a child.

"My lord . . . The kidnapping."

"That's a bit of fiction. The baron's soldiers absconded with our best beehives. 'Twas done before the clover was pollinated." Shaking his head, he added, "We suffered a poor harvest."

"You retaliated by stealing something of his."

Was that hope he saw in her eyes? Imagine her, a romantic. Imagine him, exploring the feminine facets of her. Oh, but he couldn't, for duty called. Blinking like a fool, he perjured himself. "Me? A Border reiver? What a novel thought, but off the mark. I gave the farmers grain from the storehouses and acquired new hives for them."

Her voice dropped. "You never retaliate?"

With absolute honesty he said, "Duncan Armstrong Kerr is a scholar. He battles with pen and ink, not guns and bullets." He shuddered. "The sight of blood makes me ill."

"I'm sure. Anything else?"

The tapping of her fingernails, which had ceased, seemed her only peculiarity. He didn't even remember seeing her blink. Lord, she could teach a parson patience. He made a show of hesitating, as if he couldn't say what was really on his mind.

"Please, don't be shy, my lord. I'm here to help you."

And he was the bloody king of France. What could a well-composed and finely constructed redhead do to solve the problems that began centuries ago when a pack of hungry, pelt-clad Saxons took a shine to Scotland? The malleable woman who currently occupied the throne was merely following the lead of her predecessors in trying her hand at settling the Border. Only this time Anne had sent a minion who pleased the eye and challenged the intellect.

"You could continue your list now, Lord Duncan. What's so terrible that you can't speak of it?"

He didn't reply, for Mrs. Elliott stepped into the room, her eyes averted. "Excuse me, my lord. I've brought cider for you and Lady Miriam."

That was the signal. Lookouts had spotted visitors from Sinclair approaching Kildalton. They'd be here in an hour.

Duncan would be gone, though, for he couldn't let his enemies see him disguised as a bumbling idiot. He didn't like the idea of his leaving Lady Miriam either.

He thought of a solution. "I say, Lady Miriam, would you perchance want to see for yourself what the baron has done? We could take the carriage and the cider. I could show you some other things, too—Hadrian's Wall, and a dozen species of butterflies. We could make an afternoon of it, if you will."

Gray eyes glittered with pleasure, and her mouth tipped up in a genuine smile. "That would be splendid. May I bring a friend along?"

The facade of bumbling idiot shifted. Duncan's true nature surfaced. "Of course. So long as it's not a man more handsome than I."

An enchanting expression of confusion eclipsed her smile. Blinking, she said, "But my sleuthhound is a female."

Inwardly Duncan groaned. Miriam MacDonald possessed a logical, calculating mind and the body of temptress. But she had no sense of humor.

Before this beauty left Scotland, Duncan intended to give her one. Among other things.

3

A cloak over her arm, Verbatim on a leash at her side, Miriam left the kennel and stepped into the castle yard. The sounds and smells of country living filled the air. The alehouse rocked with raucous laughter and singing; the blacksmith hammered out a tune of his own. At a trough beside the well, a group of women rolled up their sleeves and plunged into the laundry. Nearby, the children played at peevers and tag.

Small herds of black-faced sheep bleated their way down the hay-strewn thoroughfare to the lush carpet of grass in the outer bailey. A pleasantly brisk breeze fluttered the Kerr pennons that framed the open gates.

Only a handful of soldiers wearing Highland bonnets and colorful Kerr plaids patrolled the walls. Where were the others? Searching the yard she spotted Malcolm near the portcullis. Brandishing a wooden sword and shield, the lad battled a tree stump.

Hoping to get a closer look at the courtyard where she'd glimpsed the mysterious shadow last night, Miriam walked to the rear of the castle. Passersby called out greetings as if they'd met her before. None came too close, but then strangers never did when she had Verbatim at her side.

A rickety cart, pulled by a fat jennet and stacked high with peat, rumbled across the yard. As a child, she had loved to stare into the shiny brass brazier filled with glowing clumps of peat.

"Doona get too close, pet," her nanny would say.

Pain squeezed Miriam's chest. The Glenlyon Campbells had bludgeoned poor Nanny to death.

Verbatim tugged on the lead.

Taking a deep breath, Miriam moved on. A stair tower with fishtail arrow slits stood at the back corner of the castle. She stopped at the ten-foot-high wall surrounding the courtyard. From beyond the barrier came the sound of rushing water. To get her bearings, she studied the windows until she located the green velvet drapes that marked her chamber.

Then she located a squat wooden door in the garden wall. She pulled on the iron handle. Well-oiled hinges emitted not a whisper of sound. "Stay close," she said to the hound, then ducked under the portal.

Heat from Verbatim's massive body seeped through Miriam's dress. She rested a hand on the dog. Beneath her fingers she felt the sturdy chain of backbones and the bow of Verbatim's ribs. Her other senses were fixed on the cozy garden before her.

A trysting place, she thought, staring at the fountain that housed a trio of naked marble nymphs emptying urns into a pool. Benches carved with vines and horn-shaped flowers ringed the fountain. The lush motif was repeated on a dozen mosaics set into three walls of the enclosure. The castle proper formed the fourth wall. Against it stood six Grecian urns as tall as she and overflowing with herbs. The perfume of basil, thyme, and fennel sweetened the air. Between the fountain and the castle wall was an elegant flower bed laid out in the shape of the clan symbol: a blazing sun. Bright yellow gorse formed the flames, frost-tinged daisies the center.

Verbatim tugged at the leash, her keen black nose sniffing the ground. Miriam let the slack out of the leash. Head down, the dog picked up a scent, followed it around the giant urns, and discovered a door in the castle wall.

Who else save the lord and lady of the keep would warrant direct access to the private garden? Had Duncan Kerr crept from the castle last night?

Verbatim scratched at the door and whimpered.

"Shush, girl," Miriam whispered.

She tried the door. It was locked. Tonight they'd return, and if she was lucky, she'd find out who used it.

She returned to the castle yard. A pair of dappled grays harnessed to an open carriage emerged from the stable. The earl held the reins. He sat straight and tall and confident, much like a ruler surveying his kingdom. From a distance, he appeared handsome, in a general sort of way. His neck appeared thicker, his shoulders broader.

Spying her, he slumped and sawed on the reins. The team veered right and headed her way. Scoffing at the alluring picture she'd made of him, Miriam vowed to keep her imagination in check.

Traffic on the thoroughfare stopped. The castlefolk and the laborers paused in their conversations to doff their caps. Some called out greetings to the lord of the keep. Smiles wreathed their faces, except the tinker, who stared in awe.

They like Duncan Kerr. She wondered how so eccentric a man had attained their respect and devotion. Could they truly admire his obsession with fishing lures and his blithe indifference to his son? Of course they could; when it came to raising children, the earl was no different from the rest of the nobility. They cared little for children, leaving them to cruel nannies and later, stern governesses for the girls and strict academies for the boys. When she had children, she'd love them, respect them, and be a part of their daily lives.

As the earl approached, his spectacles glinted in the sun. Miriam tried to picture him conducting assizes and passing out harsh judgments. She failed.

When the carriage reached her, he dropped the reins and climbed down. He wore unadorned shoes, on the proper feet, and a coat and long breeches of dark green wool. Over the wig, he wore a sheared beaver hat that sported a cluster of badly frayed peacock feathers. His longed-for birds had better arrive soon.

He was two steps away when Verbatim bared her teeth and growled. Gasps sounded from the crowd. The earl stopped. He swallowed noisily. "Is she vicious?"

Miriam pulled on the leash and ordered the hound to sit. Smiling, she spoke loud enough for all around them to hear. "Actually Verbatim is very gentle once she knows you. May I have one of your gloves, my lord?"

Gingerly, he removed the right one. She remembered the blisters. "How is your hand today?"

"What?"

"The blisters on your hands, my lord. How are they?"

The castlefolk closed in. The horses started to wander.

The earl's eyebrows rose in surprise. "You remembered." Then he waved his hand. "'Tis nothing. Mrs. Elliott gave me a poultice."

Miriam held the glove before the dog's nose. "Friend." Tail wagging, soulful eyes trained on the earl, Verbatim held up a huge paw.

Ohs of surprise and ahs of approval spread through the crowd.

Miriam returned the glove. "She wants to shake your hand, my lord."

As if reaching into a roaring furnace, the earl extended his bare hand. Staring at Verbatim's mouth, and probably expecting the animal to bite off his fingers, he said, "She's . . . uh . . . quite an engaging beast, and lovely in a way."

"To some, I suppose," Miriam said, patting the dog's head. "Good girl."

Verbatim barked. The earl jumped back and fell against the carriage.

The onlookers roared with laughter, yet none went to their master's aid.

The earl righted himself and his spectacles. To the people he said, "Yes, well, carry on, everyone, and keep watch for that fellow with the peacocks. I expect him any day now. Shall we go, my lady?"

"Of course, my lord. We can continue our discussion later."

Duncan cursed himself for not expecting straightforwardness from her. The solicitous query about his silly blisters had caught him off guard.

I never forget anything.

Grumbling inwardly, he handed her into the carriage and was pleasantly surprised at how slight she was, how delightful she smelled. His pretty little diplomat wore an exotic fragrance that reminded him of crisp winter days in the mountains. He climbed in beside her, remembering to stumble on the step. He could be thorough, too, when the situation demanded it.

Verbatim leaped into the opposite seat and sat in ladylike elegance.

Duncan shrank back. Making sure his hands trembled, he flicked the reins. As the crowd parted, he decided his people deserved a boon for their performance; none except the newly arrived tinker had expressed surprise at his appearance or his exhibition of cowardice. Angus had schooled them well. He'd also ridden out earlier to prepare the farmers for a visit from their laird. The excursion would proceed without a hitch.

The instant the carriage passed through the outer curtain wall, Lady Miriam said, "Out, Verbatim."

The sleuthhound bounded from the carriage, put her nose to the ground, and began a systematic mapping of the terrain. Her sleek, golden-red coat glistened in the sunshine.

Seated comfortably in the open carriage, the afternoon breeze ruffling his outlandish wig, the queen's minion his captive audience, Duncan reviewed his plan. By day's end she'd be convinced that he and his people were innocent, defenseless victims of Baron Sinclair. She'd report back to the queen. Baron Sinclair would be revealed as the villain he was. Life, albeit peaceably, would go on.

Duncan said, "Did you train the hound?"

She gazed after the dog, affection softening her features. "She needed little, actually. Sleuthing is bred into her. Do you mind if she stays in my room? I promise she won't misbehave."

If it made her happy and kept her occupied, Lady Miriam could bring a litter of squealing pigs into his pantry. "Please, feel free."

"Thank you. I noticed that you have a number of terriers from the dales of Aire and a litter of foxhounds in your kennel."

He glanced down at her and smiled. "Is that what they are? Terriers and foxhounds," he repeated much like Malcolm when he learned a new curse word. "To me they're scruffy creatures with heaven knows what in their fur. None are so fine or elegant, I think, as your Verbatim."

As if he'd made small talk about the weather, rather than a diatribe about dogs, she said, "I forgot, my lord, that you prefer fishing to hunting."

He knew that for a lie; she never forgot anything, and if she thought to trip him up, she'd be vastly disappointed. "Verbatim looks swift enough to outrun a horse."

"Thank you. She's an excellent traveler. Did your father teach you to drive a team?"

Duncan tensed. The horses slowed. Her attempt to turn the conversation might have charmed him, if she had chosen any subject except his father. Kenneth Kerr had been an impatient, cold man who was highly skilled and inventive with a strap.

Flicking the reins, Duncan said, "No. I'm afraid we didn't get on well at all. He was such a crude fellow. He used to say he'd sooner stroll the halls of Holyrood Palace in stays and a farthingale than ride in a carriage. Can you imagine such a thing?"

"Did he also fight with Baron Sinclair?"

Duncan wondered if she practiced that smile in a mirror. Was she attempting to distract him? Or trick him with wily questions?

Answers would have to wait, for Duncan needed to keep his wits about him. Wits! He almost laughed out loud; he was supposed to be witless. "Also? You don't think I'd sink to the baron's level? Heaven forbid. Violence brings on the grippe. I prefer fishing, but then you know that. Did I ever tell you about the boot I mistook for a salmon?" He twisted his face into a self-effacing grin. "Bent my hook and destroyed one of my most valuable lures. I call it the spangle-dangle. Took me a whole day to make another."

"How clever of you to name them."

She stared at the horses, but Duncan knew she wasn't thinking about the grays. He'd trade all the salt in Kildalton for a peek at her thoughts.

"Are you named for your father?" she asked.

Duncan spoke from the heart. "No. For the king MacBeth slew. My father was a rough Scotsman who embraced the clannish ways. A likable, bold chap, I suppose—if you favor that sort. They called him the Grand Reiver."

"He raided, then?"

"Until the eve of his death."

"How old were you when he died?"

He had expected her to ask personal questions. He just wished he could return the favor. He wanted to know why she'd never married. If she were betrothed? Was she the mistress of some well-fixed peer? Were her nipples pink, and did they pucker when suckled?

"If the subject makes you uncomfortable, my lord . . ."

Duncan marshaled his lustful thoughts. "Not at all, my lady. I was twenty and in Rome at the time." Sheepishly, he added, "I've always enjoyed studying the Romans. The aqueducts fed some of the finest trout streams in Italy."

"Ah yes. I'm curious," she said, toying with the leather lead. "Why does the baron accuse you of raiding?"

"Why, it's as obvious as the scales on a bass. He accuses me to cover his own ghastly crimes. Surely someone of your vast experience and knowledge understands that."

He might have been a spy lurking in her wardrobe, she eyed him with such suspicion. He almost chuckled, for that's exactly what he intended to become.

Sunlight turned her irises to sparkling gems of blue and gray, and her hair to golden fire. She powdered her face, he decided, for he could discern a faint spattering of freckles across her nose and cheeks. How adorable. Perhaps he should powder his face too, or ask her what cosmetics she preferred. The carriage hit a bump. He turned his attention to driving the team and playing the fool.

"Where shall we visit first?" she asked.

Pretending spontaneity seemed a good tactic. "You've seen the MacLarens' croft—or what's left of it. Do you truly want to see the other farms Sinclair has burned? You'll muss your dress and dirty your hands."

"No. But I should like to meet a few of the farmers. Not, of course, that I don't believe you, Lord Duncan."

He should have expected the request. Considering her reputation for composing detailed trade agreements, Lady

Miriam wouldn't take the pope's word for the date of Easter. Ah, but she was newly introduced to Duncan Kerr.

He almost laughed. "I should be flattered that you think me capable of subterfuge. Do you speak Scottish?"

"Aye. I'll be able to converse with the people." In his language, she said, "You hesitated before answering me. What were you really going to say?"

He loved playing verbal hide-and-seek with her. In English he said, "Oh, Lady Miriam. I fear you already think me foolish."

"If you don't tell me, I might think you're hiding something."

Duncan snatched an outrageous topic. "If you must know . . . I was wondering if dogs could be taught to fish."

She looked like a child tasting a lemon for the first time.

To keep from laughing, Duncan said, "I told you 'twas foolish. You'll forgive me, I'm sure. It's just that fishing is such a marvelous pastime. I'm always inspired to improve upon my technique. I'm a very progressive thinker, you know."

Skepticism lent an angelic quality to her features. God, did the woman never laugh?

"I'm sure," she murmured.

They visited two cattle farms and three shepherds. At every croft they were met first with cheers and then straight faces. Angus had done his job well. The women wailed of crimes committed by the baron. The men knotted their fists and called Sinclair names that would have made a lesser diplomat than Lady Miriam blush. Goodwives fawned over Duncan as if he were incapable of caring for himself. Everyone spoke of the dreadful twist of fate that required him to wear spectacles. He was proclaimed a saint, a savior, and a gentleman among men.

Blessed Scotland, his people were magnificent.

Except for Lettie Melville.

Later in the afternoon, they had stopped at the croft belonging to the Melvilles. Duncan had been pulled aside by Finlay, a wiry shepherd who had lost a hand while protecting his flock from Sinclair's raiders. As he listened to Finlay praise the sleuthhound, Duncan watched Miriam. She chat-

42

ted amiably with Finlay's wife, Lettie, but her attention and her bewitching gray eyes constantly strayed to him.

"Oh yes," said Lady Miriam, as charming as Malcolm on the day before his birthday. "I understand Lord Duncan's lures are all the rage."

"Sure as the good Catholics eat fish on Friday, milady," said Lettie, bouncing her son on her knee. "Ladies come from as far as Aberdeen to get a taste of his 'lure.'"

"I beg your pardon," said Lady Miriam. "You mean they come to fish with him?"

Finlay burst out laughing.

Lettie huffed and said, "Oh, he's been known to hook a few ladies all right. All they suffers is a broken heart."

Miriam turned so fast that her shock of hair swung over her shoulder. The look she shot Duncan said, "You, a heartbreaker?"

If she were as easy to bed as she was to fool, they'd be buck naked and going at it like newlyweds. The image kindled a fire in Duncan. He pictured her languishing on his feather mattress, her glorious hair blanketing his pillow, her slender arms extended in invitation. His loins swelled with need.

It was time to get back to bamboozling her.

Once they returned to the carriage and headed toward Hadrian's Wall, she said, "You and Mr. Melville seemed to find much to whisper about."

As he had since the excursion began, Duncan discarded his natural response and thought of what a bumbling coward would do. He held his breath to make his face turn red.

"Don't be shy. Tell me about today's chat." That trouble line reappeared in her forehead. "Are you blushing?"

Tucking his cheek to his shoulder, Duncan did his best to look embarrassed. "Oh my. I couldn't possibly repeat it. 'Tisn't suitable conversation for a fine lady."

Her chin came up. "I'll be the judge of that."

Oh, she'd regret it, for Duncan relished her reaction. Would she blush in soft pink or red to match that enticing satin jerkin? Guilt stabbed him, for Duncan realized he liked her. Still, he had a role to play.

"Finlay wanted to send his bloodhound courting your Verbatim—when, uh, the time is right," Duncan blurted.

Surprise smoothed out her features, and her skin blossomed in an enchanting shade of pink. "I see."

A master actor in a play of his own creation, Duncan added, "I told you so. Now you'll think me crass, when I want more than anything to be cooperative." Almost more than anything; he wanted *her* cooperation in a very different matter.

She cleared her throat. "No, not at all. I did, as you say, ask for it. Thank you for your cooperation."

Duncan wondered if she ever had fun. He could make a vocation of entertaining her. But as diverting as the prospect might be, it was impossible, for he couldn't go on being the witless earl forever. Or could he?

Studying the landscape, she said, "Why are the farms smaller on your side of the wall?"

She recovered quickly, he'd give her that. Squinting, he peered over the rims of the spectacles. "A man can only work so much land—or so I'm told."

"But I've seen entire families working in the fields, both here and on the baron's land."

Were she truly knowledgeable about the baron, she wouldn't make such a statement. Unless, she'd only viewed his holdings from the London road. Those he kept prosperous, for show. Cautiously, Duncan said, "You know the man?"

She stared at the dog, who was chasing a hare. "He brought the complaint against you."

A hedge, if Duncan ever heard one. Could the renowned Lady Miriam of Her Majesty's diplomatic corps be so unprepared and uninformed? She hadn't known that the baron only arrived in the Border eight years ago; she'd asked if Duncan's father raided the baron. Duncan had to find out how much she knew. "Complaint?"

"I told you. Robbery, vandalism, kidnapping, and bodily injury."

Duncan decided to fish. He thought of Adrienne. "That's laughable. You do know that in June he offered one of his stepdaughters to the magistrate as an inducement to dismiss a charge I brought against him."

"'Tis a father's obligation to arrange his daughter's marriage."

44

Happy thoughts of Adrienne carrying her first child made Duncan smile. "Unfortunately, the magistrate was already married at the time. A cruel trick to play on a well-bred girl."

Her eyes narrowed. A moment later, she said, "You were telling me what you know about the work ethic of the crofters."

What would it take to shock her? The Border Lord could find out. He tried to imagine the life she'd led, the experiences that could bring about such iron control. No wonder the queen praised and valued Miriam MacDonald. Why, then, had no one briefed her on the problems here? He'd find out, but he'd pick his time to ask, for Duncan had learned a thing or two about diplomacy himself.

"The crofters, my lord," she prompted.

The carriage clipped along at a brisk pace, wheels whirring, harnesses jingling. Fields sped by. "Sinclair works his poor families to the bone. But in Kildalton, the children don't work in the morning. They attend school."

Her gaze whipped to him. "All of them?"

"Most. I provide the school and the teacher—nothing elaborate, or so my steward tells me. But no one forces the children to attend. I like to think their favorite subject is nature study. Imagine a whole crop of youth learning about fish and fowl." He preened. "That was *my* idea."

She waved a gloved hand toward a field that had been plowed in stick-straight rows. "Yet the farms in Kildalton prosper."

He dare not tell her how hard he and his tenants worked to implement new farming techniques and try new crops. Instead, he chose a defensive stand. "None of the farms near the wall do as well as they should, because of Sinclair's vile raiding."

"Does the baron also provide a school?"

Duncan had to work at stifling his anger. He flipped the reins. Summoning nonchalance, he said, "I can't trouble myself with his agenda. I have my own interests. Do you know about the ruins near the wall? 'Tis a wondrous place the Romans built. I've been exploring there since I was a child."

Successful diplomacy required a certain amount of compromise from all parties involved. Duncan waited, hoping she'd do her part.

"Then you must have had an interesting childhood."

Again he wondered about her life. To which MacDonald clan did she belong? Where had she grown up? But his role didn't allow for familiarity with the queen's minion. His next words tasted bitter. "Oh, a very interesting childhood."

Hadrian's Wall came into view. Guiding the team off the road, he steered them toward a bracken-infested vale that contained two stone walls and a well.

"Behold . . . the remains of Virgin's Gate," he said.

She stepped from the carriage and approached the well. Peering over the edge, she said, "Hello . . ."

Spoken into the well, the word sounded hollow, distant. Duncan didn't move from the carriage, for his eyes and his senses suddenly fixed on her slender ankles and shapely calves. Her hips were narrow, too, he suspected. Silently he begged her to bend over just a bit more.

The dog joined her, front paws braced on the lip of the well. "Listen, Verbatim." She spoke playfully, smiling at the dog. "There's an echo in there."

Tail swishing, her regal head cocked, the dog listened in rapt attention.

Duncan sneaked up behind them. Cupping his hands around his mouth, he said, "Woof."

The dog yelped and jumped back. A startled Lady Miriam froze. "Quite diverting, my lord. Go find something, Verbatim."

The dog lumbered off. The woman turned toward Duncan.

His breath caught. She looked the picture of feminine charm, an alluring virgin. Or was she? The Border Lord would find out.

God, he wanted her.

"Tell me about the well."

She wanted to know about a stupid well.

His groin aching, Duncan didn't have to pretend to stumble on the rocky ground. In a voice pinched by longing, he said, "It was built in A.D. 120, but destroyed twenty years later."

"Who destroyed it and who fixed it?" She eyed the structure.

Duncan eyed her. "The Scots destroyed it. An engineer named Severus rebuilt it. This was a fort once. The Roman soldiers brought their families."

He dragged her along, showing her the spots where he'd found treasures, and laughing over the rubbish he'd carted home. She listened intently, even sifted through rubble for a treasure of her own—the handle to a teacup.

"Once," he said, sitting on the lip of the well and drawing her beside him, "after scavenging for the better part of a morning, I found what I knew to be a priceless vase belonging to old Hadrian himself. I was eight, as I recall, and destined for what I knew would be international acclaim." He chuckled so hard, his shoulders shook. "I hauled the heavy thing home and spent days cleaning it up. Only to discover that it was a chamber pot from a pottery concern in Worcester."

She tilted her head. The sun sparkled in her eyes, which were soft with concern. "How can you laugh?"

How could he reply without tripping himself up? He'd let down his guard and stepped onto dangerous ground.

"You must have been embarrassed to your toes," she said, her expression solemn.

"Oh, I was," he admitted. "But only Angus saw it and he'd never betray me."

Her keen gaze locked with his. "The burly fellow? I thought you didn't know any of your soldiers' names."

Duncan instantly regretted his confidence. She was too quick to catch a slip of the tongue.

"People always betray themselves," she said. "'Tis the way of things."

Was the cryptic statement a warning? How odd, he thought, that she could snatch up a single word in a sentence and create a beatitude, albeit a dangerous one.

Duncan didn't comment, for out of the corner of his vision he saw the sleuthhound nosing around the wall. "You should call the dog back," he said. "Badgers and snakes nest around here."

She tunneled her hand under her thick hair and lifted it

off her neck. Taking a handkerchief from her pocket, she dabbed at her nape. "Don't worry. Verbatim avoids snakes, and a badger's no match for a sleuthhound. Besides, she won't kill game. She only tracks and finds it."

Fear jolted through Duncan, for the dog could accidentally unearth the lair of the Border Lord. He rose. "All the same, she could be hurt or scarred in the scuffle. Not to mention the badger."

As he approached the dog, Duncan watched her put to use the fine qualities of her breed. She darted in and out of the bracken, and once, jumped on the wall. Long ears flapping in the wind, she sniffed and investigated. Then she bounded to the ground and into the bushes very near the door that led to an underground chamber. Dirt began to fly.

Heart thumping, Duncan yelled, "Stop that digging."

Verbatim's head popped into view. Dust coated her black muzzle and burrs clung to her long ears. A moment later, the dog went back to her excavation.

Frantic, Duncan went in pursuit.

Lady Miriam whistled. One hundred pounds of eager dog dashed from the bushes. She ran so fast in her haste to reach her mistress that she almost plowed into him. But not so fast that he missed the swatch of black silk hanging from the dog's mouth.

Duncan's heart skipped a beat, for the dog had found the black scarf of the Border Lord.

How had he been so careless as to lose it? Bloody hell, the answer wasn't important. Like a dervish, his tortured mind whirled in search of an explanation. *The scarf belongs to a traveler. It's the property of a grieving widow.* Yes, of course. Duncan would offer to locate the poor creature.

Wait a minute. Miriam couldn't know who the scarf belonged to. Duncan's anxiety eased. He sucked in a deep breath and felt his heart slow to normal.

The dog had found a plain black scarf. So bloody what?

If he acted guilty, Miriam would fix those gray eyes on him and persist until he came up with a satisfactory excuse or tripped over his own foolish tongue. Act natural, he counseled himself. Then he laughed and banished the word natural from his mind. Duncan Kerr had a bumbling earl to portray.

Mincing over brambles and rocks, he returned to the old well. He retrieved his own handkerchief and began brushing debris from his long trousers. To his surprise, he saw Lady Miriam tying the scarf around the dog's neck and praising the animal.

Delight sparkled in her eyes. "Doesn't she look dashing, my lord?"

He'd only met her last night, but instinctively Duncan knew that Miriam MacDonald didn't often express herself so freely. An honest, open conversation with her sounded very appealing, and impossible. Sadly Duncan did what he must, what he hated.

He let his mouth drop open and propped his hands at his waist. "You should have the maids clean that filthy rag first. Goodness knows what creatures infest it."

An imploring expression gave her a girlish appeal. "Verbatim's only playing, which she seldom gets to do. You yourself said 'twas naught but a rag. Don't be such a spoilsport, my lord."

Unable to live with the constant reminder of his dual identities, he forced himself to insist. "I couldn't allow the animal inside the castle with it on."

Her cheerful expression wilted like daisies in a freeze. She yanked the scarf free. "Of course, my lord. Rest assured I'll have the twins bathe her and wash the scarf as soon as we return."

Duncan felt as if he'd taken a cannonball in the chest. Damn. He'd buy the blasted dog a scarf in every color of the rainbow—anything to put the light back in Miriam's eyes.

During the return to Kildalton Castle, he fabricated fish stories to entertain her, to make her smile. He might as well have tried to reform baron Sinclair.

Silently Duncan cursed.

The cool diplomat sat inches from him.

The laughing woman stood miles out of reach.

He consoled his guilty conscience with facts. She was here to gain evidence against him. What proof did he have that she would be fair? Certainly not the English justice system. She could knock his life into the hazard. That done, she'd pack up and move on to wherever the queen sent her.

He'd better stay one step ahead of her. He knew just the

way. After the evening meal he'd slip into the secret passageway, stand behind her wardrobe, and listen and watch. She'd never know he was there.

Encouraged, he patted his stomach. "Mrs. Elliott's preparing umbles of deer and fricassee. 'Tis a favorite of mine. I prefer fish, of course, but one can't eat it every day. I'm certain we'll have dessert, probably berry tarts with clotted cream."

His constant chatter rattled Miriam. She could abide his eccentricities, he was entitled to those, but didn't he ever shut up? Keeping her voice light, she said, "Sounds delicious. I love kidneys and heart."

"Splendid. Perhaps my peacocks have arrived. Oh, I do hope so. Are you familiar with the mating habits of peacocks?" He laughed and didn't seem to expect an answer. "The male puts on a show that is pure entertainment. They'll be molting now, though. Poor fellows seem so despondent without their pretty feathers. They mope around like a buck without a doe. I'm doing a study on it, you know."

At least deer fought for their women, and defended them, she thought morosely.

By the time they entered the castle yard she wanted to scream. She almost did when a shepherd approached, a lifeless sheepdog in his arms.

"The baron's men did it, my lord." Tears pooled in the old man's eyes. "'Tweren't no cause to kill my ol' Barley. I give 'em my chickens and all the acorns I'd collected to sell to the swineherd."

"Oh, you poor, poor man," said the earl.

Her heart breaking over the sad man and his burden, Miriam turned to the earl. "What will you do?"

Blinking innocently, he said, "Why, I'll find him another dog. Would you care to help me locate one?"

Galled by his cowardice, she didn't trust herself to answer. Instead she climbed from the carriage and took Verbatim to the kennel so the twins could bathe the dog. Then Miriam went in search of solitude.

Later that night she stood at the window looking down on the garden. Behind her a freshly washed and recently fed Verbatim snoozed by the fire.

The side door opened. Alexis came in, a rueful smile on her face. "Had enough peace and quiet?"

Guilt plagued Miriam. "I'm sorry I snapped at you earlier, but I simply couldn't help it. After the earl's chattering, I needed solitude."

"Apology accepted." Alexis knelt beside Verbatim and stroked the long velvetlike ears. "Anyone who works as hard as you should be allowed an occasional touch of bad humor."

Miriam let the drape fall back in place. "I thought I wouldn't know humor if it crept under my skirt."

"Which you're still wearing. Not sleepy again?"

The candle flame flickered. Miriam shivered, wondering if architects designed drafts into castles. Rubbing her arms, she said. "I can't stop thinking about that poor, dead sheepdog."

Alexis's hand stilled on Verbatim's head. "If it's any consolation, the earl helped bury the dog and promised the shepherd he'd find a replacement."

"How magnanimous of him."

Alexis sighed. "He's not your Sir Lancelot, Miriam. But don't judge him unfairly."

"I'm trying not to judge him at all."

"I know, and he's lucky the queen sent you. Shall I help you undress?"

"No. I'm going to investigate the garden."

"I'll go with you."

"Thank you, but no. I'll take Verbatim."

The dog barked and jumped to her feet. Head cocked, she stood perfectly still. Then she lifted her long blunt nose and sniffed. A moment later she went to the open wardrobe and poked her head inside.

The candle wavered wildly in another draft of air.

Alexis raised an eyebrow. "Something strange is going on. Maybe we have a ghost—"

"Shush." Miriam crossed the room and threw open the other door to the wardrobe. "What is it, girl?" she whispered to the dog.

The hound's head disappeared between the folds of a lavender day dress and an emerald evening gown. After rummaging through every item of Miriam's clothing, the dog backed up and sat.

For the thousandth time since acquiring the animal, Miriam wished Verbatim could talk.

"Would you like to go for a walk outside?" Miriam asked.

A loud bark was her answer.

Miriam picked up the leash and her cloak. "Don't wait up for us," she said.

"I wouldn't dream of it." But Alexis sat at the vanity and began brushing her hair.

Her scribes had explored the castle today. Following Saladin's directions, Miriam found the back stairs and exited the castle through a door that faced the kennel. The air smelled of rain, and clouds masked the moon.

Torches lined the wall, illuminating the guards on patrol. She counted twenty armed men. In Scottish, they spoke of a storm to come.

As if she were out for a casual evening stroll, Miriam made her way slowly to the garden gate. Looking left, then right, she bent low and tiptoed inside, Verbatim on her heels.

She started across the garden, but stopped at the sight of a tall dark shadow. Her heart hammered.

He stood near the giant urns, which now seemed as small as flower pots.

Verbatim growled.

Miriam clutched the leash and started backing toward the door.

The shadow moved. "Doona be afraid, lassie."

The rich burr in his voice sent shivers down her spine. The crunching of his boots on the stone pathway echoed off the garden walls.

Swallowing hard, she said, "Who are you?"

"A friend who means you no harm," he said in Scottish.

When he was only an arm's length away, she saw that he wore a hat pulled low over his forehead, the wide brim effectively shielding his face from view. A muted tartan cape fell to his knees. She squinted, studying the pattern of the plaid, but couldn't discern the design or his clan.

"What are you doing here?" she asked.

He chuckled, deep and natural, as if laughter came easy to him. "I could ask the same of you."

Feeling foolish and frightened at once, Miriam said, "I'm walking my dog." She yanked on the lead. "Who happens to be extremely vicious."

"It doesn't look vicious." He squatted in the path. "It looks like a fine wee beastie to me."

In the dim light, a rakish plume waved over his hat. Was he a cavalier? A guest of the earl?

"Animals love me." He extended a black-gloved hand to Verbatim.

"Don't!" Miriam stepped back, dragging a growling, quivering Verbatim with her. "Easy girl."

The dog sat.

The man said, "Can you shake my hand?"

To Miriam's surprise, Verbatim held up a paw.

The stranger chuckled and stood. "I've been told I have the same effect on all women."

Miriam craned her neck. Fear snatched her breath. Dear Lord, he was tall and broad-shouldered. She whispered, "Tell me who you are."

He bowed from the waist. "I'm the Border Lord."

"The what?"

"The Border Lord. Doona tell me you've never heard of me?"

He reeked of feudal nobility. She remembered the tales told to her by the innkeeper in Bothly Green. He proclaimed the Border Lord a legend. "What are you doing here?" she asked.

"Living out a prophecy, I trow. You, lass, have the look of a MacDonald about you."

Her throat closed. No one ever mentioned her family. "I do?"

"Aye." The sound rumbled in his chest. He reached out and took a strand of her hair. "'Tis like silky fire. MacDonald for certain."

Good judgment told her to flee from this dark stranger with the ominous name. Fascination made her blurt, "I'm Lady Miriam."

"You must be a Highland lassie," he said thickly.

She thought of her childhood home. A snow-covered glen. A river of blood. A little girl wandering aimlessly. Tears welled in her eyes. She sniffled.

"Doona cry, lassie. 'Tis too bonnie a night for tears."

Then his hands touched her shoulders, and Miriam saw the invitation in his eyes.

4

Duncan held his breath. Anticipation coursed like vintage wine through his veins. Would she take the bait and come willingly into his arms? Could he play the rogue and woo her into confessing her plan to make peace? Darkness intensified his doubts, for he couldn't see her clearly.

He squinted, trying to make out her features. In the dim light he could discern only the shape of her lips and the line of her jaw. She neither smiled nor frowned. Yet one thing was certain: In darkness or light, deception or innocence, Miriam MacDonald was a beautiful woman.

Instinct compelled him. He tugged gently on her shoulders. "Come, lass, and bide a wee. 'Tis time you had a proper Scottish welcome."

"I shouldn't. I don't know you."

Standing behind the wardrobe, he'd heard Lady Alexis say that Miriam longed for a Sir Lancelot. Duncan thought of something a gallant knight would say. "Look into your heart, lassie. You know who I am."

She stepped closer. He held her in a loose embrace. She

55

felt kitten soft against his chest, her glorious head bowed, her delicate hands clutching the fabric of his cape.

The old familiar yearning for a woman of his own gnawed in Duncan's belly. But Miriam MacDonald was not the one for him. Still, he had a job to do. He stroked her back. "You're cold. Let me warm you."

"I don't usually embrace strangers. I don't recognize your plaid."

"I'm no stranger. Not to you."

He'd come here to gain her confidence, to charm her, to learn her secrets. But she was doing her own prying and quite enticingly, too, from the way her fingers traced the weave of his cape.

Over the gurgling of the fountain, he heard the dog lapping water. The resident bullfrog croaked to his lady love.

Conscience nagging, Duncan thought of the ways he encouraged Malcolm when the lad grew shy. "You feel safe with me, don't you, Miriam?" he queried softly.

A subtle change occurred in her bearing, and while Duncan couldn't precisely name it, he sensed she was judging him. "You're very forward, Sir Border Lord. What is your given name?"

The special boots added inches to his height and allowed Duncan to rest his chin on her head. Her clean, fresh fragrance permeated his senses. The word companionship flashed in his mind. He whisked it away, snatched a name for himself, and got to the business at hand. "'Tis Ian. Tell me. What brings such a finely bred and bonnie Highland lass to the Borders?"

With a feather-light touch, she brushed her hand over his tartan. Even through the heavy wool his skin prickled.

During the years Duncan had donned the costume and the demeanor of the Border Lord, he'd seldom encountered a woman, let alone romanced one. Now the notion challenged him.

"I've come to settle a few matters," she said.

He might be portraying a different man tonight and view the situation through new eyes, but Miriam hadn't changed. She was still the wily diplomat. He could be wily, too. He clutched her left hand. "You don't wear a wedding ring or a widow's band. Is that the matter you've come to settle?"

"No. I've no wish to marry." Then she added, "At this time."

By modern standards she should have been wed five, even ten years ago. "You should have a man to cuddle up with on a warm winter's night, or a man to give you bairns."

She leaned back, bringing her thighs in contact with his. "You're bold."

If she got any closer, she'd redefine her opinion of boldness. His confidence soared; he *could* play the rogue. "I *am* right about you, but doona take umbrage. I'm country-bred and have little knowledge of courtly manners and such."

"Are you a farmer?"

"Aye." Nonsense popped into his mind. "I've a pig farm," he said, putting a note of pride in his voice.

"I thought pigs lived in a sty."

Lord, she missed nothing. Delving deeper into his bag of fiction, Duncan said, "What do you know about swine?"

"Little. Does your wife mind living on a pig farm?"

"I've not found the lass who'd have me—or my pigs."

"Somehow I doubt that."

"You flatter me."

"'Twas not my intention. I merely thought you a forth-right man."

Now he was on even ground. "I've been known to pursue a quest with a certain amount of vigor."

Her hand stilled. "Are you pursuing someone here at Kildalton? A maid, perhaps."

With absolute confidence in her inability to understand innuendo, he said, "Not in the castle proper."

"Then why are you here?" she asked.

"Ah. A woman who doesna mince words," he said. "How delightful and rare."

"A man who minces around questions," she murmured. "How interesting and suspicious."

"Mince?" he said defensively. "I'm standing in a secluded garden, a beautiful woman snug in my arms, and she asks me what I'm doing."

"Ha! I could be as ugly as a plucked goose and you wouldn't know it. 'Tis too dark to see."

"Aye, 'tis too dark now, but I saw you today near Hadrian's Wall."

She stepped out of his embrace. "I didn't see you."

He felt like a dancing master, skirting a lie. "I was watching you through a spyglass. Even from a distance your hair blazes like a fire on a dark moor."

"Very poetic, Sir Ian."

With disarming scrutiny, she studied him. Unease tiptoed up his spine. Wait. She didn't know that he wore the wigs and the scarf to hide his fair hair. Or that he darkened his eyebrows and side whiskers with lampblack. The brim of the hat obscured his eyes. His friend Adrienne hadn't recognized him. The stranger Miriam MacDonald wouldn't either. Relief cooled his skin. "Do you favor poets, lassie?"

"Aye. You're very tall." The smile in her voice said she liked that aspect of him, too. Faint moonlight cast her in a golden glow. "I don't recognize your tartan. What's your clan?"

Her regal nose lent her a lofty air. A result, he thought morosely, from poking it into everyone's business. She could scour the clans of Scotland and never find a family to claim the unique plaid of the Border Lord, for the weaver had designed it especially for Duncan. He hoped the mystery of it bedeviled the wits from her. She was too intelligent by half. "I doona think anyone knows all of the tartans."

"I do. I have a very good memory."

"Come sit with me." He led her to a bench near the fountain.

Once seated, she said, "Why were you sneaking out of Kildalton Castle?"

As Duncan considered his answer, a pleasant realization occurred to him. In a way he was meeting her for the first time. "I wasna sneaking. I was visiting the earl."

She stiffened and folded her hands in her lap. "Are you his friend?"

So casual was the question, she could have been asking directions to the Great North Road. But her physical withdrawal told a different tale.

"Duncan's a pleasant enough fellow," he said cautiously. "A bit odd, though, for a laird. Do you know him well?"

"Apparently not well enough, for he's never mentioned you."

She'd answered, but told him nothing. If she were as clever in the physical aspects of love as she was with words, a true rogue would chain her to his bed. The image made him feel very much the cavalier. "I'm a boor of a fellow, and I doona care for fishing."

"Then why are you here? Did you bring him the peacocks?"

Taken off guard, Duncan threw back his head and laughed.

She snapped her fingers. Pebbles rattled nearby. In a spray of rocks, the sleuthhound raced to her side.

Duncan held out his hand to the dog, but his eyes stayed fixed on the woman. "My stock in trade is pigs, not peacocks."

"Shame on you, Ian. You shouldn't mock Lord Duncan just because he's different from you."

Aha! Now he was getting somewhere. If he could keep her defending the bumbling earl, the Border Lord might distract her enough to glean her plans, earn her patronage, then facilitate her swift departure. "I was simply laughing at the idea of me delivering a pair of peacocks."

"How did you know he's expecting *two* peacocks?"

She was as sharp as a barrister at the court of Lincoln's Inn. But Duncan Kerr would not play the harried victim in the witness box. "Why are you so suspicious? 'Twas a logical assumption, Miriam. He's distraught over the loss of his birds, which he breeds with some success. His last cock could pounce on a peahen and give her his finest before she could scratch in the dirt."

She gasped. "If you're not here to deliver peacocks, why are you visiting the earl?"

"I doona think I should tell you. Duncan's a very private person."

"I'm surprised he would mention the birds, then—if he's such a private person."

"We shared a glass of wine, which makes him *less* private."

"Meaning . . ."

Blessed Scotland, she was persistent. "I'm not a gossiping stable lad. I prefer to make my own scandals."

"That's no explanation."

He sighed and, feigning reluctance, said, "If you must know, the earl has no tolerance for strong drink." Let her do with that tidbit what she would.

"Thank you for telling me. I won't gift him with any of the fine wines I brought from Europe. Actually . . ." She shooed the dog away. "You could prevent me from making any number of faux pas by telling me more about Lord Duncan." She snuggled closer.

If he weren't careful, she'd have him choosing the stones for his own cairn. But he knew she was trying to distract him with sex, and he rather liked the idea of holding her again. "Are you still cold?"

"A bit. I should go in, I suppose."

Propriety demanded she make such a statement, but decorum had no place in the life of the Border Lord. Not when he had the queen's beautiful minion exactly where he wanted her.

Wrapping his arm around her shoulders, he brought her to his side and drew the cape around them. "'Tis early, Miriam, and you have nothing to fear from me. I am interested in the 'matters' that brought you to the Border."

"'Twould bore you to tears."

Would she never talk about herself or mention the Treaty of Utrecht or her role in the affairs of England? The mediators before her had rambled for hours on their accomplishments. Ah, well, perhaps her career was a topic for the bumbling earl to broach. For the moment, Duncan would learn what he could. "Beautiful women never bore me. Give over, Miriam. Tell me why you've come to Kildalton."

She cleared her throat. "Do you know Baron Sinclair?"

"Aye, I know the man." He kept his voice even, but his stomach pitched in anticipation of her next words.

"Then I'd like your opinion of his quarrel with the earl."

She could set verbal traps with the skill of a gamekeeper. Hoping to divert her attention, Duncan began to stroke her arm. Even through the thick gloves, he felt her warmth. He wanted to touch his skin to hers, but if he removed the gloves, she'd notice the blisters on his palms.

"I understand your hesitance to discuss Lord Duncan's enemy. May my hair turn white and my scribes run off with lightskirts tomorrow if I don't." Her hand settled gently on his knee. "Please believe it's important that I know all sides of the quarrel. I commend you for speaking up."

Lulled by the tone of her voice and the eloquence of her plea, Duncan scrambled for a reply. "They'll never reach accord," he said. "Not while both of them live."

"I know how much you want to put the matter behind you. Life is too short and unpredictable for petty annoyances and feuding lairds. Who knows that better than a fellow Scot? Did the baron burn the MacLarens' farm?"

"Aye, the bastard," Duncan grumbled.

"So he is." She gave his knee a squeeze. The tendons in his leg tightened, sending a jolt of pure pleasure to his groin. She might as well have caressed his manly parts. "How has he wronged you?"

"He . . ." Duncan paused, pretending to hesitate in the hope that she'd touch him again. He needed her to touch him again.

"You're a saint to reveal your troubles to me," she said, her voice a pleasing octave lower. "I'm sure the earl will repay your loyalty handsomely. Did the baron raid your pig farm?"

With a belated flash of insight, Duncan realized that she wielded her velvet tongue with the skill of a fencing master drawing his foil. Had she not mentioned the ridiculous pigs Duncan would've poured out his soul.

"If I'm to accomplish what God intended for me, I must know your role in the problem, Ian."

Bless Saint Ninian! She was as shameless as a royal concubine. No wonder England enjoyed the most lucrative trade agreements on the globe. Given the chance, Miriam MacDonald could convince the king of France to wipe her slippers. But Duncan Kerr was wise to her tricks, and had a few of his own.

He put his hand on hers. "I want to trust you, lassie." He began to draw her hand slowly upward. "But the earl wouldna take kindly to my spilling his troubles to you."

She moved her hand back down to his knee. "I thought he wanted peace."

His own hand followed. "Everyone in the Borders wants peace, but no one knows how to begin." As he spoke he again guided her hand higher. "'Tis a powder keg to be sure."

Her fingers slid from beneath his and glided back down to his knee. "You mustn't worry, Ian. I know what I'm about."

So did he. Duncan again covered her hand and began the trek upwards. "You were saying . . ."

"I'm here to help you—if you'll let me."

Raw lust infused him, and his randy body seemed determined to meet her hand halfway. "Oh, but I will," he said, his mind eons away from Border feuds and selfish Englishmen.

"Think how wonderful it will be if we work together."

"Wonderful seems a bland word." Especially for the carnal fulfillment he had in mind. His hand continued its slow, agonizing upward journey.

"We'll begin carefully," she said.

Two more inches and she'd give him the touch he craved. He could take her here on the bench. Erotic possibilities dashed through his mind. Her skirts hiked to her waist, her pale legs parted in invitation, her silky, fragrant hair pillowing his cheek. His mouth began to water. Perspiration drenched his brow. He could lift her onto his lap, lean her back, and suckle her breasts while she rode him.

"I know you're in a difficult position."

A groan lodged in his throat. Cramps of frustration attacked his groin. He swallowed in a noisy gulp. "Difficult isna the right word either."

"Please, Ian, trust me. I work with the utmost discretion."

Distracted, he said, "Discretion, aye. We'll need that."

"The earl need never know."

Again, reality intruded. But this time he was a victim of his own desire. Regrets played havoc with hindsight. She, with her wily ways and feminine allure, had instigated the episode. It wasn't his fault she hadn't perceived his train of thought. Given the chance, she'd suck his mind dry of information and use it against him.

Oh, Christ, he couldn't make love to her. He had only

himself to blame. He'd leaped into the role of seducer without considering the consequences, and suddenly, the trappings of the bumbling earl seemed a safe harbor, albeit a frustrating one. Who would have thought a woman like Miriam MacDonald could get him so hot and bothered?

"What are you thinking?" she asked.

Futility made him say, "That I've never trusted a woman so completely."

"You're in good company, for I've never trusted a man so completely. Let's make a bargain, you and I."

Mischief pervaded his dilemma. Hell, he was desperate to gain control of the situation and rule this conniving red-haired wench. "I favor bargains. 'Tis tradition between a fair maiden and an errant knight to seal a bargain with a kiss."

She turned to face him, bringing her lips dangerously close to his. Blinking, her face wreathed in confusion, she said, "That's not the sort of bargain I meant—"

"Good." With her sweet breath wafting across his face, he could no more stop himself from kissing her than he could save Hadrian's Wall from the ravages of time. "The Border Lord sets his own bargains," he said, bringing her hand home.

Relief eased the aching fullness of his loins. He fitted his lips to hers, and as he expected, she tried to pull away. "Shush," he whispered, "and kiss me."

She gasped and withdrew her hand. Pushing against his chest, she said, "Let me go."

He clutched her shoulders. "You wanted me to kiss you, so doona be denying it now."

She shook her head. "No. You misinterpreted my intentions."

Even in the faint moonlight, he could see her discomfiture. "Did I?" he drawled. "You put your hand on my knee. You caressed my leg."

She twisted free of him, shot to her feet, and backed away. "'Twas only a friendly gesture. I never meant anything by it."

He stalked her to the garden wall. "'Tis also a friendly gesture to fondle me."

Her hands flew to her breasts. *"You* did that."

"Nay. You did, and we both enjoyed it." Leaning forward, he forced her against the wall. Bracing his hands on the cool tiles, he demanded, "Did you protest?"

"Yes. I mean, I am now. I was merely—"

"Merely what?"

She took a deep breath and blurted, "The queen sent me to make peace between the earl and Baron Sinclair. I'm a member of her diplomatic corps."

"Do you always use your feminine wiles in negotiations?"

"Most men I negotiate with are not lusty rogues."

The admission did little to soothe his fury. "Then know this, my sneaky wee diplomat. The only man in the Borders who can aid your cause is me."

Pride brought her chin up. "For a pig farmer, you're very sure of yourself."

"Oh, aye." The need to outsmart this too intelligent, overalluring woman consumed him. "I'm more sure of you, Miriam MacDonald."

"What's that supposed to mean?" she said, as prissy as a spinster on May Day.

He stoked his raging desire with aggression. "You wanted me to kiss you. And you can deny it until your hair turns white and your scribes find their lightskirts, but it wilna change what you feel in here." He brushed her hand aside and lay his gloved hand on her breast. "Your heart beats for me."

Miriam stared up at him. "You're wrong." She grasped his wrist and tried to dislodge his hand. Her heart didn't just beat for him, it hammered with an intensity so wild she almost leaped into his arms. Raw desire mocked her purpose and her protest.

"You may have deluded those dandified fops at court," he said. "But your scheming machinations will cost you dearly here. Are you willing to pay the price?"

"What price? What do you have to sell? Why should I be willing to pay?"

He loomed over her, a dark and dangerous shadow. Perspiration glistened like diamonds on his upper lip, giving evidence of the control he exercised over his passion. She remembered the feel of him in her hand, pulsing with life

64

and vigor. Even now, his power held a part of her spell-bound, but for too many years she'd resisted courtiers and cavaliers more wily than he. The irony was, she usually did the angry protesting, then turned it to her advantage. A challenge beckoned. She drew strength from it.

Capitulation seemed a good place to start. "Very well. I admit the prospect of kissing you interested me. But you lured me with what I thought was an honest offer of friendship."

His heated gaze remained steady. "'Twould take a blind man to ignore your charms."

"But you lured *me.*"

"'Twas a mutual allure, lass." He rubbed himself against her. "Still is."

Desire and confusion clouded her thoughts. Pushing those weakening emotions aside, she latched on to the lifeline of domination. "If you could pry open that stiff jaw long enough to discuss our situation reasonably, we could stop yelling at each other and start—"

"Taking off our clothes?" he said in a silky whisper.

Shock paralyzed her mind, but her body responded with a wanton yearning she couldn't master. Her muscles grew listless, her skin flushed.

"You want me." His leather glove crackled as he caressed her breast. "Admit it."

She slapped him. "I want your cooperation."

He grinned, his teeth a slashing white line in a disarmingly handsome face. "'Tis yours."

She'd faced angry ministers and petulant kings and mustered the wherewithal to prevail. Her skills couldn't desert her tonight. "For a price, you mean?"

"I'd call it a reward."

"Let me be sure I understand. In exchange for information which may or may not help me achieve peace on the Borders, I'm to receive a boon in the form of your manly prowess?"

He squeezed his eyes shut. "I'm a man who cares little for the useless maneuverings of politics. Keep your diplomacy, Miriam MacDonald. I want the woman."

Her knees grew weak. No man had ever disregarded her

reputation and expertise. Quite the contrary, her position had lured them like dying sinners to redemption. But they wanted an alliance with England.

"What's this? A diplomat with nothing to say."

She stared at the straight slope of his nose and the gentle flare of his nostrils. "I want you to be reasonable."

He leaned closer. "I want to nestle with you before my hearth and hear your favorite verse. I want to see you garbed in your favorite color. I want to know your dreams and be a part of them. I want to protect you, cherish you."

Flabbergasted, she said, "How can you expect to know that's what I want? We've only just met."

"How does a golden eagle choose his lifelong mate?"

Prior knowledge compelled her to say, "He's influenced by the rut."

Hearty laughter rumbled in his chest. "Bless Saint Ninian, Miriam MacDonald, when you shed that conniving nature, you've a humor to light the bleakest night."

Humor? If acumen were measured in wealth, she was the poorest wretch in Christendom. Obviously the Border Lord was easily entertained and knew little of the animal kingdom—outside his precious pigs. Still, she felt a rush of pride that he'd found her interesting in a personal way.

"Come, love. Show me more of that MacDonald humor."

Temptation pulled at her. She had a mission here, and her duties did not include trysting with a lusty stranger. But she liked the reckless abandon he made her feel.

Reason won out. If she didn't succeed in Kildalton, she'd never convince the queen to punish the Glenlyon Campbells. "Perhaps another time. I was sent here for a reason. I did not come to socialize or pour out my troubles on a stranger."

"And your responsibilities to England come before dalliances with rogues like me. Unless, that is, I tell you all you want to know about Baron Sinclair and the earl of Kildalton."

"Aye. My work comes first." The word tasted bitter.

He stepped away from her. "'Tis a pity. For squabbles between Englishmen and Scots are a way of life here. I promise you this, lassie. You'll grow old and frustrated trying to solve them." He touched the brim of his hat and started walking away. *"Lang mae yer lum reek."*

The wish for good fortune, spoken in the beautiful language of her youth, snared her heart. The sound of retreating footsteps filled her with despair. She reached out to him. "Wait."

Quick as a cat, he turned and grasped her hand. "What is it?"

"I can't bear for you to go yet."

"I'll stay, but for one purpose." He pulled her toward him and whispered, "This."

He surrounded her, a dark visage offering a haven of light. He smelled of a lush forest, unexplored and precious in its isolation. She sought shelter there and found herself welcomed and comforted by sweet Scottish words, then enticing her to cast off her worldly cares and languish in his arms.

When his lips touched hers, Miriam gave herself up to the desperation he inspired, and plunged heart first toward the fulfillment he promised.

"One touch of your honeyed lips," he murmured, "could drive a man to madness."

Endless nights of girlish dreams came brilliantly to life. Dizzy with desire, she pressed forward, cupping her hands to his strong jaw, feeling the muscles stretch when his mouth opened wide and his tongue shot forth to pillage her senses and sharpen her need. Like a primitive dance done 'round a roaring fire and to the beat of an ancient drum, the kiss evolved into a basic awareness that knocked on the door of her soul. She shuddered beneath an onslaught of feelings so simplistic in nature that give extended to take, want embraced need, sustenance obliterated hunger, and warmth banished cold.

Then her body spoke of a different need, and he answered with hands that caressed, lifted and shaped her hips into a cradle. He nestled himself there, rocking against her in a rhythmic motion that sent a spiral of wanting to her belly. Wild with the urge to touch and know, her hands roamed his face, her fingers encountering the sheared beaver of his hat, then sending it flying.

He stiffened and dragged his mouth from hers. Into the

silence of the night burst the labored rasp of his breathing. Or was it hers? She opened her eyes, only to see him slide from her line of vision. Weakness drenched her bones. The night wind chilled her skin.

With a muffled curse, he snatched up the hat and jammed it on his head. In a strained voice, thick with the burr of Scotland, he said, "That's a fair bit of socializing."

"From you, too."

He turned to go.

The garden door swung open. He stood in the shadow of the wall, the hat pulled low over his brow, his gloved hand curled around the aged wooden portal. She felt compelled to utter some meaningful, poignant phrase that he would carry with him, that would imprint on his heart the memory of a woman who'd never forget him.

With heartbreaking honesty she realized that outside the rhetoric of diplomacy she had no talent for the romantic. The knowledge saddened her. "Will I see you again?" she asked.

Without turning back, he said, "You haven't seen me the first time, yet."

"How will I know you? 'Tis so dark I don't know what you look like."

"You'll know me. You know my terms: No questions about the feud. Have you the courage and the time to meet them?"

Suddenly time became a commodity she possessed in abundance. Information was what she lacked. Gleaning it was her forte. Again she reached out to him. "Oh, but I do have the time. I'm thinking of wintering here."

He lifted his head. The murky moonlight wreathed his hat in a silvery patina. "Saint Ninian help us, then."

In a swirl of inky shadows, he moved through the gate. His resigned prayer hung in her mind and mingled with the sweet remembrance of his embrace.

Her arm fell to her side. A cold canine nose nudged her palm. "Well, you certainly took a liking to him."

Verbatim sat back on her haunches and extended a paw.

As Miriam made her way back to her chamber, she couldn't dispel the image of the dark, intriguing stranger. As she undressed in the privacy of her room, she could still feel his eyes on her, still remembered the gentle touch of his hands, relived again and again the soft insistence of his lips. Even as she slipped beneath covers, she felt the comfort of his embrace. And as she closed her eyes, the echo of his hearty laughter and the memory of his bold seduction made a mockery of her attempts at sleep.

Gleaning information from the Border Lord would be difficult, for he would try to seduce her in return. Wintering in the Borders suddenly represented a challenge she welcomed. Smiling, Miriam drifted at last to sleep.

Cursing, Duncan stomped into the stables. Horses nickered and poked their heads out of the stalls. Even the greeting of his favorite mount failed to deter him on his quest for sanctuary.

He passed the tack room, rife with the aroma of old leather and new manure. He stopped at the base of a darkened stairway.

As a child he'd walked this route countless times, some days with pride swelling his chest and a Roman treasure in his hands. Other days he'd come with tears in his eyes and welts on his legs.

He'd come for reassurance on the night Malcolm was born. He'd come for solace on the day Roxanne had died. Tonight he came because Miriam disturbed his soul.

He grasped the wooden railing and bounded up the narrow steps two at a time. A bar of light streamed beneath the door. With the slightest effort, Duncan pushed it open.

Angus MacDodd sat at a desk, a bone-handled knife and whetstone in his hands. The spacious room served as both his private quarters and armory. Crossbows and pikes filled one long wall; shields bearing the Kerr sun and breastplates bearing the signature dents and scrapes of battle lined the other. Interspersed with the hoard of Kildalton's defense were the ancient treasures unearthed by an inquisitive lad. Pitted Roman lances, helmets shorn of their brushy plumes, and a tub of broken pottery served as a fitting foil for the devices of modern warfare.

Angus put the tools aside and helped Duncan with his

cape, "I take it she's more interesting than a gouty minor lord with an empty purse and a mind to match." He folded the garment and laid it in a trunk.

Duncan swept off his hat and raked the scarf from his head. "Interesting?" He handed the clothing to Angus, who added them to the box. "She has a mind and a purpose to match Marcus Brutus."

Angus grimaced, "I was hoping for the gentle disposition of a Claudius."

Duncan peeled off his gloves, tossed them in with the rest of his disguise. He slammed the trunk. "She could devour him with a 'how do you do.'"

Angus went back to the chair, the light shimmering in his red hair and beard, which were generously salted with gray. Even so, Duncan was reminded of another redhead.

He must have scowled, for Angus said, "I take it she wasn't afraid of the Border Lord."

"Afraid?" Duncan began to pace the room that had been a haven for as long as he could remember. "I woefully underestimated her, Angus."

A smile and a knowing glint in merry brown eyes transformed a battle-hardened soldier into a trusted friend. "She's just a woman, lad."

Visions soared in Duncan's mind. "Aye," he growled. "So was Boadicea, but she ran the Romans out of London. Our little diplomat has a tricky enough tongue and ample charms to send a man chasing after his own tail. I doona wonder now why she's never married. 'Tis as plain as the battered nose on the face of an Irishman."

Angus put his foot on an empty chair and sent it sliding toward Duncan. "You should be happy she's not got marriage on her mind. Sit down."

Duncan pulled the chair between his legs and sat with his arms resting over the back. The position eased the lingering ache in his groin. "It's what she does have on her mind that worries me. She's also cunning enough to make a man regret he'd ever set eyes on her."

"You don't mean she found you out?"

"Nay. She's just wily."

"A challenge, then? An available challenge?"

The understatement made Duncan smile.

"Good," Angus declared. "You need that. You spend too much of your life in the role of guardian. You deserve a comely diversion now and then. Nothing like a redhead to put a skip in a man's step."

Anger subsided, leaving in its wake a determination that brought both excitement and caution to Duncan's soul. "Oh, aye. I need a comely diversion like I need another English neighbor."

"She's still a Scot, and a MacDonald to boot. Is she from Skye?"

Duncan wrung his hands. "I was too busy kissing her to ask."

"So, the Border Lord has become a cavalier? Here." Angus pitched Duncan a towel. "You've lampblack smeared on your forehead."

"Have I?" A genuine smile lightened Duncan's spirits. As he wiped the soot from his face, he related most of the details of the interlude, omitting her intimate touch and the pleasurable, erotic journey he'd made of it. The parting kiss was another matter altogether. Given time, he'd understand the tender feelings she inspired, but he'd do his soul-searching in private.

"What will the Border Lord do next?" asked Angus.

"I don't know." Duncan held up his hand. "I'm a weary, confused man with too much on his plate and no taste for the meal."

"Then have a drink."

Angus filled a tankard and passed it to Duncan. The yeasty ale flowed over his tongue and mingled with the taste of Miriam MacDonald. Heat rushed through him, and he gulped down the contents of the mug, trying to wash away the flavor of a woman he couldn't have.

After downing his own ale, Angus said, "So, the bumbling earl has his work cut out for him, eh? What will *he* do next?"

"Curse himself for donning those ridiculous spectacles."

"You look rather fetching in the disguise. Everyone says so. The people of Kildalton haven't felt closer to their laird or more entertained since your grandfather captured the Armstrong heiress and held her for ransom. He was a fine laird, much like you."

Pride warmed Duncan. "You're forgetting that my grandfather's attempt at blackmail went for naught when his captive grew big with his child."

Angus tucked his thumbs into the wide leather belt that separated a barrel-thick chest and massive arms from trunklike legs. "I was a lad at the time, but my Da said the old earl bragged about what a fine breeder she was." Fondness softened a voice perfectly suited to barking orders and upbraiding laggardly soldiers. "Then your grandsire doubled the ransom. Lord, he was a braw one, the old earl was."

"He'd never pack up his wits, don spectacles, and give a woman the upper hand."

"Don't take it to heart, laddie." Angus leaned forward, his callused index finger extended. "'Tis only a temporary setback. She surprised you, nothing more. You'll retaliate. You always do. But can you swear that you don't enjoy the masquerade?"

"At this moment, I'm sorry I locked myself into the role of bumbling earl. Malcolm's getting out of hand. Mrs. Elliott bursts into laughter every time my name is mentioned. Oh, she covers it by pretending to sneeze, but it's embarrassing all the same. The only person who doesna seem entertained by it all is Lady Miriam."

"You want to bed her."

Passion rose again in Duncan. "Who wouldn't? Have you seen her?"

"Aye, she's a bonnie one, and smart, you say?"

"Miriam MacDonald could have talked Caesar out of Rome."

Placing his palms on his cheeks, Angus stroked his thick beard into a point at his chin. "You've a task ahead of you, my lord, what with Sinclair's men pouring across the Border like Crusaders into the Holy Land."

Everyday problems crashed in on Duncan. Guarding the safety of his people was a constant task, but a more immediate concern blazed in his mind. "I've got to get rid of Miriam MacDonald," he said. "Before Sinclair does his worst."

Angus reached out and clutched Duncan's hand. "Do you truly believe he'll try to take away your son?"

"Oh, aye," said Duncan, fury rising like bile. "He'd

resurrect Malcolm's mother if he thought he could turn a profit by it. The presence of our bonnie diplomat may just inspire him to new depths of deviltry. I'm afraid that like all the other emissaries of the queen, Miriam will believe the bastard." Duncan's stomach sank, for he didn't like the notion that Miriam MacDonald might be unfair.

Angus slapped his hand over his heart. "Baron Sin will never take Malcolm."

Duncan sighed. "What if Miriam sees it differently?"

"I learned a few things about her today that might help our cause," said Angus.

Hope chased away Duncan's misgivings. "Tell me."

Angus refilled their mugs. "According to Lady Alexis, they've never set eyes on Sinclair. They don't know the particulars about the strife between you two. Nor do they know of the relationship."

Relief mingled with satisfaction. Duncan had suspected she knew little about the problems here. "Lady Alexis told you all that?"

"Give an old man some credit, lad." He leaned back in the chair, his eyes glittering with manly pride. "She's tall, you know, and carries herself with dignity, same as her father did." Angus made the sign of the cross. "God rest his pure Stewart soul. I merely asked her if it bothered her to stand so close to a fellow of Sinclair's stature."

"By God, you baited her well. He's a giant." Duncan slapped his thigh. "What did she say?"

Chuckling, Angus said, "She looked down that pretty nose at me and said a well-bred and intelligent woman didn't judge a man by his size or his lack of it. Why, if I hadn't been fishing for information about Sinclair, I'd've thought she was referring to me. Stump that I am."

"Sounds as if she was flirting with you." Duncan pictured the stately Alexis beside the good-hearted man who'd been too busy caring for a lonely, mistreated lad to find himself a wife.

Angus's smile faded, replaced by an expression of understanding that Duncan had seen often in his life. "Nay, lad. I'd not expect Alexis Southward to flirt with me."

"Why not?"

"Let's just say I'd question her motives. She's a Stewart

princess, no matter what side of the blanket she was born on. I won't go lusting after her, either."

Duncan couldn't let lust cloud his reason or influence his decisions, for the welfare of his people and the future of his son hung in the balance. "Good advice, Angus."

"Lady Miriam got your blood up. I see it in your eyes and . . ." His sly gaze dropped lower. "Elsewhere."

Duncan ground his teeth and focused on a Roman helmet he'd spent weeks restoring. "I'm a widower, not a monk."

"Forget the ache in your lady crackers and guard your heart, lad, for if what my brother said about Miriam MacDonald is true, she hasn't the capacity for affection—not the kind you're seeking."

Disappointment weighted Duncan's spirits. "What else did the good tinker allow?"

"He swears, according to the trustworthy chambermaid in the household of the mayor of London, that the MacDonald lass is a cold fish and wouldn't know humor or passion if they ambushed her in the road."

Duncan remembered the feel of her mouth moving beneath his, and the pleasurable sensations of her satiny tongue gliding between his lips. Renewed lust rocketed to his groin. In retrospect, he could recall the precise moment when she yielded to passion and became its eager student. He hadn't known then that the experience was a new one for her. Now he sorely ached to initiate her fully in the joys of physical love. But the risk was too great. She mustn't find out he was the Border Lord. She mustn't stop him from defending his crofters and his own son.

"Have you nothing to say?" asked Angus.

"Aye." Duncan downed the remainder of his ale and slammed the tankard on the table. Getting to his feet, he said, "If the tinker said she was a stranger to passion and humor, he was right on only one count."

5

"You can't possibly intend to winter here," said Alexis.

"Keep your voice down," Miriam whispered, not breaking stride in her journey down the main stairway of the castle.

In the entryway, a housemaid sloshed a rag mop into a pail, then twirled the handle between her flattened palms. A servant boy carrying a brimming ash bucket paused to talk to the girl. Miriam went on her way.

Alexis hurried after her, her calf slippers making soft rustling noises on the stone flags. "You can't, Miriam. The queen will be furious."

"She's furious now." The aroma of freshly baked bread drew Miriam toward an arched corridor. Her stomach growled. "This way. I'm famished."

Alexis clutched her forearm. "Say you're jesting."

"I never jest, and you know it." Except once last night, but she'd erred royally in all other aspects of the evening. She'd learned nothing and experienced everything.

"There's something you're not telling me," said Alexis. "Don't ask me to guess, 'tis too early in the morning."

"Then I won't."

"Oh, drat you," she grumbled. "Unless . . ." She snapped her fingers. "It's about that man you saw in the garden, isn't it? Who is he?"

Miriam took great pleasure in saying, "He's a pig farmer who tried to seduce me."

Alexis tilted back her head and gave Miriam a stern glance that reeked of motherly disapproval. The expression also made her look exactly like the state portrait of her father. "You let a swineherd kiss you?"

Miriam thought of the dark stranger. Conflicting images tweaked her mind. One moment he soothed and comforted with gentle words and coaxing hands, the next he seduced and bullied with bold threats and vulgar ultimatums. She knew that her queries about the earl had caused the change in the Border Lord's mood and methods, she just didn't know why. Unless they were in collusion. But his parting kiss had nothing to do with territorial disputes and everything to do with cheap seduction.

"You must tell me," said Alexis.

Confused, Miriam whispered, "Later, Lexie," and walked into the lesser hall.

To Miriam's delight, the elusive housekeeper stood at a trestle table, her arm pumping as she sawed a loaf of brown bread into thick slices. She wore a sturdy woolen frock beneath a crisp, linen apron, shiny from starch and wear.

"Good morning, Mrs. Elliott," said Miriam, taking a seat at the long bench by the table.

A smile puffed out the older woman's cheeks. Blinking, she said, "You remembered my name, Lady Miriam. Thank you."

People were surprised by the small gesture that came effortlessly to Miriam. "You're welcome. Is that bread I smell?"

Mrs. Elliott sent a maid to the pantry for plates. "Aye. What will you have to drink, my lady?"

"Honeyed milk, if you please."

Alexis slid onto the bench and said, "I'll have watered wine." When the housekeeper offered her a slice of bread, Alexis shook her head, a pained look on her face. "Thank you, no. I couldn't eat a thing so early in the morning."

Miriam slathered the bread with butter and candied pippins. Although she intended to compliment the food regardless of the quality, the rich flavors made her sigh with pleasure.

Alexis, usually grumpy before noon, groaned, "Oh, please."

Mrs. Elliott said, "Can I get you anything else, my lady?"

Miriam hoped to glean information on the mysterious pig farmer who called himself the Border Lord, if, that is, Mrs. Elliott would cooperate. To that end Miriam made a great show of considering her answer. "A thick slice of fresh roasted pork would be grand."

The housekeeper's smile faded and her hands worried a stack of crumbs. She seemed wary, or was she just uncomfortable with visitors? The earl said he didn't often entertain. "I'm sorry, my lady. We haven't any fresh pork today," she said, "but there's salted ham and oat pudding."

Silently rejoicing, Miriam said, "The ham will be fine." When the meat was served, she exclaimed, "What a beautiful ham. You must have a fine pig farmer in Kildalton. Send him my compliments."

Mrs. Elliott's brows made a chevron in the center on her forehead. "It comes from the butcher. I'll tell him."

Honey ran over the edge of the bread. Miriam caught it with her finger. "The butcher raises his own stock. How enterprising." She popped her finger into her mouth.

"He don't raise it, I'm sure," said Mrs. Elliott. "I'll fetch you more milk."

Sensing her chance was slipping away, Miriam said, "Alexis, do you remember that eccentric French count who raised pigs in his keeping room?"

Alexis paused, the tankard an inch from her lips. She rolled her gaze to Miriam, searched her face, then took a drink. "I believe you said his castle smelled wretched."

Turning slightly, Miriam winked. To Mrs. Elliott, she said, "Imagine that, will you? Squealing piglets underfoot."

The woman's wariness turned to stiff-necked disapproval, deepening the dimple in her chin into a cavern. "You won't find swine in this castle."

"Not the cloven-hoofed variety," Alexis murmured into the tankard.

Ignoring her, Miriam said, "Of course not. I believe I met one of your pig farmers."

"You did?" the housekeeper said.

"Aye. He said his name was Ian, but he also called himself the Border Lord."

Mrs. Elliott scooped up her apron and sneezed into it with the gusto of a tavern keeper. Turning her back, her shoulders shook with the force of the sneezes. Slipping one hand free, she waved it at Miriam, curtsied, and rushed out of the room.

"You should be ashamed," said Alexis, staring at the empty doorway.

"I must know more about him. The Border Lord knows both the earl and the baron. He could be useful."

Alexis shook her head. "'Tis a crime for a mind to work so deviously at this hour of the morning."

After so many years, the familiar barb didn't prick at all. "'Tis not, so long as I succeed."

Miriam finished the ham and was describing to Alexis the tartan of the Border Lord when Alexis said, "Shush!" and picked up her tankard.

Mrs. Elliott returned, her eyes still watering and her nose as red as a China poppy. "Forgive me, my lady. 'Tis the time of year." She began separating the comb from a crock of honey.

Grasping the tried and true tactic of aggression, Miriam said, "Before you left you were telling me about the pig farmer who goes by the name of the Border Lord."

The sieve slipped into the crock. The cook sniffed and held her apron at the ready. "I don't generally deal with the farmers. We have markets here, so everyone can trade freely." Her voice sounded strained.

"But you know where he is."

"Aye," she choked out, and again hid her face in the apron. Through the cloth she said, "There's a swineherd in Sweeper's Heath." Then she dashed from the room once more.

Miriam's spirits soared. She would find the Border Lord, and in the light of day.

"I take it," said Alexis in weary resolution, "that we're

78

going on an excursion to the quaint little village of Sweeper's Heath."

Miriam was already mapping out a strategy for dealing with the mysterious Border Lord when she said, "Aye, but first we must visit the weaver."

"Why did I bother to ask?" said Alexis, with a royal wave of her hand. "We always visit the weaver before we see the swineherd."

Puzzled, Miriam said, "We've never been to a swineherd."

Alexis got to her feet, mumbling, "I had such hopes for you. You were such a bright child."

Duncan yanked up the full black periwig and slammed it on his head. He had intended to spend the day with Malcolm, for according to Mrs. Elliott, the lad was taking his role of indulged brat much too seriously. But thanks to that meddling, I-never-forget-anything redhead, Duncan had to forgo his fatherly duties and chase her down before she made the grievous mistake of looking for a swineherd who didn't exist.

Stupid, stupid, stupid. Perverse, too. He'd dreamed up the story to mock Miriam and her lack of a sense of humor. The plan had backfired, and a moment's satisfaction last night had become a joke on Duncan. He wanted a different sort of satisfaction from her, one that prohibited clever repartee and involved tussling naked and nibbling on the delicacies of the flesh.

A knock sounded at the door.

"Enter at your own risk," Duncan grumbled.

Angus strolled inside, his thick hair still bearing the imprint of the visored helmet he now held in his hand. "What is it, my lord?"

Duncan stifled his anger and frustration; he had only himself to blame. But Blessed Scotland, he hated being one step behind in a game of his own creation. "Do you remember when I told you what occurred in the garden with Lady Miriam?"

"Aye, my lord. I remember every detail." His lips twitched in the effort to hide a smile. "First you stomped into my quarters with a hard-on to rival an oak branch and your lady crackers aching. Then you confessed that you told her you were the Border Lord and a pig farmer. Oh, and you quaffed two pints of ale in the doing."

"How is it," Duncan said, trying to keep his voice calm and his anger in check, "that the duke of Cromarty, who rules all of the Highlands, manages to earn the loyalty and respect of his clansmen?"

Undaunted, Angus replied, "I wouldn't know, my lord."

In spite of himself and the dire situation he faced, Duncan chuckled. "'Twould seem our merry diplomat cornered Mrs. Elliott this morning and grilled her on the whereabouts of a certain swineherd."

Angus spat a Scottish curse and rapped the helmet against his thigh. Over the rattling of forged steel, he said, "What will you do?"

"I'll wring her pretty neck!"

"I'm sure you have a better plan."

"Tactic, Angus, that's the operative word." Duncan snatched up his clan badge and secured his tartan over his shoulder. "Everything to do with that wily witch involves tactics. She's too bloody smart for her own good—or mine."

"Aye, sir. I'm sure she is. But if appearance means aught, you'll dazzle her with your kilt. The wig adds a nice touch."

"You needn't placate me." Duncan walked to the standing mirror and donned his bonnet at a jaunty angle that all but obscured the right side of his face.

"Nay, my lord. I wouldn't think of it."

Studying his reflection, decked out in Kerr regalia, Duncan thought of the differences between him and his forebears. "I doona ken why I'm worried. She's probably halfway to Sweeper's Heath by now anyway."

"No, she isn't."

"She's most likely cornered the real swineherd and talked poor Ian into baring his soul and damning mine to perdition."

"She ain't in Sweeper's Heath."

"I should have sneaked into the corridor this morning and listened to her plans. Er—what's that you said, Angus?"

"I said, she ain't in Sweeper's Heath."

"How do you know that?"

"Because she can't be in two places at once."

His nerves jangled, Duncan said, "Then where, for the love of Scotland, is she?"

Blithely, Angus said, "At the weaver's. I saw her on my way here."

Duncan went weak with relief. He grabbed his coat and headed for the door, the sporran slapping against his groin and thighs. "Go to Sweeper's Heath. Tell the real swineherd that if a conniving, dangerous redhead asks him about the Border Lord, he's to . . ."

"To what, my lord?"

Duncan took a deep breath and prayed to the patron saint of Scotland. "He's to tell her the truth about the Border Lord."

The helmet hit the floor. "What?"

"Just do it," said Duncan before he changed his mind.

Angus scooped up his battle gear. "Oh, aye, my lord. Straightaway. I'd love to be a midge on the wall when she hears the tale."

Duncan threw open the door. "Thank you, Angus. I'll be certain to buzz right back and tell you how she reacts."

"My lord," said Angus, grinning like a Turk. "You forgot your spectacles."

The weaver's shop smelled of dank wool, but the sharp odor was offset by the earthy aroma of the lichens and plants used in the making of dye. To Duncan, the place inspired pride in himself and fondness for the proprietor. At the age of five Duncan had stood stiff as a soldier while Mr. Murdoch draped him in the Kerr family tartan and spent the better part of a morning showing an eager lad how to pleat and tuck and secure his first kilt.

The pleasant memory took the edge off his anger. The sight of Miriam MacDonald alone in the room and bending over a box of tartans gave him a start. From behind a curtained doorway drifted the sound of voices and the clickety clack of the looms, but Duncan couldn't take his eyes off the woman.

She wore a full-skirted gown of ocean blue velvet over a mountain of lace-trimmed petticoats, all visible thanks to both her diligence in rummaging through the box and his vantage point just inside the door. By lifting his chin and peering through the spectacles, he could see in minute detail the weave of her white silk stockings and the blush of skin beneath.

Engrossed, he tipped back his head and through the magnifying lenses followed the flare of the skirt up to the base of her spine where the lacings of the dress began. He had touched her there. He'd caressed a particular vertebra in the small of her back. Her knees had wobbled. From that moment on she'd participated in the kiss and become a damn fine explorer herself. What would she do if the earl peeled off her clothing and tasted her sensitive spots?

"Good morning, my lord. How was your trip?"

Startled, Duncan turned to see Alexis Southward standing inside the curtained doorway, a knowing smile on her lips and a Royal Stewart plaid draped over her forearm.

Damn! She'd caught him ogling Miriam, who was still immersed in her task.

He wiped what he suspected to be a leer off his face and said, "Good morning to you. That's a lovely plaid."

"As is yours," she replied, eyeing him from head to toe.

For some reason Duncan became aware of the soft wool against his bare buttocks. Now he wished he'd worn trews beneath his kilt, for he felt exposed. But that was silly. Only in the dead of winter did he defy tradition. He willed his blush away. She'd simply surprised him. Once he regained his composure, he could get on with the business of escorting Miriam to the swineherd.

He bowed from the waist. "You're very kind, Your Grace."

"Please," she said, stroking the most revered plaid in Scotland, "call me Lexie. I severed my ties long ago with the duke of Challenbroke. I consider myself an ordinary citizen."

Over her shoulder, Miriam said, "Ha! How many ordinary citizens have the blood of kings in their veins?"

"Thanks to my father . . ." said Alexis, "many."

Miriam whirled to face her friend, a tartan in her hands. Gray eyes glared with disapproval. *"Honte a toi,"* she said. "You should not say such a thing."

Alexis lifted an eyebrow. *"Touché, mon amie.* Now practice the good manners I taught you and greet our host."

Miriam opened her mouth, then closed it. Looking at Duncan's bonnet, she said, "Good morning, my lord. You're up early today."

When her eyes didn't meet his, Duncan grew wary. What if she recognized him? Suddenly he felt naked again. He had to slip back into the role of bumbling earl. He pulled a petulant frown and waved a slip of paper. "I had no choice but to rise early. I must get supplies for my most alluring fishing lure, the flippity-flop. I'm going salmon fishing next week."

Alexis sniffed, then coughed.

"What's that in your hand?" asked Miriam.

"Malcolm's *nom du jour.* I've written my shopping list on the back."

Miriam glanced at the plaid, then returned it to the box. "How is little Llewelyn?"

"My son is quite busy, actually," Duncan said. "Off somewhere practicing being a Welsh king." And testing his father's patience.

As casually as an old friend asking after his health, she said, "What an interesting way to learn history, my lord. Was that clever idea yours?"

An unsuspecting man would wallow in Miriam's cordiality. But Duncan was growing wise to her flattery. "Just so, my lady. But I fear I've failed with the lad. He can't tell a salmon from a trout. Did you find the cloth you were looking for?"

She started, then wiped her hands. "Lexie wanted a new plaid. I just happened to accompany her."

And Duncan Kerr just happened to live in a pigsty. She'd been looking for something in that box. He walked to it and peeked inside. Dozens of tartans lay in a pile in the waist-high box. He picked up the one on top. The soft wool still held the warmth of her touch.

Watching her expression closely, he told her a truth. "I

can't tell one tartan from the other. Give me a box of fishing lures and I'm right at home. These look like so many swatches of cloth to me."

"Not to Miriam," trilled Alexis, still blocking the door to the workroom. "Why, she's a veritable expert. Aren't you?"

A self-conscious smile blossomed on Miriam's face. "Please, Lexie. I'm sure he's not in the least interested."

"Oh, but I am." Duncan sheepishly shuffled his feet. "It's been a long time since we've had a lady as bonnie as you, Miriam, in our castle. I'm interested in whatever you're doing."

"How nice of you to say."

To Duncan, Alexis said, "One look at those and she can name the clan it belongs to. In her mind she can conjure a detailed map of Scotland and match the clan to its territory. She's always been fascinated by puzzles. 'Twas near impossible to pull the wool over her eyes, so to speak, even when she was a child."

Duncan sensed a double meaning in her words, or perhaps a warning. "How enormously clever of you, Lady Miriam."

"'Twas nothing."

An eerie thought crept into Duncan's mind. *She's too smart for me. She'll serve up my head on a platter to the Lord Chancellor.* Manly pride balked. "I don't usually examine the plaids so closely."

She reached up and touched his hand. "My lord, your voice sounds odd. Are you ill?"

He was so captivated, he'd forgotten to speak in the high, clipped voice of the bumbling earl. "Nay," he said. "'Twas the haggis I had for breakfast." Then he looked her in the eye and added, "I hope it doesn't give me the wind, too."

Alexis coughed. "Down wind, I hope."

Miriam frowned. "Why do you eat it if it makes you ill?"

"Because . . ." He snatched at an absurdity. "It was what the cook served me. Kippers would have been ever so tasty, but I haven't been fishing lately."

She stared at the badger pelt on his sporran. "Oh. I thought that was where you were going today."

The beast beneath his tartan roared to life. Knowing he had to find out what she was up to, Duncan dropped the tartan in the box and picked up a different one. "Tell me about this plaid."

Glancing from the cloth to his spectacles, she said, "'Tis the Murrays of Atholl."

And very much like the cape the Border Lord wore, now that he considered it. So *that's* what she'd been investigating. A waste of time, Duncan decided. "I always thought the Murray plaid dull and drab."

"You do? I rather like it," she said in a dreamy whisper.

Drawing his bottom lip between his teeth, Duncan said, "This tartan reminds me of another I've seen. Last year when I went to the fishing tournament at Loch Ness. I saw a fellow wearing— No. I must have been mistaken."

Interest sparkled in her eyes. "What's the fellow's family name?"

"She knows them all," said Alexis.

With the aid of the glasses, he could see perfectly the sweep of Miriam's eyelashes and their golden tips. She still wanted to know the Border Lord's family name. He'd evaded the question before. He'd evade it now. He just wished he could see all of her thoughts so well. "I believe I've forgotten the name of that clan. But I have so much on my mind. Being out of my flippity-flops just puts me in a dither."

Miriam leaned closer. "Does the family live around here?"

"I can't remember but can almost picture the cloth."

"Of course you can. Could they live in a place like Armstrong Moor or Sweeper's Heath?"

Hallelujah! She'd walked into his trap. He snapped his fingers. "Sweeper's Heath. What a coincidence that you should mention it. I'm going there this morning."

"Why?"

He grasped an absurdity. "Pig's hair."

Her hands fumbled with the twine, turning it into a mass of knots. "Pig's hair?"

"Aye." He made to consult his list, but watched her from the corner of his eye. "'Tis a very important element in the flippity-flop, but only when plucked from behind the left ear of a nursing sow. Well, the blue seal fur is equally important, of course. But I haven't any of that. The weaver, though, assured me that he has some dyed wool that I can substitute for the seal fur. Do you think the fish will know the difference?"

Alexis said, "The wool might give them wind."

Duncan coughed to keep from laughing. "I'm sure I couldn't say if the fish . . ."

Miriam shot Alexis a withering glare, then threaded her arm through his. "I'd love to come along on your outing. May I?"

Her guileless smile didn't fool Duncan. Neither did the coy gesture of pressing her breast against his elbow. Sweat popped out on his skin. The spectacles began a slow slide down his nose. He righted them and turned to Alexis. "Will you join us? We could make an excursion of it. Maybe we could stop and view one of my favorite fishing holes."

Her eyes crinkled with suppressed laughter. "Thank you, no. I promised to give the twins a fencing lesson."

"Fencing?" Duncan raised his voice. "With a real sword?"

"A foil, my lord." She smiled, held up one arm and made to lunge with the other. "You know. Long and slender, very sharp, and very deadly."

Like Miriam MacDonald's tongue, thought Duncan. Feigning fright, he stepped back, pulling her with him. "Please, my lady," he whined. "Practice if you will, but I beg you, do it in the old tilt yard or the walled garden. If you bloody up the keeping rooms, Mrs. Elliott will fuss and take to her bed. Supper will be late. She does go on about rowdiness."

"Lexie doesn't mean it, Lord Duncan," said Miriam. "'Tis another of her silly jests. We haven't drawn blood for years. Tell him so, Lexie."

The bastard daughter of the late and last Stewart king sheathed the imaginary weapon. "Forgive me, my lord," she said, heading for the front door. "I'm never at my best in the morning. You two go along and enjoy your excursion to meet the lord of the pigs. Just beware of Baron Sin."

The door closed. Miriam fell still at his side. "Will we be safe in Sweeper's Heath?"

"Of course," Duncan said expansively. "I'll bring along a guard."

"But you didn't when we visited Hadrian's Wall. Why not?"

"Please, Lady Miriam." He patted her hand. "That burly soldier lectured me for hours for being so careless. Don't you too remind me of my folly."

"You mean Angus MacDodd."

"Aye. I haven't your gift for recall."

She flushed with pride. "When shall we leave?"

Duncan considered how much time Angus would need to prepare the swineherd. "An hour from now. Meet me in the walled garden. You'll need to change your clothes."

"What's wrong with my dress?"

Everything, he thought. The neckline, the cinched waist, the enchanting color that turned her eyes to storm-cloud blue. "'Tis too fine for tramping through pig muck."

"Very well. I'll find something suitable."

He felt jubilant. She'd played right into his hands.

6

Forty-five minutes later, Miriam stood between two of the giant urns in the walled garden. At her feet sat Malcolm, dressed in a too large tunic, his bare legs and face painted in Celtic symbols. As Llewelyn he wore gloves with the fingers snipped off, and in a white-knuckled grip he held a Welsh longbow like a pike. His eyes, as big and bright as summer daisies, followed the activity going on near the fountain.

The slice of steel sliding against steel and the huffing breath of exertion filled the air. Alexis, in leather breeches, jackboots, and a padded leather vest, fended off a fierce attack by Saladin, who was similarly dressed, and crowned by his pale blue turban.

The walls of the garden played host to a score of curious onlookers. Even some of the earl's soldiers had come to watch the unusual participants in a fascinating display of swordsmanship.

Studying the men, Miriam counted five Kerr tartans, three Armstrongs, two Elliotts, and a lone flashy MacMillan, but not the muted black and green plaid of the Border Lord. Frustration made her edgy. She'd molded her hands to his

88

face, and could feel the shape of his features, picture the bow of his lips, but in the light of day she wouldn't know him from Louis XIV.

To search for him among the castlefolk was fruitless, for if he spoke the truth he lived on a pig farm. Still, she couldn't help herself; the man and the mystery about him intrigued her.

The crowd gasped. Alexis had pinned Saladin against the wall, the rebated tip of her foil pressing his leather vest. A pained grin exposed the space between his front teeth. Miriam could almost hear the hissing of his breath.

"Yield, stripling," said Alexis, leaning close.

Saladin clamped his lips shut.

Admiration shone in the eyes of the spectators.

Grimacing, Saladin shoved Alexis back. Startled cheers erupted. The contest was hot again.

Salvador, who stood with Verbatim near the garden door, yelled, "Brother mine! Show her the kind of stripling you are."

"Aye, show her!" shouted Malcolm, losing his grip on the bow, which was half again as tall as he.

With everyone's attention focused on the contest, Miriam eased behind the urns. If she found the door open, she could see how the Border Lord had gotten into the earl's room.

She stepped back until her hand touched the hidden door in the castle. She found the place where wood met stone. Cool air seeped through the opening.

Keeping her eyes fixed on the back of Malcolm's head, she made a wish on her lucky star and wedged her fingernails into the narrow space. Her nails bowed. One snapped to the quick. She ignored the stinging pain and tugged gently.

The door moved on silent hinges. Hooray! She had fifteen minutes to explore. Jubilant, she slipped inside. Into an inky blackness. She tottered like an overspun top, and had to spread her feet to keep her balance. Over the pounding of her heart, she heard the muffled cheers of the crowd.

Curiosity and the need for haste pushed her onward. If she could learn the layout of the tunnel, she could follow the Border Lord on his next visit.

Flattening her palms against the cold, scratchy surface of the wall, she felt her way along the corridor. Her hand touched a sharp piece of metal. A nail? Then her fingers closed over a key. Not stopping to question her good fortune, she put the key in her pocket. As blind as a Frenchman to English reason, she continued her exploration.

Time and again, she squeezed her eyes closed, but when she opened them, the world remained a mass of black pitch. When she'd traveled about twenty small steps, the wall played out. In an alcove, she found a door. Locked. She tried the key, but the door didn't open. She moved onward, following the downward slant of the passage. She found another door, then another. Each locked as tight as a spinster's hope chest and impervious to the key.

Damn. How could she discover what the Border Lord had been doing here if she couldn't find an exit to the tunnel?

Bracing one hand on the wall, she stepped to the left and reached out for the opposite wall. Just when she found it, just when she stood spread-eagled and in a place where she didn't belong, light flooded the corridor.

She froze, her eyes fixed on a door some thirty paces ahead and the man who held it open.

The earl of Kildalton.

Blast him for being early.

He stood in the tunnel, the grouse feather in his Highland bonnet touching the ceiling, his head turned toward the light. In profile he didn't seem so bookish or awkward. A serious expression added intelligence and strength to his features.

He pulled the door to close it.

Quick as a spooked squirrel, she dashed into one of the alcoves and melted against a door she'd explored just moments before. The corridor went dark again.

Not daring to breathe, she listened with eerie expectation, as he started toward her. Each footfall brought him closer. The sound of her own heartbeat thrummed in her ear and settled in the tips of her injured finger.

He passed her, a smooth black shadow against an even blacker backdrop. His footsteps were sure, his stride smooth, as if he'd walked this corridor a hundred times.

"Where's the bletherin' key?" he cursed.

Light and the noise of the crowd poured into the passage-way.

Hopelessness pressed in on her. If he returned and searched, he'd find her. He'd know she'd been snooping. She couldn't go back the way she'd come. She knew not what lay ahead. But she had to find out. One exit awaited her. She had to take it.

Before she could change her mind, Miriam hurried down the corridor to the place where the earl had emerged. Once there she took a deep breath and plunged again into the unknown.

Relief drenched her, for she found herself in the corridor outside the lesser hall. She slipped the key in the lock, but it didn't work.

Stifling the urge to run, she strolled to the main staircase and out the front door. As she walked the path that led her back to the garden door, she hummed a lively tune.

She was still humming the refrain hours later when the earl helped her from his carriage and brought her face to face with the swineherd named Ian. The song died on her lips.

Stoop-shouldered and shorter than Miriam, the man doffed a cap to reveal a pate as slick and shiny as polished ivory.

"How do you do, Ian?" she said, straining to keep from stammering.

"Fair as the heather in God's sweet July, my lady," he replied, with a toothless grin.

He must be the father of the Border Lord. Disappointed, she busied herself with smiling and examining his farm. It consisted of a round straw and wattle house with a thatched roof that almost met the ground. A wellhouse and tiny dovecote stood nearby. Both were dwarfed by a new barn and pigsty. The swine appeared as great brown lumps in a fenced and noxious quagmire.

The earl touched her shoulder. "Are you ill, my lady?"

His solicitous tone and worried frown brought her to her senses. "Absolutely not, my lord. I'm having a bracing good time."

He sniffed the tainted air. "Bracing is hardly the word.

What an idiot I was to bring you here. Mrs. Elliott tells me I never think of aught but my fish. Do you forgive me?"

His honesty warmed her. "I'm fine, truly."

Raising his eyebrows, he said, "You wouldn't lie to me, would you? You look distressed."

She wanted to ease his concern. "Please don't give it another thought. I love the country."

Touching a finger to his cheek, he said, "You didn't have haggis for breakfast, did you?"

Breakfast seemed eons ago. "Nay, my lord. I had the ham, and thank you for your concern."

"Haggis has a way of staying with you, you ken?"

Embarrassment threatened her control. "Speaking of which, I'd best be sure Verbatim isn't chasing a pig. Excuse me, won't you?" She moved out of his reach.

"Is it this wee beastie yer lookin' for?" said the swineherd, pointing at the earl's heel.

More regal than a queen on parade, the traitorous Verbatim sat, soulful eyes fixed on Duncan Kerr.

"Will you feast your eyes on this?" he said, patting her head. "I do believe I've made a new friend. Just yesterday I thought she'd gobble me up for scraps."

He had a fine, capable hand. Verbatim squirmed with delight under his ministrations. Miriam wondered how his hand would feel against her skin. The wayward thought shocked her. "She must realize you mean no harm, my lord." She clapped her hands. Verbatim jumped up and bolted to Miriam's side.

"Come for a tuft o' hair from my Quickenin' Sally, have ye, my lord?" the farmer said.

"That I have, Ian. Can't make a flippity-flop without it."

A cackle emerged from the swineherd. "Ye named it well, my lord. Flip 'em on the bank and flop 'em into the fire. Um hum." He rubbed his belly. "Ain't no finer eatin' outside the taste of roasted pig, ye ken."

"I certainly do, Ian. As a matter of fact, just this morning my guest was expressing to Mrs. Elliott her fondness for fresh pork."

"Were ye now? Got me a barren sow ready to put to the stick anytime. How'd that suit yer palate, my lady?"

Miriam sifted through his words and sorted out their

meaning. "I can't think of anything I'd like better. Does your son help you stick the pigs?"

"Son?" He looked in confusion to the earl.

The earl swallowed noisily. "Uh, Ian doesn't have a son. His wife ran off years ago with the driver of a peat wagon. He's been alone ever since."

Shocked and dismayed, Miriam wondered where the elusive Border Lord was. "I'm sorry," she said. "I'm sure the rest of your family has been a comfort to you. Your nieces and nephews—the other pig farmers."

"Ain't no other pigmen in Kildalton, 'ceptin' myself."

So the dark stranger had lied. She felt gullible, used and tricked like an inexperienced maiden.

"Your color's coming back, my lady," said the earl. "Must be the country air."

"Would ye be carin' fer a drink of water, my lady?"

Seizing the chance to speak alone with the swineherd, she said to the earl, "Will you be so kind, my lord? I'm fair parched."

He hesitated, watching her. Oddly enough, he seemed reluctant. Could the earl be taking seriously his role of escort? Was he protective of her?

"Wait right here." He minced off toward the well, where their guard watered the horses at a trough.

Once he was out of earshot, she said, "Ian, I suppose you know everyone around here."

"Aye, I ain't never been more 'n a pig's walk away from Sweeper's Heath."

The familiar role of diplomat settled about her like a cloak of confidence. "I suppose, then, that you'd know a fellow who calls himself the Border Lord."

He slid a glance at the earl, who fumbled with the well bucket. "No," she said. "Not Lord Duncan for heaven's sake. The Border Lord."

"You mean the one the womenfolks tells the tales about? The man who sets their hearts aflutterin' and has 'em pinin' at their doors on Hogmanay?"

Miriam's own heart skipped a beat. She shouldn't have been surprised that so bold a cavalier had a reputation. "I seem to recall that the person who mentioned him said he had a certain . . . manly appeal."

Squeezing one eye shut, he whispered, "Did they tell of 'is caped tartan and a hat with pitch black feathers?"

Excitement raced through her. "Yes, I believe so."

"An' did he come to 'em in the night with the burr of Scotland on his lips?"

The memory of the musical cadence and deep pitch of his voice echoed in Miriam's mind. She clasped her hands to steady them. "Yes, that could be said of him."

"An' he called himself the Border Lord? Yer certain o' that?"

"Quite certain. Er, my *source* was quite certain, that is. Have you seen him?"

"Seen him?" He smacked his lips. "Can't nobody see the Border Lord."

The creaking of the windlass sliced through the country stillness. "Oh, really. Why not?"

An expectant gleam twinkled in the old man's eyes. "'Cause the poor man was killed by the English more 'n a hundred years ago."

Logic rejected the words. Miriam leaned against the hitching post. A denial leaped to her lips. "Then we're speaking of someone else. This man's given name is Ian."

The swineherd picked a piece of straw from his battered cap. "Did he say he was a shepherd from Barley Burn?"

"No. He's a swineherd." Miriam felt as if they were talking in circles. "That's why I thought you might know him."

"Oh, aye. I know *of* him." He nodded slowly, staring at the earl's clansmen who had moved from the well to the shade of a rowan tree. "Full o' stories, that one. Come to my grandmother at the first frost o' winter in her fifteenth year. The Border Lord told her he was a cooper from Whitley Bay. Had her all dreamy-eyed, my grandsire said. Stayed that way 'til Whitsunday, she did."

"Then it can't be the same man."

"Yer a Highland lassie, are ye?"

"Aye. A MacDonald."

"I'd've said so myself." His wizened gaze fixed on a spot over her left shoulder. "'Cause o' yer hair. Makes sense he'd come to ye then. Always visits the bonnie ones, he does."

Miriam began to pace. "You're very kind. I appreciate your telling me where I can find the man I was speaking of."

"Nothin' to that. Find trouble and you'll find the Border Lord. Just ask our fine laird."

Miriam wasn't certain which statement was more preposterous. That the man she'd met last night was a ghost or that Duncan Kerr held the respected position of laird. If her suspicions about both men were true, any information from the earl about the dark stranger would be untrustworthy.

She decided to try another line of questioning. "What kind of trouble?" she asked.

The swineherd studied his hat again. "Same as been happenin' since the Great Bruce was a pup. 'Tis the way o' things in the Border."

"You mean the raids, the slaughter, and the burnings."

He jerked his head toward the well. "Here comes the laird. He can tell ye better'n me."

The earl shuffled toward her, a pail of water in one hand, a cup in the other. "For you and the dog." He gave her the cup, then put the pail before Verbatim.

"Thank you," she said.

"Did I miss something?" he said, looking from her to the swineherd. "You look upset, Ian. Don't tell me you couldn't find that sow."

The stone cup felt ice cold against Miriam's palms. "We were just discussing the Border Lord."

Grinning expansively, he said, "Everyone in Kildalton has a jolly tale of his ghostly derring-do. I never tire of hearing them myself. Why, my first governess swore he gifted her with sprigs of heather. She always wore them in her hair—until my father sent her away for telling ghost stories to an impressionable lad."

"I met a man who calls himself the Border Lord, and I assure you, he was no ghost."

He smiled indulgently. "How delightful. You'll have a fanciful story of the Border to pass on to your children, won't you?"

His placating tone irritated her. She gripped the cup so tightly her torn fingernail ached. "I have never been fanciful, my lord." Even if she had, it was none of his affair.

"Then we're kindred spirits. Fairy tales and romantic fiction bore me to tears. I prefer a history text or an exhilarating treatise on the modern techniques of animal husbandry."

"I wouldn't dream of keeping you from sharing your exhilarating stories with our host."

"You're too gracious, my lady. Too gracious, indeed, for country bumpkins like us. Wouldn't you say so, Ian?"

The swineherd swallowed loudly, probably embarrassed to have his opinion sought by a nobleman. "I'll be fetching Quickenin' Sally."

The earl rubbed his hands together. "Splendid. We'll see about plucking a bit of sow's hair." He turned to go, but stopped. The spectacles wobbled, and the wig swung about his shoulders like a mane. "Unless you'd like to watch, my lady? I shouldn't care to be a neglectful escort."

She'd sooner watch Torquemada interrogate a heretic. "I'll just put these back." She scooped up the pail and headed for the well, Verbatim on her heels.

She'd only gone a short distance when Miriam realized her mistake. Fairness and objectivity were the tools of her occupation. She'd been accused of much worse than being fanciful. Growing defensive in the face of so petty a charge wouldn't serve her at all. Ghosts didn't exist. The Border Lord was a real, flesh and blood man who made her feel very much a flesh and blood woman.

She'd find him. She had the key to the tunnel door, and she was a master at waiting and watching. If the swineherd spoke the truth and the baron sent his men to raid Kildalton land, the Border Lord would appear. She'd be waiting for him.

From the edge of her vision, she watched the earl and the swineherd walk toward the sty. Duncan Kerr towered over the older man, but so did she. Yet Lord Duncan cut a fine figure, dressed as he was in full Kerr regalia. The red and green kilt barely covered his knees and drew attention to his legs, which appeared surprisingly muscular for a man who spent his time attaching feathers to hooks. Without the green jacket, his waist seemed trim, his hips slender. The elaborate sporran and its finely tooled belt added to the illusion of male virility.

Her admiration, she decided with a smile, stemmed from his Scottish attire and her affinity for it. The queen's court teemed with Scotsmen. Even the pudgy, bowlegged Argyll looked resplendent in his hated Campbell plaid.

Lord Duncan draped his arm over the swineherd's shoulder in a casual affirmation of male camaraderie. The swineherd spoke. In response, the earl gasped and slapped a hand to his gaping mouth, effectively shattering the masculine image.

Confused by her conflicting images of him, she turned away. To his credit, he somehow maintained the respect of his people and his soldiers. What would his enemy say about him? Unanswered questions and inconsistencies nagged her. Once she met Baron Sinclair, she would better understand both men. Then she could steer them toward reconciliation and peace.

Verbatim barked, lunged a few feet away, then stopped and barked again. "All right, girl," said Miriam. "Go find a stick."

As powerful and loose-limbed as a tiger, the sleuthhound raced for the rowan trees. The band of clansmen grew silent and, as one, watched the dog canter across the yard and straight to a fallen branch. Barely breaking stride, her long ears flapping like bonnet ribbons, Verbatim snatched up her prize and dashed back to Miriam.

She'd find out who the stranger was and why he visited the earl. She'd spent her adult life prying vital information from men who were much more clever than the Border Lord. A pig farmer was he? Bosh. With each toss of the stick, Miriam thought of another insult. She'd singe his ears. In a game of verbal throw and fetch, he didn't stand a chance.

Duncan stood outside the pigsty, but his attention stayed focused on the queen's emissary. He'd angered her with the remark about having a tale of the Border Lord to pass on to her children. She'd clutched the cup so tightly her knuckles had turned white, drawing his attention to her bruised fingertips, one nail broken to the quick.

Under different circumstances, he would have played the cavalier and kissed and bandaged her injury. Then he would have catered to her every need and fulfilled a burning one of his own.

"We fooled her good, my lord," Ian said.

Duncan thought of her perfect memory and her skill at catching him off guard. "Doona be so sure, my friend. She isna like the others."

Ian sat astride the sow, his hand poised on the animal's ear. "Ye take me fer bein' old *and* blind? I can see she ain't like those money grubbin' ne'er-do-wells. She's got pride and dignity, and a fair set o' motherly necessities."

Duncan remembered the softness of her breasts and the way she'd leaned into his caress. "Aye, she does."

Concentrating on the task of grabbing a handful of hair, Ian said, "What'll ye do with her?"

A midnight fantasy played out in Duncan's mind. "Not what I'd *like* to do with her, I assure you."

Ian grunted, then leaped free of the squealing sow, a tuft of umber-colored hair in his hand. "She's easy on the eyes, fer sure. Here, my lord."

Duncan laughed, but without humor, and took the sow's hair. "I'm trying to forget the way she looks."

"But yer lady crackers keep remindin' ye, eh?"

Painfully so, thought Duncan. "You shouldna listen to Angus MacDodd, much less quote him."

"Yer pardon, my lord." Ian touched his forehead, but his smug expression belied the show of apology. "I been knowin' ye since the day the Grand Reiver strapped ye to his saddle and brought ye 'round for all to see. I say the MacDonald lass will go the same way as those gin-soaked lords the queen sent before 'er. Ye've done yer best to make peace with Baron Sin. Yer bonnie redhead can't do better. I'll wager my Sally's next litter on it."

Loyalty so freely given inspired Duncan. Yet in his heart he hoped Miriam could bring about a peace. He was weary of strife. "I'll hold you to that bet, Ian. But now I'd best get back to being the bumbling earl."

"'Tis a fair job yer doin' of it, my lord. You were born to bumble."

Duncan groaned and stuffed the pig's hair into his sporran. His fingers touched something scaly. It moved. Looking inside the pouch, he spied a fat newt. Malcolm's handiwork, no doubt.

Vowing to take the lad to task, Duncan gathered Miriam

and the dog into the carriage and headed home. The soldiers rode ahead and behind.

Five minutes later, she said, "You have a special friendship with the swineherd."

As if facing a long climb up a craggy hill, Duncan gathered his strength and his stupidity. "He's a generous fellow. Always willing to pluck his best sow so I can have my fishing flies."

"What would you do if the baron raided his farm?"

Duncan affected a pout. "I'm no Lancelot," he whined. "I'd protest most vigorously, but I'm hardly the type to go bounding over the countryside, brandishing a sword in defense of the downtrodden."

"You could hire someone to fight your battles."

"I do. That burly fellow sends some of those men." He fluttered a hand at his clansmen. "They help clean up the debris."

She stared pointedly at his gloved hands. "Who buries the dead sheep and dogs?"

Sly, conniving creature. "Heavens, not I. I'm busy at my desk doing what any decent and law-abiding overlord would do. I write to the local magistrate."

"Who is he?"

"Avery Chilton-Wall. Do you know him?"

"He's originally from York." She stared at her injured finger. "A short man, rather portly. He has brown eyes, a long face with a rather bulbous, red nose. He takes snuff . . . frequently. He likes peas and biscuits and French brandy. His wife's name is Mirabelle."

"Then you know him well."

"Nay. I met him once about three years ago. He was in London for his daughter's coming out. The duchess of Richmond sponsored the girl. I attended a dinner given in her honor."

Drat her memory! If minds were arsenals, the woman beside him could make Guy Fawkes look like a schoolboy. "Chilton-Wall is a hunter, not a fisherman. So we seldom speak of anything but business."

Miriam shrugged and picked at her finger until it began to bleed. "Where is he?"

"Probably at Baron Sin's. They're thick as ditchbank

thieves. They ride to the hounds together. Birds of a feather, and all that. The baron bankrupts himself to entertain the magistrate, who always sides in the baron's favor."

"You say you've written to him to voice your complaints. Do you keep a record of your correspondence?"

"Of course. I'm as meticulous about crimes as I am about the entries in my fishing journal. I hope someday to publish my collective works on the spawning cycle of the red-finned salmon."

"I'd like to see it."

He knew precisely what she meant, but couldn't help saying, "Certainly, but not until next week."

"Why not now?"

The carriage hit a rut. The bonnet flopped low over his brow, but Duncan made no move to right it. "Because the baron's men are fishing the Tyne today. We mustn't take such a risk, even for red-finned salmon."

"I meant," she said, her voice laced with patience, "your journal."

"Oh, silly me. Be my guest. But you already are. I'd let you read my fishing entries, but I'm very protective of my research. You understand, of course."

"Of course. Why do you share fishing rights to the river Tyne?"

"Share?" He tried to control his anger, to keep a loose grip on the reins. His fingers knotted. The horses reared. "I don't do it by choice," he grumbled, trying to settle the team. "The river's on Kildalton land, but Sinclair pays no attention to boundaries or laws."

She reached out to steady the sleuthhound, who teetered on the opposite seat. "I see."

Duncan didn't relax until the towers of Kildalton Castle came into view. The moment they entered the castle yard, Angus broke away from a crowd of farmers and rushed to the carriage.

His relief at being home fled when Duncan saw the rage burning in Angus's eyes.

The soldier darted an uneasy glance at Miriam and said, "May I see you alone, my lord?"

Duncan dropped the reins and made to leap from the carriage. Angus stopped him with a hand on his knee. "I wouldn't distress you for all the heather in Scotland, my lord. I know how easily fashed you are."

Catching the warning, Duncan settled back into the seat. "Very well, then. What's happened? Why are all those farmers gathered in the yard?"

"The baron came. When you weren't here he went away peacefully enough. But on his way home his men raided the Lindsay farm and made off with the man's wool."

Betsy Lindsay broke away from the crowd and ran to the carriage. Tears and misery wreathed her face. "Oh, my lord. 'Tis my Mary Elizabeth," she wailed, clutching his tartan with hands that were scratched and bruised. "She's gone! When the raiders come, I put her in the springhouse and told her not to make a sound. The bastards must've taken her, 'cause she wasn't there."

Overcome by the conflicting urges to kill and comfort at once, Duncan acted on instinct. He stepped from the carriage, took Betsy's hands, and pulled her into his arms.

"My lord!" warned Angus under his breath, his eyes again darting to Miriam MacDonald.

Duncan whispered, "Doona fret, Betsy. We'll find the lassie. She's too spry to come to harm. Will you trust me?"

Her head bobbed beneath his chin. The angry crowd milled, the men brandishing pitchforks and shepherd's staffs. Feminine whispers blended with angry male threats.

Taking a deep breath, Duncan feigned indignation. "I say, this is an outrage of the meanest sort. This poor woman is beside herself. Do something!" he shouted to Angus. "Order those men off the wall and go after the brigands."

"But what about the little girl? Can't you do something?" Miriam's voice, hoarse with outrage, poured over Duncan.

Betsy drew back and gazed over Duncan's shoulder. "My husband says she's gone. But she does like to wander. Oh, Sweet Saint Ninian, she's only three years old."

The carriage squeaked and shifted. Miriam stepped down. "Do you have some article of her clothing, Mrs. Lindsay? Something that Mary Elizabeth has touched?"

Hope glimmered in Betsy's eyes, then faded. "Her shawl. She didna even have it on."

Duncan said, "She'll be cold, the poor lambkin."

"The sun is warm today. Please don't worry," said

101

Miriam, pushing Duncan out of the way and wrapping her arm around Betsy's shaking shoulders. "You'll have your daughter back before nightfall." She snapped her fingers and the sleuthhound bounded from the carriage. "Do you see this dog, Mrs. Lindsay?"

"What's a dog got to do with my poor, lost bairn?"

"Well," said Miriam, as chipper as a lark in spring. "This dog happens to be the very animal that rescued the duke of Orleans from a band of gypsies. Haven't you heard about it? 'Twas a very daring act."

Besty's cheeks sagged in confusion. Before she could speak, Miriam said, "Verbatim tracked their caravan, and His Grace was happily reunited with his duchess. If you'll find Mary Elizabeth's shawl and let Verbatim smell it, you and I will get in that carriage and follow the hound. She'll lead us to your daughter."

Speechless, Duncan looked on as fresh tears poured down Betsy's cheeks. Agony roiled in his gut, for if he dared help, he'd wreck his disguise.

Betsy gazed at the dog. Verbatim held up a paw. "God bless you," Betsy said.

Miriam turned slowly toward Duncan. Disdain tightened the corners of her mouth. "Excuse us, my lord. Please tell Lady Alexis I've gone to fetch a stray child. No one else seems so inclined."

They walked to a box wagon, where Betsy found the tattered shawl. Miriam guided her back to the carriage. They climbed in, and without a backward glance, she flicked the reins and drove the team away.

"You'd best get inside, my lord," said Angus. "I'll go with them."

Duncan's feet stayed rooted to the dusty ground. "I canna shirk my duty. No matter the risk."

Angus gripped Duncan's arm. "Everyone knows 'tis not like you to sit back and let others do the work, my lord. But you have no choice. You dinna want the queen's wench to discover the truth."

Duncan scanned the faces of his people. He saw compassion in the pursing of Mrs. Elliott's mouth and acceptance in the shaking of the tinker's head. "If any harm comes to

Miriam or Betsy or Mary Elizabeth, I'll have the hide of the man responsible."

"I'll gladly be the one to bring him to you," Angus swore and called for his horse. Then he raced after the rescue party.

Duncan dragged himself to his study. Helplessness ignited the fire of his fury. He yanked off the spectacles and threw them on the floor. They bounced on the rug and landed facing the fireplace, the flames turning the lenses to discs of light. He ripped off the bonnet and wig, and tossed them in a corner. Reaching for the decanter of brandy, he discarded the top and took a long swig. Then he began to pace the floor.

The pillar clock ticked off the passing minutes. Inactivity chipped away at his restraint. He'd make the baron pay dearly. Tonight the Border Lord would ride with a vengeance.

He stopped and caught his reflection in the cheval glass. His blond hair hung about his shoulders in a wild tangle. His shirt had come free and lay bunched and wrinkled beneath the sash of his tartan. He looked a fierce sight, a kilted Scotsman poised to defend his domain.

That thought brought a sorry laugh to his lips and a pain to his heart. *He* should be leading his men to the rescue. Not Miriam MacDonald.

He ticked off her faults on his fingers. She was far too distracting. She was too intelligent. She had no business snooping in his affairs. But how could he stop her?

Snooping.

Like a draught of fresh air, Duncan remembered the missing key to the tunnel door. Earlier today he'd found it open and an empty nail where the key should have been. According to Malcolm, Miriam had stood beside him in the garden watching the fencing duel, then suddenly she'd vanished.

A purpose beckoned. Here at last was something he could accomplish, and he'd never have a better opportunity away from her too observant eyes.

He traded the bottle of brandy for a lighted torch and a spare ring of keys. With a twist of his wrist, he turned the wall sconce and triggered the ancient mechanism that opened a secret door in the wall between the fireplace and the bookshelves. Holding the torch high, he wound his way through the warren of tunnels until he reached the outside door.

On his knees, he searched for the key. He didn't find it, but much to the delight of his bruised and battered pride, he discovered a more condemning piece of proof—a broken fingernail.

Feeling assuaged and eager for another bout with the flame-haired diplomat, he returned to his study and the brandy. Sometime later he heard a cheer from the soldiers on the curtain wall. Then Malcolm burst into the study.

"Come quick, Papa. You won't believe who's riding through the gate."

7

Although Duncan had his suspicions, he said, "Who?"

"You'll see." Malcolm grabbed Duncan's hand. "We'll watch from the tower."

He let himself be pulled out of the study and to the tower door. Grunting, Malcolm pushed it open. They started up the circular stairway, the boy's short legs pumping. "Hurry. We'll never make it," he said between gasps.

"Make it to what?"

Malcolm stopped and flapped his arms in exasperation. "To see what's happening outside."

"Very well." Duncan swept up his son and propped him on his hip, the same way he'd carried him as a babe. Eye to eye with Malcolm, Duncan said, "But hold on tight."

Malcolm grinned and thrust his arm upward. "Go very fast. Faster than Rob Roy when Sassenachs are chasing him."

After five hours of waiting for Miriam's safe return, Duncan nearly ran up the stairs, his bouncing son squealing with delight. At the top, Duncan kicked open the door and stepped into the cool night.

Distant cheers erupted. Shifting his son higher on his hip, Duncan leaned into a chest-high arrow slit. A score of people carrying torches had formed a double line outside the gate. From the castle yard, hundreds more poured through the human column, lighting torches as they went. In minutes, a flaming yellow gauntlet stretched from the mouth of the portcullis to the curtain wall. In the inner bailey, bleating sheep scattered and sheepdogs raced to herd them.

"Papa, isn't it wondrous?"

The crowd hushed. Anticipation hung like rain clouds in the air. From the darkness of the outer bailey came the jingle of harnesses. From the depths of Duncan's soul came a silent plea: *let them be unharmed.*

Angus rode into the light, his bay horse gleaming like polished mahogany, his smile as broad as Armstrong Moor.

"Look, Papa!"

Behind Angus pranced the sleuthhound, her head high, her tail a banner of high-strung dignity.

The people cheered again. As if to punctuate the excitement, the torches wavered.

"There's Lady Miriam, Papa!" Malcolm said in awe. "She's got Mary Elizabeth and her mother."

"Indeed," said Duncan as he focused on the open carriage and the woman holding the reins. Her unbound hair shone like a nimbus of fire, the yard-long tendrils licking the breeze.

Envy and misgivings descended on Duncan. Instead of waiting in safety like a brow-beaten goodwife, he should have led the rescue party. As laird, he had a duty to the citizens of Kildalton. As a man, he wanted to command the soldiers and instill pride in the horde of smiling people. But fate had denied him these things.

"What's wrong, Papa?" Malcolm's worried expression tore at Duncan's heart. "Are you angry?"

"Nay, son." The noise in the castle yard grew deafening. Duncan almost yelled, "I couldna be happier." Unless, he added to himself, the baron was within striking distance of his fists. Sinclair would rue the day he'd allowed his henchmen to endanger a child from Kildalton. "Mary Elizabeth looks very brave, don't you think?"

106

Malcolm screwed up his face. "She's just a bairn. Besides, lassies are mewling and troublesome, and they grow up to be tart-tongued wenches. They get scared and run away. They can't be brave." Puffing out his chest, he added, "Not like lads."

"Who told you that?"

"I thought it for myself."

"I think," Duncan said firmly, "you've been doing too much thinking for yourself lately. You've also been listening to the soldiers."

The boy's gaze darted guiltily from the carriage to the soldiers lining the wall.

"Lassies can be just as brave as lads," Duncan said.

The boy's chin puckered with stubbornness.

"Malcolm . . . ?"

"Llewelyn. I want down."

"I want down," Duncan mocked the whiny tone. "Now who's acting like a bairn?"

He stiffened. "I'm not a bairn."

"Then be reasonable. If I put you down, you wilna be able to see. Look there." Duncan pointed to the carriage. In complete command, Miriam drew back on the reins and slowed the team to a walk. Betsy Lindsay waved to the crowd. Between the women sat the toddler Mary Elizabeth, her eyes drooping with fatigue, her cheeks smudged with dirt. "Don't you think Lady Miriam was brave to go after Mary Elizabeth?"

Grudgingly, the boy said, "Yes, but Angus went with her. I wanted to go, but he said Baron Sin's reivers would love to get their filthy paws on me."

Parental responsibility weighted Duncan's shoulders. "Angus told you the right thing. But you're evading the subject. Lady Miriam didna run away, did she?"

"No. Saladin said they rode horses all the way from London." His face brightened. "Can we ride horses all the way to London someday?"

"Aye, and all the bonnie ladies at court will kiss your forehead and pinch your perky cheeks."

His hand flew to his face. "I won't let them. I won't show 'em my lady crackers, either," he said, as serious as a butcher on slaughtering day.

Duncan sighed. His son's disrespect and vulgar language had gone on long enough. "Son," he began ominously.

"Look," Malcolm squealed, leaning into the embrasure.

Over the boy's head, Duncan saw Miriam guide the horses beneath the portcullis and drive them to the stables. The castlefolk swarmed the carriage. The lathered horses reared. Angus stormed through the throng, shoving the spectators aside. He grasped the harness to hold the team steady, then waved the crowd back.

A cool breeze ruffled Duncan's hair, reminding him that he'd left the wig in his study. Suddenly he felt exposed.

Miriam stood and scanned the crowd. Malcolm stuck his arm through the arrow slit and yelled her name.

Duncan leaned back, out of her line of vision. He had to return to his study before she came looking for him. He pulled Malcolm back and set the boy on his feet. "Come along, son."

"No." Malcolm crossed his arms, his face a picture of defiance. "You can't make me."

Anger ripped through Duncan. He took the boy by the arm. "You seem to be forgetting one vital piece of information, my foul-mouthed friend."

"I ain't your friend. I'm your son."

"You'll bletherin well start acting like it." He turned Malcolm around and pointed him toward the stairs. "Walk!"

They retraced their steps. In the hall outside his study, Duncan yelled for Mrs. Elliott. When the housekeeper appeared, he said, "Should Lady Miriam ask to see me, tell her I'm at a crucial moment in the wrapping of my flippity-flops. I canna be disturbed."

A sly grin blossomed on her face. "Aye, my lord."

Duncan ushered Malcolm into the study, then indicated the chairs by the hearth. "Sit down, son."

"No. You tie your auld flippity-flops. I want to go out in the courtyard with everyone else."

"That's unfortunate. Sit."

"But . . ."

"Sit!"

Like a scolded pup retreating to the corner, Malcolm

shuffled slowly across the room and wiggled into the farthest chair. Duncan took the other.

"Where is your essay on Llewelyn Fawr?" he said.

Malcolm began fanning his legs. "I dunno."

Duncan counted silently to ten. "You didna write it, did you?"

"No. I had to watch the duel," he said, as if the activity were a matter of life or death.

"You know the rules. You'll either write it before you go to bed or answer to your own name for a week."

Mouth open, the boy shot out of the chair. "A week! No. I won't do it. You can't make me."

His control hanging by a thread, Duncan yelled, "Sit down!"

Malcolm plopped into the chair, a sullen expression making him look very much like his mother. The resemblance cooled Duncan's anger. If he were to succeed at being both mother and father to Malcolm, he had to keep a level head. Didn't a motherless boy deserve a bit of indulgence? No, not at the expense of good character.

Calmly, Duncan said, "You seem to have forgotten who gives the orders around here. You've become disrespectful, rude, and vulgar. You've taken advantage of my disguise. Gainsay me again, son, and I'll forbid you your game of names altogether."

The boy swallowed loudly and lifted his head. Great tears pooled in his eyes. "I'm sorry, sir."

Duncan's heart constricted, and he almost ended the reprimand. But that would be doing Malcolm a disservice, for the lad must learn to respect others.

Duncan held up a finger. "No more mentioning your lady crackers in the presence of females."

With the back of his hand, Malcolm brushed aside his tears. "Nay, sir. Never again. I promise."

Duncan held up another finger. "No more sassing me—even when I'm in disguise."

Malcolm sniffed. "I won't, sir."

"No more snakes nailed to the door of the women's privy."

Mouth open, the boy said, "Who told you?"

"Never mind that. Your word, please."

Swallowing loudly, Malcolm said, "I promise."

"No more newts in my sporran."

A gamin smile brightened Malcolm's eyes and teased the corners of his mouth. "If I had a baby brother, I wouldn't have to play with newts."

Duncan's dream of marrying again and siring a large family had died long ago. But Malcolm needn't know that. "If you had a baby brother, you'd have to share all of your toys."

"I would, Papa." Eagerly he sketched a cross over his heart. "I'd give him every last boat and soldier."

Tenderness welled up in Duncan. "I'll do what I can, lad. Please fetch me my wig and spectacles. Lady Miriam wilna wait all night to see me."

Malcolm bounded from the chair and did as he was told. Duncan put on the wig, then held out his hand for the spectacles.

"May I put them on for you?" Malcolm asked.

"Be my guest, just doona be pinching my nose."

Using great care, the boy placed the spectacles on the bridge of Duncan's nose. Standing back and squinting to see if the glasses were straight, Malcolm said, "I know a secret about Lady Miriam."

With great interest, Duncan leaned forward. "What's that?"

Pride puffed out Malcolm's chest. "Saladin and Salvador swear she fences even better than Lady Alexis. She has leather pants, too. Can I have leather pants?"

Duncan pictured her long legs encased in flesh-tight doeskin. "We'll visit the tanner."

Malcolm's smile wilted. "You'll be busy with those foosty feathers and hooks. Or taking her somewhere. You always are."

Since Miriam's arrival, Duncan had spent little time with his son. Regrets besieged him. "Do you know why?"

"So the queen will think you're a braw man."

"Aye." Duncan laid his hand on Malcolm's head. "I love you, son."

Malcolm smiled, endearingly sweet. "I love you, too, Papa. And I promise to write my essay."

The tenderest kind of affection infused Duncan. "I know you will. How do I look?"

"Funny. The wig is crooked." He reached up to right it.

Seizing the boy's vulnerable position, Duncan tickled him. Malcolm squealed and tried to dart away, but Duncan followed, thrumming his fingers on the boy's ribs. They tumbled to the floor, and scuffled like children, rubbing the paint off Malcolm's legs and rucking Duncan's kilt up around his waist.

He almost lost the wig, and when he reached up to secure it, Malcolm plopped on top of him. "I'm the tickler now," the boy declared, and dug his fingers into Duncan's ribs.

Flat on his back, the spectacles askew, Duncan bent his knees and bucked, trying halfheartedly to bounce Malcolm off. He grunted with exaggerated effort. "Aye, you're a braw laddie."

Skinny knees straddling Duncan, Malcolm said, "Dost thou yield to Llewelyn Fawr, the High King of Wales?"

Feigning fright, Duncan pleaded, "I yield, your kingship. I yield."

Just then the door opened, and Lady Miriam strolled inside. "My lord, didn't you hear my knock—" Mouth open, she stopped. Her gaze traveled up Duncan's bare legs to his fully exposed manly parts. A lovely shade of crimson blossomed on her cheeks. She gasped. "Excuse me." Then she whirled and fled the room.

Mortified, Miriam raced down the hall toward the keeping room. Just outside the door she stopped, her heart pounding, her senses reeling.

Sweet Saint Margaret, beneath his kilt he wore . . . nothing. She had seen marble statues of nude men and admired the sculptor's work. She'd seen Italian frescoes and Moorish mosaics, blatant in their depictions of the human form. But seeing a classic rendering in pale stone or tiny chips of tile and viewing a man in hot living flesh were different experiences altogether. Lord, the statues seemed innocent, benign by comparison. The earl, in his natural state, was a powerful sight to behold. Even the Lancelot of her dreams hadn't been so well made.

Could she ever look at Duncan Kerr in the same way? As

an ordinary man? He'd made her feel anything but an ordinary woman.

Had he been naked all day, even when he'd found her at the weaver's and escorted her to the swineherd's? The probability made her shiver. She cast out the disturbing thought and became aware of noises in the room beyond. The twins and Alexis were in there.

Pressing her hands to her flaming cheeks, Miriam focused her thoughts on Baron Sinclair's latest raid on a Kildalton farm and the tricky task of confronting the earl about his cowardice. Secure in the safe topic, she strolled into the keeping room.

Saladin, his head swathed in a turban, and Salvador, wearing Alexis's Highland bonnet with a Stewart crest badge, sat on a rug in a corner with an exhausted Verbatim. Alexis, garbed in a fashionable gown of garnet-hued velvet, sat on one of the two straight-back benches that flanked the massive stone hearth.

On the mantel sat a pair of hundred-eyes lanterns with thick tallow candles. The ancient lamps cast a spray of dotted light on the gilt-framed painting of Kenneth Kerr which soared to the beamed ceiling. A kettle of bayberries simmered over the fire, the steam perfuming the air with the fresh holiday scent.

"What's wrong?" Alexis peered up from the book she was reading.

Miriam's vulnerability returned in full force. She walked to a side table that held a brace of candles and a dish of dried rosemary. "Why should anything be wrong?"

"You looked . . . well, for a moment you looked disoriented. Did you see the earl?"

In perfect detail Miriam remembered just how much of him she'd seen. A penis. Good Lord, she'd seen his penis, and she'd stared in awe at the fleshy, weighty sacks beneath.

The muscles in her abdomen tightened. Taking a handful of the dried herbs, she crushed them between her damp palms. "Yes, I saw him. He and Malcolm were tussling on the floor."

"The earl?" Alexis tossed the book aside and came to stand by Miriam. "That's odd. I've never seen him take an interest in the boy."

The need to defend him rose sharply in Miriam. "So? Most parents can't be bothered with their children. I was glad to see them laughing and tickling each other, same as any country gent and his lad."

Alexis glanced at the twins, who were picking burrs from the still-sleeping sleuthhound. "'Tis odd," she said, "how different he and the boy are. But I'm sure you've noticed that Malcolm is boisterous and bold, while the earl is quiet and passive."

"They seemed very much alike a few moments ago. But I hardly know Malcolm." The boy could shed a new light on the father. But the idea of using the lad to gain information pricked Miriam's conscience.

"After your daring rescue of that child tonight, I'll wager the boy will dog your heels for days. He's woefully in need of a hero to worship. A heroine might do."

Miriam pictured Malcolm giggling with delight in the company of his unexpectedly playful father. "We should have taken him along on the adventure. There was no danger at all."

Just above a whisper, Alexis said, "What did you learn from the swineherd?"

"That the man I met in the garden is supposed to be a ghost."

"Truly? Do you think he is a ghost?"

Miriam remembered his seductive words and hot kisses. She related the romantic tales of the Border Lord's appearances. "According to one and all, the earl included, the man was hanged by the English a century ago."

Alexis tapped her teeth with a fingernail and gazed thoughtfully at Kenneth Kerr. "What do you make of it?"

Again Miriam sifted through the possibilities, but the conclusion always remained the same. "I think someone has taken on the identity of this folk hero. Why would he visit Kildalton Castle at night unless his purpose were a nefarious one?"

"What did the swineherd say?"

"He said the Border Lord pops up whenever there's trouble."

Alexis scoffed. "Then where was he when little Mary Elizabeth and her family needed him?"

The inconsistency nagged at Miriam's logical mind. "He obviously picks his battles. Or maybe he only rides at night because of his disguise."

"Do you think the earl knows who he is?"

"Logic tells me yes."

"Well, then," said Alexis as if she were ordering a meal, "you'll just have to use that dangerously clever mind of yours and persuade him to tell you."

She wasn't sure she could face the earl just yet. She needed time to banish the image of that thick penis sprouting from his muscular loins. "I may have better luck seeking out the Border Lord on my own. Now that I have the key to the tunnel door, I intend to lie in wait for him tonight."

"What makes you think he'll come?"

Herb dust clung to Miriam's damp palms. She rubbed at it until her sore fingertip began to throb. "The swineherd said he always appears after a raid by the baron."

"You're so clever, Miriam. But you must be careful." Alexis looked again at the hound. "Verbatim won't be any help to you. She's fair toil-worn."

Miriam recalled the dog's tireless searching and that instant of relief when the animal had barked, signaling she'd located her quarry. Betsy's heartfelt declarations of gratitude and the cheers from the crowd still filled Miriam with joy.

Alexis hugged her. "You looked like Boadicea in her chariot driving that carriage. I cried when I saw you come through the gates."

Fighting off a wave of melancholy, Miriam hugged her back. "It felt good to see that little girl in her mother's arms again."

"Of course it did. You always do the right thing, Miriam. You always have."

The familiar praise warmed Miriam. "Let's just hope the Border Lord makes an appearance tonight, since I seem to be riding a high wave of luck."

The sound of Malcolm's laughter echoed down the hall.

"Come," Alexis whispered, pulling Miriam to the hearth. "This painting," she said, louder, "is of Lord Duncan's father. They're very different don't you think?"

Just as Miriam was about to agree, Malcolm bounded into

the room. A moment later the earl shuffled in, a large book under his arm, a curled white feather in his wig.

Her gaze strayed to his kilt, now modestly concealing his manly parts. The first thought that popped into her mind was an inappropriate question: Didn't he get cold in the winter?

"I'm awfully sorry to have kept you waiting, Lady Miriam," he said, setting the book on the mantel and warming himself by the fire. "I must admit, though, with my spectacles askew, I didn't know who had come in the room. It could have been the queen herself. Malcolm told me 'twas you."

"I'm sorry to have disturbed you." She rose and joined him, her eyes straying to his magnificent badger sporran. She knew what lay behind it. "I should have knocked louder."

With a self-deprecating smile, he said, "I confess that we're regular ruffians on occasion, Malcolm and me. Surely you've learned that we have no locked doors in this castle. 'Tis a part of Scottish hospitality, you know."

From the corner, she heard Malcolm and the twins cooing over Verbatim. "Your hospitality is exemplary, my lord."

"Mine?" He dropped his chin and busied his hands with adjusting the spectacles. "I simply told Mrs. Elliott to refuse you nothing." He glanced at Alexis. "Good evening, my lady."

Glancing up from the book, she said, "My lord. How are the flippity-flops?"

"So kind of you to ask." Chuckling and rubbing his hands together, he said, "They're ready for a fat salmon. However, I'm thinking I might just try one out in my favorite trout stream."

Miriam studied his strong hands. The healing blisters appeared as smooth pink circles on his broad palms. They were strong hands, made for wielding a sword instead of cleaning feathers, yet perfect for tickling a boy into giggles and stroking a woman's flesh.

"Have you supped, Lady Miriam?" he said. "You deserve a feast, you know, for your daring rescue of that poor child. Cook will have a bone for Verbatim, too."

Miriam's stomach growled, but she had matters other

than food on her mind. "I'm fine, truly. I'd hoped we could talk about the raid."

A frown marred his broad brow. "I brought my journal," he said absently. "But that can wait. What kind of host would I be if I showed my appreciation by letting you go hungry?"

"I think the damage to the shepherd and his family today is more important. Mary Elizabeth had a dreadful scare. Their entire harvest of wool was stolen."

"Then let's strike a bargain—or is that your line?" Laughter sparkled in his eyes and rumbled in his throat. At her puzzled frown, he said, "Never mind me." Then he tucked the ledger under his arm and took her hand. "We can adjourn to the lesser hall. I'll have Mrs. Elliott prepare you a plate. While you eat, we can talk. Good night, Lady Alexis." He glanced pointedly at Malcolm and the twins, and whispered, "Some details of the baron's crimes aren't fit for everyone's ears. I intend to reveal everything to you."

Her hand felt snug in his, and unexpectedly, a sense of security infused her. "How thoughtful, my lord."

He shrugged and dropped his chin again, a shy gesture she was coming to associate with him.

"Please," he said, as clumsily charming as a bashful cavalier, "call me Duncan."

Suddenly the idea of being alone with him appealed to her. She smiled. "If you'll call me Miriam."

He led her from the keeping room and once he'd settled her in the lesser hall, he excused himself. He returned a few moments later and put a covered tray before her. With a flourish, he plucked off the cloth. "Haggis and neeps 'n tatties," he announced, steam rising from the food and fogging his spectacles, "and a tankard of fresh beer."

Miriam's mouth watered, but she held out the napkin. "Here. So you can clean your glasses."

Flapping a wrist, he said, "'Twill evaporate by itself."

"Please, let me do it for you."

"Oh, no. Don't trouble yourself. Eat."

Thinking he was probably self-conscious about his poor vision, she picked up the fork. He watched her take the first bite, an air of expectancy about him. The mashed potatoes and turnips, flavored with butter and honey, melted on her tongue. "Delicious."

He grinned and clapped his hands like a gleeful child would. "I believe in exposing myself to different foods, but who can resist good, unadorned Scottish fare?"

"I've eaten snails with crowned heads of Europe, but this pleases me more." Throughout the meal, her attention kept straying to him as he leaned over the journal, his face only inches from the page. His thick eyebrows had a manly arch that drew attention to the high bridge of his nose and the pleasing line of his temples and cheekbones.

Again she wondered if his hair was truly black like his wig and Malcolm's hair, or if it was the same golden brown as the hair that covered his legs? She shuddered, thinking about the other pelt of hair she'd seen. It had looked like silky sable, lush and soft, a vivid contrast to the thick penis and ponderous sacks.

"Are you cold? The drafts do chill a body."

Mortified, she almost choked on a mouthful of tatties.

"I'll just build up the fire." He went to the hearth and bent over to add another log to the flames. The kilt rode dangerously high in back, revealing muscular thighs and straining tendons. Again her lower abdomen went taut, and her mind conjured images of his penis. In a flash of insight she knew how he could ease the tension within her. She saw naked legs entwined, felt heated flesh against flesh, anticipated touching his manly parts, having him touch her where she felt hollow and damp.

Dizziness engulfed her.

Abashed at the vivid pictures and her own preoccupation with them, she took a long drink of the beer and lectured herself on the importance of maintaining her objectivity.

She heard the crunch of coals and the twang of the fire iron on the grate. The fire hissed, popped, and flared.

"There." He stood and strolled toward her, the sporran flapping against his—No. She exiled the thought and concentrated on the motions of his hands as he swiped palm against palm.

"All done?" he asked, as chipper as a moorhen in a field of heather.

The image of him naked returned. "Thank you, yes. 'Twas delicious."

He picked up the journal and helped her from her chair. "Let's sit by fire, shall we?"

Think about the raids, she told herself. Kidnapping. Thievery. Vandalism. Punishment for the clansmen who'd made her an orphan. "That would be lovely, Duncan. 'Tis a fine blaze you've built."

He shook his finger at her. "Miriam, you'll strip me naked of my pride with such flattery."

Naked. She pivoted and almost ran to a chair by the hearth.

He sat cross-legged in front of the fire. "The light's better here," he said and opened the book. "You'll be able to see everything."

The firelight shimmered on his white silk shirt and turned the hair on his legs to gold.

"Now," he said, pulling a lead pencil from the binding and thumbing through the pages until he found the last entry. He drew a line across the page and wrote today's date. "Please tell me about the raid—how much wool did the baron's men steal, what damage they did, etcetera. I'll put it all down here."

His casual acceptance of the crime baffled Miriam. "Aren't you curious about what happened to Mary Elizabeth?"

His shoulders drooped. "Please don't think me crass, but I thought you'd want to get straight to the business of the baron's crimes."

"You did?" With stunning clarity she saw herself through Duncan's eyes. She wanted to cry, for he perceived her as cold, single-minded. Had others seen her that way? Suddenly it seemed vital to change his opinion of her.

"Have I said something wrong?" His earnest expression made her feel worse.

"No, Duncan. You said the truth, and I thank you for it."

A puzzled frown marred his brow. "I thank you for rescuing her."

Feeling so at ease with him, Miriam wanted to touch him. When his gaze dropped to the pencil in his hand, she stifled the urge. "Verbatim found the girl asleep in a haystack."

"Then she wasn't truly in any danger? The baron's men didn't kidnap her?"

"I don't think so. When the robbers searched the spring-house, where her mother left her, Mary said she scrambled through a hole in the floor and ran away as fast as the wind." Thinking of the brave tot's tale, Miriam added, "She's a precocious mite. It all seems a great adventure to her now."

Smiling, Duncan said, "Good. She gets that brawness from her father. Two pints at the alehouse and he can weave a tale of derring-do that makes Rob Roy MacGregor look like a petty highwayman."

"I'm surprised he doesn't tell stories about the Border Lord," she said. "Everyone else seems captivated by the man."

He surveyed her curiously. "Are you captivated by so romantic a legend?"

Disquieted by his close scrutiny, she picked at her ragged fingernail. "I don't believe in ghosts."

"I suppose that's just as well. A woman in your position can't afford such fanciful notions."

There it was again, a delicately worded but honest ap-praisal. Instinctively, she knew he considered her lack of whimsy a shortcoming. Didn't he understand that she had responsibilities? She couldn't afford to fail here; her future and her heritage hung in the balance.

Fighting off a wave of sadness for the jesting, charismatic woman she could never be, she said, "Just so, Duncan. But aren't you curious to know if anyone saw the thieves, so they can be identified?"

"They're always the same." He flipped back a couple of pages and angled the book to the light. "Ah, here 'tis. The leader is a stick of a man who's missing a tooth in front. Some say he speaks like a Cheapside man. Another fellow is average in all things, except he's bald, having a high forehead. They say he smells like a peat bog. A third man—"

"Please," she interrupted. "You needn't go on with the descriptions since I didn't see the men. How do you know they work for the baron?"

The earl looked up at her, a quizzical expression on his

face. "The toothless one runs the baron's cattle. Or, I should say, mostly *my* cattle which he's stolen over the years."

His blasé attitude baffled her. From her vantage point she had a perfect view of his eyes, which appeared more hazel than green today. He's very attractive. The observation shocked her, but after her earlier discovery, she shouldn't have been surprised. The clumsy earl had some smooth parts. She was surprised by her attraction to such a coward. Or was he simply a peaceable man?

"Is something wrong, Miriam? You're all aflutter. I wouldn't want to strip you of your dignity."

"No. Nothing at all." She recalled the situation at the shepherd's farm. "Twenty bags of wool were stolen, and the shearing shed destroyed. The bandits also made off with a hairbrush. Mrs. Lindsay was beside herself over the loss of it. It bears her clan badge, a swan rising from a coronet."

He switched back to the fresh page and began to write. "My, you *do* have a perfect memory."

"Four ewes and the shepherd's best ram were taken. Two of Mr. Lindsay's sheepdogs were killed."

"Oh, no." He sighed, his shoulders drooping. "I'm sure the man is distraught. Perhaps there's another litter on some other farm. I'll see—I'll have someone go and see. What else?"

"Isn't that enough?" Miriam said.

"Did I say something wrong?"

Weariness set in. She'd probably fall asleep in the corridor waiting for the Border Lord. "Nothing's wrong, my lord."

"Well it must be if you've stopped calling me Duncan." Sadly, he added, "I thought we were becoming friends."

Friends seemed a dangerous word tonight. "We are, Duncan."

"But you'd like me better if I were more forceful." When she opened her mouth to object, he held up his hand. "Don't deny it. I've been thinking about the kind of man I am, and I've decided to learn to use a sword."

He looked so pleased with himself, Miriam didn't quite know what to say. "Just be careful that you don't injure yourself. May I see the book? That way you won't have to read it all."

He clutched it to his chest. Apologetically, he said, "It's

rather like baring my soul. But, then, I've nothing to hide from you. Still, I'd rather you didn't."

At the unintended double meaning of his words, she wanted to flinch. Years of practicing emotional control kept her hand steady. "If you're embarrassed, I won't persist. If you'll excuse me, I'm very tired."

"Oh, of course, how thoughtless of me." He got to his feet and offered her a hand. "You completely denude me of my composure."

He pulled her from the chair and kissed her hand. "You smell of rosemary. How delightful." Then he walked her to the main staircase. "Sleep well, Miriam. I hope you have pleasant dreams."

She murmured thanks and started up the stairs, her thoughts strangely torn between the polite man she was beginning to respect and the dark stranger who set her blood on fire.

Would the Border Lord come tonight?

8

Alone, Miriam slipped through the squat wooden door and stepped into the private garden. From beyond the wall she heard the faint laughter of soldiers manning their posts and the comforting shuffle of sheep and cattle bedding down for the night. The sky blazed with stars. A grinning face on the quarter moon mocked the feeble clouds that tried to obscure the view of a Scottish castle and a woman bent on stealth.

Tucked into the pockets of her hooded cloak were a candle, flint and steel, and Saladin's brass compass. If the Border Lord followed his routine and arrived just before midnight, she had an hour's time to map out the corridors and lie in wait for him.

The fountain burbled gently. The crunch of her footsteps on the pebbled ground sounded a warning, but there was no one to hear her passage into intrigue. Even if she were caught, she had little to fear; what better pardon for perfidy than the command of the queen of England?

Verbal meddling came easily to Miriam. Physical stealthing both invigorated and frightened her. Keeping to the shadows, she made her way past the urns, to the castle wall and the entrance to the corridors.

Although no bigger than a paring knife, the ancient key felt like a battle lance in her hand. She felt along the wooden door until she found the cool iron of the lock plate. For security, the door had no handle on the outside. On impulse, she slipped her little finger into the keyhole and pulled. On silent hinges, the door opened.

Logic told her the earl had another key, but if so, why hadn't he locked the door tonight? Because he was expecting a visitor who used back entrances to conceal his comings and goings and hid behind ghostly tales to glorify his escapades of revenge.

Common sense told her the earl hadn't locked the door because he couldn't pull himself away from pig's hair and owl feathers long enough to admit his caped mercenary. Shame descended on her. Perhaps he wasn't the utter twit she had imagined. Less than an hour ago, he had revealed his plans to learn a soldier's skills. An hour before that, he'd revealed himself completely.

Miriam didn't need a flawless memory to recall the earl's manly parts. The tightening, curling sensations that coiled in her belly reminded her in a more vivid way. Worse, she was beginning to feel attracted to the gentle earl, a man who bore no resemblance to the charging, gallant knight of her dreams.

The Border Lord.

The realization both frightened and exhausted her. Without objectivity she might fail. That she couldn't afford, because too much was at stake.

Fighting off untimely fantasies, she eased inside the door, lighted the candle, and began mapping the corridors. Using the tunnel door where she'd entered and the tapestry-draped door near the lesser hall as points of reference, she cited each exit from the musty tunnel. This morning she'd hidden in an alcove and quaked with fear as the earl passed her. Now she knew that she'd been standing by the door to the stair tower. The earl had entered the tunnel from his study. She resisted the urge to search his room for evidence of his involvement in the raids on Sinclair's land; she'd have time for that later.

She'd also have time to explore the stair tower that spiraled into graying darkness. Using the same deductive skill that allowed her to look at the weavers sticks and picture the plaid the pattern would weave, Miriam diagrammed the dark passages. When she had fixed in her mind a picture of the warrenlike tunnels, she stepped out into the garden and locked the door.

She found a hiding place in the shadows. She sat back against the wall, her knees drawn to her chest, the cloak pooling around her. She had yawned only twice when the Border Lord entered the garden.

Her heart clamored in her breast and a slow heat brought dampness to her skin. Years ago in a Russian forest, she'd sat in an iron-barred wagon and watched a snow leopard stalk a reindeer. Danger had consumed her then; it fascinated her now.

In unhurried, powerful strides, the Border Lord passed the fountain. His cape billowed, and he appeared a liquid shadow, moving past the urns and out of sight.

The crunching of his boots on the gravel stopped. Silence, save the soothing sound of rushing water, fell over the night. Miriam's pulse accelerated.

"Bletherin wench!" he spat and kicked or pounded on the door. "She locked the door."

Confidence shaved the edge off her anxiety. She decided to observe him for a while. Cupping her hands over her mouth, she breathed deeply, the metallic smell of the ancient key still on her hands, the anticipation of the man filling her senses.

What would he do?

He paced like a caged animal. He cursed her in the language of her youth. He called her a meddling harlot with the common sense of a Cornishman and the stubbornness of a Highlander. He swore to wring her neck and teach her a lesson about meddling in his affairs.

Let him try, she thought. She could handle him.

Suddenly he stopped and seemed to stare straight through her. Then he marched to a bench near the fountain and plopped down, his elbows braced on his knees, his palms supporting his chin. Like a mask, his hat brim cast a curving shadow over his eyes and the bridge of his nose.

"What to do," he mused. "What to do."

The despair in his voice called across the few feet that separated them. She longed for the sunlight or even the flame of the half-burned candle in her pocket. She couldn't risk detection, yet the unknown aspects of the dark stranger played havoc with her judgment. Why was he here? What shade of dark brown were his eyes?

Despite the dim light she could tell he'd been blessed with appealing, manly features. Soft, insistent lips that had kissed away her maidenly objections were now pulled in tight anger. Broad shoulders and the strong arms that had caressed and sheltered her, were now slumped, weighted by some heavy burden. A burden she craved to lift.

But unlike composing betrothals and divvying up shipping routes, eavesdropping on a man in such obvious misery suddenly seemed a dishonorable act.

"You've brewed yourself a bonnie kettle of fish," he said, the burr in his voice like a melancholy song. "If you canna get the wench from your mind, how in the name of Saint Columba, can you get her to see the truth? She isna different from the other silk-stockinged macaronis who footle into the Borders and swear they can strike a peace." He chuckled without humor. "Except that she doesna ease her lust on the chambermaids or fatten her purse on Kildalton's gold.

"Why?" he beseeched the moon. "Why did you send us a kinswoman who rescues lost lassies and devils my nights? I canna decide what to do—strangle her or love her to death. God a'mercy, auld heart. We want the lass."

Stunned, Miriam swallowed to ease the tightness in her throat. He spoke with pained ambivalence and longing. Her heart ached with the need to comfort him and to believe him.

Sighing, he slapped his thigh and smiled. "Bonny wrappings or no, she'll decide in the baron's favor. She canna help herself." Glancing over his shoulder, he stared up at her window. "Nor can I."

He shot to his feet and retraced his steps. Bracing his hands on his waist, he tilted back his head and growled a wicked taunt up at her window. A moment later he snatched up a handful of pebbles and tossed them.

Rocks tinkled against glass. Verbatim appeared at the window, her black nose framed between the velvet drapes.

The Border Lord grabbed another handful of rocks. "Miriam," he whispered urgently.

A thrill coursed through her, and she hugged her knees to keep from leaping to her feet and answering his call. She had to know what he intended to do.

"I'll give her to the count of ten." He resumed pacing. "If she doesna open the window and give me that bletherin key, I'll make her sorry she stepped her dainty feet in the Borders."

Miriam's high spirits sank like a stone. He didn't want her. He wanted the key. But how did he know she'd taken it? The earl had told him. That possibility fostered a dozen more questions and twice as many suspicions. Just how close were those two men?

"Stop dallying, you nosey beastie," he called up to Verbatim, "and fetch the lass." Again he showered the glass with pebbles. "One . . ."

Verbatim dashed away from the window. The curtains fell back into place.

"Two . . ." Silhouetted against the gray stone, the Border Lord looked an imposing figure. He radiated anger, impatience, and manliness that lured her like a miser to a gold mine.

Verbatim came back to the window, her head cocked in question.

"Rouse her, you overgrown lapdog."

Verbatim whined, her breath fogging the panes. Miriam fumed. Even if the Border Lord was acting out her romantic fantasy, he was doing it for the wrong reasons. How dare he say he wanted her one moment, then insult her the next? It was time to teach this despotic Scotsman a lesson in manners. Yet a part of her longed for a man strong enough to match her own will and honest enough to admit he desired her.

She pushed back the hood of her cloak and prepared to reveal herself, but stopped, for the Border Lord began to scale the castle wall.

Miriam's breath lodged in her throat. How could so large a man find purchase in the smooth stone?

In the pearly moonlight, his arms stretched over his head, he moved like a leopard climbing a tree. She almost called him back, for if he injured himself she'd feel responsible. On the other hand, he deserved to see where a fit of angry impatience would land him.

His grunts of exertion echoed off the stone walls. Between breaths he continued to call her names and promise retribution.

She got to her feet and tiptoed to the squat door in the garden wall, the fountain masking the sound of her steps. She had to make him think she was just entering the garden and had not overheard his dilemma. Let him believe she came running at his command.

From her vantage point she saw him struggle, now about ten feet in the air, but at least another ten feet from the window. When he was an arm's length from the ledge, he lost his footing. He plummeted like a wounded bird and landed on the ground with a grunt and a whoosh of air.

Panic held her motionless. Never had she caused another person pain. What if he were paralyzed? Or dead?

"Damn bloody female."

Relief swamped her.

He struggled to his feet and reached again for a handhold. "I'll turn her over my knee and whack that delectable bottom until she begs for mercy. She wilna sit for a week! Or poke her perky nose where it doesna belong."

Incensed, Miriam ground her teeth. Whack her, would he? Let the miserable cur try.

His curses and insults continued as he slowly retraced his vertical path. His hand touched the ledge below the window.

"Rouse yourself, my wee, meddlesome diplomat," he said in a harsh whisper.

Miriam said, "Impossible, for I'm wide awake."

"What?" He grunted. In a swirl of dark shadows and flailing arms and legs, he tumbled to the ground again. His torso lay between the box hedges, his booted feet exposed to the moonlight.

Fear cut a path through her triumph. She rushed to him.

A heap of cloth and lost dignity, he didn't move. His hat had come off, and his hair lay like a black cap over his head. His face looked inordinately pale against his ebony clothing, the arching of his black eyebrows distinctive even in the dim light.

She dropped to her knees and felt his throat for a pulse. The throb of life brought a slight relief, but the warmth of his skin, his distinctive male scent, and the stubble on his jaw stirred her in a different and feminine way.

Leaning close, she turned her cheek to his face and felt the slow rush of his breath. His eyes opened.

"You came to me, lassie," he whispered. "I didna think you would."

Miffed, she said, "How can you speak such romance when you're lying flat on your back? Are you hurt? Have you broken anything?"

He slipped a hand around her neck and pulled her toward him. "Only my heart, Miriam," he said, a fevered tremor in his voice. "'Twas your doing. Heal me."

The seductive words fanned the embers of her desire. But practicality had for too long been her soulmate. She drew back. "No. You lied to me about who you are."

"Ah, lassie. 'Twas but a wee stretch of the truth, and one you shouldna hold against me."

"You're no swineherd. Who are you?"

"I'm a man with few choices and fewer joys. Be my joy tonight."

Temptation dragged at her. He was the embodiment of her fantasies. He was a silver-tongued devil. "You want the key to the castle, not me."

"I'd hoped for both."

"If you want to go into the castle, why don't you knock on the front door? And don't concoct another lie about sow's hair for the earl's fishing flies."

"Because the housekeeper claims I'm her great-grandsire."

"Mrs. Elliott is much too practical for such nonsense. Tell me the truth."

He freed a strand of her hair and brought it to his nose. Inhaling, he said, "I'd rather talk about your hair. It smells like a summer garden. 'Tis a truth I'll swear to."

Like the tide raking the beach, his tender words dragged at her will to resist. "I don't trust you."

128

"Trust doesna come so quickly to people like you and me."

"What do you mean?"

He tugged gently on the lock of her hair, pulling her over him again. "You're a fighter, Miriam MacDonald. You wilna stand by and let others wage your battles. The only battle you fight is with yourself. Over your desire for me. You'll win, lassie. I trow you always do."

She hadn't expected praise from this rogue. "You're bold."

"Aye," he said, the warmth of his lips teasingly close. "I'm fair smitten. Kiss me. I need you."

Lost and weak with yearning, she touched her mouth to his. Like a long awaited reunion with a cherished friend, the moment stretched out, the anticipation driving away reason and logic, leaving her with a longing so real her body strained to get closer, to get caught up again in the spell only he could weave.

When his mouth slanted across hers and his tongue stabbed past her teeth, her eyes drifted shut and she gave herself up to his demanding mastery. Nimble fingers cradled her face and held her still while he performed a ravishing dance of advance and retreat. Keenly attuned to him, she felt his desperation, and ignoring the consequences, sought to feed his desire.

"You taste like paradise," he murmured, and drew her over him.

Thrilled by his words and emboldened by the feel of his long body beneath hers, she admitted, "I want to taste you, too."

He half-chuckled, half-growled. "Doona expect resistance from me, love. I'm as agreeable as a Cameron on campaign."

She settled herself on top of him, legs tangled with legs, chest against breast. She moved slightly. Something stabbed her in the ribs. Sliding her hand between them, she searched his belt and encountered a hairbrush. How odd. Angling it toward the moon, she tried to examine it. "Why are you carrying this?"

His hand closed over hers and slid the wooden handle

from her palm. She felt the carving of a swan rising from a coronet. The badge of clan Lindsay. It was Betsy's brush.

Miriam had known he would avenge the crime, same as he had before. A part of her hated that she'd been right; another part of her applauded his deed.

"Doona trouble yourself over it," he said and pulled her close again. "'Tis nothing."

His evasive tone sparked her annoyance. She scooted an arm's length away. Desire evaporated. Looking into the shadows, she tried, without success, to gauge his expression. "Nothing but Mrs. Lindsay's hairbrush, which was stolen by the baron's men. How did it end up in your breeches?"

"I have far more interesting things in my breeches than a hairbrush."

"That's preposterous. The hairbrush is a family heirloom. Where did you get it?"

He sighed. "I found it near the Wall. I thought the earl would know who it belonged to. Then he could return it, benevolent laird that he is. He's always concerned about getting possessions to their owners. He's persnickety about the rights of his people."

"He's a fine man. You shouldn't belittle him."

"In truth, lass," he said, his voice rife with exasperation, "belittling Duncan Kerr is the last thing on my mind." Leaning up, he grasped her around the waist. "I'd rather make love to you."

She squirmed, but couldn't free herself from his hold. "A pity, for you've broken the mood. Have you spoken to him about the brush?"

He chuckled, the sound a seductive rumble in his throat. "If you make love half so well as you interrogate, we wilna stop all night."

At his seductive words, a shiver played over her skin.

"Why do they say you're a ghost who fulfills women's fantasies?" she asked.

He heaved a sigh, and with little effort, pulled her onto his chest. "I canna control what other people say."

"You're very much a flesh and blood man."

He placed her hand over his chest. "Who should know that better than you, Miriam?"

"You haven't adequately answered me."

130

"I canna. Now tell the truth. You want to kiss me."

Heaven help her, she did. "I only want to kiss you. Nothing more."

Giving him her weight, she cupped his face in her palms. The manly drag of his unshaven jaw made her skin tingle to the tips of her fingers, the lobes of her ears. Following his lead, she tilted her head and began a slow, delicious feast of his mouth. He tasted of unrestrained lust, and he promised the sweet fulfillment of a thousand nights of maidenly dreams. She charted the curve of his lips, the slick, heated skin that beckoned her deeper into a banquet of sensual delights. With the slightest of entreaties, his tongue frolicked with hers, darting away and enticing her on a merry chase that ended in a swirling union so divine she stifled a moan of pleasure. She grew damp and demanding in places that cried out for relief, yet at the same time she begged for him to stoke the fire.

Then his hands slid from her face and rummaged through the bulk of her cloak until he found her arms, her waist, and her hips. Easing his legs apart, he cradled her there, his palms kneading, caressing, mapping her bottom, urging her closer to the stark evidence of his desire.

The circling motion of his hands, sliding the soft wool of her dress against the sheer silk of her chemise, turned her body to liquid need.

Pulling back, she opened her eyes and focused on his parted lips, now slick from their ardent kisses. Again, she wished for the light of day so she could learn his expressions, watch emotions play upon his features. Even as close as she was to him and as intimately as she felt she knew him, she would not be able to pick him out in a crowd.

He smiled, revealing straight white teeth. "How's that for a ghost?"

"Well . . ."

"You want more, don't you?"

"Tell me what to do," she said.

His hands stilled. The smile faded. An agonized groan passed his lips. "Doona tell me you're a virgin, lass. Not now."

Hearty and strong, his manhood throbbed against her. She felt empty, desperate. A half-truth came to mind. "I've never been ravished in a garden 'neath the light of the moon."

His eyes narrowed. "There isna enough moonlight for an owl to forage, but I doona need the sun to tell me the truth."

Her confidence waned, but her body waxed. "Which is?"

He lifted her off him. "You're an innocent."

His rejection stung. Rising to her knees, she said, "Ha! I'd hardly call myself that."

He sat up and began rubbing his thighs, as if he had a cramp. "Have you stood naked before a man?" One of his hands caressed her breast. "Has he suckled you here?"

Her nipples tingled. "You've no right to ask me that."

"I think," he said thickly and slid his hand lower. "That no man has brought an ache to your belly and touched you—" His fingers wedged their way between her legs. "Here."

Her backbone turned to jelly, and she grabbed his wrist to dislodge his hand. "What are you doing?"

His other hand tunneled beneath her skirts to touch her bare leg. "Proving a point."

Her knees trembled and yet an odd languor engulfed her. She wanted his touch and his sweet words, not a challenge. "'Tis a silly point when you said you wanted to make love to me."

"Is it now?"

The flowing of the fountain and the rustling of leaves filled the silence. His hand snaked higher until the warmth of his fingers touched her intimately.

Drenched in a downpour of erotic sensation, she stifled a moan.

At last he said, "Give me the key to the castle."

Distracted by the pleasure he inspired, she said, "Why?"

One of his fingers played over her woman's flesh, and to her surprise, she felt a wetness there. She grew lightheaded and a cool flush blanketed her skin.

Leaning close, he said, "Spread your legs a bit."

She did, and when his finger slid into her, she sucked in her breath. Fire raced through her, and her hips surged against him, opening herself and giving him easy accessibility. He instantly took advantage, and with a twist of his wrist, captured her completely. Magic fingers moved to and fro, tracing flesh that tingled and swelled, but the movement of his thumb against her secret treasure pushed Miriam toward the edge of fulfillment.

"Now will you give me the key?"

Through a fog of delicious excitement, she sought to understand his words.

"If you give me the key, lassie," he whispered against her cheek, "I'll carry you inside and love you properly."

His hot breath flowed over her skin. But a smidgen of rebellion remained. "What if I don't?"

His thumb moved in quick circles that made her dizzy. "You'll have bruises on your back from the ground." He spoke softly, yet urgently. "You'll get leaves in your hair. You'll get dirty. We canna have that, can we?"

Involuntarily, her head moved from side to side. Her hand fished in her pocket for the key. Just when she would have given it over, his thumb stilled.

"No!" she cried out, feeling as if she were teetering on a narrow ledge.

"Shush." He brought her hand to the bulge in his breeches, slipping the key away as he did. "Feel how much I want you?"

He pulsed with vigorous life beneath her palm, straining against the soft leather of his clothing, but selfishly, her mind stayed fixed on her own body and his wretchedly motionless thumb. "Please," she said.

"With pleasure," he said, his lips closing over hers, and he resumed his glorious play.

She leaned into him, yielding herself completely. His tongue darted into her mouth, then retreated, while his fingers performed a matching motion. The erotic sensations were multiplied when his thumb stepped up the intoxicating spiral. In reflex, her hand curled around him, eliciting a growl that sounded part pain, part bliss, all undeniably male.

He rocked his hips against her hand, pushing himself closer, then drawing back, and with each lunge she felt him grow stronger, harder, his chest laboring to draw breath, his mouth threatening to devour her.

Miriam gloried in his spontaneous show of sensuality and reveled in her own ability to rouse such passion in so bold and forceful a man. But his expertise soon dominated her budding confidence, and the wizardry he worked sent her thoughts flying to a goal just out of reach. She groaned in frustration.

"Think of paradise, love," he murmured urgently. "Imagine you're standing on the bank of a deep blue loch."

From the delirium, she dredged up a few words, but had no idea if they made sense.

Against her ear, he said, "Aye, you can. Trust me. Do you see the water?"

Afraid he would stop, she conjured an image of the glassy, black waters of Loch Leven.

"Do you see it?"

"Aye," she breathed, clutching him tighter.

He trebled his assault on her virgin flesh. The garden and Kildalton faded, and her mind latched on to the man and his magical image of silky water.

Then he said, "Jump in."

In her imagination, she sprang from the bank and plunged into the icy water, but in reality, her body burst forth in a heat that sent a tremor from the crown of her head to the soles of her feet. Like a cinder leaping from the flames of a mighty fire, she jerked and swayed, riding the currents of a gusty wind, letting it take her where it would.

"To paradise."

"Did I not say 'twas so?" he said in a strained whisper.

Her eyes drifted open and focused on the appealing slant of his nose and the thick brush of his lashes. His eyes were brown, she decided, the warm, rich hue of an oak.

He planted a quick, wet kiss on her forehead. "Put your arms around my neck."

Too happy to wonder why, she did as he bade, barely noticing that his hair wasn't slicked back with pomatum as she'd thought, but covered with a scarf and tied at the nape of his neck.

He swept her up and carried her past the urns, and with the ease of a seamstress plying a needle, he unlocked the door to the castle and took her inside.

9

Absolute darkness and the mustiness of damp stone greeted them. Without faltering, he carried her through a second door, then started up the stair tower.

The circular, upward journey had a dizzying effect. Her head grew light, and she nestled her cheek against his neck. He smelled clean and earthy, like fallen leaves, freshly cut timber. Beneath the pleasant aromas, she detected the odd odors of dank wool and something burned. At the absurdity, she focused her thoughts on the man himself, his allure, his vitality.

She seemed as light as eiderdown to him, his steely arms cradling her, his thickly muscled chest a wall of strength.

"You know this castle well."

"To make you mine, lassie, I'd gladly brave the fires of hell."

His seduction called to mind a classic conquest of the heart and everlasting love. In her fantasies he'd been cast as a fair-haired and honor-bound knight fettered to goodness by virtuous deeds. But what was a little tarnish, she reasoned. With her help, this errant knight could turn his back on subterfuge and race back into the fold of the righteous.

Inspired by so noble a challenge, she said, "Where are you taking me?"

"To the first soft spot I find."

"Where?" she insisted.

"To a storage room in the tower."

He stopped, but she knew they hadn't traveled far enough to reach the top. Dipping his shoulder, he leaned into the stone wall. As if by magic, the wall moved.

Her heightened senses were filled with the sweet aromas of basil, sage, and rosemary. She had a moment to wonder if they had come full circle on their journey, for the herbs were the same that grew in the giant urns in the garden.

But when he relaxed his hold and let her slide down the length of his body, thoughts of fragrant plants fled like morals at court. Just as her feet touched the floor, he pulled her against his chest and kissed her again, murmuring Scottish love words. The satiny feel of his lips on her neck rekindled the desire she'd thought he'd extinguished. The tender phrases enticed her into blissful surrender.

Before she'd felt anxious. Now she felt empty, wanton. And in love.

Love. Her logical mind stumbled on the word. Did she love him? Yes, her heart answered. He was the man of her dreams.

"Take off your cloak," he whispered, "and give it to me."

Languishing in her newfound passion, she did as he bade and heard the rustle of wool as he removed his cape. Missing his solid strength and warmth, she said, "What are you doing?"

"Making a soft place so I can love you properly."

The burr in his voice drew her like an entrancing melody. She stepped deeper into the inky darkness and reached for him. As he whirled toward her, his movement stirred the perfumed air. Never, she thought, had any bride enjoyed a sweeter bower of love.

Her eager fingers touched the coarse homespun of his shirt and pulled him closer. His hands roamed her back, tracing her spine, cupping her bottom and lifting, introducing her once more to his blatant and erotic male need. The rasp of his breath close to her ear sent tendrils of desire cascading over breasts that begged for his touch and to legs that seemed too weak to hold her.

Emboldened, she unbuttoned his shirt and splayed her hands on his chest. The springy, silky hair curled around her fingers as if to caress her in return. She pictured them lying naked and imagined the feel of his crisp chest hair against her taut nipples. Her belly grew tight at the thought. "I want you now," she heard herself say.

"All in good time. 'Tis too soon, love." He nipped her shoulder. "Think of something else while I take off your clothes. According to legend, I've waited for you one hundred years. I'll not be rushed."

Oddly, she considered the pelt of curly hair that covered the earl's groin, and as her fingers explored the Border Lord's chest, she thought of his easy sensuality and the differences between the two men. The fair, bashful earl and the dark, alluring lover.

But when he freed the laces of her gown and eased it off her shoulders, she forgot about the gentle nobleman. When he stripped her of chemise and petticoats, she remembered that her lover was still dressed.

She pulled his shirt from the breeches and unbuckled his belt. The leather felt soft and warm, a contrast to the hot, hard length of him that lay beneath.

He groaned. "I should've worn a kilt."

Confidence filled her. "You'd be loving me now if you had. Because you wear nothing under it."

He froze. "How do you know what the Border Lord wears or doesna wear beneath his kilt?"

The sharp words surprised her. "'Tis common knowledge that Scotsmen wear nothing under their plaids. Are you jealous that I might have seen another man's nakedness?"

His hands started roaming again. "Aye, lassie. I canna bear to think of you with another man."

A hint of humor flavored the agreement. Miriam's inability to understand innuendo kept her from grasping why.

He tore at the buttons on his breeches, then began working them down. She rested her hands on his slim waist and the rippling muscles there. Like a path, a trail of hair led to the niche of his navel and lower, to the swollen maleness that strained and pulsed with life.

Her fingers closed over skin smoother than silk velvet. He sucked in his breath and surged forward, his rock hard manhood jutting through the circle she'd made of her hand, the crown of him nudging her belly.

Since she couldn't actually see him, she envisioned the earl's exposed manly parts. In comparison, the Border Lord had been overly blessed by nature.

As she plied her newfound knowledge, her mind wandered to the reason behind the differences in men; perhaps a bold man required a greater organ than a timid one. Could courage have a bearing on a man's sexual prowess?

"Enough," he growled and grasping her waist, he lifted her, snatching her thoughts from the earl and planting them firmly on the Border Lord.

Weightless and supported only by his strength, she clutched his shoulders for balance. But when his mouth touched her breast, she went limp, all of her perception focused on his lips and tongue and the wildly erotic sensations he aroused. A connection was born between her breasts and her woman's core, and like a silken cord, twisted and strung tight, the bond weaved its magic.

He laved and suckled, opening his mouth so wide she feared he might, then prayed he would, devour her. A new wetness flourished between her legs, and deeper, an aching hollow begged for fulfillment. She bit her lip to stifle a keening cry.

Drawing back, he blew gently on the pebbled peak of her breast, sending a shiver to the soles of her dangling feet.

"Speak your mind, Miriam," he whispered. "Doona grow shy on me now."

Unable to comply with his reckless request, she shook her head. Her hair swished around them.

Using delicate bites, he plucked at her nipple. "I canna be certain what you like if you doona tell me."

A sound, half laughter, half frustration, passed her lips. "I too much like what you're doing. I want more."

He chuckled and lifted her higher. "I would gladly give all, but I canna stop kissing your breasts."

The long, heavy heat of him throbbed against her thigh, yet he continued to lavish his attention on her nipples. In pleasurable agony, she grasped his head to pull him away, and was surprised when her palms met soft fabric. She raked off the scarf and threaded her hands through the thick mass of his shoulder-length hair. Even without light, she knew it was black, same as his brows and side-whiskers.

"Unless you'd care to . . ." he began.

"To what?" she said.

Against her breast he answered, "Unless you'd care to whisper your secret desires in my ear."

Needing no further coaxing, she leaned close and in Scottish said, "Make me yours."

He shivered so hard she thought he might drop her.

"Please," she added.

"My pleasure." He lowered her to the makeshift pallet.

As she lay back on a bed of soft wool over bundles of dried herbs, she became aware of his every movement. Even though she couldn't see him, she could hear him kick off his boots and peel the breeches from his legs. His belt buckle rattled loudly on the stone floor.

Then he was beside her, enveloping her, devouring her with hungry kisses that fed her desire and filled her with longing. The enticing drag of his crisp body hair rubbing against her skin heightened her impatience. "So this is how the Border Lord makes love," she said, thinking of the wild disparity between reality and her girlish dreams. "You don't feel like a ghost."

"How do you know how a ghost feels?" His legs slid between hers, spreading her and saturating her imagination with visions of the joining to come. When he had settled himself to his satisfaction, he tunneled his arms beneath her shoulders, taking his own weight and hugging her to his chest. His manhood brushed her.

"Are you truly experienced, lass? Doona lie to me."

An awful possibility occurred to her. "Do you promise not to stop?"

"Miriam," he said on a pained sigh, "I couldna stop, even if the dragoons were scaling the walls."

Relieved, she said, "I'm not ignorant of the workings of men and women." To accentuate the point, she lifted her hips, eliciting a gasp from him. "But to be exactly truthful, I haven't been . . . Oh, bother it. I'm still a virgin."

"In truth, lassie, I'm very happy. I'll go slow." His lips brushed her cheek. "You'll find pleasure in our loving. I give you my solemn word as a Scotsman."

Her dream knight had always spoken similar declarations. Through her fantasies, she knew about honor among men. She turned so their mouths touched. "But I want you now."

Her words so excited Duncan that he almost threw caution to the wind. He burned with the need to claim her, but the idea of deceiving her pricked his conscience. Deceiving her? Christ, from the moment he'd seen her huddled in the garden, he'd begun to play the role of cavalier. He'd even climbed the castle wall.

If she ever learned his true identity, she'd be angry, but worse, she'd be hurt. Wounding the bright diplomat didn't bother him. Harming the untried woman did. He told a small truth. "In a moment you may regret your eagerness, but 'tis said the pain goes quickly."

Her hands traced his nose, his brow, and his cheeks. Her palms would be stained with lampblack. With her loving gestures she had inadvertently stripped him of every vestige of his disguise. Later he would wipe her hands with his shirt and hope for the best.

"I trust you," she said.

Her honesty stopped him. He'd never bargained for her trust. Or had he? As Duncan, he needed her to believe in him, but the Border Lord required no such allegiance. Or did he? One identity bled into the other. Confusion and passion warred within him.

The movement of her breasts against his chest and her softly spoken, "Please . . . I want you," ended his emotional battle.

With a shaking hand, he guided himself into her and felt a moment's regret. But then his thoughts scattered and her maidenhead beckoned. Lust caught him in its grasp. Exerting gentle and constant pressure, he broke through her veil of innocence.

She didn't cry out, but spoke the name Ian in a heavenly soft whisper. Still, the quick heaving of her breasts and the feel of her teeth gently scoring his shoulder told him he'd hurt her. Bridling his own raging passion, he reverted to Scottish, and murmured every lovers' phrase he knew. Between promises and pledges and the quelling of his own need, he managed to soothe her. To keep his own lust in check, he let his mind wander.

The mantle of the Border Lord had never been heavier, and of late, Duncan found himself wondering which man he was. Now more than ever, he simply wanted to be a man ruling his kingdom and raising his son.

She felt small beneath him, her narrow hips a perfect cradle, her slender legs a soft frame for his larger form. But he couldn't forget her other admirable qualities—her intelligence, her independence, and her loyalty to a country that, more often than not, relegated women to the kitchen or the marriage bed.

Suddenly he was proud to be the first lover of a woman who had risen to glory in a profession reserved for men.

The man who captured Miriam MacDonald's heart would be a lucky bastard indeed. She'd bear sons to stand at the right hand of kings. She'd bear daughters to stand at the left hand of kings. Sadly, Duncan Armstrong Kerr would not be that man.

"What are you thinking?"

He almost laughed at the irony of her question, but she wouldn't understand his response, and the last thing he wanted right now was to alienate Miriam MacDonald. "I was thinking that being inside you is so pleasurable a thing 'twould drive a sane man to madness."

He felt the curve of her lips against his cheek. With a smile in her voice, she said, "I thought you wanted an experienced woman."

"You're different," he said, and realized it was true. Never before had God made a woman like Miriam MacDonald. "And you doona qualify anymore."

She moved against him. "You kept your word, my gallant knight. You didn't hurt me."

"Good. For now I intend to pleasure you royally."

"Tell me what to do."

Primed and eager, he surged forward, burying himself

completely. His breath caught. Her sweetness surrounded him, clutching him in a velvet vise of excruciating pleasure. So great was the urge to give himself up to the passion, he had to squeeze his eyes shut and grind his teeth.

Long moments later, when he'd mastered his control, he said, "Bend your knees, and do what your body tells you."

She proved an apt and inventive pupil, and when the strain of near completion again threatened to overpower him, he felt her stiffen. Hidden feminine muscles contracted, squeezing him, enticing him to spill his seed. He did, and as the heavenly spasms began, he wondered how he'd ever let her go.

He awoke to the news that she was gone.

Shaking off the cobwebs of sleep, Duncan bounded from his own bed. "If this is your idea of a jest, Angus, 'tis not funny."

Wearing a breastplate, leather breeches and boots, his gauntlets tucked under an arm, Angus stepped back. "I'd love to claim I had a part in her leaving, but 'twas none of my doing. When the news reached me, I was in the old tilt yard testing that new lad from Lanarkshire. Here." He tossed Duncan a sealed parchment. "She left you a note."

Miriam was gone. The morning after he'd made love to her. Duncan didn't know whether to charge after her, drag her back by her hair, or rejoice and bid her fare-thee-well. But she'd said her good-byes hours ago to the Border Lord. He'd led her down the tower stairs and to the door outside the lesser hall. Drunk on passion and physically exhausted, he'd made his way to his chamber, stripped off his clothes, and slept the sleep of the dead.

"What time is it?"

"Almost nine o'clock, my lord."

Duncan pried off the seal and stared at the words she'd written.

I have gone to Baron Sinclair. Should the need arise, you may reach me and Lady Alexis there.

Need? Sweet Saint Ninian. He needed to strangle her. He needed to lock her in that tower room. He crumpled the paper and threw it in the hearth.

The chill of morning brought gooseflesh to Duncan's naked skin. Inside, however, he burned with rage, for the taste of her lingered on his lips, her essence lingered elsewhere. "How dare she leave today."

Lines of confusion scored Angus's forehead. "My lord, why are you angry? 'Tis what you wanted."

His pride in tatters, Duncan walked to the table by the hearth and snatched up a water pitcher. He drank deeply. "She canna go traipsing off without asking me."

"I think," Angus said ruefully, "she's a woman who comes and goes as she pleases."

Duncan slammed the pitcher against the mantel. With a dull crack, a spray of pottery shards rained on the hearth. "Well it doesna please me!"

"I see," Angus murmured, eyeing Duncan from head to toe. "Would you like your robe?"

Torn by conflicting emotions, Duncan started for the wardrobe and his clothes. A shard of pottery punctured his big toe. "Ouch!" Hopscotching through the debris, he hobbled to a chair.

The rumble of Angus's laughter broke the silence.

"Doona just stand there," Duncan said. "Do something."

His lips contorting to hide a smile, Angus opened the door and yelled for Mrs. Elliott to send up a bath and a maid to sweep.

Grasping the sliver with his fingernails, Duncan pulled it free. A drop of blood seeped from the wound and ran between his toes. "I doona need a bath."

"Aye, you do, my lord. You've lampblack smeared all over your face and hair, and—" He cleared his throat and stared at the beamed ceiling. "And . . . uh, dried blood on your lady crackers."

The memory of loving Miriam MacDonald diffused Duncan's anger. Staring at his manly parts, which indeed bore traces of her virgin blood, he was again reminded of the sweet feel of her beneath him, yielding. The sound of her soft cries, rejoicing. His body responded.

"I take it you didn't hurt yourself there," Angus said, his eyes squinted with worry.

Duncan leaned forward, not out of any need to shield

himself from Angus, for he had nothing to hide from the man who'd been both a mentor and a friend, but suddenly he felt weary. He rolled the inch-long piece of pottery between his thumb and forefinger. "Not the kind of harm you're speaking of, but I doona think I advanced the cause any."

With the toe of his boot, Angus began nudging the broken pottery into a pile. "One thing's for sure. Being the Border Lord has given you a knack for the cavalier ways, eh?"

"'Twas the woman, Angus, not the disguise."

His eyebrows raised in surprise, Angus said, "She seduced you?"

"I canna recall for sure. It just happened." Three times, he vividly remembered. Had he driven her away with his lust? He'd been surprised himself at his ardor, but she hadn't protested or complained; she'd been as eager as he.

"What will you do now?"

"Clean my battle wounds and tend to business . . . until she comes back."

"She went to the baron's."

"Aye." Duncan tossed the shard into the hearth. "I expected as much, just not so soon."

"Look on the bright side," Angus said. "Sinclair'll fill her head with tales, offer her a fat bribe—"

"'Twill be a mistake on his part. She wilna care to be bought."

"Then let's hope he does pull out his purse. Maybe she'll side with us."

Until now, Miriam's knowledge of the feud had involved outside events: reiving, burning, and general villainy. But now the dispute would become dangerously personal. "He'll tell her about Roxanne. He'll tell her I kidnapped Adrienne."

A look of loathing lent a feral quality to Angus's strong features. "Kidnapping," he spat. "You saved the lass from a life of shame and dishonor at the hands of the magistrate. 'Tis a pity your bonny diplomat will never learn *that* truth."

Exhaustion swept over Duncan. He threaded his hands through his hair. A trace of oily lampblack coated his palms. "I told her about the baron's plans for Adrienne. Miriam won't forget, and bless her memory for that."

"You mean you told her you helped Adrienne and her beau flee the baron?"

"Nay. Only the baron's threats to Adrienne. But Miriam knows too much about me as it is."

Angus went to the storage chest and returned with a towel. "Here. 'Tis best the maid doesn't see that soot on your face."

On a half-laugh, Duncan said, "She might mistake me for the Border Lord and accuse me of seducing her grandmama." He began wiping the remains of the disguise from his face and hands.

Angus whacked the gauntlets against his thigh. "'Tis the cleverest of your tricks, my lord. A good thing, too, for the people are fair enchanted by the Border Lord's return. Gives them hope, you ken? They believe justice will prevail."

Duncan thought back to the time of his wife's death, the bloody raids that followed, the senseless destruction, and the havoc Baron Sin had wreaked on the people of Kildalton. Not since the bloody time of Kenneth Kerr had the Border seen such destruction. But the resurrection of the Border Lord had evened the odds and spared Duncan from being likened to his father. One day soon the Border Lord would settle the score. Unless Miriam's interference destroyed his plans.

"Well." He got to his feet. "I've a mountain of work to catch up on. Send out the word that I'll hear any disputes this afternoon in the keeping room. I've a hankering to dress as myself again. Lord, those wigs and spectacles are a bother."

Angus rushed to his side. "You can't give up the disguise, my lord. Lady Miriam left one of the twins behind."

"Which one?"

"Saladin, the Moorish lad. He's out in the tilt yard teaching Malcolm to wield a scimitar."

The joy of the moment faded as Duncan considered the responsibility he'd heaped on his son. "Stay with them, Angus. We can't expect Malcolm to watch his every word."

"You had a talk with him, didn't you?"

"Aye, he needed discipline, no thanks to you and the other soldiers."

Angus pulled a scrap of paper from his gauntlet and

handed it to Duncan. "Let him be a lad, Duncan. Allow him the childhood the old laird denied you. He hasn't cursed once this morning, or mentioned his unmentionable parts."

As always, Duncan wondered if he was raising Malcolm properly. But a little indulgence wouldn't spoil the lad. Glancing at the paper he saw his son's familiar scrawl and his *nom du jour.* "Suleiman," Duncan said. "The magnificent?"

Angus roared. "Gloriously so. He began the day as King John, but when Saladin brought out his sword, Malcolm dashed inside and came back with a handful of these notes and one of his mother's lace shawls wrapped around his head for a turban."

The picture amused Duncan, but a serious ramification could result. "What if Miriam instructed Saladin to pry information from Malcolm?"

"Is she so devious as that?"

Duncan's first response was no, but he realized loving her colored his judgment. Loving her. The notion shocked him and spurred an argument with his conscience.

Did he love Miriam MacDonald?

He'd *made* love to her, that was all.

He'd taken her maidenhead.

She gave it willingly.

But why to the Border Lord, unless she fancied herself in love with him?

She wanted information that would gain her greater fame at court.

She'd asked no questions last night.

She called him her gallant knight.

She'd had too much beer with supper, and she was already drunk on praise from rescuing Mary Elizabeth.

She harbored a deep affection for him.

"Is she, my lord?"

The urgency in Angus's tone snatched Duncan's attention. With regret, he said, "'Tis possible she could use the young scribe."

Angus jerked on his gauntlets. "Then she's no better than a camp whore if she'd use a child for her own gain."

The comparison troubled Duncan. Could Miriam be so cold and selfish? He wasn't sure. "Leave the woman to me.

You befriend the lad. Turn on that MacDodd charm and teach him a few things about being a man."

"But that's stooping to her level!" Angus objected. "At the expense of the lad. Saladin's only twelve years old, Duncan. He's alone here now."

The informal address spoke volumes about Angus's mood. Throughout Duncan's childhood, he had basked in Angus's unconditional love. "He'll be a finer man for any time spent with you."

"Bah! You've been spending too much time with that silver-tongued diplomat. She has you believing any means justifies the end."

The jibe hit home. Duncan retreated. "Very well, Angus. Forget I brought it up."

Angus scratched his beard. "He's a bright boy, but if you asked my opinion, the Lady Alexis coddles him overmuch."

"Then while the good duchess and our wily diplomat are gone, he'll profit from your tutelage."

"What will you do?"

The challenge beckoned. Rubbing his hands together, Duncan added, "I intend to serve the people of Kildalton again—and not as a bumbling earl. 'Twill be your task to keep the lad Saladin occupied elsewhere."

Angus sighed, his mighty shoulders heaving. "Just this morning I heard him ask Malcolm where his mother was."

Shocked, Duncan gripped the arms of the chair. "How did Malcolm answer?"

Angus shook his head. "At the time he was still calling himself King John, so he said his mother was Eleanor of Aquitaine and she was buried at Fontevrault Abbey."

Once Miriam found out who'd given birth to Malcolm, she'd be madder than a wet cat. Out of revenge she might try to enforce the codicil to the marriage agreement he'd innocently signed eight years before. But Duncan was prepared to fight the devil and all the demons in hell to keep his son. "If she sides with Sinclair, we'll let her have a peek at the family Bible. For now, send a messenger with the tinker to Sinclair's. I want to know everything that goes on there. Oh, and get me Mrs. Elliott's key to the tunnel door. I've misplaced mine." A lie, for it wasn't missing at all. After they'd made love, Miriam had filched it again.

"I hope it works."

Feigning innocence, Duncan said, "The key?"

Angus raised his eyes to the ceiling and sighed.

Duncan chuckled. "I canna remember a time when you disappointed me, Angus."

The soldier turned and walked to the door, mumbling, "Would that I could return the compliment."

During the following fortnight Duncan settled disputes ranging from a minor quarrel between the swineherd and the butcher to a major feud between his Armstrong and Lindsay cousins over a broken betrothal.

Duncan thought of Miriam and wondered how large a dowry her father would offer. Sadly he realized he didn't know who her father was.

The messenger wore out a path and nearly winded his horse on the two-hour ride between Sinclair land and Kildalton. He related that Lady Miriam had ridden to the hounds with the baron. Lady Miriam had been crowned the Queen of the Frost Fair. Lady Miriam had danced three minuets and a twosome reel with the duke of Perth, who'd stopped on his way home from London. Lady Miriam had gone a-hawking with Avery Chilton-Wall. Lady Miriam had lost at chess to the baron.

Duncan thought of the many nights Miriam had spent under his roof and castigated himself for never testing her skill at chess.

Leaving Angus in charge of the castle defense, Duncan took a small force of clansmen and the local doctor, and visited every village in Kildalton. In preparation for winter, fuel shortages were alleviated, fences mended, roofs thatched.

Back at Kildalton Castle, he found himself in the garden at moonrise. The darkened window of Miriam's chamber reflected the bleakness in his heart.

He missed her.

Tormented by the bittersweet revelation, he trudged into the tunnel. He needed no light to find the secret passageway outside her chamber; he'd traveled these tunnels from the time he could walk. Sliding open the panel behind the wardrobe, he was seduced by the bracing fragrance that

lingered in the gowns she'd left behind. His senses heightened by the absence of light, he stroked the garments, feeling
the nubby texture of brocade, the furry nap of velvet, the
airy delicacy of watered silk.

Elegant gowns, costly gowns, gowns to charm a foreign
king. But in her quest to snare a Border Lord, she garbed
herself in modest frocks of serviceable wool. Then she'd laid
siege to his heart.

Would Duncan Armstrong Kerr yield? Not with so formidable an ally as the Border Lord.

Thoughts of his dark persona demanded a bold new
strategy. Patting himself on the back, Duncan returned to
his chamber, donned the clothing of the Border Lord and
planned his next seduction.

10

Duncan never got the chance to carry it out, for at dusk Mrs. Elliott came to his chamber to announce the unexpected arrival of the duchess of Perth.

"Tell me it isna true," he said, a lamp chimney in his hand, his fingers coated with lampblack.

The housekeeper twitched her button nose and stared at the black scarf draped over his shoulder. "As you wish, my lord. 'Tis not the duchess of Perth leading an entourage through the gate, but Eleanor of Aquitaine come to claim her firstborn son, who's now purging the buttery of infidels."

Duncan put down the cylinder of glass, wiped his hand, and grasped a moment's respite before his life erupted into chaos. "Should I discipline young Richard the Lionheart before or after I receive the good duchess?"

Her brown eyes crinkled with mirth. "'Tis not for me to say. But I will remind your lordship that when last she visited you said conversing with Her Grace was like bartering with a Turk over the very last horse."

Duncan winced at the memory. Lord, the duchess could meddle. "Why is she here?"

"The messenger said she's on her way down from Perth to join her husband at Sinclair's. It's to be a hunt and a ball."

"Last week 'twas a frost fair." Where Miriam was crowned queen, he thought sourly. "Perhaps the duchess will be so anxious to see the duke that she wilna stay long."

"I'm sure the housemaids are praying for the onset of her wifely devotion, my lord. They're tidying the large suite now."

He bowed from the waist. "Then I'll change clothes and prepare to dodge her verbal arrow."

Mrs. Elliott sniffed and plucked at the lace on her apron. "Why is she so insistent that you marry again, my lord?"

"I suppose she canna stand to see a man happy."

The housekeeper turned to go but stopped. "My lord . . ." Her voice dropped. "'Tisn't fair to the lad Saladin, the way master Malcolm's acting. The Moor can't help the way he was taught to worship."

Her sense of fairness pleased Duncan. "What did Malcolm do?"

"He makes fun of the lad, who doesn't eat meat or take spirits. Malcolm also dances around the Moor when he's praying."

"Thank you, Mrs. Elliott. You're a woman of justice. Tell Malcolm and Saladin they're to stay the night with Angus, and report to me in the morning. Oh, and give the housemaids the honey I brought from Dearcag Moor."

Standing taller, she grasped the door handle. "Aye, my lord. Honey or no, you'll hear nary a quibble from anyone while the duchess is here. We need no bribes. We're loyal to you." Glancing over her shoulder, she stared at his black clothing. "If I may say so, you cut an especially braw figure tonight as the Border Lord."

Flattered, Duncan watched her leave. As he exchanged the black raiments for his Kerr tartan, he tamped back disappointment. Tonight's raid to retrieve his stolen cattle would have to wait. The duchess wouldn't. Only one aspect of the evening pleased him; with the scribe Saladin out of the castle, Duncan could forego disguises.

By the time Duncan reached the dining hall, the duchess reigned at the head of the table. The panniered skirt of her white gown billowed around her, obscuring her chair and the table legs. Ropes of pearls hung in triple festoons from her bodice, which was cut barely an inch above her nipples. Current fashion, it seemed, was the duchess's only saving grace.

The observation surprised Duncan, for he couldn't remember ever noticing her feminine assets. Slowing his steps, he thought of Miriam's fancy gowns in the wardrobe upstairs and wondered if the bodices had been fashioned to accentuate her feminine charms. How many men had seen her so daringly revealed?

Jealousy seared him. Why didn't she dress that way for him?

Halfway across the room, he stopped, but like a hunter on the prowl, his male pride went in search of a victim.

"What's wrong, Duncan?" The duchess put down her tankard. "You looked peaked."

Her waspish voice reminded him that he had bigger problems than jealousy. He smiled and approached the table, his hand extended. "I'm fine, Your Grace. I simply canna remember seeing your charms displayed in so bonnie a gown."

She snatched up her fan and tapped his knuckles. At forty years old, her graying hair hidden beneath a powdered wig, the duchess could still play the coquette. "Since when do you play the flatterer, Lord Duncan? You've never cared a farthing for fashion or flirting."

The truth of her challenge gave him pause. But he had no time to examine the changes that were ripping his life apart. He drew back his hand. "Life on our side of the Border isna conducive to fancy frocks and courtly manners. 'Tis all we can do to put food in our bellies and hold on to what little our forebears left us."

Curiosity glittered in her eyes. "Something's different about you, my lord."

Had someone disclosed his dual identity? No. It was only her dreaded verbal haggling. He took the seat at the other end of the table. "I canna imagine what you mean, unless I need a barbering."

"Not that. You seem so . . . so determined and comfortable with yourself."

152

Trying not to smile, Duncan laid his napkin in his lap and lied. "Because I'm hungry and glad to see you?"

Her eyes rounded in surprise. Her fork clattered onto the pewter plate. "There. What you just said. That's what I mean. You're not usually so . . . cordial and gallant."

He had been remote, he supposed, but visits from the nosey duchess and her kind were always a trial. Invariably they were journeying to or returning from the pomp and boredom of Anne's court. Common decency made him offer her and other travelers hospitality; protocol forced him to endure her company.

Mentally arming himself for a battle of words, he poured himself a mug of beer. "I hadna noticed, Your Grace, but come to think of it, we havna had so many visitors since Anne took the throne."

"You were a child then."

Astounded, he said, "Your Grace, I'm thirty-six years old. The queen took the throne eleven years ago. I was hardly a child."

She stared at the fingers on her left hand, moving them in sequence as she tried to make the simple subtraction.

He reached for the pitcher. "More beer?"

She gave a guilty start, then sighed dramatically. "Ah, Duncan. Why must you shun my efforts to be your friend? I only want to help you and liven your life."

"You're kind to do so. 'Tis dreadfully boring in the Borders."

"Oh?" She tapped her little finger with the tines of the fork. "Adrienne Birmingham disappeared." She tapped her ring finger. "You turned out your mistress." The fork touched her middle finger. "Miriam MacDonald has been staying with you. Hardly boring occurrences. Shall I go on?"

He couldn't have felt more exposed had she watched him use the privy. For years he'd allowed her to meddle in his life because of her rank, and it was easier than arguing with her. He thought of Miriam and her mastery of conversation. He'd trade all the salt in Kildalton for a fraction of her expertise. What would she do in a similar situation? The answer inspired him.

"You're prying again." He picked up his fork and tapped his finger in imitation of her. "Adrienne Birmingham is old enough to go off on her own. I tired of my mistress. Miriam MacDonald is here on an official assignment."

She toyed with her pearls. "You're defending yourself, and rather aggressively. Why?"

An angry retort leapt to his lips, but he refused to utter it. He would keep his temper in check. But if he were to use Miriam's methods, he had to use them all. "You're too observant."

"You're so charmingly blasé, my lord," she chided. "I have only your best interests at heart."

"Then you've succeeded, for your visit makes me extraordinarily happy."

"That's news. Perhaps you could make me *extraordinarily* happy by telling me you've found another wife."

He had found a woman to love, he thought sadly, but if Miriam learned the truth about her lover, he didn't stand a beggar's chance at winning her. What a coil he'd gotten himself into. Saddened, he said, "When I do chose a wife, I wilna draw breath before informing you."

A frown wrinkled her brow and puckered her painted lips. "You have always been far too secretive about personal matters. But this boldness, Duncan. I don't know what to make of it."

As if it were in her jurisdiction to do so. Seizing the opportunity to lighten the conversation, he said, "You could make a feather of it and put it in your cap."

The fan flew to her mouth, but didn't muffle her laughter. "Your wit grows bolder, too. But what, I wonder, do you truly think of Lady Miriam?"

From the knowing look in her eye, Duncan suspected she could provide information about Miriam MacDonald. Expectation made his blood race, but he schooled his features into blandness. "She's another of the queen's minions here on a fruitless task. Besides, she isna here at all. She's off to Baron Sinclair's."

Like a merchant trying to drive up the price of her wares, the duchess underplayed the situation. "She's beautiful and brilliant, and she has no interest in marriage."

A lie slipped easily from his lips. "Then we have one thing in common."

Seriousness smoothed out her features. She leaned forward, exposing the crests of her nipples, which she'd rouged. "She's never failed at a diplomatic task, Duncan. She struck a peace between France and England."

She'd started a war in his heart. He wondered just how much the duchess would reveal about Miriam. "I doona ken why the queen rewarded so brilliant a negotiator with a sojourn in the Border," he said and speared a leg of rabbit he didn't want. "Sounds very much like punishment to me."

Her expression turned cool. She sipped the beer. "Indeed it was. Lady Miriam was impudent. She angered the queen."

Every exchange in the conversation seemed a piece on a chessboard. He must think ahead and play skillfully. But the exercise was exhausting. Miriam spent her life in such contests. He both envied and sympathized with her. "So? How did she manage that?"

The duchess shifted in her chair, her attention riveted on the bones on her plate. "I'm not at liberty to divulge that."

Ha! The nosy biddy didn't know. "If Lady Miriam's so clever, surely she could sway the queen. Anne isna our most stalwart sovereign." Duncan took a bite of the hare.

"Ah, Duncan. You are so thoroughly countrified."

"Thank you, Your Grace. I do but try."

Real interest sparkled in her eyes. "Lady Miriam has no resources, other than her friendship with Alexis Southward and her skill as a diplomat. If Lady Miriam fails to strike a peace between you and the baron, the queen will marry her off to the minister of Baltic affairs. He's rather in his prime, the duke says. Which means he's a dottering old lech."

Duncan's mouth went dry, the meat suddenly as tasteless as rowan bark. Had she been eager for a last fling with a younger man? If so, he'd given her a bonnie dose of passion. A more painful possibility occurred to Duncan. What if she'd been trying to weasel information from him? Then he laughed to himself, for in that area only, she'd gone away disappointed, for he'd spoken lovers' phrases.

"Don't you find her situation interesting, Duncan?"

"So much so, I shall give her my felicitations and a pair of warm mittens."

Sputtering, the duchess groped in the folds of her gown for

the napkin. "There's other trouble between Miriam and the queen, an old matter neither will discuss. Aren't you curious, Duncan?"

He washed down the hare with a long pull on the beer. "I doona see why I should be. The secrets of women are of no consequence to me. The queen could marry her off to the pope for all I care." He laughed. "I'd probably offer a dowry for the wench. Since she's without."

"Wench?" she squealed. "Dowry? What's gotten into you?"

Feeling used and vengeful, he made a show of wiping his mouth with his napkin. At length, he rested his elbows on the table. "While I sympathize with the plight of our lovely, dowerless diplomat, I'm fair weary of English interference in Border affairs."

"Plight? You don't know the half of it. Your life is a harvest fair compared to hers."

Then she told him a story about Miriam that broke his heart.

Hours later as he lay awake in bed, Duncan thought about an orphaned lass who had survived a devastating childhood, overcome an adolescence filled with tragedy, and matured into a woman who could challenge a queen. And capture the heart of a Border Lord.

Blessed saints! During her diplomatic career, Miriam had had ample opportunities to lose her innocence. She'd just never faced consequences so dire.

The urge to possess her, to confirm her affection rose fiercely in him. His bed was cold, lonely. His life confused, unsatisfying. He wanted her back at Kildalton. He'd drag her back here by her hair. He wanted her under his protection. He'd teach her to dally with his affections. He wanted to obliterate her childhood tragedy. He'd chain her to his bed. He wanted to give her children of her own.

He wanted her for his wife.

The only man she wanted was a product of his imagination. She favored a bold adventurer who thrived on danger and conquest, not a country earl who struggled for peace and harmony.

As the aching in his heart grew, Duncan considered telling

her the truth, but a part of him cried, "Hold on to her while you can."

In the face of so fervent a plea, his gentle nature yielded to the darker, more insistent side of him. He would yield again tomorrow night, and the next, and the next. The duchess of Perth would depart on the morrow. At nightfall Duncan would banish the country earl and don the disguise of the Border Lord. Then he'd ride into England and reclaim all the baron's men had stolen of late. One glimpse of his dark form and the English would scurry for the safety of their houses and cloak themselves in prayer. He'd retrieve his stolen flax and salt, then return to Kildalton.

He would continue to practice swordsmanship with Angus. Miriam wanted a warrior. Duncan would oblige her.

He smiled and fluffed his pillow. He knew the way to win her heart: a love letter to arrange a tryst at midnight in the shadow of Hadrian's Wall. The messenger would keep Duncan apprised of her plans. When she concluded her visit with Baron Sinclair, she'd be furious with Duncan Kerr. But she'd fall into the arms of the Border Lord.

She slapped him so hard he fell against the Roman wall.

"You thoughtless barbarian," she shouted loud enough to make the sleuthhound scurry for the safety of the bushes. "How dare you send a love note to me at Baron Sinclair's?"

Shocked, his cheek smarting, Duncan didn't know whether to kiss her or turn tail and run. Lord, she could get angry. Even the hood of her cloak quivered with a rage she didn't try to control.

She stood on tiptoe. Starlight added to the fire in her eyes. "Have you nothing to say for yourself, *Sir* Border Lord?"

Her sweet breath fanned his face. Safe in his disguise, he feebly murmured, "I thought my note said it all."

"A note the damned maids could've read, you dolt," she hissed, all injured feminine pride. "How dare you compromise my position and threaten my authority? What if the maids had told the baron about your ridiculous note?"

The insult stung. He'd apologize for many things, but not for loving her. He grasped her shoulders. "The baron's maids doona read. Forget them. You have kept me waiting on this spot for an hour. 'Tis bletherin cold out here."

In the moonlight, her serene smile boded ill. "Too cold for you? That's odd, since you spend your nights on that horse terrifying the poor citizens of Sinclair."

Thanks to the duchess of Perth, Duncan knew that Miriam had come to Scotland ignorant of the facts of the feud. Now that she'd heard the baron's side, the gentle Duncan was in for a battle. The Border Lord had to even the odds. "Did the poor citizens of Sinclair tell you I turn cattle into sheep and deflower virgins only at the full of the moon?"

"The English are more gullible than the Scots, for they fear you. Stop changing the subject. Where were you a sennight ago?"

I was listening to the duchess of Perth tell me how your parents died. I'm sorry, he wanted to say. Instead he prevaricated: "I shared a pint with my black cat. He's my familiar."

"Do tell. Someone raided a farm near Cooper's Mill and almost made off with a herd of the baron's spotted cattle. I suppose you'll swear that neither you nor the earl had anything to do with it."

He wanted to beg her to see the truth, but weakness and groveling wouldn't work with Miriam. Reason and finesse would. "Spotted cattle, you say? A rare breed in these parts. The earl bought such a herd last fall. He even has the bletherin papers on the beasts. He talked of nothing else for months. His pride and joy, they were."

"A convenient story since the earl's a fellow Scot. Did he pay you to raid that farm?"

An owl sailed over the wall, its talons clutching an English prey. It had ever been so. From mice to men, every creature in the Borders struggled for survival and dominance.

"Well?" she demanded.

He'd come here hoping to salve his pride and make her love him again, but she seemed eager to fight. To dominate, he thought ruefully. "The cattle belong to the earl. If you doona believe me, ask him. Or look in that record book of his. He'll prove he owns the cattle and tell you the date the baron took them."

"Rest assured," she said, "I intend to deal with his

lordship, but now we're speaking of you, Ian. Or whatever your name is. You lead the raids on Sinclair land."

She radiated determination, her shoulders squared, her chin held high, her luscious mouth softly pursed. But he knew about her now, and he had to get her mind on sweeter subjects. A wee truth and a fair dose of seduction seemed a good starting place. "I was christened John, but the Scots use Ian. 'Tis the name you called out when I made love to you."

She stared at Hadrian's Wall, melancholy in her eyes. At length she said, "You're a rounder to remind me of past indiscretions." With a shake of her shoulders, she pulled free of him.

"Indiscretions? Tell the truth, Miriam. You wanted me."

"Since you're in a mood for honesty, Ian, tell me what you know about a shipment of salt that disappeared from the baron's barn on Tuesday last."

"Where did the baron acquire salt?"

"I'm asking the questions. I'm also concerned about the twelve cartloads of flax that were stolen from the baron's tenants in Wickham."

He felt like a pot ready to boil over. "The earl, not the baron, owns the salt. He's been selling it to the duke of Cromarty for a decade."

"You're very knowledgeable about his affairs. That's odd, since you yourself named him a private person."

He reached for her. "Drat your memory, and to hell with salt and flax."

She knocked his hand away. In a low, insistent voice she said, "What of the flax?"

Cursing himself for losing his temper and forgetting how smart she was, Duncan struggled for control. The hood of her cloak framed her face in miniver. He ached to touch her. "I hadna thought to talk of business tonight, lassie. I saw a bonnie rainbow today. It reminded me of your beauty."

A cloud passed over the moon, throwing her face in deep shadow. Her gaze didn't waver. "I'll verify the salt. Tell me about the flax."

His confidence plummeted. "I'd rather hold your hand and take you for a stroll in the moonlight. I havna seen you in weeks. Doona play the diplomat tonight, Miriam."

Her teeth closed over her bottom lip. He could sense her weakening. He searched for the right words. When he spoke, it was from the heart. "I meant what I said in the note. You rob me of sleep. I've missed you sorely. Be my love again."

She faced him, her intrepid mettle a shield. "The flax."

Resigned to failure, he said, "'Tis grown near Loch Lockerbie. The baron's land hasna the water to support so thirsty a crop. He stole the flax from the earl. I got it back."

"Tell me this, is your life worth a sack of salt or a cartload of flax?"

"Do you care so much for my life?"

Like a soldier in battle, she had wiped away all sentiment, every scrap of emotion. His respect for her trebled. But by the bones of Saint Ninian, she would lose this battle. She had her strengths. He bletherin well had his.

He folded his arms over his chest. "So you do care whether I live or die."

"Of course I care. But I cannot respect a man who does not value his own life."

Duncan took small encouragement from her words, but he hadn't come here to discuss midnight raids. "You've forgotten your folklore, Miriam. Ghosts doona give a second thought to mortality."

She sucked in her breath. "How dare you be so glib?"

"I'd rather be sweet and loving, but you wilna give me the chance. Let's not quarrel."

"Quarrel?" She raised her arm as if to slap him again. A second later, she decided against it. "I never quarrel. I spend too much of my life patching up the squabbles of prideful men and deceivers like you. Good night." She spun around, her swirling cape casting a long shadow on the rocky ground.

Alarmed, he shouted, "Miriam!"

She stopped and snapped her fingers. The hound raced to her side. "Have you ever seen a pack of hungry mastiffs fell a deer?"

His stomach floated like a cork. "Aye, 'tis a gruesome sight, even to the stout at heart."

"Come near me again and I'll make certain you learn why even a starved mastiff fears a sleuthhound."

Reason and finesse be damned! He ripped off his gloves

and holding them in one hand, he grabbed her with the other. Exerting pressure, he spun her around.

Time slowed to a crawl. She turned, drawing a breath and parting her lips to utter the command. He jammed the gloves into the dog's muzzle and covered Miriam's mouth with his hand. She stiffened. Her chin came up. The hood fell back, exposing her glorious hair.

"Doona lecture me about dogs, Miriam. The Romans brought their beasties here. The Norsemen brought theirs." He tipped his head toward the wall. "The Romans played a game. They tossed bread over the wall to coax the children near. When the hungry bairns had come close enough, the Romans loosed their 'pets.' Over the pitiful cries, the soldiers laughed and made wagers over how long 'twould take the children to die. Border folks learned to deal with dogs centuries ago." His hand dropped to her shoulder. "I doona fear your Verbatim."

"You're trying to shock me."

"Nay. I'm trying to befriend you. You doona ken the trouble here."

"I know all I need to know."

"To do what?"

"To be fair."

Frustration dragged at his good intentions. "You canna be fair, Miriam, for there are no fair solutions. It's been tried before."

"Not," she ground out, "by me."

"Why are you different from the others?"

"Because I'm better than the others. I made the Treaty of Utrecht for crissakes! I've heard more convincing lies from the lowliest page at court than I've heard from the baron or the earl. The truth is the place to start."

If assurance was the harbinger of victory, she would succeed. The possibility filled Duncan with ambivalence. "One of them speaks the truth."

"You know which one, don't you?" she mocked. "You've taken sides."

Duncan grew desperate to make her see reason. "Aye, the side of peace."

"I'll win a peace here. Only a Scot can."

Her simple declaration bounced off Duncan's temper like raindrops off a mallard's back. "Even a Scot canna always understand the Border. Heritage doesna make you a Scot, lass. 'Tis what's in your heart that counts. You've met the earl and the baron. Which man do you believe?"

"Both of them, and neither of them."

Disappointment seared him. "You speak, but say nothing. Will you act and do nothing?"

"If you knew anything about me, you wouldn't ask that question."

"Oh, I know about you, lass." He did. He knew a story that even today brought tears of shame to any decent Scotsman. "I know that you shiver in your sleep and dream dreams that make you weep and whimper like a lost child. You never sleep the night through, for sunrise finds you pacing the floor. I think you spend your days running from your nights. Let me help you stop running."

"Ha! Spoken by a man who is always on the run, a man who won't reveal his true identity." She turned away, her profile limned in silvery moonlight. "Where do you spend your nights?"

"When I'm lucky . . . with you."

She stared at their horses grazing nearby. "'Twas only the one night."

"A memorable one, aye?"

Her tongue slipped out to moisten her lips. "Aye."

He took her in his arms, his mind spinning with thoughts of the bloodbath she'd witnessed as a child and how he could make her forget it. "'Twas heaven lying with you," he whispered against her temple. "Feeling you beneath me, your hands clutching me, your soft sigh when I made you mine."

"I belong to no one."

True, he thought. A clan of favor-seeking Highlanders had seen to that. "Because you wilna allow yourself to need anyone."

"I cannot fail. There *must* be peace here."

True. Because for her the consequences were too dire. "Peace is relative, you ken? A forest once covered this land. The Romans created a desert here and called it peace."

She jerked away and threw her hands in the air. "You're just like the earl."

Duncan's heart skipped a beat. Had she guessed? Calling her bluff, he said, "I doona ken why you'd make so ridiculous a comparison."

"You're like the baron, too. You see things in black and white, right and wrong. You're all stubborn and deceitful. You think you can trick me because I'm a woman."

Duncan burst out laughing. "Doona compare me to a stick of an Englishman who thinks the world owes him a living or a niddering poltroon who prefers brook trout to women."

"At least the earl doesn't bedevil poor folks into draping their mantels with leeks and pouring chicken blood in the corners of their homes as you do."

He'd made the mistake of letting her goad him earlier; now he was wise to her methods. "I canna be responsible for people and their superstitions."

"The baron tells a different tale. He says you frighten them apurpose. He says you're a spirit from the pits of hell. His people swear you're a devil who vanishes at will."

"What do you think?"

"The answer to that will cost you."

Good Lord, would he never stop underestimating her? She had changed the destiny of England. Duncan longed to change hers. "I doona want to bargain or argue with you. I want to love you."

She eyed him cautiously. "You're an opportunist, and I *doona* believe you."

"Then believe this." He slid his hands down her arms and threaded his fingers through hers. The warm softness of her skin, the frailty of her bones made him think of how much he needed her and how desperate he was to keep her. "My life changed the day you came to Scotland."

She looked down at their joined hands. "Yes, it did. You're in grave danger now. I can have you arrested for thievery."

"By the magistrate?" He laughed. "The coward'll nae come after me. He couldna catch me."

"You're speaking of Avery Chilton-Wall?"

When she used that silky tone, he wanted to hide behind a shield. He wanted to hold her close and learn the secrets of her past. And he would. But not now. "Aye, Avery Chilton-Wall bribes easier than a Glenlyon Campbell. God rot their wretched souls."

Her eyes grew wide, then narrowed with scorn. "Then I'll replace him."

Would she never broach the subject of her past? And the clan of Campbells that had ripped her childhood to shreds. He wanted to comfort her, but all she could talk about was warring men. "You haven't the power to replace the magistrate."

Silence.

Christ, she did have the power. Now more than ever, he had to secure her loyalty. Malcolm's future and the safety of Kildalton depended on it. Logic had failed. Pray God seduction succeeded.

He grasped her waist and lifted her. "The greatest danger I face is losing my heart to you."

She clutched his shoulders for balance. Now that they were on a level, he could see the wariness in her eyes. Softly, she said, "Heartaches are a part of life."

For certain heartaches had been the lion's share of her life. He'd change that, too, if he could. "Happiness should be a bigger part, Miriam."

The night wind rustled her hair, sending silky tendrils across her face. "You know nothing about making a woman happy. Honesty is what *I* want."

He couldn't give her honesty but he could show her she was wrong. "I know that you like it when I kiss you here." Tipping his head to the side, he touched his lips to the curve of her cheek. "And here," he whispered into her ear, then sent his tongue exploring the delicate whorls.

Her fingers tightened on his shoulders, reminding him that she'd nipped him there at the instant he'd breached her maidenhead. A moment later, she had breathed a soft sigh against his skin and said his name. Later still, she had gasped, straining for breath until she cried out her pleasure, then lay against him, sated and so femininely soft, he'd taken her a second time, and a third.

Desire and need filled him, swelling his loins and bringing an ache to his belly. His legs began to tremble, and when his lips found hers willing and eager, he forgot that she might deny him and remembered that happiness had been a stranger in her life. Tonight he would make it her boon companion.

Clutching her tightly to his chest, he reveled in the feel of her tongue dancing with his, her hands moving to his neck and his jaw. Too many clothes separated them, but like the other obstacles in their path, Duncan intended to strip them away, one by one.

Duncan. She wouldn't call out that name in passion. At the unwelcome consequence of his disguise, sadness enveloped him. He must find a way to make her want the man he truly was. But with desire ripping at his gut and the promise of soul-deep satisfaction so close at hand, he banished plans and schemes and set about seducing Miriam MacDonald.

He kissed her deeply, drawing her tongue into his mouth and suckling gently in imitation of the way her body received him. Her breathing grew ragged, her hands busy in their exploration of him. When she inadvertently sent his hat flying on the wind, Duncan had to act before she stripped him of the scarf and spied his fair hair.

He swung her into his arms and made haste for Hadrian's Wall.

"Where are you taking me?"

Looking down at her, the moonlight wreathing her in a silvery glow, her lips damp from his kisses, Duncan thought himself the luckiest man in Scotland. "A familiar place. To paradise, my love."

His words and the promise they contained sent a thrill through Miriam. Yet the irony in what he'd said made her smile.

"What's so funny?" he asked.

Feeling carefree and happy, she said, "Paradise in the Borders. Imagine that."

He flashed her a grin that brightened the night. "'Tis no fair making me laugh just now. I could drop you in the dirt."

She had made a jest. Glory be! Inspired, she said, "I told you I could make you laugh."

A quizzical expression arched his dark eyebrows. His shoulders shook with laughter. "For a woman with no sense of humor, you're doing a damned fine job of entertaining me."

Languishing in his arms, the starry sky overhead, the beloved soil of Scotland beneath, warring men forgotten, Miriam felt at peace. At home. For the first time in her life.

Joy filled her, and over the crunching of his boots and the soft whistle of the wind, she heard her own heart hammer with anticipation of the pleasure to come. Reaching up, she laid her hand on his cheek. He turned and placed a kiss on her palm.

Shivers of desire tickled her scalp and vibrated in the soles of her dangling feet.

Then the shadow of the crumbling wall fell over them, trapping them in a net of darkness. He turned and leaned his shoulder into the barrier. Stone grated against stone. In a state of stupefied splendor, she felt the wall give way.

Cool air, perfumed with hay, wool, and a long dead fire rushed to meet them. Possibilities flitted through her mind: perhaps he *was* a ghost who appeared from nowhere and disappeared into nothing. He could be the ghost of some Kerr ancestor, for he often reminded her of the portrait of the dark and oddly handsome Kenneth Kerr.

Before she could explore his identity or her dark surroundings, the Border Lord put her on her feet and began stripping off her clothes. His seductive Scottish words, whispered against her lips, obliterated rationale and inspired her to divest him of scarf, cape, and shirt. But as she slipped off the scarf, she again found herself wondering who he really was. She opened her mouth to ask him, but his lips smothered the words.

She fumbled with the buttons on his breeches, her mind fixed on what lay beneath. Her petticoats whooshed to the floor at the same moment his manhood sprang free. Temptation lured her from her task of undressing him. She flattened her palms on his waist, then slid her fingers beneath the warm leather, moving down until her hands were filled with him.

In frustration, she said, "I wish I could see you."

"You know me well enough, lassie." He groaned and rocked his hips against her, showing her vividly how her touch affected him. "Ah, Miriam, you've magic in your hands."

His soft, manly pouches had become rock hard, and his jutting maleness had grown bold in its size and insistence. Pride and confidence infused her. "Enough magic," she said, "to cast a spell—even on a ghost?"

He chuckled and lifted her chemise so he could caress her bare bottom. "Aye, or bring out a worse goblin in me."

Her womb became a tight coil of desire and her breasts ached for his touch. He hunched his shoulders and ran his hands over her back and buttocks. When he glided lower, spreading her and teasing her sensitized skin, she felt a familiar sheen of wetness.

Eager to expand her own exploration, she made a ring of her hands and slipped it over the crown of his manhood. She encountered a drop of moisture and realized that, although as different as night and day, their bodies reacted in much the same fashion.

"No more teasing, love," he said, laying her down on a straw-filled mattress that crackled under her weight.

She heard him peel away his leather breeches, yank off his boots and toss them aside. The inky darkness robbed her of sight, but her other senses grew keenly aware of him, looming above her, radiating heat, and offering a passion she could not deny despite her misgivings about succumbing to a man who remained a mystery to her, a man who would soon flit off into the night and vanish, perhaps forever, leaving only wistful memories.

Reaching out, she pulled him down, and when she opened her legs and bade him enter, he rasped, "Nay, lassie, I've a craving to love you in other ways first."

Then he set about showing her the marvelously diverse ways a man could use his lips and tongue, fingers and teeth. He left a trail of wet kisses from her breasts to her navel, from her ankles to her inner thighs. But when he'd lifted her legs over his shoulders, parted the folds of her womanhood, Miriam gasped in surprise. As his lips closed over her aching flesh she wilted in surrender. The hungry laving of his tongue and the gentle nibbling of his teeth revived her. Suddenly paradise seemed a run-down shanty compared to the heaven that lay ahead.

He groaned, and the low vibration of his voice against her sensitized skin triggered the first in a succession of climaxes that rocked her to her soul. Just when she thought the pleasure had ended, he opened her wider and murmured, "More, Miriam. Give me more." Then he stabbed fiercely with his tongue and suckled her until she gave him what he sought.

His quest fulfilled, he rose above her, driving deep, grinding deeper. Her languor vanished and she felt compelled to hear him gasp and groan and cry out his pleasure, too. Once, twice, she brought him to rapture, then forced him to stop. Then he reversed their positions and commanded her to ride him to glory. Sitting astride him, his manhood robust and buried to the hilt, she quaked again. He grasped her waist, lunged, and sought his own release.

Once their breathing had slowed, he lifted her and brought her to his side. Nestling against her, he said, "Sleep awhile with me, love. Hold me close and dream only of me."

Hours later, limbs and senses still mired in euphoria, they donned their wrinkled clothes and emerged from Hadrian's Wall.

Verbatim sat sphinxlike, a black plumed hat and pair of gloves resting on her paws. The waning moon cast long shadows on the earth. The Border Lord lifted Miriam into her saddle and rode alongside her to Kildalton. As the towers of the castle came into view, the horizon grew ripe with the promise of sunrise. With it, reality returned.

In a few hours she would face Duncan Kerr and give him the shock of his life.

11

Miriam dawdled at her toilet, her thoughts ambling from the meeting ahead to the rendezvous past to nothing at all. Depending on the topic, she felt listless, invigorated, and challenged. Sometimes she shivered and felt her knees go weak; other times she ground her teeth and prayed for patience. Once she cried. Never did she regret.

After her arrival hours before, she had thrown open the drapes and stood at the window, watching the sun creep into the sky. Then she'd paced the floor until the maid had come to build up the fire and draw her bath.

Now, she dragged the brush through her still-damp hair and wondered how she'd get through the day, or how harshly she should deal with the earl, or how her body could speak so eloquently to a dark stranger who wouldn't reveal his true identity. Or how he could know her so well.

You shiver in your sleep and dream dreams that make you weep and whimper like a lost child.

Someone scratched on the door. Miriam sighed, smiled, and said, "Come."

A plump maid bustled into the room, a covered tray in her

hands, a bundle of dried heather under her arm. "Morning, milady." She dipped a neat curtsy and deposited the tray on the bedside table.

The smell of food triggered a raging hunger in Miriam. Her mouth watering, she put down the brush and went to investigate the food. Beneath the ironed napkin lay a feast of kippers, tatties, scones, and oat pudding. A frosty pewter goblet brimmed with icy cold milk.

As if today were Fat Tuesday, she devoured the crunchy fish and feather-light pastry. The maid stoked the fire and tossed in the heather. The burning plants filled the room with the sweet smell of summer.

The maid began fluffing the pillows. Miriam dove into the tatties and oat pudding.

"Would ye be carin' for more kippers, milady? There's fish aplenty, thanks to his lordship."

An odd thought seeped into Miriam's euphoria. She looked at the maid, who was frowning as she stripped the case from a pillow. "What's your name?"

Flipping the pillowcase over her shoulder, the maid said, "My given name's Faith, but they all calls me Saucy."

Food momentarily forgotten, Miriam rose. "Well, I'd call you a mind reader, Saucy. I was famished."

The maid reached for another pillow. "His lordship said 'twould be the case."

Miriam grew exceedingly curious, for the earl couldn't have an inkling as to her mood. She hadn't seen him in weeks. Had the Border Lord crept into the castle and told the earl? Probably so.

"Oh?" challenged Miriam. "Is his lordship a mind reader, then?"

Saucy's jaw grew slack and her gaze darted from the pillow to the rumpled counterpane, to the empty tankard. "Ah, would ye be carin' for more milk, milady?"

Hiding a smile, Miriam said, "No. But I wonder . . . How did the earl know I'd take breakfast so early—and in my room?"

The maid opened her mouth, closed it, then leaned over the bed. "Will you look at these stains?" With a loud pop, she jerked the pillowcase from her shoulder and began rubbing vigorously at the sheet. "Looks like soot, it does."

She stood and headed for the door. "I'd best tell the laundry maid 'afore the stains set."

What was the girl hiding? Obviously something about the earl. "Did you say the earl had been fishing?"

Her back to Miriam, her hand on the door, the maid stopped. "Oh aye, milady. Fishes all the time, he does. He just come back yesterday from Barley Burn. 'Afore that 'twas Loch Horseshoe. He's a real fisherman, the laird is. Feasted himself on kippers just this morning, he did."

The overdone explanation, delivered hastily and without sentiment, sounded like a lecture. Obviously the earl had told Saucy what to say. If he thought to elude a reckoning with Miriam by going fishing, he was in for a surprise.

"Where is his lordship today, Saucy?"

A square of paper appeared beneath the door. Saucy snatched it up and eased toward Miriam. "Practicing at swords in the old tilt yard with Angus. Here."

So, the earl had carried through on his promise to learn a soldier's skills. He'd become a better leader and for that she was glad. But one truth did not an honest man make, especially when the man had lied to Miriam outright and by omission. He'd be sorry as sin that he'd underestimated Miriam MacDonald. "What name has Malcolm chosen?" she asked.

Saucy unfolded the paper. Frowning, she said, "Another Englishman. Thomas à Becket."

So, even servants in Kildalton could read. The earl hadn't lied about the school. But he still had much to answer for.

Miriam took the paper. "Thank you, Saucy. You may take the tray with my compliments to the cook, and send young Salvador to me. But don't disturb Lady Alexis."

"Nay, milady." She picked up the tray and hurried to the door. "Mrs. Elliott'll have my hide, should I wake her ladyship 'afore ten o'clock."

Miriam fetched the brush from the vanity, then sat on a tapestry stool near the fireplace to dry her hair. Her thighs, sore from the hours of lovemaking, protested; so she stretched out her legs and curled up her toes. She became aware of differences in other, distinctly feminine, parts of her body: her breasts felt heavy, the nipples still tingling from the touch of his lips, his ardent suckling, and the drag of stubble on his cheeks. He'd kissed her in more intimate places, too. At the remembrance, she felt hollow in the place where he'd loved her with his mouth, then filled her, time and again, with his manhood. Her womb contracted and she drew her legs together.

The Border Lord. Her lover.

You never sleep the night through, for sunrise finds you pacing the floor. I think you spend your nights running from your days.

Maybe, she thought, but once she'd solved the problems here her own troubles would be over. The queen would keep her word and Miriam's quest for justice would come to an end. The Glenlyon Campbells would pay for their treachery of twenty years before.

Lassitude swept over her. She stared into the fire. Atop the smoldering peat sat the remains of the heather, the stems glowing bright red, the ashes floating upward on a stream of toasty air and disappearing into the blackened chimney.

Black. Her mind darted to the sooty stains on the bed. Twice she'd so soiled the sheets and her dresses. Each time she'd been with the Border Lord. He was clean, but the places he took her were dark and dusty. What could she expect? She was in a country castle, not some spit-and-polished palace. She giggled, for she didn't know exactly where she'd been last night and doubted she could find his lair again. Or had he turned into a spirit and carried her through the wall?

A knock sounded at the door. Expecting Salvador, she was surprised to see Saladin, wearing a turban and tunic, stroll into the room.

Hands clasped, he bowed, touching his steepled fingers to the widow's peak in his forehead. "May Allah's blessings be upon you, my lady."

The familiar greeting, delivered in sibilant tones, made Miriam smile. Saladin's outer tranquility served as a perfect foil for his fiercely competitive nature. He'd been an enigma since the day she'd plucked him and his brother from an auction block in Constantinople. At seven years old, they had been as surly and as filthy as camel drivers. At twelve, they were confident youths, highly skilled in their abilities, thanks to Miriam, and secure in their futures, thanks to Alexis Southward.

Miriam returned the greeting and patted the rug beside her. "Come. Sit here and tell me where Salvador is."

He sauntered toward her, knee-high red boots and saffron tunic contrasting vividly with the homey decor. He sat cross-legged facing her, an incredulous expression making him appear younger than his twelve years. "His ribs are hurting. Is it true that he let a girl—a mere child—tie him up and beat him with a stick?"

Miriam had forgotten the unfortunate episode with Baron Sinclair's odious niece. "I'm afraid Alpin hurt him dreadfully. But I hardly think he 'let' her get the best of him. A meaner, more wicked child I've never seen."

"Alpin. That's an odd name for an English girl."

Miriam had thought so, too. "Kenneth mac Alpin was king of Scotland in the ninth century. To show his good will to the earl of Kildalton, the baron changed the girl's name."

With a shrug, indicating that old Scottish kings were unimportant, Saladin said, "One time she blacked Malcolm's eye, he says." Scoffing, he added, "Her father should beat her. Muslims control their women."

With concealing black robes and pretty prisons they call harems, Miriam thought, remembering her struggle to open diplomatic channels between King Ahmed and Queen Anne. "Well, she hasn't a father or a mother, Saladin. Only an uncle and a brood of cousins. I suppose a six-year-old girl gets lost in the shuffle."

"Salvador says the baron has more children than a sultan."

Thinking of the noise, the hustle and bustle, and the crush of people at Sinclair's, Miriam felt relieved to be back at Kildalton. "They're not all his children, per se. Many of them are poor relations with nowhere else to go."

"Then he's a kind man?"

"Not exactly kind," she said, thinking of the baron's misguided generosity. "Just accepting of life in general."

Still sitting, Saladin took the fire iron and poked idly at the clumps of smoldering peat. "The earl's been practicing swordplay with Angus MacDodd since you've been gone."

"And fishing, I'm told."

Stirring the fire and sending a whoosh of sparks up the chimney, Saladin grunted. "He cavils on like a camel driver." In a poor imitation of the earl, the boy said, "My flippity-flop did the trick today. The salmon fair clamored after the hook."

Knowing the boy would never speak so disrespectfully in public, she let the insult pass. "But has he learned to wield a sword?"

A wry grin exposed the space between Saladin's teeth. "I pinned him to the wall on Tuesday."

"I'm not surprised, but do you think 'twas proper?"

"He laughed, my lady," said Saladin, as if it were the most ridiculous of reactions. "Then he minced off to quaff a pint with the soldiers."

Curious, Miriam said, "Tell me what else happened while I was away."

His report held few surprises for Miriam until he said, "The earl told Malcolm and me to stay with Angus MacDodd the night the duchess of Perth came. At first I thought we were both being punished for one of Malcolm's silly pranks, but Angus showed us a chest full of dirks. That's a Scottish dagger."

Miriam had first met the elegant and verbose duchess in Edinburgh while living with the then Princess Anne. Once she had taken up the scepter and crown and moved to London, Anne was often attended by the duchess of Perth. When the duchess had arrived at Sinclair's last week, she and Miriam had sat in a solar, sipping precious lemonade and discussing Duncan Kerr's bachelorhood.

"She only stayed here the one night," Saladin offered. "But the next morning . . ." He cleared his throat and studied the soles of his boots.

Intrigued by his hesitance, Miriam said, "The next morning, the duchess did what?"

"Oh, not the duchess. She left. But the earl summoned us, and reprimanded his son for making fun of me because I'm a Muslim. He made Malcolm memorize a page from the Koran and write the Ten Commandments fifty times."

"I'm surprised," she said. "Are you?"

He nodded, giving her a full view of the top of his

perfectly wound turban. "What surprised me was how much he knew about the Prophet Muhammad."

"May he live ten thousand years," she added.

"The earl?"

She laughed. "No. His flippity-flops."

"His flippity-flops?"

Feeling self-conscious, Miriam said, "I actually meant the Prophet Muhammad."

His mouth fell open. "You were jesting?"

Incredulous as it seemed, she had twice made a jest. Intentionally. Inordinately pleased, she said, "I suppose I was, but I meant no offense."

"But you never jest."

"Well I do now."

He smiled and jumped to his feet. "Wait'll I tell Salvador. He'll be sorry he missed it."

"Saladin," she called after him.

He skidded to a halt and turned. "Yes, my lady?"

"Bring me Salvador's transcription of my meetings with Baron Sinclair, and after your evening prayers, please join me here. I must dictate a letter to the queen."

His enthusiasm faded. He picked at the stitching on his tunic. "Is the feud settled? Are we to leave Scotland soon?"

Leaving Scotland was the last in a natural progression of events. Miriam always knew she would leave when her work here was done, but she hadn't counted on falling in love with a mysterious rake who claimed to be a ghost. She hadn't counted on loving Scotland so much, either.

Seeing Saladin so apprehensive about her decision gave Miriam pause. "Don't you want to? We'll go to Bath. You love the jelly shops and searching the ruins for old daggers."

Not looking up, he said, "There are ruins here. The earl offered to take Malcolm and me exploring at Hadrian's Wall."

Miriam had done some exploring of her own at the wall, and thinking about her erotic discoveries brought a lightness to her stomach. "You'll have time for your excursion before we leave. I promise."

That made him smile. "Thank you, my lady. Until after my evening prayers." He dashed through the door.

Moments later, her hair in a single braid, Miriam donned

her fencing habit, chose her favorite foil, and went to the tilt yard in search of the earl of Kildalton.

She found him spread-eagled and face down in the dirt, his sword blade a broken stub, his shield rolling like a wheel toward the castle gates. The burly soldier Angus MacDodd was bending over him.

A dozen kilt-clad soldiers stood nearby, and closer to the wall, a group of castlefolk crowded around the tinker's wagon. Children tossed a leather ball in the yard. No one seemed interested that the laird had fallen; they all watched Miriam.

Suspicion made her alert. It seemed as if they were waiting. But for what?

A bold clansman stared pointedly at her legs, then winked. Miriam relaxed. They weren't staring for any secret reason or waiting for anything. They couldn't know she was about to take their laird to task. They were simply shocked by her leather breeches and vest.

Decked out in boots, tight-fitting hose, and a short leather jerkin over a mail shirt, the earl looked more like a real warrior than a niddering poltroon who favored brook trout to women, as the Border Lord had called him. Like a second skin, the hose molded his muscular thighs, cupped his taut buttocks, and outlined his manly sacs. With her newfound knowledge of male anatomy, she couldn't help comparing him to the generously endowed Border Lord. She found the earl wanting.

But she'd underestimated Duncan Kerr, given him the benefit of the doubt. She wouldn't do so again. Her greatest challenge lay in keeping her temper in check.

That's why she'd chosen to face him with a foil in her hand. The distraction of a contest would take the edge off her anger. It would also teach him a lesson about telling the truth and trusting.

"What's happened here?" she demanded.

Angus flipped up the visor on his helmet. Sweat dripped from his nose. He glanced at her, then patted the earl's back. "My lord, how are you?"

"Chipper as a spawning salmon," came the muffled reply.

"Are you hurt?" the soldier asked.

The earl groaned and struggled to a sitting position. "Only my pride, Angus. 'Twas a devil of a blow you dealt. Teach me that move next or at least a decent defense. Lord, this soldiering taxes a body."

"You're making excellent progress, my lord," said Angus.

With a gauntleted hand, the earl raised his visor. His spectacles tumbled to the ground. A mail coif covered his hair and framed his face, which was coated in dust and sweat. He squinted up at Miriam. "Who's that? Is it the new lad from Lanarkshire?"

Although innocently spoken, his mistake touched off a blaze in Miriam. She wanted to stomp her foot and smash his corrective glasses. She wanted to rail at him for being the uncooperative oaf he was. Her own integrity as a diplomat stopped her.

She slid the rebated tip of her foil under the nosepiece and offered him the spectacles. "No, my lord. 'Tis Miriam MacDonald."

"Oh, well! Pardon my ghastly manners." Fumbling to remove the gauntlets, he snatched the glasses, which were slightly bent and very dusty; then he blew the dirt from the lenses and made a clumsy job of working through the helmet and coif to fit the crooked frames on his nose. Blinking, he studied her from head to toe. "That's a striking costume, my lady. Most becoming."

He looked so unusual, a knight garbed for battle, yet wearing thick spectacles and spouting compliments, that she felt a twinge of pity for him. "You needn't resort to flattery, my lord," she said. "I find this attire quite comfortable, when I'm in the mood to fence."

Angus held out a hand and helped the earl to his feet. "If you'll excuse me, my lord—my lady. I'll have the blacksmith repair your sword." He clicked his heels and marched off.

Shaking his finger at her, the earl said, "I thought we'd agreed you would call me Duncan."

"That was before I visited your neighbor."

"'Tis another of his crimes then."

His bitterness puzzled her. "Why do you say that?"

"I thought we were becoming friends, you and I."

The sentiment first pleased then angered her. "Friends don't lie to each other."

"Speaking of liars—how was the baron?"

If he was being snide, she could match him in that. "Your father-in-law is fine. He sends you his best."

"Ha! Sinclair's my former *step*father-in-law, and the only thing he can send me is that herd of spotted cattle he stole. I spent a fortune on the beasts."

His aggression surprised Miriam. The Border Lord had defended him in the matter of the cattle. The baron had known nothing about a herd of spotted cattle. Where were the beasts? Later she would ask to see the earl's receipt for the animals. Then she'd find the damned herd and discover who had stolen them in the first place. "You should have told me you married his stepdaughter."

"I thought you knew I married Roxanne. You know everything else about me."

At Sinclair's, the duchess of Perth had said the earl had changed, grown bold. She'd been eager to tell Miriam stories about Duncan's ruthless father. But Duncan himself remained a puzzle to Miriam. "Quite the contrary, my lord. I don't know you at all. Would you care to fence?"

"No, I wouldn't, Miriam," he said. "Bad eyes and all that. But I'll wager you'd like to best me at it."

So much for teaching him a lesson. Still she was taken aback because he'd read her intent. "Why do you think that?"

"Because." He whacked the gauntlets against his jerkin. Dust clouded around him. "I think you're angry with me, and I worry the people of Kildalton will suffer for it. After you make me suffer."

Miriam's thoughts scattered, emotion playing havoc with logic, duty squaring off against discretion. Beyond her personal war, she heard the soldiers speaking among themselves. From the outer bailey came the ringing of a sheep's bell and the high-pitched bleating of hungry lambs. Children squealed and laughed and boasted in the language of her youth.

Feeling exposed and confused, she said, "You *are* different. You seem more forceful and you've developed a burr in your speech. You've changed."

He started, stared at her legs. "You have, too." Then he laughed. "The duchess of Perth said the same about me. Angus swears 'tis the soldiering. Mrs. Elliott believes a bad ham is at the root of it. Malcolm says 'tis time and past."

To Miriam, he seemed at ease and surprisingly appealing in his knightly garb. For lack of anything else to say, she asked, "What do you think brought about the change in you?"

He tucked the gauntlets into his sword belt and held out his arm. "I think . . . we should discuss it over a barrel of beer. I'm fair parched. I also ache in unmentionable places. What say you, Miriam?"

The invitation, delivered with such charm and honesty, dissolved her confusion and reminded her of the first rule of successful negotiation: both parties thought their causes just and their actions necessary. It was up to her to find a workable medium. Her own objectivity was the key.

"What a splendid idea." She laid her hand on his mail-clad arm. The metal felt warm against her palm, the muscles beneath well formed. The soldiering had honed his strength.

As they started across the yard, he limped. "Have you hurt yourself?" she asked.

He looked down. His mouth turned up in a smile, and behind the lenses his eyes appeared dreamy, unfocused. "Too much exercise in the wee hours of the morning," he said.

The soldiers disbursed. The tinker expounded on his wares. Hands clasped, the children skipped in a ring, caroling a tune about the escapades of Mrs. MacKenzie's mischievous cat. Miriam seemed to coast through it all, her body reminding her of the extraordinary way *she'd* passed the night, her heart yearning for a repeat of her tryst with the Border Lord.

Once inside the castle, the earl said, "If you'll excuse me, I'll shed this heavy garb and ask Mrs. Elliott to serve us in my study."

The statement triggered Miriam's curiosity. "How did you know I'd welcome breakfast in my room this morning?"

"Oh, that." He waved his hand. "When Lady Alexis arrived with Salvador yesterday evening, she said you'd been detained. This morning when I went to remind the guards to look out for the peacock man, I was told you didn't get in until nearly dawn. I thought you'd be hungry." Glancing at the door, he shook his head. "I do hope he arrives soon with those birds."

"But I thought you never rose before noon?"

He squared his shoulders. The jerkin grew taut across his chest. "'Tis my new schedule. I was wide awake and vigorously exercising this morning. I prefer it in the morning, don't you?"

He seemed excited, and genuinely interested in her opinion. She hoped he would cooperate fully after all. "With me, it's when I have the time to exercise and if it's appropriate."

He made a slow inspection of her legs. "Yes, I can understand. Of course I'm equally agreeable to nighttime. That's very appropriate. Now that I'm in training, I must rise with the dawn. According to Angus, that's the first commandment of soldiering."

Charmed, she said, "What's the second?"

He chuckled, sweat streaming off his brow. "Ah. That's the pleasant one: chivalry toward the weaker sex."

Let him think she was weak; most men did. They all regretted it. "Do you follow all of the commandments?"

"A novice must, and to the letter!" He made an elaborate bow. The visor slammed shut. The gauntlets plopped to the floor. Scooping them up, he said, "I'd best get out of this contraption before I hurt myself or break the furniture."

In the interest of good relations, she touched the foil to her forehead. "I'll wait in your study."

"I won't be long." Duncan fumbled as he collected his gear, giving her time to head down the narrow hallway. Her bottom swayed deliciously in the snug-fitting leather breeches. Her slender legs carried her with fluid grace. In the wee hours, he'd cupped her naked buttocks in his hands, felt her thighs clutch his waist. From top to bottom, her skin felt as smooth as a baby's cheeks.

Baby. The word jolted him out of his lustful observation and sent him hobbling in the direction of the kitchen. The thought of siring another child, and with Miriam MacDonald, both excited and troubled him. He'd done well enough so far in his attempt to temper the earl's cowardly bumbling and become the gallant knight she favored. He'd wanted to broach with her the subject of conception, but how could he, when he wanted her to believe the Border Lord a ghost? She might even believe the fantasy, but not if she were carrying her lover's child.

Still, when they were belly to belly and giving each other the pleasure of a lifetime, he couldn't bring himself to withdraw from her. A selfish part of him wanted her to conceive. Then as the earl, he could do the noble thing and offer to wed her. But as his wife, she'd find out everything about him. She'd be angry and feel betrayed. She might side with the baron out of spite. Duncan would lose Malcolm.

If she refused his proposal, she'd have to marry someone else. Duncan's unborn child would belong to another man.

Either choice was unthinkable. Only one fact remained: he wanted her with the zest and fervor of a youngling lapping up his first taste of passion. He'd have her again tonight, too. He'd bring a bone to distract the sleuthhound, and enter her room through the wardrobe. Then he'd strip naked and crawl into bed beside her—

"What can I get you, my lord?"

Mrs. Elliott's voice put a halt to his daydreaming. He must face Miriam, the diplomat, and he'd need all his faculties. She'd already tried to goad him into a fencing match, which she unfortunately thought she would have won. Thanks to Kenneth Kerr, Duncan could duel with the best of swordsmen.

What would she try next?

After requesting a pitcher of beer be sent to his study, he went to his bedchamber, quickly bathed off the dirt and grime, and donned a modest white wig and a green suit. Looking in the mirror, he thanked his mother for the gift of hazel eyes. Today they appeared as green as summer clover.

Then he put on the spectacles and tromped to his study.

Miriam lounged in a chair by the hearth, one leg slung over the arm. When she saw him, she sat up, her knees as tightly closed as a devout spinster's. Lord, he loved those knees, and her trim inner thighs and the secrets they concealed.

She waved a hand at the tray on the table before her. "Shall I pour?"

He took the chair facing her. "Please. My mouth is as dry as a smoked salmon's."

She laughed, the sound warm and enchanting. And new to Duncan. With delight, he watched her pour the foamy beer with the grace of an honorable Mayfair miss serving the matrons of nobility. Her fake smile troubled him. As the Border Lord, he'd seen her smile with genuine happiness, but now she pasted on her diplomat's expression of pleasure. Thank God he knew the difference.

When she handed him a tankard, he said, "I'll forgive you a small prevarication, if you'll forgive me one."

She stopped, the pitcher poised over her mug. "I don't prevaricate."

He clutched the cold tankard when he'd rather be clutching her. "But you did. You told me you didn't have a sense of humor."

Confusion brightened her eyes. "I never said that to you."

Oh, Christ, she hadn't. She had said it to the Border Lord. Buying time to cover the slip, Duncan took a long drink. "You said you never jest."

Deep in concentration, she studied the Kerr emblem on the pewter mug. "Yes, you're correct. I did say that."

Her memory would be the death of him and the ruin of his people. "The point is, you have a bonnie laugh."

"Thank you, but . . ." She shifted in the chair, her leather breeches sliding noisily against the leather upholstery. Smiling shyly, she dragged her thick braid over her shoulder. The gesture was so totally feminine, Duncan felt his body respond. The reaction surprised him, for after their hours of lovemaking, he hadn't thought himself capable of more.

A moment later she put down the mug and leveled him a look devoid of emotion. "You will agree that humor has no place in this discussion. We must talk about you and the baron."

Lack of sleep and the futility of the topic sapped his strength. He leaned back in the chair. "Yes."

She leaned forward. "I've asked you before to trust me. I'll ask it again. Please be honest."

As the man who'd taken her virginity and ignited her desires, Duncan wanted to be honest with her. As the man who loved her and wanted to marry her, Duncan thought it his duty to tell her the truth. But as laird of clan Kerr and a man who risked the loss of his son, he would have to tread carefully.

"You won't be prejudiced against me because I didn't tell you I was related to the baron by marriage?" he asked.

Pain softened her eyes, and her lovely lips pursed with disappointment. Duncan was reminded of the hurt in Malcolm's eyes the first time he'd punished the boy.

"We're starting anew, my lord," she said with the dignity of a queen.

Duncan thought about her life as a diplomat, the slander she'd faced, the spoiled heads of state who probably treated her no better than a servant. He cringed to think she might group him with that selfish lot. He quaked at the thought of putting his fate and the future of all he held dear in her hands.

Pledging caution, he smiled tentatively and gave her a salute with his mug. "To a new beginning?"

She nodded and returned the salute. "What started the trouble between you and Sinclair?"

Duncan stared at the empty scabbard above the fireplace. "None of the other mediators cared."

"I do. There's more to peace than boundaries and legal writs. There are feelings—pride, revenge. There's the past and those who set the troubles in motion. I'm here to stop it. Help me, Duncan."

The years rolled back, exposing Duncan to the pain of his childhood. "Do you remember when we talked about my father?"

"Um hum." Kindness twinkled in her eyes. "The Grand Reiver who favored farthingales to carriages and scorned a lad who liked to scour ruins. Tell me more about him."

How could she, with a few words, make him feel like pouring out his heart to her? *I'm better than the others,* she'd said last night. He was beginning to think it was true. But could he truly trust her when her future was also at stake? He didn't know.

He told her a common fact. "As if it were his right, my father raided Birmingham lands—they were called that until the baron arrived. In an attempt to expand his kingdom, Kenneth Kerr drove out English farmers, then

183

uprooted Kildalton tenants and forced them to settle the vacated lands. He separated families and violated betrothals. The seventh earl was a merciless, uncaring man."

"Not at all like you," she said, a note of reassurance in her voice.

She could have stroked his cheek, so comforting were her words. "After my father's death, I called on Birmingham and offered to return the land between here and Hadrian's Wall and move the tenants back to Kildalton. He was a fair fellow and more interested in his family and his coal concern in Newcastle than he was his Border lands."

With her fingernail, she drew a line through the condensation on her tankard. "He refused your offer?"

"Aye. He wanted peace, said let bygones be bygones. So we did. But I saved all my profits from those lands for Birmingham's two daughters."

"They would be Adrienne and Roxanne."

"Aye." Duncan had no intention of telling her that last summer he'd given the money to Charles as a dowry for Adrienne. The money had helped them start a new life in Barbados, the girl's only letter had said.

"How long did the peace last?"

Fond memories turned sour. Duncan drank deeply of the beer, but even his favorite brew couldn't wash away the bitterness. "Until a year after his death. Then Birmingham's widow married Sinclair. The raids began, and the first of your predecessors appeared."

Unaffected, she said, "Who was the mediator and what happened?"

Duncan had been so naive at the time. It had cost him dearly. "He was Avery Chilton-Wall."

He expected surprise from her. She merely nodded. "What happened?"

"Sinclair offered him a bribe. I offered him a greater sum. He took both and bought the post of magistrate."

"I'll replace him with a fair man."

Duncan studied her beautiful features, her luminous blue eyes, her sensuous lips, her glorious hair. What would it take to sway her? He didn't know. "Can you truly? Have you the power?"

She held her thumb and forefinger an inch apart. "Last

spring I came this close to having the constable of France removed. He thought it prudent to change his views on the placement of French troops."

Fascinated, yet realistic, Duncan said, "You won't change Baron Sinclair."

Challenge glittered in her eyes. "I changed you. What happened next?"

"The baron brought in mercenaries—I described the leaders to you. Then the war began in earnest."

"You told me earlier you never retaliated. Would you care to amend that statement?"

He wondered when she'd bring up the Border Lord. "Aye. I hire a fellow named Ian."

Her eyes drifted out of focus. She was remembering last night. So was he, and fondly.

"He calls himself the Border Lord," she said, still staring at nothing.

Duncan put his empty tankard on the table. "What does the baron say about him?"

Suddenly alert, she filled the mug. "Here. I shan't tell you what he said. 'Twould only anger you, as your statement would him."

He took the mug when he wanted to throw it across the room, throw her over a horse and disappear into his lair in Hadrian's Wall.

"Drink up," she said. "You told me you were as thirsty as a smoked salmon."

Was she trying to get him drunk? Yes, he decided. The Border Lord had told her the earl couldn't handle strong drink. Considering all the roles he'd played of late, a tipsy nobleman seemed easy.

"What did you do while Ian was retrieving your property?" she asked, giving him that trumped-up smile.

"I again went to Chilton-Wall for help. He said for a price he would intervene. So I started selling salt to the duke of Cromarty in order to pay off the magistrate."

"Did the raids stop?"

"No, but the killing did—for a time."

She lifted her eyebrows. "What started it again?"

"The baron had the bletherin gall to try to blackmail me. A Scot! 'Twas unthinkable."

Interest smoothed out her features. What had he said that concerned her so? "Why are you looking at me like that?"

She took a drink, then used a napkin to clean the moisture from the bottom and sides of the mug, and wipe a ring from the table. She took great care to fold the napkin. "'Twas nothing. Please go on."

If her look meant nothing, then he was the Great Bruce come back to life. "Tell me."

Her eyes met his and she studied him so closely he almost squirmed. "Very well," she said reluctantly. "I think, for all your clipped English speech, you're a Scotsman at heart, Duncan Kerr. Even though you try your best to hide it, you ken? You *have* changed—for the better."

Her insight and quickness astounded him. Her smile and cordiality affected him in a more intimate and base way. If she only knew how much he was hiding, he'd be dungeon deep in the Tower of London. When he wanted to be eight inches deep in her.

Remembering the half-witted earl he was trying to reform, Duncan said, "I won't be grouped with barbarians."

She laughed again. "There's no chance of that, I promise you. I haven't seen a true barbarian since I visited the steppes of Russia. Tell me what happened next."

Lulled by her cordiality, Duncan stared at the framed tapestry on a stand by the fireplace. He thought of the long hours of their lovemaking. Their closeness. The passionate Miriam clutching him, calling him a scoundrel for denying her the hasty release she craved. The surprised Miriam, proud of herself at making a jest. The sated Miriam, shy about discussing her pleasure and naively inquisitive about his.

"Duncan? You were telling me about the baron's galling attempt to blackmail you. What happened after that?"

Taking a deep breath, he dredged up the biggest mistake of his life.

12

With mixed feelings, Miriam watched him struggle to say the words that obviously pained him. She loved many aspects of her work. Prying into a person's sorrow was not one of them. But for all his declarations of innocence, the shy, charming earl could still lie, and very convincingly; any man trying to maintain control of his kingdom would. It was up to her to sift through his words and find chips of information with which to bargain.

Softly she said, "A lasting peace may hang in the balance, Duncan. Please tell me what you did to solve the problems."

He put a hand to his forehead as if to rake his hand through his hair. Just as his fingertips touched the wig, he stopped. Again she played a guessing game about the color of his hair. Brown, she decided, same as his eyebrows.

"I made an offer of marriage for Roxanne Birmingham."

Miriam remembered the framed likeness of the countess of Kildalton that hung in the portrait gallery at Sinclair's. Captured for eternity with a maidenly smile and haunted brown eyes, the jet-haired beauty had looked infinitely lonely to Miriam. The earl seemed haunted, too, at the mention of his lost love. But Miriam had to know just how deeply the baron had offended Duncan Kerr. Only when their pride had been salved could she engineer a peace that would satisfy them both.

Compassion came naturally to Miriam; she'd learned early in life to say good-bye to those she loved. "Your countess was a beautiful woman. I'm so sorry she died."

Brackets of anger framed the earl's mouth. "I wish the baron had shared your sentiments. He mourned the loss of her as countess of Kildalton—grieved over losing the title more than the passing of the woman."

Miriam looked beyond his pain to decipher the essence of his meaning. "Are you saying the baron tricked you into offering for her in order to get your title?"

"No." He shook his head sadly. "I made that folly on my own."

Folly? According to the baron, his stepdaughter had wanted the match. He, however, had wanted her to marry a wealthy merchant who resided in London. The baron had bragged about using Duncan's first marriage contract for kindling. "What did the baron say? Did he refuse your first offer?"

On a half-laugh, the earl said, "He tossed the contract into the fire, but I had a duplicate. Roxanne cried and locked herself in her room until he relented."

So, on the matter of the contract, Duncan and Sinclair both told the same story. It was a small step, but a significant one, for it meant they could occasionally see things from the same perspective. "Roxanne loved you."

He grew pensive. "I suppose. She'd known me all of her life. She was a shy, quiet lass who favored books and chess and country life." A sad and guilty sheen appeared in his eyes. "She wed me to escape a marriage to a London merchant the baron had arranged for her." In a barely audible murmur, he said, "No great passion blazed between us, but we were comfortable. We were friends."

Miriam compared the two households, so different in ambience and style. The peaceful order of Kildalton contrasted with the noisy disarray of Sinclair. The word "friend" lingered in her mind. For a short time, Roxanne had been fortunate in her marriage. "I imagine you made her very happy."

Fondness wreathed him. "She gave me Malcolm." He grinned, looking unexpectedly handsome. "Although at times I'm tempted to give him back."

Miriam's heart ached. For five short years, she'd been the joy of her parents' life. But a Dutchman cum English king and a band of merciless Highlanders had stolen her family and all she'd held dear. Without even a reprimand, the Glenlyon Campbells had gone on their merry way. But not forever.

Shelving those thoughts for later, she said, "He's a fine boy. Thanks to you, he knows more about the great men of England than most of the queen's ambassadors. Thank you for encouraging him to respect Saladin's religion."

Like casting off a cloak, he threw off his melancholy. "There's a braw laddie. That Saladin almost ran me through with that wicked scimitar of his. Did he tell you about pinning me to the curtain wall?"

A second truth. Miriam smiled. "He's made great progress in only a few years."

"I don't understand."

She did something she'd never even considered before meeting the earl of Kildalton; she told a stranger about that day at the slave market in Constantinople.

Pale with shock and indignation, he crossed his legs and said, "You mean the man bidding against you would have . . . have unmanned them?"

"Yes. They would've become eunuchs before you could've said, 'hand me a flippity-flop.' "

"To think I defended the Muslims to Malcolm. I'll not make that mistake again."

His misguided vehemence wouldn't do at all. " 'Twasn't religion but custom that almost cost the twins their manhood."

"Truly?" His brows shot up and his green eyes glittered with interest. "Do tell me more about the Byzantines. Malcolm wrote a glowing piece on Suleiman, you know. The Magnificent."

As she drank from the mug, Miriam phrased a dissertation on the politics of King Ahmed III, but stopped short of speaking when she realized the earl had gotten her off the subject of his marriage agreement. Had he done it on purpose? She searched his pleasant features for a sign of subterfuge. She found a curious, handsome man. Surprised by the observation, she said, "'Twould bore you to tears." When he looked as if he would argue, she said, "Another time, then. But now we have the matter of Baron Sinclair's claims to discuss."

"Claims?" he scoffed. "That brigand takes what he wants and burns what he can't carry. You must stop him."

The baron's opinion of the earl had been patently similar. He claimed Duncan Kerr was a deceiving Scotsman cut of the same ruthless cloth as his father, the Grand Reiver. Avery Chilton-Wall had corroborated the statement. The duchess of Perth had deferred to her duke, who'd curled his lip and ranted about the despicable crimes of Kenneth Kerr. By turn, each man had cursed the seventh earl and condemned, by heredity, the eighth.

Miriam discounted the magistrate's opinion and thought the duke spoke to hear himself talk, but the baron's comparison of the current earl of Kildalton to his cruel father troubled her. Duncan hadn't led those raids on Sinclair's land, Ian had. Yet as the Border Lord, her lover had been accused of nothing more than turning a cow's milk sour and stealing the affection of women prone to melancholy. If the earl was hiding a darker side, she'd be surprised and disappointed. Judging character was her strong point.

In some aspects, the baron and the earl were alike. Both wanted peace, but their approaches to the problems were vastly, culturally different. One similarity lay in the fact that they both hired out their raiding, which she intended to stop. The other problems between them required all of her expertise.

Expecting an outraged reaction, she said, "He wants you to return his stepdaughter's dowry." He wanted Malcolm, too, but Miriam wasn't ready to broach that appalling topic.

The earl fell back in his chair, his hands dangling over the arms. "Now *that* would start a war a dozen Border Lords couldn't finish."

Caught off guard at the mention of her lover, Miriam

moved to set her mug on the table, but it slipped. Trying to catch it, she only succeeded in tumbling it. "Oh!" Pewter clattered against the hearth. The remaining drops of beer sizzled on the warm stone.

"I've frightened you," he said. "Do forgive me. But I told you about Ian. He's no ghost."

She grabbed the fallen tankard and put it on the table. *You hurt my feelings,* she wanted to say. *You laughed at me. You called me fanciful.* She'd come here to help him, and he'd made a fool of her. She'd been treated with disrespect before. Then, as now, she must put aside her personal feelings and get on with the job.

She took a deep breath and thought about her reward. "You didn't frighten me, and I agree with you."

His interested gaze held her immobile. "Do you know him well, Miriam?"

She tried to stop herself from blushing. She failed.

He grinned.

Annoyed at herself for equivocating and piqued by his amusement, Miriam picked up the thread of the conversation. "We were speaking of the dowry."

"Roxanne willed her land, which lies between here and Hadrian's Wall, to Malcolm. She, too, wanted peace. Everyone does. Except the baron."

Years of practice had taught Miriam to ignore bickering insults and find the solid, legal facts on which to build a compromise. "Have you her wishes in writing and properly witnessed?"

He leveled her a look that said, What do you take me for, a niddering poltroon who favors brook trout to women? But he said, "Of course. I have the other copy of the marriage contract, too."

Through the jumble her thoughts had become, real success beckoned. "May I see the papers, please?"

He grasped the chair arms, sprang to his feet, and went to the desk, all traces of a limp gone. Pulling a key from his breeches pocket, he unlocked a drawer. Paper rattled. When he returned, he handed her two rolled documents, aged and beribboned.

Her palms grew damp as she unfurled one of the yellowed parchments. Adorned with official seals and illuminated by an overly fanciful scribe who favored primroses and broad-leaf ivy to the more traditional cinquefoils and Celtic knots, the marriage agreement confirmed her dowry: the land from Hadrian's Wall north to Kildalton. Reading the other parchment brought a thickness to Miriam's throat. In her own swirling hand, the late countess of Kildalton had indeed bequeathed the disputed land and her pearl necklace to Malcolm. Her clothing, embroidery frames, and bride's chest she had passed on to her younger sister, Adrienne.

Miriam dropped the documents in her lap where they again curled into rolls. A pearl necklace. The simplicity of a dying mother's one personal gift to her infant son made Miriam want to cry.

"Well?" said the earl, impatience making him look very much like the portrait of the Grand Reiver that hung in the keeping room. When, she wondered, had she stopped seeing him as the bumbling earl? The answer banished her pity. She'd begun seeing the earl as a man the instant he'd begun to behave like a kind and decent fellow instead of a niddering poltroon who favored brook trout to women.

"What's wrong, Miriam?"

"Nothing," she rushed to say. "These are quite in order. It was very clever and generous of you to ask only for the land your father took as Roxanne's dowry. You made amends for your father's crimes when you could have asked for more."

He stared at the smoldering coals in the hearth, giving her an unobstructed view of his elegant profile. He seemed so at home in the room filled with books, heavy furniture, and Kerr memorabilia.

"I wanted an end to the dispute," he said at last.

Casually, she said, "Where is Adrienne?"

He turned so fast he almost slung the spectacles off his nose. "Uh . . . I wish I could tell you. Unlike her sister, Adrienne was ever headstrong. I couldn't possibly hazard a guess about where the lass has gotten herself to."

Disappointed, Miriam strummed her fingers on the arm of the chair. He was lying. "According to her personal maid and the baron, Adrienne considered you her brother. Both say she spent weeks here after the death of your wife. She came here often until the time of her disappearance."

"Did you meet anyone at the baron's who *didn't* want to leave his house?"

He had a point. Miriam recalled the overcrowded parlor, the elbow-to-elbow dining, the young men sleeping three to a bed, the girls packed like herring in a barrel. The poor harried servants. Miriam's heart went out to each of them. But she couldn't let her personal opinion hinder her investigation. Big families always suffered. So did orphaned children, the little girl in her said.

Swallowing back self-pity, she said, "We were speaking of the whereabouts of Adrienne Birmingham. Did you kidnap her?"

His mouth drawn in a tight line, his eyes narrowed, the earl stared at the documents in Miriam's lap. "I'm hardly the type."

Miriam wasn't so sure anymore, now that she knew him better. "Then what happened to her?"

"She was in love with a fellow named Charles—a glazier, I think, from Bothly Green."

"Did he make your spectacles?"

He started, his over-large eyes blinking behind the lenses like a startled maiden. "No. The tinker gets them for me." With obvious reluctance, he added, "You could ask after Charles in Bothly Green. They say the innkeeper is a fountain of information. That's all I can tell you."

"Can or will?"

He finished off the tankard, then licked the foam from the corners of his mouth with the tip of his tongue. "I doona know anything else."

She gave him a refill, hoping another pint would loosen that tongue. Besides, he became more charming when he lapsed into that Scottish burr. Much like another man she knew with a deeper, huskier voice. But thoughts of her lover were too distracting. The Border Lord had no place in this discussion.

"Find Adrienne's fellow and you'll most likely find her."

The baron had said nothing about Adrienne having a beau, but he had looked guiltily at the magistrate, Avery Chilton-Wall, who'd cupped his private parts at the mention of Adrienne, the woman he'd wanted for his mistress.

The earl reached for the tankard. "We can share mine. Will you make Sinclair return my spotted cattle?"

She took great pleasure in saying, "Yes. If you'll give me the certificate of ownership and tell Ian to stop raiding Sinclair land."

Putting the tankard aside, he reached for the papers in her lap. His hand grazed her thigh. "Pardon me, Miriam. But I've become very protective of what's mine. I'd best keep it under lock and key. Rest assured I'll speak with Ian."

For a moment she sat riveted by the suspicion of a double meaning. But no, the earl was talking about the papers. She scooted back in the chair and watched him stroll to the desk. An image flashed in her mind of another man—a dark stranger sauntering toward her with seduction on his mind and magic in his hands. Passing off the notion as pure fancy, she hid a smile and sipped the fresh beer. The Border Lord was definitely a more virile man.

Duncan rummaged through a stack of papers, sending a occasional feather flying from the desk. "I know the dastardly thing is here somewhere." Not looking up, he said, "Have you seen evidence of Ian's raids on the baron's land?"

If she weren't careful, she'd lose the ground she'd gained, and parroting the baron's exaggerated accusations was a sure way to alienate the earl. "I heard testimony from his tenants."

"Did you now?" He glanced up. The spectacles sat low on his nose, giving her a clear view of his eyes. Framed by thick eyelashes and thicker brows, his clover green eyes glowed with an intensity she hadn't seen before. Her gaze dropped to his mouth and the subtle points of his upper lip, the deep indentation that led to the tip of his nose, the perfect turn of his nostrils, the suddenly appealing planes of his cheek and jaw.

"You stayed at Sinclair's for weeks. He took you to their farms and showed you the destruction?"

Rather than actually hearing him, she read the words on his lips. His very attractive lips. Absently, she said, "I'm not at liberty to say. You tell me what Ian did."

"You didn't take the baron's word for the crimes, did you, Miriam?"

Seeing her name on his lips and reading the accusation in his eyes jolted her. Again he'd snatched control of the conversation and compelled her to reveal what the baron had said. The diplomat rebelled. She had no intention of telling him what she'd seen, for he'd pick the details to pieces, and in the doing, lose sight of the primary issue: solving the problems.

Men, she thought with disdain and impatience. How had they managed to work together long enough to carve the first wheel? A perfectly reasonable explanation occurred to her. A woman had done it. Inspired, she gave him a detail to pick at. "You said you have proof those spotted cattle are yours."

He snatched up a page. "I most certainly do. Baron Sin can't be bothered with buying stock and improving blood-lines, not to mention providing occupations for his people. All he cares about is putting beef on his table and wine down his gullet. Here."

Applauding herself, she said, "You're very cooperative."

An arm's length away, he stopped, his features serene with understanding. "You're very patronizing, Miriam MacDonald. Am I so transparent?"

Miriam fought the urge to squirm. Partial honesty, she decided, must prevail. "Let's just say you're a man with troubles." Smiling her most winsome smile, she added, "I'm very good at alleviating trouble between men. But only if you help me."

He threw the paper in the air and laughed. A very charming laugh. "Why do I try to pry information from you?"

Laughing, too, she said, "I don't know, Duncan."

He scratched his chin. "You won't tell me what you saw at the baron's. But I keep asking."

"No, I won't, and yes, you do."

"Must be the soldiering that makes me want to know what my enemy is up to."

It wasn't the soldiering; it was his gender. But she wasn't about to tell him that. "I'm certain it is, and now that we've settled that—"

"You're patronizing again. . . ."

Miriam sighed. He was dangerously close to understanding her methods. If he did, she might as well give up hope of winning a peace here. Throw him a bone, her experience said, but do it respectfully. "I apologize. It must be all of the company I've been keeping. Good lord, the baron's house is busy."

She watched his ruffled feathers settle nicely. Then he picked up the paper and handed it to her.

"Would you care for a game of chess?" she asked. "I could set up the board here in front of the fire." She often drew men into a chess match and let them win. They were always so involved in the individual moves, the strategy, that they invariably dropped their guard. Some of her best sleuthing had been done with a rook in her hand. Such had been the case with Baron Sinclair. For once, though, she'd like to meet a man who could outplay her and keep his secrets.

Did the Border Lord play chess? She'd have to challenge him to a match. That way he'd have to show his face.

"I'll just clean the table," she said.

"I'll get the chess set." He went to the bookcase.

She picked up the large pitcher. It was almost empty. She'd had only a small portion. He'd probably be drunk soon. To be certain, she topped off his mug.

"I'll wager you've played against some interesting fellows," he said.

"A few." Turning, she saw him standing before a wall of books, a chessboard under one arm, the other extended to a high shelf and a carved wooden box. Over his shoulder, he said, "I keep the set out of Malcolm's way. My grandmother made it."

Good, thought Miriam, he was already relaxing and making her task easier. His pose, though, struck her as odd. He looked as if he could scale the bookcase, much the same as the Border Lord had scaled the castle wall. The comparison surprised her. "Did she teach you to play?"

"Aye." He stepped down and put the box on the board, then walked toward her with the dignity of the archbishop of Canterbury carrying the crown of England. "But don't tell Malcolm we played. He'll whine for days and days. The set is quite precious and too delicate for his eager hands."

His easy familiarity warmed her. "I can keep a secret," she said, thinking of her lover.

"Who knows that better than I?" He opened the box and put it on the table.

Nestled on a bed of worn white velvet lay a young boy's treasures, cleverly fashioned into playing pieces. Sixteen smooth stones, eight dark, eight light, represented pawns. Mounted on tall squares of wood were the kings, a jagged dark shell for the black, a clump of snowy quartz for the white. On slightly shorter wooden dowels sat the queens; one a pearl, the other a garnet. The bishops were wishbones, one polished, the other painted black. Carved miniature horses, one caparisoned in white, the other in black, were the knights. Castles were arrowheads driven into pin cushions; one dark, one light.

The significance of the chessmen awed her. *His grandmother had made it.* Sentiment choked Miriam. "It's wonderful."

He grinned boyishly. "It's not very fancy. I'm sure you've seen the finest sets of ivory and jasper and solid gold—in your travels."

His childhood lay spread out before her, lovingly preserved. The orphan in her coveted the set. The diplomat told her to get back to business.

She scooped up the dark pebbles. "I'll take black."

Once she learned his strategy, she'd slow him down enough to distract him. She moved a pawn. "I understand you commerce in salt with the duke of Cromarty."

He slid a white pebble forward. "Who told you that?"

"A friend." She moved another pawn. "May I have a drink of your beer? It's really quite good, but you know what they say about Scotsmen and beer."

He handed her the mug. "Aye, we brew the best beer in the world. This friend is someone you trust? Someone you admire?"

Her feelings for the Border Lord were much more visceral. A lie seemed apropos. "Implicitly."

He nudged another pawn into the fray. "I imagine trust is very important to you, isn't it?"

Heartened by his conservative play and cordiality, she handed him the beer. "Why do you say that?"

He turned up a work-worn palm. "I assumed you travel

much of the time. Common sense tells me the nature of your work lends itself more to passing acquaintances than building lasting friendships."

So, the earl was a philosopher. She liked that aspect of him, but felt the need to defend herself. "I have Alexis, Saladin, and Salvador. We're great friends, a family, if you will."

Slyly, he said, "I imagine you've turned down a horde of marriage offers—foreign princes and the like."

The sad truth of the matter sat like a stone in her stomach. To allay the uncomfortable feeling, she laughed and said, "I wouldn't exactly call their propositions offers. They're hardly fit for mixed company."

"Then they were fools," he declared. "For you're far too intelligent to fall for such knavery." He cleared his throat. "You're very beautiful, too."

The compliment, delivered with shy hesitance, started a glow in Miriam. "Thank you."

Mirth twinkled in his eyes. "Highland women generally are. Not that you're general in any way. I simply meant that your hair lends a certain fire to what I'm sure is a . . . an altogether sensible demeanor—" He bit his lip. "I'm botching it rather badly, aren't I?"

Embarrassed for both of them, she held up her hand. "You were telling me about the salt."

He swallowed, drawing her attention to the powerful muscles in his neck. Why hadn't she noticed them before?

"The baron intercepted the last shipment."

Like the crack of a whip, his accusation snapped her thoughts back to reality. "I'll need to see any correspondence on the arrangement between you and His Grace of Cromarty and any other papers on the enterprise."

"Certainly." He took a long pull on the beer. "I'll take you to the mine. You're even dressed for it. Mining salt's a nasty concern."

"I'm sure it is. But thank you, no." She moved a wishbone. "It won't be necessary." The prospect of bouncing around in a carriage made her tender parts protest. "I'm rather tired today."

"Oh?" he said, all concern, his hand poised over an

arrowhead. "Did you pass a bad night? The watchman said you were out very late and alone."

Miriam felt herself blush. "My night was rather pleasant, actually." Her words were a monumental understatement.

"I'm so glad you're enjoying yourself in Scotland. If you'll tell me about your night, I'll tell you about the sunny trout I caught last week. Without my peacocks, I had to resort to using a shapely beetle. I had to pounce on the creature, wrestle it to the ground and strip the wings from it—and all before I could bury my hook. I snagged three panty fish before exhausting my beetle. A bracing, unforgettable adventure, it was."

Comparing her night of lovemaking with the Border Lord to the earl's fishing expedition seemed absurdly funny. Her newly found sense of humor suddenly had its disadvantages.

"Couldn't you sleep?" he asked.

"I'm fine. Truly. You needn't trouble yourself on my account. I do have a few more questions to ask you."

His cheerful expression dissolved into wariness. "Ask away."

"Could you possibly be confusing the baron's soldiers with someone else? Common marauders? Brigands? It's your play."

Studying the board, he frowned and murmured, "Rather difficult to think just now."

Knowing precisely what he meant, she said, "You were speaking of the baron's raiders."

"You mean those two criminals who call themselves cowherds? More like *cowards,* if you ask me."

"How do you know they're criminals?"

He twitched his nose, jostling the spectacles. "Because they came to the Border reeking of Newgate."

The possibility of hard evidence spurred her on. "Have you proof?"

"I had a signed affidavit from the warden."

"Had?"

He made a tisking sound. "I foolishly gave it to Chilton-Wall."

"What did he do with it?"

"What else? He lined his pockets."

She laughed at the picture of the portly magistrate with papers jutting from the pockets of his velvet jacket.

"'Tisn't funny," he grumbled.

Ashamed, she said, "No, of course not. Forgive me."

"I will if you'll replace Chilton-Wall with an honest man."

So the earl wasn't above doing a bit of bargaining; she liked that aspect of him, suddenly felt at ease. "I'll ask the queen straightaway. Checkmate."

In more ways than one, Duncan thought, his heart in his throat. "The queen? Are you leaving?"

"No. Alexis is. She's taking my report and my preliminary recommendations to London."

But not before Duncan had a peek at them. "Have you penned it already?"

She glanced at the clock. "No, but I've plenty of time. I'll dictate the report to Saladin after his evening prayers."

He remembered the other lad, who'd limped into the castle yesterday. "I'm sorry about Salvador. I had Mrs. Elliott make him a poultice. That Alpin is a terror."

Miriam sighed, her breasts swelling nicely and filling out the leather vest. "'Tis a shame about the girl."

"You condone her wicked behavior? She's a devil."

"She's just lonely. No one pays any attention to her."

He sensed a deeper meaning in the statement. Latching onto it, Duncan said, "I'm sure you know more about families than I . . . being a MacDonald and all. 'Tis a mighty clan, the branch from Skye."

She turned away and stared at the crackling fire. Her fingertips strummed a silent tattoo on her thigh. "I'm not from Skye. I usually don't speak about myself." Quietly she added, "Please don't press me."

Duncan felt like Pandora reaching for the lid on the box. Pray God he too found hope in the cache of Miriam's past. Casually, he said, "Not Skye? Then from where do your people hail?"

Suddenly agitated, she rose from the chair and walked to the standing globe. Absently, she set it spinning. "My home is wherever the queen sends me," she said much too casually.

The soft whooshing of the sphere on its axis intensified the silence. He could read her pain in the gentle slump of her shoulders, as if the weight were too heavy to bear; in her tightly clenched fists, as if she were armed for battle against an invisible foe.

He considered dropping the topic. But it was her complete withdrawal, her expertise at keeping the pain to herself that troubled him so. In the dark of night, she'd given freely of herself. In the light of day, he felt honor bound to do some giving of his own.

He got to his feet and moved to stand behind her. He reached around her and turned the globe until Scotland faced them. "We could play Malcolm's guessing game," he said for want of anything else. When she didn't speak, he said, "Show me. Your home must be infinitely more peaceful than the Borders."

His dare worked, for like an aged cloak, her courage began to unravel. She lifted a shaking hand and touched a fingernail to the most beautiful glen in the Highlands.

"Glencoe?" he whispered.

As if to obliterate the memory of the bloody massacre, she slapped her palm over the whole of the British Isles. "Yes. A rather gruesome day in Scottish history, no?"

Beneath her flippant tone lay a lifetime of suffering. Yet Miriam MacDonald's tragedy only touched upon the inhumanity to the northern clans. During the seven ill years of King William's reign, proud Highlanders had been reduced to begging. The English sat in their cozy cottages and blamed early frosts for the bad harvests. Scots were found dead with grass in their mouths. The English turned a blind eye.

But in February of 1692, English indifference soared to new heights of cruelty when Lord Advocate Stair, eager to bring the weakened clans to heel, demanded the Highland chieftains pledge allegiance to William. Miriam's father hadn't come forward quickly enough to suit the power-hungry Stair. In a devilishly vile move, he turned Scot against Scot by promising wealth to the Glenlyon Campbells if they'd butcher the Glencoe MacDonalds, a small clan least able to defend itself.

How, Duncan thought miserably, had she managed to survive? She'd hate him for asking now, but someday he would.

Hoping he was doing the right thing, he placed a hand on her shoulder. Vehemently, he said, "May the Glenlyon Campbells burn in hell 'til the day after forever for what they did to your family."

"Yes, well . . . They certainly haven't paid for it yet. Everyone has forgotten the Glencoe massacre." Her voice wavered and she sucked in a breath of air.

"Not I." Duncan gave up the fight, turned her around, and pulled her into his arms. Her cheek fit perfectly in the crook of his shoulder. He stroked her back, thinking that without his high-heeled boots, they were of a complimentary height. "I'm so dreadfully sorry for what was taken from you."

Her quiet breathing, coming in the choppy cadence that spoke of soul-deep hurt, almost brought Duncan to his knees. He thought of the ways he comforted Malcolm when the lad grew melancholy. "What would your mother say about you being so sad, so secretive, Miriam?" he queried softly. "Please share that day with me."

In a voice devoid of feeling, she said, "It was very cold in the glen that winter. Papa had taken me to the cottages in town. Six score Campbell soldiers were quartered there. Two of them gave me biscuits and taught me to play at dice. I was four years old. They thought I was older.

"They came when it was still dark. Nanny was with me." She grew taut as a bow string. Duncan rubbed the caps of her shoulders.

"I was hiding under the bed, but I saw them beat Nanny with a club. I didn't know it at the time, but my mother was already dead. The door opened. Papa stood there, his nightcap on crooked, his sword in his hand. There was blood all over the front of his favorite robe. He killed those two soldiers, then called to me.

"I wiggled out. He picked me up and hugged me. I felt his sticky blood soaking my nightgown. He shook me. 'Run, Poppin,' he said. 'Run and hide and remember.'

"I remember hiding in a peat bin, but I don't know how I got there. They found me the next day. It was the soldier who'd given me a biscuit and told me I'd break a great laird's heart someday. He must've thought I was hurt or dying—because of the bloodstains. I don't know what he thought. But he put me in a cart with the bodies of my mother and father."

Duncan's heart clenched like a fist in his chest and his throat grew so tight he couldn't have spoken, even if his life had depended on it. He squeezed his eyes shut and willed her to go on.

"The grave digger pried my hands from my mother's hair," she said, detached. "A church woman bathed and fed me. Sometime later—" She shook her head. Her shoulders quivered. "Days, maybe weeks, I'm not sure of how long. Anne sent Alexis to get me."

Devastated by her story, Duncan suddenly knew a hatred that made his trouble with Baron Sinclair seem like a petty quarrel. Choked with emotion, he said, "Bless Saint Ninian, you're a brave lass, Miriam MacDonald. Hell's too good for the Glenlyon Campbells."

Then a subtle change occurred in her bearing, and while he couldn't precisely name it, he sensed she was fighting her demons. There it was—one, long, deep, steadying breath. "I've never told anyone."

A very special kind of pride infused Duncan. "I know you haven't. Thank you for choosing me." He rocked her from side to side and touched his lips to her temple and lower. "Your mother would be proud of you, you know. Your father's sitting on high boasting over the accomplishments of his lassie."

Against his cheek, he felt her smile. Good Lord, he thought, no warrior possessed more strength than the slender woman in his arms. He wanted that strength, for himself, for Malcolm, for all the people of Kildalton, forever. He wanted children from her, a flame-haired son he would name Alastair, to honor her father and keep his memory alive.

At the prospect of loving her, his body came stirringly to life. Heat spiraled through him, settling in his loins. Sweat popped out on his brow. His spectacles began to fog. The spectacles. The bletherin spectacles!

Frustration seared him. He couldn't make love to her now, not as the earl. Not after the story she'd told him. She might have given her virginity to him and poured out her soul, but she hadn't lost her wits. He could fool her with disguises, but he couldn't fool her in lovemaking. He wasn't that much of an actor. Or a scoundrel.

When the lenses cleared, he pulled back and guided her to the chair. Ignoring the vacant look in her eyes, he offered her the mug. She drank, drawing his gaze to the slender column of her throat and the steady pulse of life beating there.

Feeling the utter buffoon, he searched for something to say—anything to put them on even ground. Nothing came to mind, so he watched her cradle the mug in her hands, watched her throat work. He swallowed, too, and looked up to find her studying him.

"What are you thinking?" He blurted the thought he couldn't disregard.

The clock ticked away precious moments he craved to reclaim. She lowered the mug and wiped her mouth with her forefinger. "I'm thinking that I'm a very foolish woman who should keep her wretched stories to herself. My apologies."

He wanted to kiss away her second thoughts and tell her the truth. He wanted to know how she managed to compose herself so completely. "I'm thinking you've been doing that too long," he ventured.

She stared into the mug. "Doing what? Apologizing or feeling sorry for myself? Or lamenting the fact that the Glenlyons went scot-free? An interesting term, no?"

Her bitterness gave him pause. At length he said, "Maybe you should forget all of those things, Miriam. Holding a grudge is destructive to the soul."

Like a curtain, her icy shield fell back into place. "Maybe we should change the subject."

Before he could argue the point, she rose from her chair, her legs gracefully unfolding, the leather breeches creased in the most interesting of places. He watched her walk to the bookcase.

As if she were doing nothing more than searching for a text, she scanned the titles before her. "There is one more thing, Duncan."

He hated that offhand tone, for it always boded ill. Answering in kind, he said, "Oh? What's that?"

She tipped a leather-bound volume forward and examined the gilt edges of the pages. "'Tis the matter of the baron's claim to Malcolm."

Duncan's blood turned to fire. He picked up the tankard and drank deeply, hoping to douse the flames. How dare she fall into his arms one moment and accept his comfort, then in the next moment, try to rip his life apart? He wasn't sure which he hated more, himself for loving her, or life for treating her so cruelly. "Maybe we should change the subject again. Custody of my son is not open to discussion."

"You can't ignore it. Do you refute the codicil to her Will wherein Roxanne gives her stepfather the right to foster the boy?"

Her insensitivity chilled him. "The boy?" he said mockingly. "As in—the embroidery frames? The trunks of clothes? Malcolm is not an object or a commodity. And Roxanne wrote the codicil to bring peace to the Borders."

Her keen gaze bored into him. "Fostering is a common practice throughout England."

But this is Scotland, he almost shouted, echoing his father's favorite excuse for doing whatever villainy he pleased. The memory yanked Duncan back into himself. Be reasonable, he told himself, you're nothing like the Grand Reiver. Miriam wouldn't win on this point, and she might make him pay in other areas of the negotiations. Surely she felt vulnerable now.

In his most rational tone, he said, "Discounting the law, which gives me the right to govern all of my property, offspring rudely grouped with chickens and table linens, can you honestly see Malcolm living in that mess the baron calls a household?"

She quirked her mouth as if to say he had a point. "Well, thank you for your cooperation and the chess—and everything. If you'll excuse me." She headed for the door.

Shocked that she would just leave, he said, "That's it?"

She stopped. "No, there is one more thing." Glancing over her shoulder, a thick red braid against her cheek, an odd gleam in her eyes, she said, "The duchess of Perth was correct. There's something very different about you, Duncan. I'll find out what it is."

13

Later that day, standing at the window in her chamber, Miriam watched the shadow of the stair tower creep across the yard toward the castle wall. Just as the day was coming to a close, her time in Scotland was coming to an end. She hadn't expected to regret leaving the land of her birth. But she hadn't expected to find the Lancelot of her dreams, either.

Over the scratching of Saladin's quill and the occasional hiss of the peat fire, she heard Verbatim gnawing on a bone.

Fading sunlight splashed the western sky, transforming a bank of clouds into a treasure chest of amber, garnet, and amethyst. Oh, Scotland, she thought, I remember you as a bleak, loathsome place.

Thinking of that day twenty years ago, she saw once more a silent, haunted child huddled in a rickety cart between the mutilated bodies of her mother and father. The old pain, heartbreaking and bone-deep, seared Miriam. She bit her lip and began the drill that always chased her demons away. But recalling her accomplishments and counting her blessings couldn't banish her melancholy. She knew why. Earlier today the earl of Kildalton had enticed her into dredging up her painful past.

In a moment of weakness she'd come close to jeopardizing her career and her future. Thank God she hadn't cried out her frustration, for once the tears had begun, they would have flowed unchecked. Yet even now, the comfort of his embrace reached out to her, urging her to tell him the tale. A crushing weight had robbed her of breath. Duncan Kerr had extended the hand of friendship. He'd showed her his most precious childhood treasure, the chess set. He'd seemed different today. Yet so familiar.

She remembered vividly the moment solace had become yearning. When his lips had touched her temple and his arms had held her fast, her feelings had taken a decidedly passionate turn. Only one man had held her so. And she'd never considered telling her lover about her past. Why, then, had she told the earl? Because she desired him, too? She couldn't want both men; logic and her own morals told her the folly in that.

Still, the incongruity plagued her.

The gentle, bumbling earl had blundered into her heart as easily as the mysterious, domineering Border Lord had stormed her defenses. One offered passion and ecstasy, the other peace and understanding. In his attempt to soothe her, Duncan had spoken of her mother. It was the kindest gesture imaginable, and one Miriam would never forget.

A draft sailed through the room and stirred the open drapes. She shivered and rubbed her arms to chase away the chill. Verbatim whined.

Turning, she saw the dog leap to her feet and race across the room. Tail wagging like a flag, the hound poked her keen black nose into the wardrobe.

Saladin looked up. "What's Verbatim doing?"

The dog lifted a front paw. "I keep her leash in there. She's anticipating her evening walk," said Miriam. "Which she won't get until we're done. Where were we?"

Saladin's jet black eyes grew large. "You forgot?"

Surprised, too, she said, "Yes, it seems I have."

"But you never forget your place." He rolled his eyes. "Or anything else."

She'd forgotten more than her place in the correspondence; she'd disregarded her principles and befriended a man who would hate her when she told him the queen would most likely enforce the wishes of his late wife. Unless Miriam could work a miracle, he must surrender his child to his enemy.

She should have told him today, but indecision and her own melancholy had stopped her. He would learn the bad news soon enough, for she felt honor bound to prepare him. "Where were we, Saladin?"

Reading from the page, the scribe said, "A new magistrate, less open to bribery and better suited to the rigorous life here, will better serve the cause of peace in the Borders."

She'd forgotten diplomacy, too. "The last sentence is too blunt." She waited for him to ink the quill. "Change it to read . . . I'm sure Your Majesty will see the wisdom in dispatching, at your convenience, a new magistrate who is well-versed in local customs. Such a man will better . . . Go on from there, Saladin."

Like a double column of soldiers on parade, the problems and solutions of the Borders marched across Miriam's mind. She began to enumerate each of them out loud.

The quill scratched.

The dog whined.

Miriam ignored both, her attention straying from her dictation to the castle yard and the night shadows that swallowed up the light of day. She had the most bizarre compulsion to race toward the sun and follow it until there were no more nights.

You spend your days running from your nights.

Your mother would be proud of you, you know.

A philosopher. A good Samaritan.

"What's next, my lady?"

A moral and ethical dilemma. She had slept with a rakehell and now she longed for an earl, all in the space of one day.

The urge to run rose like a hunger in Miriam. Whirling, she began to pace. She had the oddest sensation that someone was watching her, seeing inside her soul.

Verbatim remained by the wardrobe. From his spot at the vanity, Saladin looked up. His curious gaze flitted from the dog to Miriam. Alexis was in the next room packing for her journey to London.

Verbatim barked.

Miriam stumbled on a thick rug bearing the Kerr sun.

"My lady!" Saladin dropped the quill and shot to his feet.

"I'm fine." She held up her hand to stay him. "Let's get on with the letter. And you!" She pointed at the dog. "Get down and be quiet!"

In a heap of gangly legs, the dog crumpled to the floor, her cowed expression a comical farce because her alert black eyes kept straying to the wardrobe and the leash.

Wiping her thoughts clean of spoiled dogs, lusty lovers, and earls who were not what they seemed, Miriam cleared her throat. "On the matter of the disposition of the late countess's dowry . . ." She waited for Saladin to take up his quill.

But he shuffled through the papers. "Do you wish to change the wording, my lady?"

"Aye, if I could," she said, impatience once again gnawing at her concentration. "I'd name Roxanne princess of Wales. Then Parliament could settle her damned estate."

Saladin scanned a page, his forehead so furrowed his widow's peak almost met his eyebrows. "But you said Malcolm would retain title of the land—" He laughed and slapped his turban. "You were jesting again."

She'd also lost her place again. Vowing to keep her mind on business, she snatched at the theme of her report. "Yes, I was, and in very poor taste. Let's move on to the concessions."

In her no-nonsense diplomat's voice, she said, "The earl of Kildalton has generously offered the baron Sinclair fishing rights to the river Tyne one week out of each month. A precise schedule will be drawn up and approved at a later date. Both gentlemen . . ."

Hiding in the cool passageway beyond the wardrobe, Duncan gasped. Generously offered! What in the name of Scone Abbey did she think she was doing? For years the baron had fished at will on the Tyne. He considered it his right. Duncan would be damned before he'd forget the bastard's poaching, and if that deceitful redhead thought he'd step aside and let the injustice continue, she could put that clever mind to work thinking again. Christ, she was the most unfair, double-talking diplomat to ever set foot in Scotland. She was also the only woman he'd ever loved.

"Verbatim!" she shouted, startling Duncan. "If you don't get your nose out of that wardrobe, I'll chain you in the kennel with those scraggly beasts from Aire."

Duncan stood stock-still. Peering between the gowns, he could see her clearly. She stood over the dog, her fiery-hued braid dangling over shoulder, her eyes blazing annoyance. A cold sweat beaded his brow. If she looked up, she'd see the open panel behind the row of dresses. If he tried to close it, she'd hear. He could dash away, but she'd still know someone had been spying on her.

The dog whined. Miriam patted the animal's head, then slammed the wardrobe door. A blessed pool of darkness fell over Duncan.

"Be patient, girl," she said, her voice muffled. "If I don't finish my report to the queen and stop these men from squabbling, we'll be doing our walking in the tundra."

Squabbling? How dare she reduce a problem that threatened to rip the fabric of his life to the pastime of frustrated fishwives? Disgusted, he folded his arms over his chest, clamped his jaw shut, and quietly tapped his foot.

"For a time they'll pout like jilted spinsters," she went on in that condescending voice, "but in the end they'll clasp hands and fall all over each other to make retributions."

Duncan grasped the irony, and almost laughed out loud, for he *was* pouting. Still, he couldn't help but scoff at her optimism.

"Saladin, strike the sentence beginning . . . Both gentlemen," she said, sounding weary. Moving away from the wardrobe, she continued, "Just say . . . Both men are fair and desire peace. The baron can't afford to feed or secure the futures of his enormous family. The duchess of Perth has graciously offered to sponsor three of the baron's natural daughters. His four eldest sons have all reached their majority with little to show for the passage. Military commissions would benefit these men, but the baron hasn't the wherewithal to supply them. If benefactors could be found, the baron's obligations would be reduced by half. I await Your Majesty's counsel on the matter.

"As for the earl of Kildalton . . ."

Anticipation stole Duncan's breath.

"The earl . . . ?" prompted the scribe.

"The earl is . . . I'm not sure anymore about the earl."

"He's fair, my lady. Not so—so gawkish since he's learned to wield a sword."

"You like him, do you?" she said with a hint of humor.

"He's an infidel, but tries to better himself."

At length she said, "Back to the report. The earl is a beleaguered man, who unjustly bears the brunt of his father's reputation for reiving."

Some Scotsmen applauded Duncan for being gentler than Kenneth Kerr. Others smiled in acceptance of his peculiar approach to alleviating the problems in the Border. The English, on the other hand, shared the baron's low opinion of Duncan. But Miriam had seen the truth. He just hoped she didn't see too much of the truth.

During the next hour, as he listened to her identify the problems and engineer the solutions, Duncan saw the wisdom in her methods. By arranging the futures of the baron's older sons and daughters, the household would be reduced to a manageable size. By allowing the baron fishing rights to the Tyne, Duncan wasn't giving up anything at all. But in the eyes of the queen, he would appear magnanimous. As it stood now, the baron fished the river when it suited him. Once the treaty was in effect, he'd be forced to govern his fishermen or stand answerable. But to whom?

His answer came when she said, "I encourage Your Majesty to create the post of sheriff of Kildalton. Further, I recommend John Hume, a protegé to the marshal of the royal household, be dispatched immediately to fill that office."

Kildalton would have a sheriff. The fight went out of Duncan. He leaned against the stone wall, shaking his head in wonder at the genius of Miriam MacDonald.

By creating the post of sheriff and recommending the notoriously honest Scotsman, Hume, to fill it, she had raised shrewdness to new heights. God, he'd underestimated her.

With a new English magistrate to interpret the law and a Scotsman to enforce it, responsibility for the troubles would be taken out of the hands of Duncan and Sinclair and put where it belonged—in the lap of the government that made the law.

He wished he could see her face. Did her eyes glitter with pride and accomplishment, or was she so accustomed to being brilliant that she took it as everyday fare?

He'd take it—every day and every night for the rest of his life. Like survival, the need to secure her love and loyalty burned like a fire in Duncan.

The Border Lord would conveniently disappear, leaving the road to her heart open for Duncan. Just this afternoon, she'd wanted him to kiss her, had welcomed his embrace. He knew, felt in his bones, that as surely as the first snowfall was on its way, Miriam would soon welcome his attentions. It was up to him to make her forget the Border Lord and nurture her affection for the man he truly was. Excitement filled him.

"On the matter of Baron Sinclair's claim regarding the fostering of the earl's heir, Malcolm—" She stopped, leaving the statement hanging in the air and Duncan hanging on her words.

Not daring to breathe, he waited. The silence of the tunnel buzzed in his ears. He leaned into the wardrobe. Fragrant velvet caressed his cheek. Foreboding knotted his gut. The fate of his precious son rested in her hands, as did peace in the Borders. Even Duncan Kerr dared not disobey the edict of the queen's representative.

"Saladin," she said, sounding distracted. "Do you know what color the earl's hair is?"

"No, my lady. Don't you think it's black, like Malcolm's?"

"Merciful heavens!" she shouted. "No. No. It can't be."

Saladin said, "You look like you just saw a ghost."

Fingers of fear clutched at Duncan.

"A ghost? Nonsense," she scoffed. "Why didn't I see it before?"

"See what, my lady?"

"That men are not always what they seem. That scheming knave."

212

"Who?"

Yes, who? Duncan thought, his legs trembling.

"No one, Saladin. No one at all. Tell me. Has Malcolm mentioned the Border Lord?"

Her abrupt change in topic brought gooseflesh to Duncan's skin. What was that business of knavery, and when would she get back to the custody issue?

"No, my lady," Saladin answered. "But everyone else talks about the Border Lord. Just yesterday, the bootboy swore that at the last full moon the Border Lord rescued his uncle's sheep from the baron. The tanner laughed, and told the boy to go on, because everyone knows the Border Lord busies himself deflowering English virgins at the full moon."

The room fell silent. Duncan cringed. She must be thinking she isn't special, since the Border Lord seduces so many women.

"So I heard. Does Malcolm never tell tales of bravery and the like?" she asked in that quick fashion reminiscent of a barrister.

"Malcolm always tells tales. Today he was pretending to be that Norman, Thomas of Bucket, who flogged the king of England. He even ruined a whip—thrashing a mounting block."

"You know very well 'twas Thomas à Becket, the archbishop of Canterbury."

"'Twas also a very fine whip. He wasted it."

She chuckled. "Everyone doesn't appreciate weaponry as you do, Saladin."

"A man who doesn't respect his sword dies a bloody death," he recited sagely. "Why did you ask about the Border Lord? Do you believe in ghosts?"

"Of course I don't. He's a flesh and blood man, though. Not a ghost."

"You've seen him?" Saladin squeaked. "Where? When? What kind of sword does he wield? Does he have a dirk? Is it jeweled? Does he hone it himself?"

She paused for so long a time, Duncan thought she might not answer. He shifted, searching for a gap between the closed doors of the wardrobe so he could see her. But the carpenter had fitted the closure well.

"I don't know anything about his weapons," she said.

"But I'm beginning to see just how much I know about him. Tell me, has anyone ever described him?"

"They say his hair is as black as soot," began Saladin with too much melodrama. "His eyes are as dark as a moonless night. His touch can steal a woman's will." In his normal voice, the scribe added, "But their will is weak. Allah, in his infinite wisdom, said women are vessels, here to serve man and obey his every command."

"Truly?" she challenged.

"Uh. Hum," he stammered. "I believe that—it's possible that—Allah never met a lady so great as you."

"I see. He also never met Elizabeth of England. Or Zenobia of Palmyra. Or Joan of Arc. But that neither diminishes their greatness, nor erases their gifts to mankind, does it?"

"No, my lady," he said, as contrite as Malcolm when caught in a lie. "Absolutely not. The people also swear," he rushed to say, "that the Border Lord wears a tartan cape woven from the lost souls of Scotland."

"Lost souls." She seemed to ponder the words. "Did they say what colors these souls have taken on? Are they woven in green and black, or black and brown? What pattern do they form?"

"The weaver says no mortal could fashion such a cloth."

"Well someone 'fashioned' it," she said, an angry edge to her voice. "I'll wager my best foil that I can find that cape right here in Kildalton Castle."

A primitive warning rang in Duncan's head. *She knew.*

Nay. She couldn't. It was only her devious mind turning to speculation. She suspected, then.

Even that possibility turned his blood to ice.

Her voice drifted through the chilling fear that held him captive. "Let's get on with the report, Saladin. After supper I intend to pay the earl a visit. Hand me that old key in the top drawer there. I may need it."

"But he's in his study winding flippity-flops."

"Splendid."

A drawer slid open, then shut. "Here," said the scribe.

The information whirled in Duncan's mind. She had the key to the tunnels. He must wipe away her every doubt. But how? What proof could he offer her? How could he convince her that he wasn't the Border Lord? Especially if she had access to both his study and his private quarters?

Like the sun bursting over the horizon, the answer dawned.

Duncan Armstrong Kerr was the Border Lord. As she dressed for supper, Miriam cursed herself for not seeing the logic of it sooner. She'd been so intent on doing her job and bringing the Glenlyon Campbells to justice, she hadn't looked for subterfuge from the earl. She hadn't looked for passion either. Absurdly, her own arrogance amused her. Adjusting the bodice of her most revealing gown, she smiled. After years of settling complicated international disputes, she had thought the problems in the Borders simple, the players ordinary.

In retrospect, the earl of Kildalton was the least ordinary man she'd ever met. Behind his bumbling exterior lurked a cunning, deceitful man. The Border Lord. His overdone ineptness, his sniveling protestations of innocence—all of it had been a clever ploy to blind her to the truth.

But her eyes were open now, and by the time the fish course was served, she'd reveal him for the imposter he was. Still, when she pictured Duncan donning a disguise and wooing her in the moonlight, then laughing behind those spectacles in the light of day, she thought she might die of shame.

How *could* she have fallen for his deception? Because she'd been distracted, concerned about doing her job and helping the people of Kildalton. She'd continue to help the people; she had no other means of support. But when she was done, she'd gather her shattered heart and get on with her life's work. Never again would she trust a man.

An hour later, she sat fuming in frustration at the table, for the earl had sent his apologies and ordered a tray sent to his study.

"You seem disappointed," said Alexis, a curious gleam in her eyes.

Tamping back anger, Miriam toyed with her portion of clootie dumpling by scooting the raisins and currants to the sides of the bowl. "I had a few questions to ask him."

Alexis stared at Malcolm. "There's always tomorrow, unless you haven't finished your correspondence."

She referred to Miriam's report to the queen, but spoke vaguely for the benefit of the earl's son, who was too busy devouring his dessert to pay attention.

Miriam pushed the bowl aside. Her dispute with the earl was purely a personal matter now and wouldn't change the outcome of the negotiations. "I'm quite finished with my correspondence."

"Then I shall take both of the twins to London."

"No," said Saladin.

"Nay," said Malcolm.

Saladin swallowed a mouthful of raisins and dried oranges and sent Miriam a beseeching look.

"Please let Saladin stay," begged Malcolm.

A smile of friendship passed between the boys. "You might need me," said Saladin. "Take Salvador. He wants to go to London."

"Yes," Malcolm said, puffing out his chest and revealing gravy stains on the embroidered table runner he wore as a surplice to emulate Thomas à Becket. "Salvador wants to go."

"May I stay, Lady Miriam?" said Saladin, his normally arrogant features pulled into an adjuring pout.

Before answering, she said to Salvador, "You're certain you feel well enough to travel?"

Of course I am, his imperious look seemed to say. A lock of blue-black, stick-straight hair fell over his brow. With a toss of his head, he pitched the strand back into place. "I'm well enough to face any puny female who crosses swords with me."

"We could all go," piped Malcolm. "I'd ride my pony the whole way and not ever complain . . . even if the fancy court ladies pinch my perky cheeks."

"Who told you the ladies would pinch your cheeks?" asked Miriam.

Squirming with pride, he said, "My papa. He said they'd call me a braw laddie—if I watch my language and mind my manners."

"I'm certain they would," said Alexis. "But would he allow you to go?"

The boy opened his mouth, but then slumped in defeat. "Nay. I guess I'd better not even ask. He'd be lonely here without me. I think Saladin and I should keep him company."

Alexis sent Miriam a questioning glance. In answer, she shrugged, troubled again at the thought of separating father and son.

Remembering the earl's statement about how unhappy Malcolm would be at Sinclair's, Miriam felt a pang of pity for the boy. The wicked Alpin would make his life miserable, and the baron didn't care enough about the girl to teach her to behave.

Miriam knew the childless Queen Anne would make the mistake of using the boy to try to bring peace between the men. Anne had made a diplomacy through fostering. Malcolm would suffer. In the wars of adults, she thought sadly, the casualties were always the children. But if the queen met Malcolm, she'd change her mind.

"I could ask your father's permission for you to go," she said. "I must speak with him tonight on another subject."

"I want to stay here," Malcolm said with conviction and went back to his dessert.

Alexis put down her fork. "I've asked Angus MacDodd to accompany us."

Alexis had shown no interest in the soldier. Stunned, Miriam said, "I'm surprised."

"'Tis only a precaution . . . should we encounter brigands or the like on the road."

Although Alexis ducked her head, Miriam didn't miss the flush creeping up her friend's cheeks. "He's a very pleasant fellow," she said, hoping to find out what Alexis was up to.

"I'm certain he is. And in his absence, you might consider exercising with the earl—or teaching him to fence."

Miriam almost laughed out loud at Alexis's clever maneuvering. To hide her amusement, she rose from the table. "Perhaps I will. Now, if you'll excuse me, I'll go see his lordship."

"Now?" squeaked Malcolm. "But you can't. His study door is locked. He's making flippity-flops. They take ever so long, you know. He won't be done for hours."

Hours! Miriam rejoiced. She had time to search his room

for the Border Lord's disguise. Suppressing excitement, she said, "Then I'll go to my room and rest for a while." At Alexis's surprised expression, Miriam added, "You should teach the boys that new card game we learned."

"Of course," said Alexis, complete understanding on her face. "We'll be in the keeping room."

Miriam left the table. The earl's chamber was on the first floor, two doors down from his study.

In the hall, she met Mrs. Elliott, who carried a covered tray. The housekeeper curtsied. "Have you lost your way, my lady?"

"Oh, no." Assuming a casual air, Miriam put her hands in her pockets. Her fingers touched the key to the tunnel door. "I was just going to compliment the cook on the clootie dumpling. 'Twas delicious."

Mrs. Elliott's mouth curled in a tentative smile. "I'm sorry, my lady. She's left for the night, but I'll be sure to tell her in the morning. She'll be pleased you bothered."

Miriam looked pointedly at the tray. "For the earl?"

"Aye. He's in his study making flippity-flops for his fishing trip tomorrow."

Miriam could not wait until tomorrow to conduct the search; the castle would be filled with servants then. Alexis wouldn't be here to entertain the boys. Miriam smiled. "Then don't let me keep you. I'm sure he's famished."

"Wander around if you like," Mrs. Elliott said. "All the corridors eventually lead back to the hall. Except this one. It leads to the tunnel, but you probably aren't interested in that."

The housekeeper's invitation was a stroke of good luck Miriam didn't intend to question. "Thank you. I think I will look around. I love castles."

Miriam started back toward the kitchen, but stopped when the housekeeper rounded the corner to the earl's study. She hurried to the tapestry that concealed the tunnel entrance. Once in the cool corridor, she paused to let her eyes adjust to the darkness. Over the racing of her heart, she considered her options. She could wait here and listen for the housekeeper's return or she could ... try the door leading from the earl's chamber to the tunnel! He hadn't bothered to lock it that day she'd gone exploring.

Hoping such was his habit, she conjured an image of the passageways. Then she felt her way down the inky corridor. As she passed the first door on the left, she heard muffled voices. The earl and Mrs. Elliott. Fighting the urge to eavesdrop, Miriam moved on until she reached the alcove she sought. Bending, she peered through the keyhole to be sure the bedroom was empty. Guilt assailed her. She took a moment to reason out her covert actions. Had he been honest with her, she wouldn't be forced to pry through his personal things. He'd left her no choice. As the Border Lord, he had taken her virginity and stolen her heart; the least he owed her was the truth about his identity.

She grasped the handle and pushed open the door. Inside, she stopped when she spied the great wooden throne. A master craftsman had carved it from an enormous oak. On the high back, the carpenter had chiseled the Kerr sun and the traditional thistles of Scotland. The arms of the piece featured rampant lions so real she expected them to roar.

A sense of wonder stole over her. To better see the chair, she took a lamp and turned up the flame. She thought of the painting in the keeping room. In the portrait, Kenneth Kerr dwarfed the chair, but that was impossible, for the seat was roomy enough for two adults. Obviously, the seventh earl had let his pride influence the artisan.

As she crossed the thick floral carpet, she couldn't take her eyes off the chair. Although darkened with age and use, it still held a majestic quality. The empty dais in the keeping room seemed the perfect place for the throne chair. The earl, however, didn't seem the type of man to rule from a throne.

She tried to picture him perched on the throne and holding forth to the people of Kildalton. But her mind conjured the image of a shadow-shrouded man clad in a dark cape and hat. The timely reminder spurred her to the wardrobe. Certain she'd find the cape there, she threw open the doors. One shelf held a dozen neatly folded Kerr tartans in varying stages of wear. Sachets of heather and pine needles had been placed among the clothing to ward off insects. The other shelves contained stockings and gloves, shirts and handkerchiefs, all monogrammed with the Kerr sun. Her pulse raced as she explored his personal articles and inhaled his now-familiar fragrance.

No cape. Not even a stitch of dark cloth.

Disappointed but not discouraged, she went to the pedestal bed, which was draped in forest green trappings and a mountainous velvet counterpane. She peered beneath the bed, but found only a pair of slippers, and a toy sailboat. Next she rummaged through a desk cluttered with papers and feathers, but found nothing to link the earl to the Border Lord.

In an iron-ribbed trunk she discovered an array of fancy breeches and waistcoats in manly shades of brown, black and biscuit. Why did he never wear them? They were stylish, with the wide lapels and roomy pockets with flaps favored by men at court.

Puzzled anew, she closed the trunk and sat on the lid. Frustration diluted her convictions. She had been so certain that the earl and the Border Lord were the same man. Now her conviction waned.

The mantel clock struck the hour of nine. Fearful of being caught, she surveyed the room one last time, turned down the lamp, then left the way she'd come. The instant she pulled the door closed and stood in the darkened tunnel, a deep voice said, "I doona think, lassie, that I care to find you sneaking out of the laird's bedchamber."

14

Panic, and a pair of iron-strong hands held Miriam immobile. When she could draw breath, she said, "Let go of me."

His arms tightened around her. "Shush, lass." He loosened his grip, but not enough for her to pull away. "'Twas not my intention to frighten you."

His voice drifted down to her in the darkness. Keenly attuned to his every move and nuance, she thought that Duncan Kerr wasn't so tall as this man. Usually his speech was refined, and not so resonant or compelling. Only occasionally did he speak Scottish.

Doubts chipped away at her earlier certainty that the man in front of her was Duncan Kerr. "What are you doing here?"

"It isna so important as what *you're* doing here."

She'd move to Russia before she'd tell him her true purpose. "What I'm doing here is my business and the queen's. See it however you choose, but remember, I don't answer to you."

"I see," he said, all threatening male. "You make love to

221

me, but you wilna trust me with a confidence. It doesna speak well of my character. Or your morals."

"My morals?" Shocked, she tried to twist out of his grip. *"You* seduced *me.* You said as far as I was concerned you were living out a prophecy, and that one touch of my lips drove you to madness."

"You bonnie well liked my loving—over and over again. Have you forgotten the way you pushed me onto my back and explored my chest and private parts?"

The memory made her blood run hot. "Of course I remember what I did to you. I acted like a Cheapside doxy."

A chuckle vibrated in his throat. "Nay, lass. A Cheapside doxy knows well how to ride a man to glory. 'Twas your first lesson."

She groaned in embarrassment. "You're a scoundrel."

"You're as dishonest as a pack of Plantagenets if you deny you wanted my loving. You still want it."

Her pride told her to slap his face. Her heart told her to leap into his arms. History told her to take him seriously. "I don't deny that you made me want you."

"Made?" He stepped away, but one hand still rested on her shoulder. "As in last night? Or as in some plaything you're done toying with?" His hand slid down to cover her breast. "What about now, Miriam?"

Trying to ignore the floating sensations and the yearning his touch aroused, she grasped his wrist. "You're being unfair and intentionally crude to me. Why?"

"Because you havna exactly swept the stoop, ordered the servants away, and bade your man welcome, lassie."

His possessive declaration touched off a thrill in Miriam. She'd always wanted a demonstrative mate, a man who would treasure her affections. Her Lancelot would allow her the freedom to dance with another; yet when the song ended, he'd appear at her side, impatient to reclaim her.

But she wasn't at a fancy cotillion, savoring the luxuries of life. She stood in a dungeon-dark tunnel, earning her living and laying her heart on the line. If her suspicions were correct, this man could destroy her reputation, her self-respect, and her independence. "You haven't told me what you're doing here."

"Well, Mistress Barrister. Since you insist so prettily, I've come to see the earl. 'Tis ironic, nay? Since you seem to be here for the same reason. Where is the niddering poltroon?"

A clever pretense, she thought, him asking about his own whereabouts. But not clever enough to allay her reservations and certainly not clever enough to distract her. She planted her feet and stiffened her spine. "Oh, yes. You don't know where he is, do you?"

His hands tightened on her shoulders. "Nay, lass, not exactly. But I'll find him. In case your perfect memory has failed you, you just left his bedchamber. Pray he's not abed, but if he is . . ."

Had there been light, she would have watched his eyes for a sign of deception. Frustrated, she listened for nuances in his voice and heard jealousy. She leaned forward. "Next you'll tell me you've brought him pig's hair."

He leaned closer. "Goose down—dyed a bloody crimson in a caldron 'neath a full moon at midnight."

Laughter bubbled up inside her. She drew a hand to her mouth. He couldn't possibly be the earl of Kildalton. Could he? Oh God, she had to be sure. "Show it to me."

Abandoning her breast, his fingers curled around her wrist, and drew her arm down. "'Tis too dark, lassie. But I could let you feel it. 'Tis in my breeches pocket. You canna have forgotten . . ." The breathless, seductive whisper played a vivid counterpoint to the bold journey he proposed.

Her fingers itched to touch him, to trigger the passion that waited just out of reach. Her heart pleaded with her to seek more from him than physical satisfaction.

"Go on, lass. Find it. You'll get no protest from me."

Pride and inexperience held her back. She blinked, straining to make out his features and put to rest the question of his identity. But all she could see was a jet black form against a blacker world. "You should have brought a light."

"I did," he said, his mouth so close, her lips went dry. "You."

Like a strong wind at her back, need pushed her toward him. "But I want more from you than couplings in the dark," she blurted. "I want to know who you are."

"I'm the Lancelot of your dreams. I'm the man who makes your heart race and your loins melt. I'm the man who wants you right here, right now."

His words tugged Miriam into a spell she sought to break. "No. You're Duncan Kerr."

"Duncan Kerr?" He laughed without humor. "Bloody hell!" Wrapping her in his arms, he said, "Curse me for a doiled glaikit."

"You're no fool," she whispered into a tartan cape that spawned fireside tales.

He turned his face away, cool damp air replacing the warmth of his breath. She felt his uncertainty. His silence spoke eloquently of the differences between them, and worse, it made her vividly aware of how foolish she'd been to fall in love with him—whoever the devil he claimed to be.

Was Duncan Kerr holding her in his arms, and with a mere touch, stirring her passions? Had he bamboozled her in the light of day and encouraged her to relive her wretched childhood, only to seduce her in the dark of night?

Surrender clouded her logic. The lonely, accomplished woman who stood at the head of the queen's diplomatic table and watched the great men of England heap respect on her plate didn't care that this man had tricked her; she craved a respite from a life of dull conversations with shallow people and tricky negotiations with sly ambassadors.

What if this smooth-talking Scotsman wasn't the Lancelot of her dreams? Who gave a brass penny? Except for the signing and sealing, the peace here was made.

Yet the war in her heart raged on.

"What's that?" He froze, then drew her deep into the alcove. "Shush."

Ducking under his arm, Miriam peered down the corridor. The door to the earl's study stood open. Mrs. Elliott stepped out, a lighted petticoat lamp hooked over her arm. "Aye, my lord," she said. "I'll fetch tomorrow's herbs from the tower, then come back for the tray."

She moved away, then stopped and looked back into the room. "Sir?" A moment later she smiled and curtsied.

"Thank you, my lord. 'Twas no bother at all. I'll tell the cook."

Just as the housekeeper closed the door, the Border Lord pulled Miriam into the darkness of the alcove and shielded her body with his. "Be still," he whispered urgently. "Make not a sound."

Duncan Kerr wasn't the Border Lord. The earl of Kildalton was sitting in his study complimenting the housekeeper. Now was Miriam's chance to see her lover's face.

Anticipation thrummed through her. She tried to lean back, but his big hand cupped her head and held her still. Mrs. Elliott walked toward them, the lantern transforming pitch blackness to watery gray. At the top of her vision, Miriam saw that he was hatless, the black scarf tied snugly at the nape of his neck.

She drew back to see better and her foot scraped the stone floor.

"Shush," he whispered, clutching her.

Against her tightly clenched jaw, his heart thudded like a muffled drum. Peering around his shoulder, she saw the glow of the tiny lamp throw eerie shadows in the tunnel. Lacy spider webs draped the blackened ceiling. Rusting, empty sconces marched in a line down the gray stone wall and marked the housekeeper's progress.

In a rustle of skirts and unawareness, Mrs. Elliott passed them by, her head down, her attention riveted to her footing.

Slowly, Miriam lifted herself on tiptoe. Her temple brushed his chin, then grazed the muscular plane of his jaw. When they were cheek to cheek, he squeezed her to him, the rush of his breath in her ear setting her skin afire, the swelling of his male flesh against her stomach pitching her thoughts into exotic realms.

Bending, he nuzzled her neck and her throat, before settling his mouth on hers. He feared discovery; she tasted his tension on his lips. But passion had him in its grip and drove him to achieve a level of intimacy that would launch them into familiar, carnal territory.

Wrapped in a cape of lost Scottish souls and drenched in a mind-shattering desire, Miriam clung to him.

The door to the tower opened and closed. Darkness

descended again. She had lost her chance to see the Border
Lord.

He pulled back slightly. "Where were we, lassie, before
Mrs. Elliott interrupted us?"

His casual reference brought new questions. "You were
about to tell me why you didn't want her to see you."

"Me? 'Twasn't me I feared exposing, Miriam. 'Twas you."

"Bosh. You know Mrs. Elliott?"

"Aye."

He spoke with such reluctance, Miriam was inspired to
say, "Then why not knock on the front door when you have
goose feathers to deliver?"

"Because then I wouldn't meet you in dark corridors."

"Don't be glib. Tell me the truth."

Silence, save the soft, rhythmic sound of their breathing,
was her answer. Then he released her, and she felt his gaze
move away. His cape swished across her hand. He was
fidgeting. Why? "Tell me, Ian. What does the Border Lord
fear?"

"He fears himself, for he loves you to distraction," he
said, the burr thick in his voice. No dialect could mask his
frustration. He didn't want to love her. Or perhaps this was
all an act. Perhaps he said I love you to all the women.

Sick yearning tore at her heart; prior to this dark, secretive
stranger, no man had ever loved her. She'd grown accustomed to having him care for her, had clutched his adoration to her lonely heart. He'd brought her Lancelot dreams
to life, but in doing so, he'd stolen her fantasy and left her
with real agonizingly wonderful memories.

Her throat felt raw with apprehension. "What will you do
about it?"

The door to the tower room opened. Light spilled into the
tunnel. The housekeeper was returning.

He pulled Miriam to him and turned, moving to the
opposite wall of the alcove. Now they stood in shadow
again, out of the housekeeper's line of vision.

His concern for her touched Miriam. One day soon she'd
coax him into the light and see him clearly. She eased her
arms around his trim waist and held him close. In response,
he undulated his hips, showing her how much her touch

affected him. He pulsed with vitality. She ached with empty wanting.

Miriam barely noted the housekeeper's passing; she was too caught up in the man, in the mystery that surrounded him, and in the magic he made her feel.

Another door opened and closed, and like water through a sieve, the light slipped through the opening and vanished. The housekeeper was gone. Miriam relaxed.

The darkness transformed him from gallant protector to ardent lover. Past teasing and nibbling, his mouth moved on hers with gentle insistence, rousing the need she couldn't deny and bathing her in sweet promise. Tomorrow night or the night after, she'd find out who he was, for eventually he'd come to trust her.

The cold cynicism of her rationale seemed at odds with the hot desire thrumming through her, and suddenly she didn't want to be Miriam MacDonald, famed arbitrator and discreet servant of the crown. She wanted to be a woman, a woman who despised snowflakes and loved the man in front of her.

As eager as he, she raked off his scarf and threaded her fingers through his thick, wavy hair. Holding him just so, she twined her tongue with his, tasting, devouring, until they were both burning, gasping for air and desperate for the joining that would send their passion soaring.

Dragging his mouth from hers, he rested his forehead on her shoulder and hauled in breath after ragged breath. She took his weight, reveling in the knowledge that she could kindle so bold a blaze in so passionate a man.

Desire trilled a lively tune in her heart, and her soul sang with the melody of love. Putting her lips to his ear, she whispered, "I'll die here and now if you don't make love to me."

He growled and lifted her skirts. "Then you'd best put those fingers to work on my buttons, love."

Giddy with anticipation, she opened the placket of his breeches, and cupped her hands to receive him. He landed, warm and heavy, swollen and pulsing in her palms.

"Push the breeches over my hips, love, and tarry not."

She dallied a moment, reacquainting herself with the

velvety soft texture and insistent strength of him. He sought her secrets, too, stroking skin that was slick with want of him and teasing a tiny seed of flesh until it blossomed into full flower.

In agony, she put her hands to work, caressing him in the way he'd taught her, but before she'd established a rhythm, he grasped her buttocks and said, "Cease, Miriam. I canna wait to have you."

He drew back, slipping from her hands just as her feet left the ground. Instinctively she draped her arms over his shoulders and wrapped her legs around his waist. Like a cherished friend at homecoming, he nudged at her door, and she welcomed him, drawing him inside and embracing him fully. A purely masculine groan vibrated in his chest and harmonized with her sigh of feminine bliss.

He went still, giving her a moment to wonder if the earl could hear their cries and earthy moans; then he began the rocking, lifting, straining motion that snatched coherent thought and tossed her into the shining world of the sublime.

Moments later, as the rapture engulfed her, a hoarse cry rose in her throat, and his mouth was there to absorb the sound, then refine and return it twofold. Against her quivering belly, the muscles in his stomach contracted in jerky spasms, showing her the sweet satisfaction she'd given him. With his mouth still tightly fixed to hers, their breaths mingling, he dragged her hand from around his neck and placed her palm just below her navel. Then he covered it with his own.

Applying gentle pressure, he made her vividly aware of the physical aspect of their joining, of how deeply he possessed her and how completely she had captured him.

Tears sprang to her eyes at the tenderness of the gesture, and if God called her home tomorrow, she'd haggle with the devil himself to stay one more night in this man's arms.

"Oh, Ian, I can't bear to leave you. I love—"

"Hush, Miriam." His hand tightened on her bottom, then moved up to her waist. "The earl might hear."

She swallowed her declaration; there would be time tomorrow night to tell him of her love.

With a soft grunt of regret, he dragged himself from her

and set her on her feet. "Everyone except the earl will be abed by now," he said, smoothing her skirts, his hands lingering. "I'll keep him occupied. You take the main stairs to your room."

He spoke with such authority, she wondered if he hadn't lived here at one time. Was he a cousin of the earl? A papal cousin? Being a bastard brother would explain the Border Lord's resemblance to the seventh earl. Seeing him in the moonlight, she'd been reminded of the great portrait of Kenneth Kerr.

"Very well, Ian. But it doesn't matter now—if the earl or anyone finds out about us. I'm not ashamed of what we shared. I'd gladly announce it to the world."

He stiffened. "I doona ken what you mean."

"I've written a treaty. I'm very good at my job, remember?"

His lips against her cheek, he said, "Aye, and you remember this, lassie. You've naught to run from anymore. Sleep tonight and every night, and dream sweet dreams of me."

The finality in his voice frightened her. She clutched his cape. "What do you mean? Where will you be?"

His hand touched her breast. "In your heart, love, and in every breath you take."

He was only waxing poetic, she realized. Yet she needed more. After so passionate a tryst, she felt romantic, too. "When will I see you again?"

In Scottish, he whispered, "Every day, lass. Until the day after forever."

She leaned against the wall and heard him walk away. How could he love her, yet refuse to show her his face? Their future loomed like a bleak winter day.

A moment later he knocked on the door of the earl's study. She peered into the corridor. He'd already crossed the threshold, but she caught sight of his hand whipping aside his cape. The door closed behind him with a definite click that echoed in the tunnel.

On unsteady feet she stepped from the alcove. The murmur of voices drew her.

"I do hope you've . . . those feathers, Ian," said the earl. "The salmon are . . ."

Hearing only snatches of conversation, she tiptoed closer.

229

"I doona care for being used as a messenger, Duncan," the Border Lord replied in his booming voice.

"Don't fuss so. I pay you . . ."

When she reached the door, she knelt and peered through the keyhole. They sat before the fireplace in the wing chairs where she and the earl had played chess. She couldn't see the Border Lord, for he'd taken the seat facing away from her. But she knew he was there, for the edge of his cape draped the arm of the chair.

Wearing his flamboyant black wig and thick spectacles, Duncan Kerr faced her. He was holding a familiar black scarf. He worked at a knot in the cloth, and when he freed it, clumps of red-dyed goose down cascaded to the floor. Staring at the opposite chair, he said, "Just what I needed, Ian."

Miriam chuckled to herself, wondering how she'd ever been so foolish as to think Duncan Kerr was the Border Lord. They now sat face to face. She'd been preoccupied with many things—trying to achieve peace in the Borders, anticipating justice for Glenlyon Campbells, and falling in love with the man of her dreams.

Happiness infused her. He wasn't deceiving her after all. She watched the earl examine the clump of bright red goose down. Then he looked up, and her breath caught, for he seemed to be staring right at her, a sad expression in his overlarge green eyes, his mouth pulled into a frown.

Suddenly uneasy, she blew a secret kiss toward the back of the chair where her lover sat and made her way to her room.

Later, when she lay in bed, she thought of her one remaining task—telling the earl of Kildalton he better prepare himself to surrender his son to Baron Sinclair.

The next morning she sat in the same chair her lover had occupied the previous night. The earl sat across from her, the first draft of the treaty of Kildalton held up to his nose.

As he read, she absently rubbed her hands over the arms of the chair and counted her blessings. With Alexis and Salvador on their way to London, and the peace a foregone conclusion, Miriam could get on with her future. She took comfort in pleasant thoughts of the Border Lord, for in a moment the earl would read the final stipulation.

How would he react?

He tossed the parchment aside and drilled her with a look of such contempt, she shrank back in the chair. Behind the spectacles, his green eyes blazed hatred.

Good Lord, she hadn't thought Duncan Kerr capable of so much anger.

"This is a bloody farce, Miriam. You expect me to give up my son to keep Sinclair happy?"

Prepared for opposition, she said, "You have no choice. By witnessing the codicil to your wife's will, you indirectly agreed to her wishes. 'Tis not my doing, Duncan, but a point of law."

He folded his arms over his chest and leaned back in the chair. "How long have you known about this point of law?"

His chilly tone and ice cold stare unnerved her. She looked away. "'Tis an old law and common knowledge. It dates back to the twelfth century and the duke of Exeter and Prince Hal of Monmouth."

In a silky whisper, he said, "You misunderstand, Miriam. When precisely did you apply this law to me and Malcolm?"

A specific answer would enrage him even more. Unable to look at him, she said, "Does it matter?"

"I can see it doesn't to you. You've probably known for weeks that you would take my son. You've accepted my hospitality, my—" He stopped and took a deep breath, as if trying to quell his anger.

"I did not make the law."

"I did not give my agreement. For God's sake, my wife was dying of complications from the birth. I merely signed the damned paper to ease her passing."

She felt his pain, his frustration, but could do nothing to alleviate it. "I'm sorry, but legally, you acceded. I promise you, the courts will see it that way. English law is very specific in domestic matters. I believe the queen will enforce it. I've asked her not to, but I fear she won't heed me in this."

He smiled and shifted in the chair, propping his chin on his palm. "English law, you say?"

Spoken with sly emphasis, the question was meant as a challenge. "I know what you're thinking, Duncan, that English law does not apply to a Scotsman. 'Tis not so. The

Act of Union changed all that, regardless of what the Highland clans think. Scotland and England adhere to the same legal system now."

"Now is the key word. Malcolm was born on the last day of April in seventeen hundred and seven. In the event your ciphering skills fall short of your perfect memory, allow me to subtract it for you. My son is one day older than the Act of Union. Therefore, he is a Scottish citizen, and immune to the ancient English law which governs the fostering of noble heirs. He will stay with me."

Taken aback by his deduction, Miriam sat silent. The earl of Kildalton had presented her with the kind of legal abstract that was her forte. Challenges to the law paraded through her mind, but none involved a Scottish child born before the Act of Union. Still, hope infused her. A clever barrister could argue the case and win.

"Have you nothing to say?"

She thought of her letter to the queen and considered how stubborn Anne could be. Hard evidence might sway the queen. "Have you proof?"

"Aye," he growled, rising from the chair and snatching a book. "The family Bible. Unless you mistrust the clergyman who made the entry and baptized my son."

Miriam believed him. "I wish you had told me sooner."

"I would have if I'd known what villainy you'd planned for my son." He handed her the Bible. "I wish I'd never laid eyes on you," he said much too cordially. "I'm going fishing."

Stung by his words, she watched him snatch up his creel and stroll toward the door, intentionally stepping on the document that she had spent weeks composing and Saladin had spent hours illuminating. She had done her best to be fair. Spitefully, she said, "A perfect decision under the circumstances, my lord. Enjoy yourself."

Without a reply he walked out and slammed the door. Miriam stayed where she was, her mind sifting through centuries of precedents to English law, her fingers clutching the Kerr Bible. There had to be a way to challenge the queen's obligation to send Malcolm away.

A possible solution came. Putting the book aside, she

jumped from the chair and sought paper and quill from the earl's desk. Just as she sealed the letter and tucked it in her pocket, the door opened and Mrs. Elliott walked inside, a tray in her hands.

Speaking to the back of the chair facing Miriam, the housekeeper said, "I thought you and Lady Miriam would care for a pitcher of cider, my lord."

"The earl's gone fishing, Mrs. Elliott."

The housekeeper's gaze grew frantic, darting everywhere. "But he can't be gone. The baron's coming—" She dropped the tray. The loud crack of crockery smashing on the floor muffled the sound of her retreating footsteps.

Wrapped in a heavy tartan, Duncan leaned against the trunk of a beech and looked up. One golden leaf clung stubbornly to the tree. A stiff, chilly breeze rattled through the bare limbs, plucked up the lone leaf and carried it a few feet before dropping it in the slow moving water of the North Tyne.

Kildalton and the Cheviot Hills lay behind him, two hours' ride to the north; to the south lay Hadrian's Wall and Sinclair land. For centuries the property in between had been English, but now it belonged to Malcolm. By bequeathing the land to her son, Roxanne had effectively moved the English border south and deeded half of Northumberland to the heir of a Scottish earl.

Duncan chuckled, picturing the dead Scottish kings and Kenneth Kerr laughing down at him and jabbing each other in the ribs, for a shy English girl had accomplished what all their war machines and fancied-up ambassadors couldn't.

Ambassadors. He thought of Miriam. Hatred and joy ripped at his gut. He picked up a rock and threw it into the river. Water splashed the wig and spectacles which lay on a blanket near his feet. He despised Miriam, he loved her. He had expected the English crown to take back this land; he'd never considered it his. Were it not for the people and the hardships they endured at the hands of Sinclair, Duncan would've turned his back on this patch of soil years ago. He hadn't expected the queen to send a thief in the guise of a red-haired Highland lassie. He hadn't even considered that she'd trade him miles of peat moorland in exchange for a brown-eyed laddie who loved all things Scottish, except his name.

A rotten bargain. A father's nightmare.

His mind whirled with alternatives. He could take Malcolm and flee to France as many Scots before him had. No. Thanks to Miriam, he couldn't go there; since the signing of the Treaty of Utrecht, the French had become allies of the English. Was there no end to her influence?

He could go to Italy or Spain. He could go to London and personally petition the queen. He could follow his father's example and kill his English neighbor.

Faced with so many unacceptable options, Duncan let his mood deteriorate from melancholy to miserable. A decisive laird would take control of the situation. His father would have thrown Miriam in the dungeon and used her as a bargaining tool. Duncan would find another way to deal with her. Only one hard and fast decision shone in the gloom his life had become: the Border Lord would disappear.

He took a small, perverse pleasure in denying Miriam her lover. But when he thought of Miriam MacDonald, ambivalence plagued him. How could he have fallen in love with the one woman who could destroy him? How could she, of all people, have found his Achilles heel? Had the massacre at Glencoe left her so heartless that she could devastate other families and not suffer a pinch of remorse?

To think he'd pitied her. Praised her. Foolish, foolish man.

The sound and vibrations of hoofbeats drew Duncan from his black mood. He got to his feet and looked toward the Cheviot Hills. Snow clouds obscured the peaks. Icy wind buffeted him. A lone rider ran before the storm.

Minutes later, a soldier wearing a Kerr plaid jumped from his lathered mount. Breathless, he said, "Come quick, my lord. Baron Sinclair's at Kildalton."

15

Letter to Alexis in hand, Miriam went in search of the acting captain of the guard. She located him across the yard near the smithy, where he was deep in conversation with a very agitated Mrs. Elliott. Arms akimbo, her face tight with strain, the housekeeper argued vehemently, but the pounding of hammer on anvil prevented Miriam from hearing what the woman said.

From the wide black stripe in his red tartan, Miriam recognized the soldier as a Lindsay, one of the clans that swore allegiance to the Kerr family. She had often seen Alexander Lindsay in the old tilt yard overseeing archery practice.

Now he looked down at Mrs. Elliott who spoke emphatically and pointed to the clansmen manning the walls. With unmistakable finality, Mr. Lindsay shook his head no. The housekeeper threw up her arms and stormed off.

Miriam took her place. After haggling with the stubborn Mr. Lindsay for twenty minutes, Miriam finally persuaded him, on threat of imprisonment, to dispatch a rider to intercept Alexis and deliver Miriam's revised letter to the queen requesting more time. Meanwhile, Alexis would find a barrister to review the claim exempting Malcolm from the Act of Union.

As she crossed the castle yard, Miriam noticed an unusual amount of activity. From the inner bailey, a flock of sheep poured through the portcullis. Behind the bleating animals came the sheepdog, yapping incessantly and the shepherd, waving his staff. The battlements and access stairs were thick with soldiers. Like a string of ants moving crumbs, they carried crossbows and pikes. Women crowded around the well, filling earthenware pots and leather bags.

When Malcolm and Saladin emerged from the smithy, each carrying an armload of crossbow quarrels, Miriam grew alarmed. "Are we under attack?" she asked.

Malcolm, dressed in a toga and a crown of gold-tinged rowan leaves, hefted his cargo, almost spilling the arrows. "There's riders coming from Sinclair. We must to arms!"

Saladin rolled his eyes. "Malcolm, it's only a carriage and two outriders. Even Mrs. Elliott thinks all this preparation is silly."

"I'm Caesar today," he corrected. "Look! It's the baron's own carriage. What if he brings Alpin?" His face contorted in fear. "I'm taking cover." Quarrels rattling in his arms, he dashed toward the steps leading up the wall, nearly tripping on his toga.

As stoic as ever, Saladin said, "Salaam, my lady."

Perplexed at the situation, Miriam returned his greeting, but focused her attention on the scurrying soldiers and noisy livestock filling the yard. "You'd think an army was coming. The baron wouldn't dare attack Kildalton."

The scribe jerked his head toward the wall. "These stupid infidels think he will."

Although the baron had seemed amenable to peace, Miriam had learned long ago not to take success for granted until the treaty was signed by both parties. "With only two outriders? That's preposterous."

Saladin shrugged. "Even so, I'd better do as Mr. Lindsay said and take these to the guards."

Miriam watched him go, his yellow tunic and red boots easily visible in a sea of tartan-clad soldiers. His jewel-hilted scimitar slapped against his thigh, drawing admiring glances from the men who'd seen him wield the dangerous blade and curious stares from those who hadn't.

A cool wind sailed through the yard, making her shiver. She looked up and saw a bank of snow clouds in the northern sky. Fear crawled up her spine. Winter loomed too close. She thought of her lover and the warmth of his arms, the heated passion he kindled into flame. She remembered his prophetic words about how she ran from her fears. The earl, too, had encouraged her and offered comfort. How lucky she was to have two such caring men in her life. Only now the earl hated her.

She went to fetch her cloak. She returned just as a team of four white horses pulling Baron Sinclair's high-wheeled, gilt-trimmed carriage rolled into the yard.

Again, she wondered how he afforded so costly an equipage. Considering the poor state of his household, his coin would be better spent on dowries for his eligible female relations and careers for the males. She'd seen worse spendthrifts, although none of those men and women had had so many responsibilities and dependents as the baron. With the queen's help, his financial burden would be considerably lighter.

Pulling her cloak snug about her and putting on a smile, she joined Mrs. Elliott who stood ready to greet their unexpected and seemingly unwelcome guest. Saladin and a very quiet Malcolm waited nearby.

She scrutinized the outriders, trying to match these men with the brigands the earl had described. The one on the left was a stick of man with a tooth missing in front. The other man was indeed average in all things, but did his ragged velvet cap hide a balding pate? Had those men spent time in Newgate? Why hadn't she seen them at Sinclair's?

She leaned close to Saladin and whispered, "Watch me. When I nod, you go find Mary Elizabeth's mother."

He whispered back, "I know where she is."

"Good. Bring her close enough to look at those two men on horseback. Ask her if she's seen them before. Keep her calm."

Miriam returned to her place beside Mrs. Elliott. Saladin stared straight ahead, his eyes sharply scouring the riders.

At the driver's hearty "whoa," Miriam put on a smile. In

fancy but mended livery, the driver jumped from the seat and hurried to open the door. No sooner had he pulled down the steps than Aubrey Townsend, Baron Sinclair began to emerge. The endeavor took the better part of a minute and drew the attention of everyone in the castle yard, for when he unfolded himself from the conveyance, he stood an impressive six feet ten inches tall.

Fearful children squealed and dashed for the safety of their mothers' skirts; the soldiers hitched up their kilts and exchanged nervous glances. Malcolm gulped and moved closer to Saladin.

Mrs. Elliott winked and softly said, "Don't fret, O Great Caesar. He's naught but a selfish man with two centurions. You have legions at your command."

Hope flickered in his eyes, but dimmed when the baron strolled toward them.

Miriam carefully regarded the guest, who reminded her of a hawker she'd once seen at Fenchurch Fair. On stilts, the man had towered above the throng.

Dressed in a waistcoat and knee breeches of parrot green brocade, the baron cut a fashionable, if emaciated figure. He wore white stockings with padding at the calves, white satin shoes with gold buckles, and a plumed hat over a powdered bag wig. Every detail of his appearance, from the high crown of the hat to the scroll-like heels of his shoes, had been carefully planned to accentuate his extraordinary height.

The short of it was, he enjoyed being tall.

With fingers as long as dinner knives, he rearranged his lace-ruffled cuffs and scanned the yard. When he spotted Malcolm and Saladin, he jerked his neck like an inquisitive rooster.

"Have I interrupted a costume ball?" he said, eyeing their unusual clothing, his gaze lingering on Saladin's blade.

Malcolm didn't move so much as an eyelash. Saladin spread his legs and folded his arms over his chest. Like Miriam, the lad had seen too much of the world and too many of its oddities to fall prey to the baron's intimidation. He glanced at Miriam. She nodded.

Expecting no reply from either boy, Sinclair pulled his thin lips into a smile.

Saladin walked casually away.

Not bothering to acknowledge Mrs. Elliott, the baron looked down from his great height and said, "You look radiant, my dear Miriam, even in this rustic setting."

During her stay at his home, Miriam had listened to hundreds of barbed insults on everything from the changing weather to the dances at court. Whatever the baron couldn't control, he criticized.

Disappointed that he had brought his poor manners with him, she glanced pointedly at the towers of Kildalton. "Rustic, my lord? 'Tis an odd word for so noble a structure, as I was just telling Mrs. Elliott. And I believe we agreed that you would address me as Lady Miriam."

His knees locked, but his smile remained. "You had me agreeing to any number of things, now that I think of it." He glanced at the battlements and milling soldiers, and smirked as if pleased that his presence warranted such preparations. "Where is Duncan? Manning a pot of boiling oil?"

Considering the earl's mood when he departed, Miriam felt relief at his absence. The baron's snide remark irritated her, but as a guest in the earl's household, she couldn't challenge another guest.

She deferred to Mrs. Elliott, who curtsied and said, "He's gone fishing, my lord. May I give him a message?"

The baron relaxed, his legs settling into a noticeable bow and his arms dangling at his sides. "Fishing? How creative of Duncan. A pity I've missed him. But I actually came to see Lady Miriam, and my dear grandson, Malcolm, of course. How are you, boy?"

Malcolm gasped. "I am Caesar. I don't have to answer you and I can order you out of my castle if I choose."

The baron winked at Miriam. "Choose not, O Great Caesar. I am your servant." Then he turned toward the carriage and snapped his fingers. "Alpin . . . come out, girl," he crooned, as if she were a shy animal he was trying to snare.

Malcolm began tying knots in his toga sash.

When the girl appeared in the door of the carriage, Miriam blinked in surprise. The six-year-old Alpin might pull pranks and terrorize her many siblings, but dressed as she was in a frilly concoction of pink satin decorated with red rosettes, she looked the perfect angel. Her mane of auburn curls had been ironed and braided into thick coils and wound tightly over her ears.

"Come, come, girl," coaxed the baron, motioning with his hand. "Show Malcolm what you have for him."

Yanking her panniered skirt to the side, she tromped down the steps, her slight weight barely tipping the well-sprung carriage. An angry storm roiled in her unusual violet eyes, and the set of her square jaw revealed a tightly contained fury.

Malcolm laughed at her. "Look at you all dressed in skirts."

With a flick of her wrist, she folded the steps away. "This is what I think of you, monkey-faced Malcolm." She leaned into the carriage, the steel cage of her miniature farthingale hiking up in back to reveal tiny buttocks and slender legs clad in patched leather breeches that were frayed at the knees.

"Spirited child," murmured the baron. "Takes after her mother, my dearly departed second cousin. A great loss to me, but one I've learned to bear. I, of course, saw to the expense of the poor woman's funeral and took in her child."

Alpin whirled, her delicate fingers clutching the handle of a large wicker basket. "My mother was your third cousin," she grumbled, marching toward them. "You never even set your beady eyes on her. You had her buried in a moth-ridden horse blanket."

The baron chuckled. "The child has a bizarre sense of humor."

"Huh," huffed the girl. "I didn't want to come here today. Kildalton castle stinks like a sewer."

As she came closer, Malcolm whimpered.

The baron reached down to clasp Alpin's shoulder, which only reached his knees. She jerked away and craned her neck to sneer at him. "Get your grimy hands off me, Baron Sin."

God, the little child had spunk, thought Miriam.

"Smile, Alpin, and give Malcolm the gift."

Her mouth widened in a grin so false it made Miriam wince.

Malcolm took a deep breath and said, "You—you lo-look very pretty today, Alpin."

She set the basket down. "You're a sniveling cur, Malcolm. I hate you."

He swallowed loudly. "Then why'd you bring me a present? Is it poison?"

"'Twasn't my idea. There."

As fearful as his father had been at his first meeting with Verbatim, Malcolm stretched out an arm and lifted one side of the basket. A fat brown hare, its ears laid back, blinked and wiggled its whiskered nose.

Malcolm sighed with delight and said, "Thank you. I've never had a rabbit for a pet."

"Her name's Hattie." Alpin picked up the animal and cuddled it to her breast. "She likes dried berries and fresh berries, and . . . and carrots with the tops on. Lots of carrots. Every day." Alpin bit her lip, squeezed her eyes shut, and buried her face in the rabbit's soft fur.

Miriam's heart ached for the lively, brave girl who had no real family to care about her. She glanced up at the baron, who was busy surveying the row of merchants' huts that compromised the commerce of Kildalton.

Miriam saw Saladin near the smithy, Betsy Lindsay at his side. The woman took one look at the outriders and slapped her hand over her mouth. Saladin moved in front of her, blocking her view. The feather in his turban jiggled as he spoke. Betsy nodded, then allowed him to lead her away.

Miriam had to struggle to keep her temper in check. The baron had lied when she questioned him about the two men. He would regret it.

Knowing she now had hard evidence against him, Miriam turned her attention to the meanest child she'd ever met.

"She only has three legs," Alpin went on. "But she can hop as fast as anything. Here. Take her." She held out her hands.

Malcolm took the rabbit. "Thank you. But isn't she yours?"

Alpin stared at his toga. "I don't want her anymore."

"Alpin loves to share with the other children," said the baron.

"Oh." Malcolm stroked the hare's ears. The furry creature wiggled in his arms. He sought a better hold. "What
happened to her leg?"

Dusting her hands and trying desperately not to cry,
Alpin said, "She lost it in a trap, but she's all healed now."

"How did you find her?"

"The Night Angel brought her to me. He watches out for
little girls and animals. He swears Hattie's not really a
cripple, no matter what anybody says."

"Always patching up some wounded beast," said the
baron. "The stable's full of them—birds with broken wings,
a blind lamb, a toothless badger. She even has a litter of fox
kits."

Alpin pretended to spit on the ground. "That's because
you and that fat magistrate ran their mother to death."

"If it were up to Alpin, hunts would be outlawed," the
baron commented dryly. "We'd all spend our leisure spinning yarns about the Border Lord."

"He's the Night Angel," Alpin spat.

"Mind your manners, child," said the baron.

To Malcolm, Alpin said, "Don't forget to scratch her—
there—under her chin. If you want to, I mean. She kind of
likes it. She's yours now. You can scratch her anywhere you
want or not at all." She sniffled a little and wiped her nose
on her fancy sleeve.

Malcolm said, "I want to. I like her ever so much."

In a thick voice, Mrs. Elliott said, "Don't you fret,
Mistress Alpin. He'll take the very best care of Hattie. We've
plenty of carrots with the tops on."

"You won't cook her?" asked Alpin.

"Alpin, please remember your manners," the baron
scolded.

A smile of pure kindness wreathed Mrs. Elliott. "Of
course we won't, Alpin. I promise." Then to the baron, she
said, "I'm certain his lordship would want me to offer you
refreshment."

It was a lie, Miriam thought, but a necessary one. Duncan
and the baron might never be friends, but they must learn to
tolerate each other. Civility seemed an excellent place to
start.

"How very hospitable of you," he said and headed up the

242

steps. Turning back, he glared at Alpin. "Behave yourself or I'll give away your fox kits."

Alpin leveled him a look that said, I dare you to try. "If Malcolm puts his smelly lips on me again, I'll wallop him good."

Malcolm blushed. Saladin, who'd returned to his place, chuckled.

All too conscious of her role as neutral observer, Miriam smiled at Mrs. Elliott. "I'll show your guest to the keeping room, if you like."

The housekeeper cast a sad glance at Alpin. "Aye. And thank you, my lady. I'll bring a tray."

Miriam followed the baron through the castle, watching him duck beneath door frames and chandeliers. He stopped just inside the keeping room and stared at the empty dais. "Where's the mighty Kerr throne?"

He referred to the great chair in the earl's bedchamber. She had wondered why it wasn't in the public room. "Throne, my lord?"

He prowled the room, picking up a silver box to examine the engraver's mark on the bottom. "A monstrosity of a thing, all carved with lions and blazing suns. It was on that dais the last time I was here." Putting down the box, he moved on to a pair of ruby glass candlesticks, which he held up to the light. A spray of crimson dots splashed his face. "Primitive in the extreme as are most things here."

"Where did the throne come from?"

He strolled to the pedestal table that held a lantern clock. Bending, he peered at the timepiece. "'Twas a gift from one of those barbarous Scottish kings, I suppose."

"The earl must have redecorated this room."

"No. This John Bowyer clock hasn't been moved, and the pre-Delian candlesticks are in the same—" He stopped and gave her a sly smile. "How clever you are."

"Clever? Hardly, my lord. 'Tis seldom I meet someone with a better memory than mine. I do enjoy our visits. After the formality of the Europeans . . ." She let the sentence trail off to see what he would make of it.

"I know precisely what you mean." Fluffing his lace cravat, he swaggered across the room and levered himself onto one of the straight-back benches, his long legs stretched out. "I must agree. People who can't remember the gist of a conversation bore me to tears."

She gave him the same soft chuckle that had proved effective in disarming him during their prior meetings. "I know precisely what *you* mean. Goodness, that dais looks bare, doesn't it?"

He didn't seem to notice that she had to remind him of the topic, for he said, "That depends on one's taste. I am surprised that Duncan would part with the beastly thing. Like his father, he loved to hold court in it, or so I'm told. Those half-naked clansmen seem to enjoy worshiping him."

The men respected Duncan, but worship was way off the mark. In demure fashion, she said, "I've been away from Scotland for a long time. I know little about the seventh earl of Kildalton, except the tidbits Lord Duncan reveals."

As if gathering an audience of children, the baron leaned forward and draped his arms over his legs. "What would you like to know? I've heard all the stories about Kenneth Kerr." Flapping his arms in exaggerated obeisance, he added, "The Grand Reiver."

He hadn't even known Kenneth Kerr except through gossip, which he'd been free with in the past. Hoping he'd shed new light on the old problems here in the Border, she said, "What kind of father was he, I wonder?"

"A rough bully, and he taught his son to carry on the family traditions. I worry about dear Malcolm. Duncan has become a master."

Miriam thought him an indulgent father, but what was the crime in that? "A master at what?"

She must have spoken too sharply, because he patted the place beside him and in a friendly tone said, "I truly didn't come here to dredge up the bitter past or tell tales on my noble son-in-law, the earl."

At least the negotiations hadn't stopped him from claiming Duncan as his relative. At Sinclair, she had used the association as an inducement to make the baron see how important it was to reach an agreement with his neighbor. "Answering a direct question can hardly be called gossiping," she said. "You know how curious a woman can be about lineages, especially noble ones."

"Don't I?" He chuckled. "With fourteen of them under my roof, I know their peculiarities well."

"You certainly deal with Alpin." And poorly, she thought.

He fished a silver toothpick from his waistcoat and began poking at his teeth and noisily smacking his lips. "She worshipped dear Adrienne. Hasn't been the same since the girl was kidnapped."

"You still think Duncan was responsible for her disappearance?"

"Well, I don't believe Kenneth Kerr arose from the dead to do it. The Border Lord didn't either."

Miriam felt her heart trip fast. But she casually said, "Who is he? Do you know?"

With his tongue, he rolled the silver pick to the corner of his mouth. "He's an excuse my tenants use to keep from paying their rents. The house servants use his presence to escape their duties. Just last week the dairy maid took to her bed all day, complaining that he'd come to her the night before and wrapped her in that magic cape. He drained her will to resist, she says, and spirited her away to Hadrian's Walls. Two days later, he seduced her sister."

Miriam's stomach bobbed like a boat adrift. Could Ian be so fickle as to take another woman to their special place? He'd said he loved her to distraction. He'd seduced her so easily. What about her feelings for Duncan Kerr? Wasn't she being fickle by desiring one man and giving herself to the other? Absolutely. Only a slut would act so disreputably.

"Then the cows' milk dried up," the baron went on. "We haven't had a dollop of decent cream since the Border Lord supposedly paid us a visit."

She put aside her personal dilemma. She'd have time later to examine her own poor behavior. "Then you don't believe the Border Lord exists."

"I don't believe the romantic tales of seduction, and I'm too practical to fall prey to the suspicions of peasants. How could a man return from the grave to seduce women and steal my livestock? I think he's a mercenary hired by Duncan Kerr."

"Why would the earl do that? I thought you said he was like his father."

He sighed, as if summoning patience. "I told you before. Because he's spiteful and greedy, and he *is* just like his father. Only Duncan's methods differ. He knows the queen won't tolerate barbarous behavior. So he pays someone else to do it. Too busy writing fish tales in his journal."

"But if Duncan were truly like Kenneth Kerr, he wouldn't hire someone to fight his battles."

"Of course he would. He'd stoop to any depths to bedevil me and trick you. But you've taught me the importance of compromise. So I've thought of a way to make sure the situation improves."

The certainty in his voice alarmed her. "How will you improve it?"

"With this. I also have a proposition of sorts." From his breast pocket, he produced an envelope.

Miriam pried open the wax seal and slipped the card free. The baron was having a ball, and to her surprise, the guests of honor were the earl of Kildalton and his heir, Malcolm Andrew Kerr.

"You're frowning," he said. "Do you think it's presumptuous of me? I mean—you made me see the logic in resolving my differences with Duncan. You *have* managed to make him see reason, haven't you?"

All Miriam had done was alienate Duncan, but since their meeting she had taken steps to correct the situation. Alexis would speak to the queen and buy some time. The baron, however, made her wary. "What do you mean by make him see reason?"

"I chose the wrong word. Surely you understand why Roxanne insisted I foster the boy."

She wasn't quite ready to address the fostering issue. "Roxanne was your stepdaughter. She sought peace by willing the land to her son. The people who live on the land between here and Hadrian's Wall want Duncan for their overlord. They told me so when I visited them."

"Roxanne was ever naive, and so are those tenants. They will obey whoever has jurisdiction over them. Who better to guide Malcolm than I?"

His arrogant presumption disappointed her. Lord, now she'd have to coddle him out of his black and white thinking. She couldn't summon the patience. She was tired

246

of bickering, backbiting men. "Legally the governing hand belongs to Malcolm's guardian. I tell you, Baron, the crux of it is, the law will prevail here."

"Exactly," he said, oozing confidence. "I do so long to make a lasting peace with Duncan. Fostering his son is one way."

He believed that by fostering Malcolm, he would gain control of the land. He was correct; all of the revenues from a minor's property reverted to the guardian, and all Baron Sinclair cared about was the money. Because Malcolm was born before the Act of Union, he might be viewed as a Scottish citizen and exempt from the law. His mother's wishes wouldn't matter. But the baron needn't know that.

Until she heard back from the queen, Miriam had no intention of making a commitment on custody of the boy. "Peace will be made, Baron. Mark my word."

Mrs. Elliott entered the room carrying a tray with goblets and a pitcher of beer. Under her arm she carried a bunch of carrots with the tops on. She served the beer, then quietly left the room.

"We're fortunate," said the baron, holding up his mug in salute, "that the queen sent you to strike the peace. Will you come to the ball?"

She ignored his patronizing comment. The event was a fortnight hence. By that time Alexis would have done her work. The queen would send word to Miriam. Then she could pen the formal treaty and present it to both men for signature. She prayed Anne would heed her advice. "Certainly. I'd love to. Now, tell me about your proposition."

"It concerns my niece, Caroline. I believe she can help patch up this whole ghastly mess."

Miriam sifted through the names and faces of all the women in his household. She saw a diminutive golden-haired girl of ten and eight with warm brown eyes and an easy smile. "How can she help?"

He began jerking his neck again. "As I told you, I hold no grudge against Duncan. To show my good faith, I'm willing to offer him the hand of my dear Caroline in marriage."

Miriam rebelled at the thought of Duncan marrying. He'd done that once to gain peace. But she was fooling herself if she used his past marriage for an excuse. As capricious as it seemed, she didn't want anyone else to have Duncan Kerr. Confused by her possessive attitude, she decided to hedge. "I'm not sure another alliance between your families will solve anything, my lord."

"What objection could you possibly have? 'Tis the perfect solution."

She couldn't answer him, because her objection was purely personal. She'd given her heart to the Border Lord, yet she couldn't bear the thought of losing Duncan Kerr's affection. She also couldn't tell the baron he was wrong. "What if it compounds the problem? I suggest you wait until the negotiations are completed."

"I insist you approach the earl with my offer. Avery Chilton-Wall concurs."

Swallowing back disgust, she said, "Chilton-Wall's approval is neither here nor there. The queen is replacing him. And hiring a sheriff, too."

The baron leaned back against the bench, which he dwarfed. "I'm surprised you would throw away the queen's money on a sheriff? Duncan and I can settle matters around here. I've given you the perfect vehicle. You know, Miriam, you really should think things through before acting so rashly."

His puny attempt at an insult amused her. "As I explained to you, my lord, at the request of Her Majesty, I'm simply affording you and the earl time to get to know each other again. You won't be burdened with the taxing business of enforcing the law or passing judgment. They're hardly fitting tasks, after all, for men of noble birth. Don't you agree?"

He laughed, a high cackling sound that made her ears ring. "I'd agree to tying my own cravats if it would keep my family in clothes and food, and my poor, frightened tenants safe."

His overdone tale of woe garnered no sympathy from Miriam. "I thought the only thing they feared was the Border Lord."

"Oh, they do fear him."

He'd left her the perfect opening. "But they don't fear the two criminals you brought with you today?"

"Criminals?" He spat the word. "Those men are my bodyguards."

She told him about Betsy Lindsay. "Shall I fetch her here, my lord?"

Red-faced, he said, "No. I believe you. What shall I do with them?"

"Don't let on anything's amiss. When you get home, have the magistrate arrest them. Lord Duncan will press charges when he returns."

"Very well, but I hope you don't think I'm to blame."

She did, but the courts would call his crime omission.

"Lady Miriam!" Mrs. Elliott stood in the doorway, the wilted carrots in her hand, her face a picture of alarm.

"My lady!" Saladin raced around the housekeeper and skidded to halt before Miriam. His swarthy skin was as white as bleached parchment. "Please. You must come. I think Alpin killed Malcolm."

16

His cheek a scant inch from the neck of the galloping
stallion, Duncan squinted into the biting north wind and
raced for home. His thighs ached from gripping the horse.
His fingers cramped from clutching the reins. The messenger from Kildalton had long since fallen behind.

Duncan's mind swirled with reasons for the baron's
unannounced visit. One possibility kept nagging at him.
Miriam had ignored his defense and enforced the codicil to
Roxanne's will; the baron had come to claim Malcolm.

Duncan burned with murderous rage. The pounding of
hooves matched the hammering of his heart. He'd ceased
trying to contain his anger. If he arrived home to find
Malcolm gone, he'd make Miriam MacDonald sorry she'd
come to the Borders to brew her diplomatic poison. Peace
with Baron Sinclair would become irrelevant, for if that
thoughtless bastard so much as parted Malcolm's hair
wrong, Duncan would wage a campaign of destruction that
would make a Viking raid look like a May fair.

By the time the towers of Kildalton rose like great black

shadows against the late evening sky, Duncan had honed his anger to a fine, lethal edge.

The stallion stumbled. Duncan eased the pressure on the reins and sat back in the saddle. The horse slowed to a half canter and blew loudly, the heaving breaths billowing like a spring fog. Duncan panted, too, sucking in frigid air. Icy snowflakes settled on his face and hands, cooling skin that radiated his inner fury.

A torch flickered in the distance and seemed to float across the inner bailey. At the curtain wall, the light winked out, then popped into view again. It bobbed over the road toward Duncan, bringing trouble.

Only the direst of straits would compel Alexander Lindsay to send out a man to meet Duncan. For a moment the angry warrior within him grew silent. The loving father took the fore. Fear clogged his throat and squeezed his chest. The unfairness of his situation besieged him. Only God should have the right to separate a man from his son.

Under the baron's control, the spry, cheerful Malcolm would grow despondent and wither like a plucked weed. No one would care that he sometimes blamed himself for his mother's death. Who would comfort him when he fell to his knees at the side of his bed and called God a foosty scunner for taking his mother to heaven? Who would find the time to nurture his bright mind without starving his lively imagination? Who would call him by his *nom du jour*?

Who would teach him to be generous and understanding? Who would teach him right from wrong? Who would teach him to earn the respect of his fellow man? Who would teach him to woo and befriend the woman of his choice?

Tears blurred Duncan's eyes. He saw his own miserable childhood. He remembered the solemn vow he'd made to a squalling, motherless Malcolm: You'll never want for companionship and love as I did.

When the torch-bearing soldier rode within earshot, Duncan again summoned the angry warrior inside him. "Is Malcolm all right?" he demanded.

The soldier halted his mount. The torch light illuminated his face. Alexander Lindsay. Oh, Lord. The situation must be worse than dire. "Has the baron taken Malcolm?"

The soldier whirled his mount alongside Duncan's. "Nay,

my lord. I'm afraid 'tis far worse than that." He stared straight ahead, abject misery pulling his features into a grimace. "The girl Alpin. She tied the lad to a tree and—"

"And what?" Duncan's blood ran cold. "What did she do to him?"

Alexander swallowed loudly. "The foul-mouthed besom put hornets under that toga he was wearing. His manly parts are . . . Dammit, sir. His lady crackers are swelled up as big as your fists. The midwife says he'll never sire a child of his own."

Absurdly relieved, Duncan wilted in the saddle. He'd thought his son dead.

Sweet Malcolm. Stung by hornets. Duncan's own manly parts throbbed in sympathy and his knees hugged the horse. With the midwife to nurse him, Mrs. Elliott to coddle him, and his father to nurture his wounded pride, Malcolm would mend. But what of protection for a lad who'd been taught to cherish the gentler sex? Malcolm would sooner answer to his own name than raise a hand to Alpin—even in self defense. Hell, he always tried to kiss her.

Duncan must continue to keep his promise to Adrienne and find a new home for Alpin, preferably a world away. Barbados. Aye, Barbados and the care of Adrienne. He'd miss seeing the look of joy on Alpin's face when the Border Lord brought her food or a wounded animal. Or showed her the smallest kindness.

"I'm deeply sorry, my lord. But rest assured, the lassie paid dearly. The baron yanked her up by the hair and dragged her into his fancy carriage. The watchman swore he could still hear her screaming long after they'd passed the curtain wall."

Duncan felt pity for a child in a threadbare smock and ragged shawl who spent most of her nights in a chilly stable, feeding her meager supper to a wounded or sickly beast. On the night he'd freed a pretty brown hare from one of Sinclair's traps and brought the frightened and bleeding creature to Alpin for help, she had offered the Border Lord her only pair of shoes in exchange for a bunch of carrots with the tops on.

The next night he'd brought her a bushel of vegetables, a supply of medicinal herbs and clean bandages, and a pair of leather breeches that his son had outgrown. She'd cried like a baby and called him God's Night Angel.

Poor Alpin. Poor Malcolm.

Suffer the little children, and bugger the brutal times that had made a curse out of a simple homily.

"Where is Malcolm?"

"He's abed, my lord. Lady Miriam and Mrs. Elliott are with him."

So, thought Duncan, she hadn't given away his son. Or had Alpin's mischief merely postponed the diplomat's treachery? He'd find out soon enough.

"Uh, my lord?" Alexander hesitated, his mount sidestepping. "The housekeeper said I was to remind you to—uh—to wear the wig and the spectacles."

Sensible Mrs. Elliott. Duncan reached into his sporran, but when his fingers touched the wig, he stopped. He'd already decided that the Border Lord should disappear, but vengeance made him rethink his plan. Miriam MacDonald would never belong to Duncan Kerr; how could she love a man who had deceived her? How could he continue to love a woman whose sole purpose in life was to ruin his?

God and all the saints help him, because he could no more stop loving her than he could unite the Highland clans.

All things considered, the matter of her knowing the true color of his hair seemed inconsequential. He would continue to wear the spectacles, though. He wanted a good close look at her when he told her the horrible fate of the Border Lord.

Half an hour later, a wigless Duncan stood on the threshold of his son's room. Mrs. Elliott had fallen asleep in a chair; Miriam sat on the narrow bed, Malcolm's hand in hers. In a voice as clear and pure as the wind off the Cheviot Hills, she crooned a Highland lullaby about a bairn who was so well loved and by so many, the king had given the lad his own clan.

Duncan couldn't see his son's face; Malcolm's knees were bent and the bed linens draped over him in tent fashion.

Bracing himself for the worst, Duncan walked to the bed and stared down at his son.

A cruel hand squeezed his heart.

Malcolm's closed eyes were puffy, the lids blotchy red. Tracks from the tears he'd shed ran down his cheeks. He'd bitten his bottom lip, for it was swollen and bore the bruised impressions of his teeth.

He looked small and helpless, his hair too black and thick for a face so fragile and fair. He looked very much like the shy woman who'd died only days after bringing him into the world.

Duncan swore that nothing would ever force him to abandon this lad. Neither war, nor inept monarchs on any throne, nor diplomats would cause him to leave Malcolm at the mercy of others.

Duncan dropped to his knees beside the bed and said a silent prayer.

Her singing stopped.

Unwilling to look at Miriam just yet, Duncan glanced at her left hand, which lay palm up and joined with his son's. What he saw through the thick spectacles shocked him.

Four small, boyishly dirty fingers, the knuckles pasty white, curled in a death grip. Dried blood caked her palm where the lad's nails had scored her tender flesh.

Feeling miserable to the depths of his soul, Duncan followed the line of her delicate wrist where her pulse pounded quick and steady. He felt her staring at him, compelling him to look up, and even though silence hung in the room, he heard her unspoken plea: Forgive me, Duncan, for letting harm befall your son.

Temptation dragged at him. His gaze moved past her wrist to the lacy webwork of veins that embellished her forearm. She'd rolled up the sleeves of her gown. Stains marred the costly sea green velvet. The color would enhance her eyes and complement her extraordinarily lovely hair. Her beauty would draw him. Her mood would soften him, temper his anger, then with clever words, she'd knead his attraction into full-blown desire.

"Duncan . . ." Her entreaty weakened him.

And awakened Malcolm. "Papa . . . ?"

Thoughts of yielding to the desirable woman fled his mind like forest creatures scurrying from a fire. His gaze swept to Malcolm. A new kind of heartache wrenched him.

His face contorted in agony and fresh tears pouring from his eyes, Malcolm held up his arms. "Oh, Papa. Hold me."

Duncan leaned down and scooped up his son, cradling him against his chest. Malcolm's narrow shoulders quaked and his chest heaved. His heartfelt sobs cut Duncan to the core.

"I know, sweet son. I know," he crooned in Scottish. "I'm so sorry you're hurt, but we'll fix it. I'll stay right here until you're well. Mrs. Elliott will make you a broonie tomorrow. I'll read you all your favorite stories. You'll be better before you know it."

Malcolm's wracking sobs turned to soft moans and gasping hiccoughs. Careful of the boy's injury, Duncan held him gently, murmuring reassurance and pledging love.

The mattress shifted, and he knew Miriam had stood. He thought about the marks on her palm. "Thank you for staying with my son," he said, his gaze fixed on the indentation in Malcolm's pillow.

She sniffled as if holding back tears. Don't cry, he silently begged; I have enough misery, right here in my arms. Yet a part of him wanted to comfort her and be comforted in return. Another part of him wanted a return to the times when he could leave this castle and his responsibilities, if only for a day, and know his son would be safe. He needed the freedom to sit beside his favorite trout stream and dream of finding a woman to share his bounty. He deserved the time to exercise his God-given right to teach his son the importance of dreaming.

He needed a woman to bring the dreams to life. A woman like Miriam.

"I'll just say good night, then." Anguish lent a husky quality to her voice.

Duncan hardened his heart to the woman who could force him to yield up his son to Baron Sinclair. "Good night."

Malcolm whispered, "'Night, Lady Miriam."

Miriam roused Mrs. Elliott, who patted Malcolm's head and gave Duncan's shoulder a gentle squeeze. "Wake me," she said, "should you need me."

Duncan heard them leave, the door clicking shut behind them. Then he rocked his son to sleep and settled in for the longest night of his life.

Near dawn, when Malcolm had fallen into a deep sleep, Duncan eased from the room and visited the butcher. Then he went to the empty quarters of Angus MacDodd. He pulled the cape of the Border Lord from the trunk and prepared his revenge for Miriam MacDonald.

He spent the morning with Malcolm, who was faring much better than expected. The lad ate three scones, slathered with butter and honey, and insisted Saladin be allowed to visit him. He offered only a token resistance when the midwife returned to change his dressings. As the fresh cloths soaked in a cool decoction of coltsfoot and mugwort were applied to his tender and swollen parts, the boy actually sighed, dropped his head on the pillow, and fell asleep again.

Saladin moved to the window and studied his worn copy of the Koran.

Duncan sent word for Miriam to join him in study.

Considering her parting words and sympathetic mood of the night before, he expected a subdued Miriam. Her squared shoulders, draped in a lively tartan shawl, and her blunt, "You asked to see me, my lord?" brought him up short.

Had she worn her clan colors to distract him? He found himself murmuring, "Won't you take a seat?" while staring at the slender column of her neck and the nicely scooped bodice of her yellow taffeta gown. As she crossed the room, the rustling of the crisp fabric vibrated in his ears and reminded him of other times, of breathless intimate moments in pitch dark places and the sounds of clothing hastily discarded.

His unexpected awareness of her femininity and the predictable response of his manly parts made him glad he'd chosen to conduct the interview from behind his desk rather than the chairs before the hearth. The spectacles, too, offered a small refuge from the allure of Miriam MacDonald.

He was pleased and encouraged to find her staring at his golden hair. "Thank you, Miriam, for coming so quickly."

"'Twas quite fortuitous, actually." She gave him a charming smile, the one she probably bestowed on the king of France before convincing him to abandon the Stewarts and recognize the Hanoverians. "I had planned to ask for a few moments of your time today anyway."

"You sound so formal, Miriam. Have you come seeking another concession from me?"

She stared at her wounded palm. "I know you're upset over what Alpin did to Malcolm. I don't think anyone suspected their enmity to go so far. They bickered at first, but their childish arguing gave me no cause for alarm. You mustn't take for gospel what the midwife said about his never fathering children. Only time will tell."

She summoned confidence as easily as she twisted words. But he knew her better now. Picking his way through the tangle of her assurances, he gleaned a curious aspect in her message: In his absence she thought it her duty to protect what was his.

And in so doing, she had fulfilled one of his basic needs. Perhaps he'd been hasty in blaming her. Maybe there was hope for them yet.

"I was hoping you'd understand, Duncan."

Of course you were, he thought, damning himself for forgetting how clever she could be. "I do understand, Miriam. Completely. Now what did you wish to see me about?"

"Two things. First you were correct about those two men the baron employs. Mrs. Lindsay identified them."

"Where are they now?"

"The baron promised to hand them over to the magistrate."

"You believe him?"

"I'm testing him."

She sounded so composed. But Duncan didn't care; he'd see the men were punished. "What else?"

She strummed her fingers on the arm of the chair. "I think you should speak now."

"Why?"

"The other thing I have to say shouldn't be difficult for me, but I find myself in the odd position of being prejudiced. I've come to cherish our friendship, and what I have to say affects you personally, and your future. So, please." She gave him a blinding smile. "Go ahead."

Second thoughts deluged him. But he'd cast the die,

figuratively, when he'd visited the butcher's shop. Now he picked up the package, but when she held out her hands for it, he couldn't bring himself to break her heart just yet. "No." He tossed the bundle to the floor. "I insist that you go ahead. Ladies and all that."

"You won't like what I've been asked to propose."

Plainly said, the statement piqued his interest. He lifted his eyebrows and tried a little diplomacy of his own. "We're friends, Miriam. I trust you."

She lowered her chin, giving him a perfect view of the glorious crown of braids resting atop her head. The style lent an elegance to her fiery beauty. The Glencoe plaid spoke poignantly of the miracle that had spared her life. But the blush creeping up her cheeks caught him off guard. Why would the mention of friendship and trust inspire so maidenly a reaction in the world-wise Miriam MacDonald? Now he was desperate to know what she had on her mind. "Please. I insist that you tell me."

She cleared her throat and locked her gaze to his. "As you know, the baron is truly anxious for peace between you and him."

Bitterness filled Duncan; she was back to business again. "Certainly. That's why he brought Alpin yesterday. To show his good faith."

Miriam turned up her hand in entreaty. "She can't help the way she is. You *do* know that Malcolm always tries to kiss her. She's unaccustomed to receiving affection. Most of the time no one even notices her. She doesn't know how to respond to Malcolm."

Duncan saw the tiny half-moon scars on her palm, but refused to be swayed. "I would hardly call loosing hornets on him not knowing how to respond. I think she knew exactly what she was doing."

"Yes, Alpin retaliated, but did you know the baron made her give up her pet rabbit? That was only a cruel example of the treatment she receives every day. He simply can't afford to feed and clothe his poor relations."

Before falling asleep, Malcolm had told Duncan about Hattie, and he sympathized with Alpin's plight. Loyalty to his son won out. "You condone what she did to Malcolm?

You should, since you've unmanned men across the continent with your diplomacy."

She balled her fists. "Of course not. But it has little to do with the baron's state of mind. He honestly wants peace. He's made another . . . gesture of his sincerity toward coming to terms and settling matters that are outstanding between you. So that the trouble will end and you both can get on with your lives, so to speak."

Miriam was babbling. Good Lord, what had the baron proposed? Sinclair's gesture had disconcerted her to the point of robbing her of her normally eloquent repartee. Duncan had to know. "If you keep dancing with words, Miriam, my curiosity will force me to agree."

"No." Her nervous gaze darted from his hair to the lamp on his desk to the tips of her fingers. "I mean, I wasn't trying to force your hand. Not by any means. 'Tis a decision you should make on your own behalf. Should you choose to make it."

Enjoying the devil out of watching her squirm so prettily, he said, "Do you think I should agree?"

She opened her mouth, then closed it. "I couldn't possibly presume to influence you in so . . . so important a decision."

"What," he said, "must I decide?"

She took a deep breath and said, "Whether or not to marry the baron's niece, Caroline."

Stupefied, Duncan slumped in his chair. He'd expected the baron to use any means to gain another foothold in Kildalton and steal Duncan's hard earned wealth. But another marriage? "Preposterous."

Miriam's smile and the lazy way she propped her chin on her palm told him she liked his reaction. But why? If she loved the Border Lord, why would she care whether or not Duncan Kerr married again? He intended to find out. He let his eyes drift out of focus. "I may have been too hasty in my refusal of the lass. I can't even remember what she looks like. Refresh my memory, Miriam."

With her thumb, she rubbed the tips of her fingers. "Caroline's not as tall as I am. She has fair hair and brown eyes and is quite accomplished on the harpsichord."

Her noncommittal tone told him nothing. "One of the women in his household has the voice of an angel, clear and—"

"Not Caroline." She spoke decisively, like the Miriam he knew. "She hardly carries a tune."

He had the strangest and most appealing notion that Miriam didn't want him to like this Caroline. To investigate further, he stared intentionally at Miriam's fine breasts and said, "Is she . . . shapely?"

Clear blue eyes regarded him. "She's quite thin. A regular stick."

"I see. Does she want to marry me?"

"She's most tractable, my lord."

"Who in the baron's household isn't?"

"Alpin."

Caught off guard, Duncan laughed.

"Then you've forgiven her?"

Alpin didn't require his forgiveness, but the careless, self-serving baron would grow old and gray before he crossed the threshold of Kildalton Castle again. Miriam, however, needn't know that.

"Have you, Duncan?"

He had to hedge. "Not enough to jump into a marriage because the baron wants my title for another of his relatives. Besides, I've done my duty to clan Kerr. The next time I marry it will be for love and friendship."

Interest flickered in her eyes. "You will?"

Suddenly wary, he said, "Aye."

"I'll tell the baron. He's having a ball in your honor and Malcolm's. He came yesterday to invite you. Will you go?"

"No. Will you?"

"I must. How is Malcolm today, my lord?"

Her eagerness to be done with the subject of his marrying someone else and traveling to Sinclair's to confirm it brought a smile to Duncan. "He's better, but he mustn't overdo. Saladin is with him. They seem to have become fast friends."

"Saladin doesn't usually make friends. I hope you approve."

Was she testing him? He'd grown so accustomed to considering his answers, he found her casual conversation suspect. He'd test her and see. "I find Saladin a fine young man, and support his friendship with my son. Oh, and I've changed my mind. You may tell the baron I'll consider his proposal."

"You will?" she squeaked, her pretty mouth open in surprise.

Artlessly, he said, "I wouldn't want you to think me uncooperative in the negotiations."

"That's very good of you." She rose and fluffed out her skirt. "I hope you find the woman you want."

Again, dark places and hastily shed clothing came to mind. "Would you care to dine with me tonight?"

She moved toward him, and through the thick lenses she appeared as a blur of yellow taffeta and red and green tartan plaid. "I'd love to, Duncan. With Alexis and Salvador gone—I—well, I'd like very much to dine with you."

He hadn't expected honesty from her. She was lonely, had probably been that way since childhood. The bloody massacre. The bloody tartan of the Border Lord.

A shudder went through Duncan. Like a blow from a cherished hand he realized the cruelty of his plan. Of all the ways to punish her, to hurt her, a blood-soaked tartan topped the list.

How could he have been so thoughtless?

He swiveled and planted both feet on the parcel.

"What's wrong, Duncan? You said that package was for me. Don't tell me you've changed your mind, for I do so love surprises."

Before he could stop her, she yanked the package loose. Too late, he saw her pull on the string. The oil cloth fell away, revealing the tartan cape of the Border Lord, caked in dried pig's blood.

Her knees buckled, and she gripped the edge of his desk for support. "Sweet Saint Ninian," she said, then pressed her lips together. The garment slipped from her hand and fell in a heap on the rug.

The cruelties he'd rehearsed died on his lips.

She swallowed hard, and her disbelieving gaze scoured his face. "You called me here to give me this?"

The reply burned like a fire in his throat.

"Is he . . . dead?"

The unspoken plea in her haunted eyes made Duncan feel like the lowest worm. But he'd gone too far to turn back now. "Aye. I'm sorry." The sorriest wretch in Christendom. "'Twas an accident. A rogue bull charged him. A cowherd found his—found him."

She choked back a sob, and her eyes drifted out of focus. What was she seeing? The answer brought him to his feet—the massacre of her parents. He crushed her to his chest and held on tight. "Don't, Miriam," he begged. "Please don't think about Glencoe."

"I wasn't, really." She rested her head on his shoulder. "I was thinking about Ian dying alone. No one should, you know. Someone ought to be there to honor the passing of a life."

Talons of agony raked Duncan's soul. "As you witnessed your father's?"

She nodded and shivered, her breath fanning his neck. "I'm always cold, you know. That's why I bought the cottage in Bath. The water's warm there all year round."

A little girl orphaned in a frozen Highland glen. A grown woman still shivering at the memory. A heartless bastard who'd carelessly brought her past to life. "Tell me about the cottage."

When he'd held this very special woman in his arms and heard her tale of a Highland tragedy, Duncan had marveled at her strength of will. She gave him reason to marvel again when she sighed and stepped away from him, her chin held high, her dignity a shimmering mantle. "Thank you, Duncan Kerr, for asking. But if you'll excuse me, I—I'll just go to my room. I'd like to be alone with my—" A sad laugh escaped her. "I'd like to be alone."

His arms quivered with the need to pull her back, to hold her and say the words that would take away her pain. But if he told her the truth now, all of it, what would she do? Was she capable of exacting a revenge as painful as the one he had heaped on her? Would spite drive her to send Malcolm to Baron Sinclair?

Duncan didn't know. He'd made a mess of things. But he'd set them right, somehow. Someday he'd win her forgiveness and her love, but if he made one false move, she'd scurry out of his life faster than she'd come into it.

Hating himself, he watched her pick up the tartan and walk from the room. Then he took off his spectacles and dashed into the tunnel. Fast as he could, he raced down the corridor and up the circular stairway to the second floor. Seconds later, he moved the panel aside and pushed open the wardrobe door.

He had just recovered his breath when she entered her bedroom and locked the door.

Like an exotic bird shedding its glorious plumage, she cast off her inherent composure. Her eyes filled with tears; her shoulders slumped. Feet dragging, she made her way to the bed, where she collapsed, the cape clutched to her breast as if it were the lover she mourned.

His own heart breaking, his fists clenched to prevent him from ripping the wardrobe apart to get to her and console her, Duncan listened to her every sob, watched her every movement, and imprinted on his mind the memory of her grief.

When she quieted, he thought she'd cried herself to sleep. But just as he turned to go, she rolled onto her back and stared at the canopy.

"At first, I didn't even know you were there," she said.

Duncan went still. Had she discovered him?

She put the tartan aside and placed both hands on her stomach. "I hadn't even considered that he might give me you."

Her meaning hit Duncan like an ax handle in his gut. He flinched and stifled a groan. At one time he had hoped to impregnate her, had wanted to force her hand.

"I guess I should tell you now, sweet babe, you've a rather odd bird for a mother. I can make peace with France, but I can't be bothered to notice that I've missed my menses. But you won't be neglected, I promise. You'll have Alexis, same as I did, and you'll love her, too. I wonder what she'll say? I know. She'll give me advice on raising you in fourteen languages."

Her bittersweet smile nearly broke Duncan's heart. She'd just been told of the death of her lover, and instead of cursing him for leaving her pregnant, she found strength and comfort in impending motherhood.

His child.

"I wonder," she said, drawing up her knees and putting her hands behind her head. "Do you think I should move to Bath and live in disgrace, little babe? Or should I find you a father?"

He bloody well has a father, Duncan wanted to yell.

"I'll tell you about the Border Lord one day, when you're older—" A sharp sob halted her. "That's another thing you should know about me, sweet babe. I'm not at all skilled at catching men. I mean, I have been courted, but the men usually have political matters on their minds and not romance."

That will change, Miriam. I promise you.

He carefully closed the panel and walked to his study. With every step, he thought of a way to woo her. By the time he was done courting Miriam MacDonald, he'd have her convinced she was the greatest catch since Elizabeth Tudor.

Katharina the shrew had been a better catch than Miriam MacDonald. Yet it was up to her to find a Petruchio of her own.

As she sat in front of the hearth in her chamber and brushed her hair dry, Miriam thought of the odd twists and turns her life had taken and how they had affected her future.

While other young girls plied their needles and perfected their fan waving, Miriam had packed up her perfect memory and plied her diplomatic wares. Her only valuables stemmed from years of poorly rewarded service to a country she seldom saw and a queen she didn't respect.

For dowry, Miriam could offer her husband a charming cottage in Bath. Rather than a bride's chest of delicately embroidered linens, she possessed a serviceable traveling trunk overflowing with a mix-match of gratuities. Among her souvenirs were a silver chalice from the duke of Burgundy, a fur-lined cape of blue velvet from a Prussian prince, and a dozen miniature portraits of noblemen who probably wished they'd never set eyes on Miriam MacDonald.

When she wasn't haggling for better trade routes or bargaining for peace, she negotiated marriage contracts. Beneath the ceremony and the business she convinced a groom to take a woman or sometimes a child to wife. Often the couple had never met.

How many brides had Miriam delivered to the altar? Twenty-six. How many had never considered they were entitled to anything above what their fathers had provided or beyond what their future husbands offered? Twenty-six.

Miriam always managed a bit more for the women: an annual visit home to Kent for the new duchess of Orleans; a stipend for an aging nun who had cared for the new countess of Vendee; a dovecote and greenhouse for the second wife of King Ahmed III.

What boon would she negotiate for herself? A name and legitimacy for the child of the Border Lord.

Melancholy sapped her strength. Her shoulders slumped and the silver-backed brush grew heavy in her hand. She raked her thumb over the boar bristles until her skin tingled. After loving a man of passion and having her heart ground to dust, she didn't want to think about matrimony. Sorrow turned to anger. Why hadn't he seen the charging bull? He should have taken more care of himself, for her sake and the sake of their child. How could he have been so thoughtless to leave her and their child? A child he'd never comfort, a life he wouldn't share, a happiness he'd never know. Then again, he'd never promised her anything. Who's to say he would have married her?

Yet when she searched her heart and scoured her memory for images of her dark lover, she saw an elusive man shrouded in mystery. Were it not for the babe in her womb, Miriam wondered if she might have imagined her Lancelot and the wild nights they had shared.

Tears threatened, prickling her eyes and tightening her throat. She took a deep breath. She must forget her grief and think of the future. She needed an understanding and reasonable man who didn't mind damaged goods and was willing to look the other way if her lying-in cut their honeymoon short. Like a well provisioned raft in a sea of broken dreams, the quest for so princely a fellow offered sad hope for her future.

But first she had to finish her work in the Borders. So she put aside her private troubles, completed her toilet and donned a heavy wool gown, then joined the earl in the keeping room.

Duncan smiled shyly and indicated a table set for two near the fireplace. "I asked Mrs. Elliott to serve us here. 'Tis warmer—what with all the snow outside. I thought we might visit first."

"How very thoughtful of you to remember that I hate the cold."

He escorted her to a chair. "I call it a Lowlander's perfection of Highland hospitality."

Once seated, she watched him stroll across the room and return with a bottle of wine. Since learning battle skills, he carried himself with a casual, yet commanding grace, his well-muscled calves neatly encased in cabled stockings that were gartered just below his bare knees. A white silk shirt with billowing sleeves set off to perfection the masculine elegance of his Kerr plaid. Wrapped in the formal fashion normally reserved for a dress affair, the tartan was tightly belted at his waist, the end draped in a generous fold over his shoulder and secured there with a brooch bearing the blazing sun of his clan. A magnificent beaver sporran, ornamented with golden tassels and a jeweled clasp, dangled from a heavy chain and lay in manly splendor against his groin.

Womanly heat spiraled through her, and with newly acquired experience she thought of what lay beneath his chieftain's pouch. The lustful reaction surprised and disgusted Miriam. No broken-hearted waif cruelly abandoned by an ill-fated lover, she responded to the earl of Kildalton with the zest of a fickle femme jilted by a passing swain. She was supposed to be grieving for the Border Lord, the man she had loved with all her heart.

The earl smiled and tucked a wayward strand of honey-colored hair behind his ear. Then he took his seat and removed his spectacles.

She stared, stunned, at the symmetry and bright green color of his eyes. The thick lenses hadn't exaggerated the length of his lashes, for they almost touched his eyebrows. "You look very different without those."

He rolled the wire stem between his thumb and forefinger, setting the glasses twirling like a whirligig. "I see differently without them, too."

Softly spoken, the vague statement contained a wealth of intimacy. "Oh?"

"Aye." He put the spectacles aside and pulled the cork from the bottle. Red wine sloshed loudly into her goblet. "From this distance I see that you just washed your hair. It shines like polished copper." Filling his own goblet, he added, "Must be the light from the fire."

If she hadn't known better, she might have suspected he had seduction on his mind. But not the earl; he was simply making conversation and befriending her. "It could be Mrs. Elliott's fine soap," Miriam said.

He closed his eyes and breathed deeply, his nostrils gently flaring. "Ah, heather. 'Tis the smell of Scotland, and my second favorite fragrance."

She held up her glass to toast him. "Second? Tell me your first choice."

His eyes drifted open, and though his gaze didn't stray from hers, he reached for his goblet. "Cheers." Pewter clinked against pewter. "The mountain mist. 'Tis an unforgettable and altogether bracing experience for the senses."

"What a coincidence. 'Tis my favorite fragrance, too."

His eyebrows arched. He extended his hand. "Truly? Let me smell."

She offered her arm, her palm up. His fingers closed over her wrist, which looked fragile and pale against his strong and work-worn hand. He leaned over and sniffed, then exhaled. Her hand trembled, her skin tingling from the rush of his warm breath. She stared at the crown of his head. His mane of golden hair shimmered like warm honey in the firelight. How could she have thought he was the Border Lord? Because she loved and missed Ian and was attracted to the earl's fair features and gentle disposition.

Alarmed at her own breathlessness, she said the first thing that popped into her mind. "You're not wearing a wig."

He gave her hand a gentle squeeze before releasing it. "Oh that. At first I thought to gain your favor with fancy dress and refined speech, but—" He shrugged. "Then we became friends, and I learned that you don't judge me for the clothing I wear or the way I speak my words. You're more interested in the person I am and the truths I tell . . . and the ones I stretch a wee bit."

His easy way with conversation warmed her more than the fire. "You look splendid in your tartan." Feeling easy, too, she added, "I remember my father wearing his plaid. He always kept sweets just for me in his sporran."

"Lucky you. Malcolm keeps newts in mine."

She laughed. "Do you know that's the first time I've spoken of my father in a cordial, normal way." The observation pleased her to her soul.

"I do hope you'll tell me more about him and you. Seems I'm always doing the talking."

It wasn't true, but the comment reminded her again of how much diplomacy Duncan Kerr had learned. She sought a safe, but friendly subject. "That's not the same sporran I've seen Malcolm with."

"Oh, no. My ancestors would rise from the dead and throw me off the family throne if I let him get his foosty hands on so prized a piece of Scottish finery."

"But you'll give it to him someday, and he'll pass it on to his son."

"Maybe." He took a long drink of the wine. The corded muscles in his throat rippled as he swallowed.

Her own mouth grew dry. "You mustn't take for gospel what the midwife said about Malcolm not being able to sire children. The eastern countries have made a science of health and medicine. There are fine physicians here, too. A doctor in Edinburgh will know better about such things."

"Well," he said with finality. "'Tis a bit early yet to worry over . . . such things."

"But surely you have cause to worry. Heirs are vital to a man of your position."

"May I speak frankly, Miriam?"

He might have asked if she liked the wine, so casual was his question. Naturally she said, "Please do."

Pushing the dinner plate aside, he propped his elbows on the table. "I think too much importance is put on the getting of heirs and too little on the feelings and happiness of the people involved. Take virginity, for instance. If a man is so desperate for bairns of his own blood, why take to wife an unproven breeder?" He set down the goblet and traced the rim with the tip of his index finger. "No decent or intelligent man should refuse to take a woman to wife because she'd fulfilled one of the roles God created her for. 'Tis my belief that a prospective husband should rejoice in finding such a woman."

How sweet and logical a man he was. She only hoped he wasn't unique, for she needed a man who shared his progressive philosophy. "I'm sorry to tell you most men are advocates of bridal purity."

"They're also fiends for gambling and bear-baiting. But not Duncan Amstrong Kerr. True, I'd love a castleful of lads and lassies, but 'tis unfair to expect a virgin to know if she can deliver them safely. 'Tis also dangerous for a woman to conceive too often."

He was thinking of his dead wife. Miriam's heart went out to him. "I'm sorry about Roxanne."

Tenderness glowed warmly in his eyes. "Don't be sad for the lass. She died doing the thing that made her life worthwhile. She wanted Malcolm more than . . . more than England wants Scotland. Or more than I want peace in the Border."

Miriam could have reminded him that the Act of Union had settled the matter of Scotland's sovereignty, but she wouldn't risk losing their congeniality. "You'll have peace here, Duncan. I promise you."

"I'll have my son, too. I trow you'll find a way for me to keep him."

Suddenly wary of his overconfidence in her limited abilities, Miriam took his hand. "Please don't expect too much. The people who govern this land and advise our queen see children as faceless pieces of property. Twice last year, our queen used children as hostages to gain peace between bickering families."

Lines of worry creased his forehead. "What families?"

She had no intention of compromising her integrity, even for a man she had come to admire. "The names aren't important. Neither is their rank. Just remember that because of the queen's chronic illnesses, she often acts rashly."

"If you ask me, I think she takes that old Stewart belief in the divine right of kings too far—a poor legacy from so noble and mighty a clan. I swear to you, Miriam, the next time I marry, I'll take an orphan to wife. I've had enough of troubles with in-laws to last three lifetimes."

Pray she found a man who shared his belief on that matter, too. "What about family loyalty? Won't you miss that?"

He stared into the fire. The reflection of the yellow flames danced in his green eyes and changed the color to blue. Changeable, she realized, had become her byword for Duncan Kerr.

"Children," he said, "should be taught respect for their elders, but they shouldna be burdened or prejudiced by their parents' opinions. Who knows? When Malcolm comes of age he may make a friend of Aubrey Townsend. Just because the baron and I have problems doesna mean that Malcolm will. I'm determined never to influence him in this. He'll pick his own friends and make his own enemies."

Miriam grew defensive, thinking about the atrocity the Glenlyon Campbells had visited on her parents and the misery she'd suffered as a result. "What of crimes that go unpunished? The law isn't always fair, and the courts are not always just. You of all people should understand that—considering your association with Avery Chilton-Wall."

"Thanks to you, the point is moot here in the Borders. The Highlands doona fare so well. Revenge and the passing of hatred from father to son are weakening the clan system. Ultimately they'll destroy it."

She understood and agreed with the principle behind his philosophy, but her particular case was different. Wasn't it?

"What are you thinking?" he asked.

Oddly she wanted to explain why it was so important to her that the Glenlyon Campbells pay for their crimes against the Glencoe MacDonalds. Odder still, the old argument sounded shallow. Confused, she chose another benign topic. "I was thinking about how much I like the wine."

He looked away, but not before she saw disappointment cloud his eyes. "I'm delighted it meets with your approval," he said, pained sarcasm in his voice.

Now was not the time to examine the reasons behind his

withdrawal or to apologize for keeping her problems to herself. So she sent her mind darting through the maze of his predicament and saw a possible solution. "I have an idea."

He poured more wine. "I'm listening. I love ideas—especially yours."

"Could you build a new residence on Malcolm's property in Northumberland—on Roxanne's dowry land? Nothing elaborate, but an estate large enough to support a modest household and a small garrison of soldiers."

His piercing gaze searched her face. "Aye, but what good would that do?"

"The baron complained to Her Majesty that you deprived him of Malcolm's company. If your son had his own place, one in close proximity to the baron's land, then Malcolm could go there from time to time—say on rent days. Sinclair could visit. He'd have no cause for complaint on that score."

Duncan's shoulders drooped. "Nay, but I would complain. What if the baron moves in and brings his household with him? That's the same as Malcolm living at Sinclair Manor."

"No, it's not. Not if the new estate is small."

Duncan grinned and snapped his fingers. "Of course. You're brilliant, Miriam. I'll design the doorways this high." He held out his flattened palm to a height that would hardly reach the waist of the towering baron. "I'll even build it near the road and offer to keep a fresh team of horses for the mail coach."

Although caught up in his exuberance, she forced herself to say, "Please understand, Duncan, that I'm not promising it will sway the queen. But I think she will see your good intentions behind the gesture. You'd also be practicing what you just preached about allowing Malcolm to develop his own relationship with the baron."

"I stand by my beliefs." He slapped his hand over his clan badge. "I do think your plan will work. But, please understand, Miriam, I love my son, and I intend to be a father to him."

A father. By modern standards the term was at best ambiguous. Most men never set foot in a nursery, and when their sons were old enough, they were fostered or shipped off to school. Not until they were adults and eligible for membership in the fashionable clubs did sons gain a passing knowledge of their sires. "I'll do my very best to help you maintain that right."

He sighed in relief, and passed a hand over his forehead. "Thank you. You may forget I said I'd consider marrying the baron's niece. My conscience won't allow me to use the girl."

Miriam, too, felt relief; a man as kind as Duncan Kerr deserved to choose his own wife. A voice inside her said take me, Duncan, take me. But it was just her broken heart pleading for comfort. "I think that's a wise choice."

He almost beamed. "As soon as we've eaten, I think we should tell Malcolm that his estates are about to double."

"You mean we'll tell Saint Francis of Assisi. That's who he's chosen today."

Chuckling, Duncan said, "Aye, and he wrote a very nice essay on the good friar. It seems he's extended his position as caretaker of Hattie, who has taken up residence under his bed. He's now lord high protector of the animal kingdom."

"I'll tell Alpin when I see her." Miriam waved a hand over the empty plates. "What are we having tonight?"

He winced. "The cook planned the menu prior to the arrival of Hattie. We're having braised wild hare and carrots."

Miriam smiled. "Do the carrots have the tops on?"

Playfully, he wagged his finger at her. "Malcolm told me about Hattie's diet, and you, Miriam MacDonald, have a delightful, if dark, sense of humor."

Happiness coiled inside her, and she basked in the glow of their friendship. During the course of the meal they talked of everything from French wine to Roman architecture. Duncan complained that the baron made a practice of tearing down portions of Hadrian's Wall whenever the stone fences on his land needed mending.

Later she and Duncan visited Malcolm. Dressed in a plain gray robe, he knelt on the bed. Saladin sat cross-legged facing him. The scribe expounded on the spiritual rewards and humanitarian benefits of the Muslim way of life. Malcolm, in his role of devoted friar, lectured on the humanitarian rewards and spiritual benefits of perfect poverty.

Upon hearing of the proposed castle, Malcolm merely shrugged and said a new house was fine with him, so long as it had a very large stable . . . "to shelter God's creatures. Be sure to build a dungeon in it, Papa . . . for Alpin."

For the next week, Miriam often found herself in the company of the earl of Kildalton. Every morning, under the charming pretense of walking Verbatim, he meandered across the snow-covered yard to remind the soldiers to keep a lookout for a messenger from the queen. He smiled and chatted in the friendliest of ways, but Miriam knew that beneath the cordial exterior he agonized over the possibility of losing his son. Without giving him false hope, she did her best to ease his torment.

Most afternoons they spent before a roaring fire in the keeping room. She learned he had a ravenous sweet tooth, and he insisted she share the many confections the kitchen staff prepared. Miriam needed little coaxing, for along with her delicate condition came an insatiable appetite.

Once he'd settled on a design for Malcolm's second home and sent for a surveyor, Duncan turned his attention to playing chess or cards with Miriam or sharing a book from his library. Day by day, Malcolm grew better but declined to leave his room. Saladin stayed with him.

Night after night, Miriam curled up in her lonely bed, and when treasured memories of her lost love robbed her of sleep, she sought solace in one-sided conversations with the child. As strange as it seemed, she often felt the Border Lord's comfort, and sometimes in the dark of night, she actually sensed her lover's presence in the room.

I'll be in your heart, love, and in every breath you take.

By all rights she should be desperate, mired as she was in the worst of life's circumstances. To the contrary, she felt at peace. She had a friend in Duncan Kerr. Motherhood loomed ahead. She'd find a decent husband; London was rife with possibilities. Everything would work out.

On Sunday, Duncan insisted she accompany him to church. When she politely declined, he folded his arms over his chest and tapped his booted foot.

"Why won't you go? Are you a Muslim, too?"

Flabbergasted at his absurdity, she blurted, "I don't like the cold—especially the snow."

"Neither do I," he said. "But 'tis quite lovely out, and I have a sleigh."

"A sleigh? How progressive of you. Imagine that, a troika in England."

"Scotland," he corrected.

"I take back what I said about progress. You're no free thinker."

"Nothing's free, Miriam." He jiggled his eyebrows. "But we could negotiate. I've learned a trick or two from you."

His bravado made her chuckle. "Be my guest, Duncan. What have you to offer?"

"I have the aforementioned sleigh, pulled by a trio of hairy-legged horses from the dales of Clyde. I had the farrier outfit the beasts with bells and blinders. Mrs. Elliott has stuffed a basket with enough food and drink to make a Frenchman forsake his homeland. The stableman put warmed bricks in the floor of our fine conveyance, and it's piled mountain-high with furs and tartans."

The invitation in his eyes tempted her more than his words. "An admirable presentation, Duncan. But I had my fill of sleigh rides in Russia."

"Scotland," he said indignantly, "is hardly Russia. I'll show you a family of badgers. We'll tiptoe to a special clearing and watch the deer feed. Come on, Miriam. Say aye. No one else will ride in it with me. 'Tis no fun to frolic alone in a sleigh big enough for a butcher's family. We'll even take Verbatim. She needs the exercise."

His charming speech robbed Miriam of objections. Besides, she had always wanted to conquer her fear of winter. Who better to face it with than her new friend, Duncan Kerr?

True to his word, Duncan had seen to her every comfort. She sat buried to her chin in an enormous pile of furs. The heated bricks warmed her feet; the good man beside her warmed her heart. The peaceful, pristine morning came alive with the jingling of sleigh bells and the whoosh of runners over the frozen road. Verbatim loped alongside the team until a scent caught her interest. Nose down, tail up, the sleuthhound dashed after her quarry, kicking up snow and leaving a distinctive trail in the winter carpet that blanketed the land.

When the towers of Kildalton faded from view and the world turned white from horizon to horizon, Miriam grew apprehensive. Duncan must have sensed her fear, for he pointed out dozens of landmarks and explained in detail the route and distance they traveled. Then under the guise of playing Malcolm's favorite guessing game, he quizzed her on finding her way home. The simple drill occupied her mind, and with ease she answered every question correctly. But the reassurance and praise of the man soothed her fears more than her perfect recall of the knowledge he imparted.

After the church service, he offered sleigh rides to the children of Kildalton. They held back, their eyes huge with fear of the modern contraption and the giant horses.

Sensing his disappointment, Miriam addressed the crowd of youngsters. "Children in Russia aren't afraid of sleighs. Sometimes they drag them into the house and use them for beds."

Mary Elizabeth, the girl Verbatim had rescued, held up her arms and declared, "I'm as brave as any Russian lass. Take me first."

With great melodrama, Duncan pointed his toe, swept off his chieftain's bonnet, and bowed deeply. "'Twould be my absolute pleasure, Mistress Mary."

The girl giggled. He swung her in the air and deposited her atop the mountain of furs. The older lads mimicked his courtly manners and assisted the other lassies into the sleigh, then whooped and whistled and clamored into the conveyance. They spent the day traversing the countryside and singing country songs. Mary Elizabeth presented Verbatim with a collar of dried rowan berries strung on a stout cord. Miriam received a fragrant garland of evergreen. Duncan was presented a crown of dried heather and proclaimed the High King of Winter.

Just as the sun began to slip below the horizon, Miriam and Duncan returned to Kildalton. The bronze glow of twilight lent a peaceful air to their homecoming. The mellow atmosphere was shattered when Miriam spied a herald pacing the castle yard, his royal blue jerkin emblazoned with the queen's coat of arms.

A weight settled about her shoulders. Her work would begin now. She must sharpen her knives of logic and carve out a compromise. She could reach Duncan. She could manipulate the baron. Whittling away at the divine right of a Stewart required a careful balance of tact and aggression.

She reached for Duncan. "The herald's name is Evan Givins."

The flush of cold faded from Duncan's face. He exhaled, his breath clouding the icy air. "You know him? You've . . . met him before?"

Turning toward him, she leaned forward so he could see her face. "I've worked with him, Duncan. He's a good man and trustworthy. Please remember, he's only a messenger. I'm certain if it were up to him, he'd rather be sitting by the fire in the Cock and Bottle Tavern, quaffing a pint of stout."

Fists clutching the reins, Duncan twisted his wrists to slow the team. The sleigh skidded to a halt. Verbatim dashed up the stairs to greet the newcomer.

"I cannot say I'm sorry he's here," said Duncan. "'Tis better done quickly, you ken?"

Was he ready to be rid of her? No, her heart cried. What will we do? Her mind demanded. We'll do what's expected of us. "Aye, I ken," she said. "Try not to worry."

His piercing gaze searched hers. "If you think I won't, Miriam MacDonald, then you've a wee bit to learn about me."

She had about a million things to learn about him. Pity she wouldn't get the chance. Her search for a husband must take precedence over friendship. If only he would marry her. She squelched the thought. A man of his noble stature would demand too great a dowry. "Trust me," she whispered.

On shaky legs, Duncan stepped from the sleigh. Trust her. He wanted to. Christ, he wanted to. Miriam MacDonald tempted him. Her confidence lured him. The woman herself captured his heart.

He grasped her around the waist and lowered her to the ground. Half his mind focused on the child she carried; the other half on the child upstairs. He escorted her up the main steps and stood transfixed by fear as she accepted the leather pouch. Duncan fought the urge to rip it out of her hands. Instead, he said, "I'll be waiting in my study."

He watched her enter the castle and disappear up the stairs, the sleuthhound at her side. After asking Mrs. Elliott to see to the comfort of the herald, Duncan made his way to his study, poured himself a brandy, and sat before the fire.

He'd known the queen's messenger was coming. He'd agonized over the herald's arrival. But out of consideration for Miriam, he'd hidden his concern. She hadn't suspected that his generosity in offering to walk the sleuthhound had been a guise. Every morning, the dog at his side, he'd gone to Alexander Lindsay and reminded the soldier to keep a sharp lookout for the herald.

Duncan searched his soul for regrets, for mistakes in his actions toward Sinclair, but even given the chance to relive the last ten years, he could think of nothing he would have changed. Within the bounds of his own good conscience, he'd acted reasonably. He'd never taken a life. In the same circumstances, his father would have cut a bloody swath through the villages of Sinclair and left with the baron's head on a pike. For a decade, Duncan had fought the demons of his upbringing and stretched his patience to the breaking point. Not once had he forsaken his principles. True, he'd resurrected the legend of the Border Lord to reclaim his property. Yes, he'd frightened English tenants. But never had he considered raising the quarrel to bloodshed.

For hours, he wrestled with the events of his past and brooded over his uncertain future with the woman upstairs. He wanted to tell her the truth, that he'd seduced her as the Border Lord and tricked her as Duncan Kerr. He wanted to confess that in either role he loved her to distraction, would love her always, even if the queen took away his son. But if he told Miriam now, she might react in anger. He couldn't jeopardize Malcolm's future. He couldn't bear the thought of losing her.

Weary, he closed his eyes and fell asleep.

A mist swirled around him, concealing him and his hiding place. "Come out, Duncan." He heard his father yell.

"You'll learn to wield a broadsword, and you'll learn now, laddie. Or I swear by Saint Columba, I'll blister your buttocks. You'll not walk for a fortnight."

The tramp of booted feet came closer. "Come here, Duncan," growled the voice of Kenneth Kerr. "Or you'll never see your son again."

"Duncan?"

The sound of her voice jarred him awake. A dream. It had only been a nightmare. Kenneth Kerr was dead. He couldn't touch Malcolm.

"Duncan?"

Miriam stood over him, a worried frown scoring her forehead, exhaustion dulling the luster in her eyes. Behind her, the windows glared like blackened doors. He wanted to reach out for her, to comfort and be comforted in return. Not yet.

"What time is it?" he asked.

"Four o'clock in the morning."

Shaking off sleep, he stretched and got to his feet. "Are you all right? Have you been up all this time?"

"I'm fine. I had work to do." She studied her hands. "I don't require as much sleep as other people."

He thought about the child she carried. "You should rest."

"I'm leaving for Baron Sinclair's as soon as it's light."

Duncan couldn't bring himself to ask what the queen had said, not when Miriam hadn't had any sleep, not when the coward inside him snatched his courage, not when he wanted to hold her, love her until she cried out his name and agreed to become his wife.

But she wouldn't call out the name he wanted to hear. She'd call out for her lover, Ian. "Miriam . . ."

"Sit down, Duncan."

Her businesslike mien and the ominous tone of her voice rattled his fears to life and sapped his strength. He plopped down in the chair. "What did the queen write to you?"

She began to pace. "I don't often make friends of the . . . of the people I'm sent to . . . to negotiate with. You ken?"

Her hesitation tied his gut into knots. Love for her was tearing him to pieces. Where in hell did she get so much strength? "Aye, lassie. I ken."

"As your friend, I will do my best to sway the queen. But as a servant of the crown I can go only so far."

Oh, God. Anne had ruled against him. "Why did she decide to enforce the codicil to Roxanne's will and let the baron foster my son?"

Anguish flickered in her eyes. "Please don't ask."

A life of now-meaningless struggles lay behind him. He'd wasted his time fighting the demons of his blood. "She thinks I'm like my father."

In a pool of pale gray wool, Miriam knelt beside his chair. "I'll find a way to prove you're nothing like Kenneth Kerr."

Crestfallen, Duncan took her hand. Her skin was icy cold. Was her heart the same? He had to warm her. "I'm worried about you, Miriam. You're chilled. You're exhausted." He longed to say, you're pregnant with our child. But he couldn't. Not yet. So he did his best. "I'll go with you to Sinclair's."

"Thank you, but no."

"What will you do there?"

She opened her mouth, then closed it. Reluctantly, she said, "I'm really very good at negotiating, especially with hard evidence. That's what I'll look for."

"Evidence against the baron?"

"Yes. I'll also decline the marriage offer and attend the ball in your honor. You stay with Malcolm."

Did she always work so hard? Taking her other hand, he rubbed them both. He studied her closely, but she so expertly masked her feelings, he saw only her serene beauty, her strength of character. How could he hope to make a life with her if he couldn't see what she was thinking? He looked deeper into her eyes, behind the intelligence, past the intense concentration. "You might need me more."

"Thank you, but no." She sighed and closed her eyes. But in that brief instant he saw vulnerability and affection.

It gave him hope. He said, "Malcolm's a sturdy lad, and healing well."

Her lips curled in a practiced smile, but no humor reached her eyes. "Then he'll need your company all the more." Quietly she added, "Saladin and Mr. Givins must go with me."

Frustration made him clutch her hands tightly. "I canna

sit back and make flippity-flops while you ruin my son's future."

She didn't wince, but a softening of her expression told him she understood. "An interesting predicament, since I'm accustomed to working alone and with great success."

She'd probably done too many things alone in her life. Duncan intended to change that and much more. "You'll be afraid in the snow. I'll send a guard with you."

She lifted her chin. "I would appreciate an escort."

He recalled the night long ago when she'd rescued the lost Mary Elizabeth and returned in triumph. The people of Kildalton had taken her to their hearts. In the alehouse, the patrons had amended the drinking songs in honor of her bravery. Mrs. Elliott had lectured him on the dangers of deceit. Angus had advised him to move cautiously with Miriam.

"None of my men can drive the sleigh."

"Duncan, I can drive it as well as I drive a carriage."

Thwarted, and angry because he felt her slipping away, he demanded, "Is there anything you don't do well?"

She gave him an enchanting smile. "'Twould take a lifetime to confess all of my shortcomings." She pulled her hands free and stood.

Duncan watched her go, her head held high, her shoulders squared, his child in her belly, his fate in her hands.

A torturous three days later, she returned.

Duncan stared, stupefied at what she'd brought with her.

18

Miriam's hands and fingers cramped from gripping the reins and controlling the huge horses. Beyond the physical discomfort of the journey, she felt torn by conflicting emotions. As she guided the sleigh through the gates of Kildalton, a bittersweet sense of homecoming lifted her spirits. But her heart ached for the sight of the Border Lord.

At their first meeting he'd sworn she could never bring the earl and the baron to accord, not while both men lived. She'd proved him wrong; yet he'd been the one to die.

Grief diluted her pride and her sense of accomplishment. Loneliness crept in. Following a ritual she'd devised of late to chase the doldrums away, she found strength in happy thoughts of the babe she carried. One day she might bring her child to the Borders.

The eerie silence in the castle yard snatched her attention. At one time she'd passed through these gates and received a hero's welcome for rescuing a little lost girl. Now, the people of Kildalton milled about in small groups and cast worried glances her way. Only the children waved. When the blacksmith's son called out to Verbatim and made a move toward the hound, his father stopped him with a stern command.

Miriam eased back on the reins. The sleigh skidded to a halt, jostling the unusual cargo. The caged badger hissed a protest. Bleating in alarm, the lamb poked his head from beneath the furs and stared with sightless eyes. Alpin's creatures.

The double doors of the castle opened. Duncan emerged, his shoulder-length fair hair rustling in the crisp winter breeze, his eyes filled with eagerness and fastened on Miriam. Mrs. Elliott stood stoically behind him, her hands clasped.

He started down the steps, tension lending dignity to his noble bearing. Originally, he'd stumbled and appeared ill at ease with the world. Today he looked as if he owned it. Bully for him, she thought, for if the queen rejected Miriam's latest plea, he'd need all the confidence he could muster.

Alexander Lindsay helped Miriam from the sleigh. Saladin dismounted and came to her side.

His fists clenched, his intense gaze still riveted to her, Duncan said, "What happened?"

Exhaustion seeped into her bones, disappointment her soul. The diplomat who'd labored on his behalf now rebelled at his insensitivity. The foolish woman who'd let friendship influence her judgment suddenly cringed at his indifference. She'd only been gone three days, but evidently long enough to make him forget the closeness they'd shared. "Could we go inside, my lord?" she said. "I'm cold, and I'd like to sit on something that doesn't slip and slide beneath me."

His expression softened. "Of course you would, and I'm a sorry, selfish Scotsman." He took her hand and led her up the stairs. "I'm very glad to see you, Miriam."

"My lady . . ." said Saladin. "What shall we do with the animals?"

The earl turned and stared in confusion at the sleigh. Then his eyebrows shot up and his mouth parted. "What are you doing with Alpin's menagerie?"

Miriam wondered how he'd known about Alpin's creatures, but the question seemed both insignificant and inappropriate. Pulling off her gloves, she said, "She asked me to care for them. She's convinced God's Night Angel will spirit her away from Baron Sinclair."

"Her Night Angel . . . ?" Then as if he understood or was distracted, he nodded. "Alexander, take them to the stable and ask the farrier to look after them. And bring him the other horse, too." To Saladin, he said, "Make yourself at home, lad."

Inside the castle, he guided Miriam to his study, then knelt before the hearth and began stoking the coals. She stood beside him, rubbing her hands until her skin tingled, and wondering what she should say first. Staring down at him, she could see his anxiety in the stiff set of his shoulders, in the way he snatched up clods of peat and tossed them on the andiron. The muscles in his thighs bulged, stretching his leather breeches as tight as a second skin. She thought of another man, a dark stranger with powerful thighs and arms strong enough to pin her to a tunnel wall.

Melancholy tightened her chest. She banished thoughts of her dead lover; she had a lifetime to think about Ian. Today she must concentrate on Duncan Kerr. Experience cautioned her to speak formally. Affection for him counseled her otherwise. She chose a little of both. "The herald is on his way to London. I submitted new evidence to the queen. Within a fortnight we should know her mind. Alexis will bring her ruling. Angus and John Hume will accompany her."

He gripped a square of peat so tightly it crumbled. "So, I'm to endure another two weeks of torture."

She almost said, I'll be here with you, but then he murmured, "I doona think my life or my household will ever be normal again."

He was probably referring to her presence and anticipating her departure. Why shouldn't he? Since the day she had arrived, his time hadn't been his own. Against her better judgment, she said, "I'm very confident, my lord."

He looked up, relief glimmering in his eyes. "Why have you stopped calling me Duncan?"

Her mouth went desert dry, and she tried but failed to remember the gist of the conversation. "I assure you. 'Twas an oversight on my part. I must have gotten lost in the circumstances—"

"No rhetoric, Miriam." He dropped the fire iron and stood. "A simple answer, if you please. Why won't you call me Duncan?"

He seemed so forthright and determined, so different from the bumbling earl with feathery lures hooked on his coat and thick spectacles on his nose. But she'd changed, too, since their first meeting. "I thought you would prefer formality."

"What I would prefer," he said, taking her arm and leading her to a chair, "is to raise my son in peace, and to hear you call me Duncan again when you explain about this new evidence and tell me what I can expect from the queen."

She settled in the chair and felt the strain ease in her back. "I found proof that the baron has raided your land. Some of your spotted cattle were penned near his slaughterhouse. I confronted him. He claimed ignorance of the situation. He also set free the two men he promised to turn over to the magistrate. I've ordered him to return what's left of your herd. I'm sorry about the others."

Taking the facing chair, Duncan leaned forward, his arms rested on his knees. "They can be replaced. But what were you doing in a slaughterhouse?"

The loose lacings at the neck of his chamois shirt exposed his throat and offered a view of the curly golden hair that covered his chest. "I was following Verbatim. She actually found them."

"How?"

"'Twas the footstool in Sinclair's library. It was upholstered in a spotted hide."

Duncan's grin made her self-conscious, but she couldn't look away. "You remembered about my cattle," he said.

"Aye."

"Remind me of the beasts if I ever again complain about your memory." He patted her hand. "What else happened?"

Matching his congeniality, Miriam lounged in the chair and stretched her feet toward the fire. "I discovered his destruction of Hadrian's Wall and reported it to the queen."

"Thank you. 'Tis a significant and irreplaceable piece of English history."

Abashed because she hadn't considered the historic value

of the wall, Miriam murmured, "'Tis also on Kildalton land."

He chuckled. "Oh, I see. Your reasoning doesna matter, so long as the wall is safe. But what makes you so confident the queen will change her mind?"

He needn't know about Miriam's bargain with the queen or how much she'd learned from him about the cruelty of prejudice and the destruction of carrying a grudge. Or did he? She studied his face, his open expression of honesty, and his handsomeness, marred only by worry over the future of his son.

"Please," he said softly, resting his chin in his palm. "Tell me."

She took a deep breath. "You made me see the unfairness in bringing to justice the people who murdered my parents."

Surprise smoothed out the creases on his forehead. "Me?"

The words formed easily. "Yes. For many years I've begged the queen to punish the Glenlyon Campbells for what they did to my family. She always refused. The last time, she grew so angry . . ." Embarrassment over her behavior that day stopped Miriam.

"She banished you to the Border," he said with a knowing glint in his eyes.

Miriam felt a burden lift, a burden she hadn't even realized she'd been carrying. "Yes. You're a victim of your father's crimes, same as the children of the Glenlyon Campbells will become scapegoats for their parents' villainy. Those men who took my parents' lives, they're old now. I like to think they've suffered all these years."

"You certainly have."

"No more. I've explained my feelings to Her Majesty. I think she'll see the parallel between your life and mine and agree that you're a good man, Duncan Kerr."

His eyes misted over. "I don't know what to say."

Warmed to her heart, Miriam smiled. "You needn't say anything—not yet, for I also told the queen what you said about letting Malcolm develop his own friendship with the baron. I expect she'll admire you for that. I also told her about Malcolm's new castle."

He nearly choked. "Castle? I can't afford another castle. I commissioned a modest manor house."

With the difficult part of the conversation behind her, Miriam sought to lighten his mood. "Oh, but I assured her you wouldn't hear of skimping on the place. I envisioned a moat, a brass-studded drawbridge, modern plumbing—even a fully equipped stable and spacious accommodations for the mail coach." At his pained expression, she added, "Did I mention the church with stained glass windows and padded velvet pews? Or the furnished parsonage with window boxes and a vegetable garden?"

His eyes narrowed and he wagged a finger at her. "You're joking, Miriam."

She was, but with the humor came the sad realization that she'd probably never see Malcolm's second home or ever learn if as an adult he made a friend of Baron Sinclair.

Sometime after midnight she awoke, and as she stared at the glowing coals in the fireplace, she again felt a presence nearby. Verbatim lay curled before the hearth. The wardrobe doors stood open, the drapes closed. Nothing was amiss. When the feeling persisted, Miriam called to the dog. "Search, girl," she said.

The sleuthhound sprang to her feet and trotted to the wardrobe, where she whined and held up a paw.

"No, Verbatim. 'Tis not time for a walk. I told you to search the room."

As if confused, the dog cocked her head and whined again.

"Oh, go back to sleep," Miriam grumbled. Then she fluffed her pillow and followed her own advice.

A bar of winter sunlight fell over the carpeted floor when next she awakened. Out of habit, she glanced toward the door and smiled when she saw a familiar scrap of paper. Out of propriety, she stifled a laugh when she joined Saladin and Malcolm at the breakfast table.

Resplendent in a blue velvet suit with a length of lace tied at his neck and draping his shoulders, Malcolm had used ashes to sketch a mustache and pointed beard on his face. To complete his imitation of Charles I, he wore a parchment crown and pitched scraps of bread to a pack of terriers.

"Good morning, Your Majesty. I trust you've fully recovered." Miriam curtsied and sat at the bench across from Saladin.

Malcolm piped, "I still got my head too, for now."

"What delightful pets." Saladin snickered. Miriam stifled a laugh.

"They're supposed to be cavalier spaniels." He nodded regally, flipping the tip of the lace collar into his porridge and toppling his crown. The dogs snapped up the paper creation and, in a frenzy of snarling and yapping, tore it to shreds.

Saladin rolled his eyes and went back to his breakfast of oatcakes, honey, and dried quinces. Miriam poured herself a glass of milk.

Mrs. Elliott dashed into the room. The normally composed housekeeper threw up her hands. Over the barking terriers, she said, "Master Malcolm! Take those dogs back to the kennel where they belong."

He surprised Miriam by gathering the dogs.

The harried housekeeper raked a loose strand of hair off her forehead. "I hope you don't mind bannocks and honey, my lady. I had planned to serve ham, but it's disappeared from the pantry."

"The Roundheads filched it!" declared the departing Malcolm. "Find that scurvy Cromwell and you'll find your ham."

She blew out her breath. "His lordship is inquiring now. He sends his regrets."

Miriam didn't see him until supper, when he informed her that a leg of braised mutton had evidently walked off the cooling rack in the kitchen. To Saladin's delight, they dined on cheese, bread, and barley soup.

After the meal Miriam took Verbatim for her evening walk. They returned to find Mrs. Elliott standing in the foyer. Tied at her waist was a heavy ring of keys Miriam hadn't seen before. She remembered the key she'd taken.

"His lordship would like to see you now, my lady. He's in his chamber." She pointed down the hall. "'Tis just past his study."

Miriam knew well the location of his private chamber;

she'd searched it to find evidence that he was the Border Lord. In retrospect, the idea seemed foolish.

"Thank you." On the matter of the key, she took a direct approach. "Oh, Mrs. Elliott, I have the key to the tunnel door. 'Tis in my room."

"So that's where it got off to," she said, seemingly unsurprised. "We haven't locked doors here since I was milkmaid. Imagine someone at Kildalton stealing food." She patted Verbatim and added, "Sorry, girl. No bone for you tonight."

"I'll just fetch the key, then," Miriam said.

Duncan sat in the throne chair and stared at the door. What was keeping Miriam? If she didn't come soon, he'd botch the whole thing. He tapped his feet. Like an old ragged tartan, his courage began to fray.

When the knock came, he jumped. Then he gathered his gumption and straightened his backbone. "Come in."

She glided into the room, the sleuthhound at her side. The icy night wind had pinkened her cheeks and mussed her fiery hair. Dressed in a gown of pale green, she looked as fresh and as innocent as a maiden in spring. But Miriam MacDonald was no maiden, he'd seen to that right enough. Instinctively, he sought some sign of the child she carried. Her breasts swelled gently above the rounded neckline of the gown, her stomach was still flat where the waistline of the dress dropped to a point in front.

"Is something amiss, Duncan?" She fluffed out her skirts and examined the fabric. "Have I spilled soup on my gown?" She lifted a mass of curls from her neck. "Have I leaves in my hair?"

"Nay," he mused. "I was thinking how much you've changed since you came to Kildalton."

Tilting her head to the side, she smiled. "More than you know, Duncan."

Oh, he knew all of her secrets, and the knowledge made him bold. "Sit down, Miriam. I have something to tell you."

Attuned to his serious tone, she sat in the straight-backed chair facing him. The sleuthhound lay at her feet. "I'm listening."

He opened his mouth, but the words wouldn't come.

"We're friends, remember?"

He almost chuckled at that. He'd lain naked with her. He'd taken her maidenhead. He'd kissed her from head to toe. He'd tricked her into believing him a buffoon. He'd put his future in her hands. Fine qualities always show through, Angus had taught him. In times of trouble, the cream of a man's soul rises to the top.

"You'll feel better when you tell me," she coaxed, a confident twinkle in her eyes.

Guilt sapped his courage. "I doona think *you'll* feel better, Miriam."

She looked him straight in the eye. "Have you lied to me?"

"Aye."

"Have you betrayed our friendship?"

She seemed fearless. Why not? She'd spent years facing clever kings and wily diplomats. "I canna say for certain, but it's debatable."

Her chin came up a notch. "Tell me."

Do it, his conscience demanded. "I'm the Border Lord."

She blinked, then put a hand over her mouth, and laughed.

Outrage nicked his pride. "Stop that."

"Oh, Duncan," she said behind her hand. "Forgive me . . . but 'tis so—so outrageous." Tears of mirth swam in her eyes.

Stunned, he pounded the arm of the throne. "Outrageous or no, 'tis true."

Between chortles, she said, "And I'm a Persian harem dancer."

Her flippant reply barreled through him like a razor-sharp dirk. "I'll prove it." From his sporran, he pulled a black scarf and tossed it in her lap.

Still sniffling, she dabbed the tears from her eyes. "Even Verbatim has one of these."

Determined, he leaned forward and drilled her with his coldest stare. "I nearly broke my neck climbing the castle wall that night you took the key and locked me out."

"Mrs. Elliott could have told you about the key a moment ago when I went upstairs to fetch it. Ian could have told you about that night in the garden. What did you really wish to tell me?"

He hadn't considered that she wouldn't believe him. "The truth, Miriam. I'm the Border Lord."

"That's the most preposterous thing I've ever heard." She laughed again, so hard her shoulders shook.

Growing desperate, he said, "I'll kiss you. That should be proof enough."

"Oh, Duncan." She stood. "I have no intention of kissing you. Come, Verbatim."

Completely lost, Duncan watched her leave. Cursing himself for a stupid fool, he decided to regroup.

The next morning Miriam hesitated before going down to breakfast. She still smiled when she thought about Duncan's confession. At one time she'd been certain he *was* the Border Lord. But no man could be in two places at once. His reasons baffled her, though. What did he stand to gain? No suitable answer came to mind.

She arrived at the table to learn that half of the meat pies the cook prepared and a full pail of milk had vanished from the pantry. Duncan didn't seem distressed over the news. From his spot at the head of the table, he made a solicitous query about her health and lamented over the small amount of milk she was served.

Throughout the meal he smiled too much and said too little. Until Saladin and Malcolm excused themselves. Over the rim of his tankard, he said, "Do you know my full name, Miriam?"

To verify the date of Malcolm's birth, she'd looked in the family Bible the day the baron had come to Kildalton. Out of respect for Duncan's privacy, she hadn't bothered to read the other entries. "Nay, I do not. Nor do I understand what difference it makes."

Looking every bit like the lord of the keep, he put down the mug and fetched the book. Standing over her, he put the volume in her lap. She stifled another bout of mirth and watched him turn the worn pages. "There," he said.

Searching the line above the tip of his finger, she read the name. Doubt trickled through her certainty.

"Read it aloud, Miriam."

The burr in his voice reminded her of stolen moments in

dark places. Suddenly she *did* know, but the realization sent her mind spinning with questions. Why had he pretended? How could he have handed her the bloody tartan and feigned indifference when he knew her heart was breaking?

"Miriam?"

She needed time to think. He was either the lowest scoundrel or the biggest fool in the realm. Or was she the fool? Confusion and hurt forced her to say, "You're Duncan Andrew Ian Armstrong Kerr."

"Ian. The Border Lord."

Mustering more courage and patience than she'd needed the day the King of France propositioned her, she lifted his hand from the page and closed the book. Then she rose and faced him. "How splendid, Ian. You must tell me about the times you seduced your own governess and left heather on her pillow or the time you wooed the swineherd's grandmother."

His mouth formed a tight, white line. "Those were tales to hide my true identity."

She could see the truth of it now. The lies. The seduction. The bloody tartan. Her hands shook so badly she thought she might drop the book. Thank God for her years of training, but even experience would carry her only so far. She had to get away from him. "Clever tales they were. Well." She slapped the book against his chest. "If you'll excuse me."

She left him clutching the book, his mouth agape. Numb with shock, she walked up the stairs and into her room.

He'd worn spectacles. He'd put his shoes on the wrong feet. He lied from the moment she'd set foot in his ghastly castle. Only when she'd told him about trying to change the queen's mind had Duncan told her the truth.

A weight seemed to press her down. She leaned against the door and fought to keep the heartache at bay. How he must have laughed at her that morning at the swineherd's farm when he'd mocked the legend of the Border Lord. Fairy tales and romantic fiction bored him to tears, he'd said.

"The wretch!" She recalled his sly innuendoes on the morning after their meeting at Hadrian's Wall. "Too much

292

exercise in the wee hours of the morning," he'd said. "I prefer it in the morning, don't you?"

Shame plunged her into despair. In the guise of a bumbling fool he'd ridiculed the love she'd given freely to a dark stranger. The passion-filled nights, the breathless whispers, the time in the tunnel when she'd confronted him.

"Me, Duncan Kerr?" Then he'd laughed and said, "I'm no niddering poltroon."

She thought of the day she'd told him about Glencoe. He'd comforted her. "What would your mother say about you being so sad, Miriam? She wouldn't want that, would she?"

Oh, God. He knew her every secret. Or did he? She touched her still flat stomach. He couldn't know about the child. His child. A child conceived in deception.

Poor baby, she thought. Poor me, she lamented.

She cringed. She was not some green laundry maid to be tricked by a smooth talking butler. She was Miriam Mac-Donald, a world-wise and intelligent woman. If he tried to sway her with seduction, she had just the keepsake to thwart him.

The moment she stepped into his study the next morning, Duncan knew he was in for trouble—her sweet smile, her glittering eyes, her confident air told him so.

She glided toward him, a vision in watered silk. The fabric rustled loudly as she perched on the edge of his desk.

"I've been thinking about what you told me, Duncan." Her hands fluttered with the grace of a butterfly. "I keep asking myself why you would confess to being the Border Lord."

Because I love you, he wanted to say and drop to his knees and beg her forgiveness. But somehow he knew if he showed any weakness she'd pounce on him like a cat on a fat, slow mouse. Aye. She wanted to toy awhile with her prey.

Resigned to his comeuppance, but determined to control the game, he put on a casual smile. "We're friends, Miriam. Do you believe me?"

She pursed her pretty lips and looked affronted. "I believe the part about our being friends. How could I not? We've shared much, you and I. After all, I told you about Glencoe."

A stab of guilt stole his breath. Why in bloody hell had she chosen to wear her hair loose, the shimmering, flame red waves falling over her shoulders and pooling on his desk. His fingers twitched with the urge to touch her silken curls, to peel off that frothy dress and kiss all of her pink spots. "I—uh—" Lust clogged his throat. He coughed to cover his discomfort. "I thought 'twas time we shared more."

She examined her fingernails. "I don't believe you're the Border Lord."

Slyly said, the statement sounded like a challenge. Well, he could be sly, too. "I wonder what I could say or do to convince you?"

"I've been perplexed by that very notion." Her gaze roamed his face before settling on his eyes. "The Border Lord knows things, I suppose."

Such as she loved him and carried his child. True, he'd acted like the most heartless of cavaliers, but damn her, she ought to forgive him. "What," he said, taking her hand and stroking her palm, "would you like to know?"

She gasped, but recovered her composure with a skill he'd witnessed and cursed a hundred times. "Where is Adrienne Birmingham?"

It was the last thing he'd expected her to ask. But leave it to Miriam to catch him off guard. He was thinking of romance. She was thinking about business. "She's in Barbados."

"Did you kidnap her?"

He laughed. "Hardly. I arranged for her and her lover, Charles, to settle in the islands. They're having a go at farming sugar cane."

"You could have accomplished her escape as Duncan Kerr. Adrienne stayed here when your wife died. You said you were friends with her. You didn't have to don a cape and disguise yourself. How did you manage the black hair?"

Hell and damnation! She'd maneuvered him into a corner. He hadn't expected direct questions on exact topics. Why couldn't she be as predictable as other women? The answer lifted his spirits. "I used lampblack." He touched his side whiskers. "Here." He touched his eyebrows. "And here."

She stared at the arm of his chair. "How clever of you."

He allowed himself one stupid question. "Are you angry?"

"Angry? Of course not." She stood up and made a production of straightening her skirts. "That would suggest I believe you."

Weary of the charade and fearful of losing her, he rushed to her side and pulled her into his arms. "If my words wilna convince you, Miriam. This will."

The instant his lips touched hers, he saw the folly in his plan. He should have wooed her slowly and built upon the friendship they'd begun. Instead he'd come on like a lusty buck eager for his first doe. But recriminations receded, became lost in the feel of her mouth opening beneath his and the gentle way she leaned into his chest. His Miriam, a prize beyond value, a woman to cherish.

Cherish her, he did. He kissed her with finesse, knowing that when he twirled his tongue with hers, she always sighed, then took the lead. Caught up in the kiss and anticipating the forgiveness he knew would follow, Duncan gloried in the embrace, pressing her closer.

Her soft sigh urged him on and confirmed what he knew in his heart—she loved him. An instant later she became the aggressor, wrapping her arms around him and slanting her lips across his to achieve a greater intimacy. Eager too, he caressed her breasts until he grew frustrated with the barriers between them. He reached into her bodice, and rather than the soft swelling mound he expected, he encountered fabric.

Confused, he pulled back and opened his eyes. Nestled between her breasts lay the black scarf of the Border Lord.

She stiffened, and her eyes fluttered open. The dreamy passion faded, replaced by a cold hard stare. In a soft, determined whisper, she said, "You don't kiss the same as the Border Lord. And he's taller than you."

"I had the cobbler build up my bootheels."

She whirled, yanked open the door and ran out, slamming it in his face.

"Miriam!" he bellowed. "Come back here!"

He found her at the base of the stairs, her fingers clutching the handrail, her charming smile bestowed on Malcolm, who wore a green bonnet with a pheasant feather.

She curtsied deeply. "Thank you, Robin of the Hood."

Malcolm kissed her hand. "I swear by my trusty bow, I'll not rest until the food thief is caught and . . . and hanged from the castle wall."

"I feel ever so safe, Robin."

"Papa." The boy brandished a quiver and short bow. "Maid Miriam said you wanted to join my band of merry men. We'll find out who's raiding the pantry."

She started up the stairs, her hair swaying, the skirt rustling. Over her shoulder, she said, "Of course, he wants to join your band. Wouldn't he make a fine Little John?"

"Will you, Papa?"

"Aye, as soon as I've finished my conversation with Maid Miriam."

At the landing, she stopped. "Oh, but I wouldn't think of taking up any more of your time."

Frustrated, and uncertain of his next move, Duncan matched her civility. "Until supper, then."

She didn't answer, but Malcolm grumbled, "If we have any."

That night Miriam locked her door, stayed in her room, and requested a dinner tray. When Mrs. Elliott brought it, she smiled apologetically. "The cook roasted a duckling with carrots and turnips, but it's nowhere to be found. So I brought you cheese and scones, and cabbage pudding. There's a full pitcher of milk."

The housekeeper had helped Duncan carry out his charade. That night in the tunnel, she'd pretended to speak to him. "Thank you," said Miriam. "This will be fine. I take it the thief hasn't been found."

Mrs. Elliott surveyed the room. Seeing Miriam's silk dress draped over the foot of the bed, she picked up the gown and hung it in the wardrobe. "Nay, and the oddest thing happened today. The stableman found pastry crumbs in the cage with that toothless badger you brought from Sinclair Manor."

Staring at the bow tied at the back of the housekeeper's apron, Miriam wondered if the woman had seen her in the arms of the Border Lord that time in the tunnel? Had she heard their cries of passion? The possibility embarrassed

Miriam, but she couldn't blame Mrs. Elliott for being loyal to her master. "The earl did tell the stableman to look after Alpin's animals."

"Aye, but the man ain't one to be feeding pastries to a badger." She closed the wardrobe doors, but they swung open again. "More like he'd eat the pies himself." Grunting, she closed the doors again.

"You're wasting your time," Miriam said. "The latch is broken."

"Oh, aye," she said, suddenly nervous. She turned toward Miriam but stared at the carpet. "Do you suppose the Moorish lad could have . . . ?"

The implication was clear, and like a mother hen protecting her chick, Miriam leaped from the bed. "Saladin is his name, and his religion forbids him to eat meat."

The housekeeper looked up, her brown eyes narrow with indignation. "Pardon me, my lady," she said without a smidgen of remorse. "I know the lad's eating habits. I'm the one who sends the potboy after quinces and nuts and instructs the cook to prepare his soup without meat. I only wondered if Saladin had a devotion for the crippled creatures. He does take special care of your hound."

Abashed but still distrustful of the woman, Miriam softened her tone. "Thank you for seeing after his diet. Others, even in his own native land, have not been so kind toward Saladin. I assure you, he is no thief. His religion forbids that, too."

Mrs. Elliott glanced about the room and Miriam noticed tears in her eyes. "I'm sorry, my lady, for . . . for . . ."

"For tricking me?"

Brackets of misery framed her mouth. "Aye."

Harboring a grudge against a servant was unfair. "I forgive you, Mrs. Elliott, but don't ask me to forgive your master. Good night."

"Good night, my lady."

The housekeeper left. Miriam locked herself in and sat down to eat. Expecting Duncan to knock on the door at any moment and demand entry so he could practice his wily ways, she jumped at every pop of the fire and rehearsed a dozen rebukes. She had just finished off the milk when the knock came.

But it wasn't Duncan with wooing on his mind. It was Saladin with Verbatim on a leash. Calling herself a fool for feeling disappointment, she said good night to Saladin and locked the door after him.

She brushed her hair, brushed Verbatim, then picked up a book of sonnets. The romantic verses depressed her even more than the duplicity of her lover. Disgusted with herself and the muddle she'd made of her perfectly decent and respectable life, she blew out the candle, drew the curtains around the bed, and tried to sleep.

Like scenes from a tragic novel, every encounter with Duncan Kerr stood out vividly in her mind. She saw him as the bumbling earl, feigning innocence, deploring violence, and befriending her all the while. She saw herself as the dutiful diplomat, believing him, trusting him, while trying to make a peace. He'd lulled her into naïveté, and when her defenses were down, he'd come to her in the night and stolen her heart. Falling in love was her mistake. She didn't blame him for taking what she so freely gave. What she couldn't reckon was the theft of her pride.

She saw him laughing at her behind the spectacles, and tried to picture herself as he must surely see her: a woman too long on the shelf, with only a perfect memory and a collection of diplomatic successes to her name. She could supply favorable references from the crowned heads of Europe, but they wouldn't buy the respect or earn the honesty of the man she had foolishly come to love.

Oh, what an oddity he must think her. Thank goodness, Alexis hadn't been here to see Miriam's humiliation. Feeling miserable, she surrendered to the tears and cried herself to sleep.

Duncan stood in the drafty tunnel and shivered with cold. He cupped his hands to his mouth and blew on his fingers to warm them. A dozen times today, he'd raced up the stairs, determined to beat down her door and demand her forgiveness. A dozen more times, he'd dragged himself upstairs and dawdled at her door, his mind awhirl with spineless entreaties. Should he play the Border Lord and force her? Should he become the bumbling earl and beg? Which man was he?

He didn't know anymore.

He'd spent so much time portraying the kind of man he thought he should be that he'd lost track of himself. Only one thing was certain: he loved Miriam MacDonald with his heart and soul. And by God, he would keep her.

He'd left orders with Mrs. Elliott that he was unavailable to everyone, even the queen herself. He intended to stay in this room with Miriam until she forgave him.

Now determined, he slid open the panel, held her clothes aside, and stepped through the wardrobe. A cold, canine nose touched his hand. He jumped and whacked his elbow on the wardrobe door. Stifling a curse, he patted the dog until his heartbeat had slowed and the pain receded. Then he tiptoed to the bed, stripped off his clothes, and climbed in beside her.

She stirred, but didn't wake. Taking advantage of her movement, he tunneled an arm beneath her and pulled her against his chest. She cuddled against him, and he breathed in the smell of her perfume, letting her freshness intoxicate his senses as easily as the woman besotted his mind.

In repose, she felt fragile and yielding, a world away from the resilient, determined diplomat. Which man did she want? She'd given herself to the Border Lord, but she'd befriended the gentle earl? Companion or lover, which role should he play?

Miriam came awake and stiffened beside Duncan. His arms circled her in a hold she couldn't break.

"What are you doing here?"

Against her hair, he said, "I wilna justify so stupid a question, lass. You know exactly why I'm here."

"I will not forgive you."

"Aye, I trow you will."

"Don't think you can woo me with your deceitful Scottish words. I've heard enough to last a lifetime."

"That, sweetheart, is precisely the reason I'm here. To discuss the rest of your life."

She clutched his upper arms and gasped. "Sweet heaven, you're naked!"

He chuckled at her outrage. The rush of her breath against his neck and the rise and fall of her breasts against his chest

300

eminded him vividly of their past embraces. "You've seen ne naked before—a number of times as I recall."

"That's a lie. You only slither into my life in the dark of night."

"Your perfect memory has deserted you, love. You looked under my tartan once when I was scuffling with Malcolm. Doona deny it."

"'Twas an accident, and not at all like . . ."

He stroked her arm. Her skin felt satin smooth beneath his roughened palms. "Like what?"

"Like the other times," she blurted. "And get out of my bed this instant or I'll order Verbatim to chew off your head."

Patience, he told himself. "She won't hurt me. You told her I was a friend, remember? She knows who I am."

At length, she said, "You cur!"

"Aye, Kerr, the name of the man you love."

Her fingernails started a slow rake down his arm. Wincing, he grasped her wrists, rolled her onto her back, then settled atop her. "We'll have none of that."

"We'll have nothing else, either." She moved against him, trying to break his hold. "Get off me!"

Passion spiraled through him and flooded his loins with need. He tried to stifle a groan, but failed. Instinctively, his hips rocked against her.

"Oh, Lord, you're—you're . . ."

"Very excited by you."

"I don't want you excited. I don't want you at all. You're a liar."

Duncan suppressed his physical needs. "I did lie, Miriam, but I believed I had no choice. I thought you were like the others the queen had sent, but when I realized I couldn't buy your favor with money, I . . ." The words died on his lips.

"You seduced me."

Frustrated at his inadequacy to explain himself, Duncan blurted, "I didna intend to actually seduce you."

"Ha! You've tripped yourself up. I knew you didn't really want me."

Softly, he said, "I wanted you enough to put my life and my son's future in your hands. I love you. Please forgive me."

301

The honesty in his voice warmed Miriam like brandy on a cold night. Weakness and love assailed her, but she was too heartsore to believe him. "Easy words for you to say, Duncan. Or are you Ian tonight?"

He jerked away from her. The mattress shifted as he moved to the edge of the bed. She'd become so accustomed to their visits in the dark that she could almost see his every movement.

His breath came out in an impatient huff. "I don't know who I am, and that's the sad truth of it."

The tangible pull of his frustration reached out to her. "What do you mean?"

He pulled back the bedcurtain and lit the candle on the nightstand. A soft yellow glow illuminated his golden hair and exposed his inner struggle. Shoulders slumped, he looked troubled to his soul, and nothing like the dark lover she had lain with so often.

She bit her lip to keep from saying the words he wanted to hear. Now was the time to listen.

"I thought," he began in a rough whisper, "that by reviving the Border Lord I could gain justice for my people without living up to the reputation of my father."

So noble a sentiment absolved him, didn't it? She wasn't sure; there was too much unsaid between them. "What of the bumbling earl who makes the finest lures in Scotland?"

He slid her a sideways glance. Smiling crookedly, he said, "He got himself hooked by a red-haired Scotswoman who's too smart for her own good."

Laughter brought tears to her eyes. "I'm not certain if that's a compliment."

He leaned over her, his powerful shoulders blocking out the light, his hands bracketing her head. "Then be certain of this, Miriam MacDonald. I love you as I love Scotland. I'm a sorry wretch who doesn't deserve you, and if you'll but give me the chance, I'll spend the rest of my life making you happy. Marry me."

Joy curled in her belly and tightened her womb. "I'm pregnant."

He flashed a broad smile. "I know. I've been watching you from a tunnel behind that wardrobe. I saw you crying the day I gave you the tartan."

She remembered the pain, the loneliness. "You hurt me."

"Aye. I'm sorry for that, too. 'Twas the poorest piece of work I've ever done." He lay beside her and spread his hand over her stomach. "Will you forgive the miserable father of this remarkable babe?"

She'd start apologizing herself if he didn't stop being so sweetly charming. "You have no idea if she'll be remarkable or rotten. Stop dodging my questions."

"She?"

Miriam couldn't help but smile at his astonished tone. "You're dodging again."

With his lips a breath away from hers, he said, "Aye, 'tis a fault for sure."

"Wait! No kissing yet. You have a lot of explaining to do."

He fell back against the pillow. "All right."

"Did you know how to wield a sword before I came here?"

"Aye. The Grand Reiver insisted I learn."

She could imagine how cruel the lessons had been. "Do you fence?"

"I wilna tell you. But after the bairn comes, you can challenge me and find out."

"You could learn between now and then."

"I promise," he whispered, "never to be out of your sight."

Happiness purled inside her. "Does Malcolm know you're the Border Lord?"

"Nay."

"What will he say about us?"

Duncan chuckled, his breath caressing her ear. "He'll probably revive the archbishop of Canterbury, turn the chapel into Westminster Abbey, and insist on performing the ceremony himself."

She shivered and snuggled closer. "Seriously."

"He'll be excited, Miriam. He needs you almost as much as I do."

"Then let's tell him now."

He groaned. "I had other plans for the evening. Besides, he's playing sentry in the kitchen."

The thief. "I wonder who's stealing the food."

His arms grew taut. "Alpin is. She stowed away in the sleigh. I thought you knew."

"How did you find out?"

"I almost knocked her down in the tunnel. She's hiding in the tower room waiting for her Night Angel to rescue her."

The candle sputtered, casting shadows on his face. "The Border Lord," she said.

"Aye. Adrienne asked me to watch out for the lass. She's so headstrong. Compared to her, you're malleable, love."

"Oh, really?"

He pulled her over him. "Aye, and don't get huffy with me."

A lifetime of happiness loomed before her. "What will you do?"

Smiling, he said, "This . . ."

Then his mouth touched hers and she forgot bumbling earls and dark strangers and kissed Duncan Andrew Ian Armstrong Kerr, the man she loved.

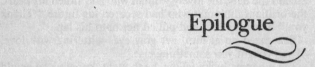

Epilogue

A week later Duncan strolled into the keeping room and sat in his favorite chair. Miriam had insisted he return the Kerr throne to the dais where it had stood since the first earl of Kildalton swore fealty to the first Stewart king of Scotland.

The ancient wood felt warm and satiny to the touch. Duncan surveyed the empty room until his gaze fell on the portrait of his father. Love, hatred, and regret seared him.

"Banish that thought, my lord!"

Covered from neck to toe in a fur-lined robe of soft blue velvet, her glorious hair trailing to her waist, her face flushed from the cold, Miriam stood in the doorway. "Alexis and Angus are coming."

Hatred and regret fled. Duncan patted the arm of his throne. "Good. Sit with me."

She hesitated, then pulled a beribboned document from beneath the robe. "I sent Alexander to meet them. He brought me this."

Duncan saw the royal seal. It was broken. Anne had exercised her divine right. Miriam already knew what the queen had decided. He looked deeply into Miriam's eyes but could not read her thoughts. Struggling to keep the fear from his voice, he said, "Has she ordered me to give up Malcolm?"

Miriam glided toward him. "No. Should you change your mind about fostering your son, you'll decide where he's to go. Her Majesty has also ordered the baron to make restitution for all the farms he's burned and the lives he's taken."

Weak with relief, Duncan slumped against the high back of the family throne. Through misty eyes he watched her ascend the dais, the lovely woman who had stolen his heart, the brilliant diplomat who had secured his future. "Thank you," he whispered, and pulled her onto his lap.

She gazed up at him, her gray eyes glittering with love. "I've brought you something else."

I'm a happy, lucky fellow, he thought, knowing he would bask for the rest of his days in the glow of her love. "What?"

Slipping the queen's official writ beneath the sash of his tartan, Miriam clapped her hands. "Sir Francis . . ." she called out.

Malcolm, in the guise of Sir Francis Drake, complete with ruff, padded doublet, and a painted-on mustache and pointy beard, shuffled into the room carrying one end of a long, covered box. Alpin, wearing a new jerkin and leather trews, carried the other end. They struggled with the cumbersome package, then set it on the floor. Something in the box moved.

Duncan bit his lip to keep from laughing out loud. Glancing down at the love of his life, he anticipated mischief. The twinkle in her eyes confirmed it. "What have you brought me?"

She rolled her head toward Malcolm and nodded. With a flourish, the boy whipped the drape off the box.

"Peacocks, my lord," Miriam said. "I remember how much you wanted them."

Once he had cursed her dratted memory. Now it would be the keeper of all their yesterdays and the harbinger of all their tomorrows.

**Pocket Books
Proudly Announces**

BORDER BRIDE

Arnette Lamb

**Coming from Pocket Books
Fall 1993**

**The following is a preview of
Border Bride . . .**

Paradise Plantation
St. George Parish, Barbados
February 1735

Lady Alpin MacKay itched to yank off her mourning veil and fan her heated cheeks. And she would, once her visitor stopped droning on about the qualities of her late cousin Charles and started reading the will.

"A sober man and a defender of the true faith," the solicitor, Othell Codrington, was saying.

Sober? thought Alpin. Poor Charles had drowned his sorrows in rum.

"A widower to envy . . ."

A man to pity. After his wife, Adrienne, passed away, Charles spent a decade grieving himself to death. As an impressionable girl, Alpin had longed to find a man who would love her as deeply as Charles had loved his wife. But Alpin also wanted a man who would not break under tragedy. Years and the reality of island life had crushed her romantic dreams.

". . . a man shrewd in business, yet fair . . ."

A misconception. For ten years Alpin alone had managed every detail of the vast plantation, from purchasing biscuit flour to harvesting sugar cane.

". . . gone to a greater glory . . ."

And the company of his late, beloved wife. Thank God.

A soft breeze wafted across the veranda and filled the air with the sweet aroma of boiling syrup. Alpin sighed. Paradise Plantation would belong to her now: the spacious two-story house, six acres of manicured lawns, one thousand acres of fertile fields recently denuded of muscovado sugar cane, fifty-six English servants, eighty slaves, scores of thatched huts, a dozen narrow barrack houses, four water wells. The wicker chair on which she sat. The copper tub in which she bathed. The carriage, the cart, the chicken roasting on the spit. The precious mill with its twin chimneys streaming smoke into the tropical blue sky. Hers.

The promise of independence sent her spirits soaring. Life on the plantation would continue as it had—except for the slaves. Five years ago she had almost convinced Charles to free them. Neighboring planters had been outraged. Under pressure, Charles had yielded. Alpin would stand fast in her beliefs.

A drop of perspiration made a slow, ticklish slide from her temple to her jaw, down her neck to the collar of her black fustian dress. She stared at the leather satchel perched on the solicitor's lap. Would he never read the will?

When he paused to draw breath, she said, "You're too kind, Mr. Codrington, to save me a trip to Bridge Town. Charles said he would trust his affairs to none but you."

He sat straighter. Sweat streamed from beneath his powdered wig and soaked his lace-trimmed cravat, turning the gentlemanly concoction into a soggy knot of wilted ruffles. "That ever was the case, my dear. Charles made an impressive go of it here." He cast a covetous gaze toward the mill. "Although none of us has ever seen the enterprise."

Let this city lawyer and everyone else think her cousin had managed Paradise and modernized the mill. Let him wonder why her rum earned a premium. Alpin needed no praise for her work, only peace of mind and security. Soon she would have both. She almost strummed her fingers in impatience. "As you say, Charles was a gentleman among men and concerned about the welfare of those in his keeping."

"I met him five years back—before he added that new

contraption to the mill." Codrington opened the satchel, which contained dozens of papers. He withdrew a beribboned document bearing a golden seal the size of a fig. "His generosity was a testament to his Christian convictions." A benevolent smile curled his lips. "He's left you a generous stipend."

She needed no allowance. Profits from the harvest would more than support her. Dumbfounded, she repeated, "A stipend?"

Like a child reading a primer, he traced each line of the document with his forefinger. "There's the usual bequests to servants. A fellowship for his club. Ah, yes. Here it is. One hundred pounds a year to my cousin, Lady Alpin MacKay."

Icy fingers of dread crept over her skin. Her throat grew tight. "And . . ."

"And passage home."

Never! she silently raged. Charles had provided the funds for a visit to the Border of Scotland and England, but only if she wanted to go. Which she didn't. "How considerate of him."

A sand fly landed on Codrington's nose. He swatted it away. "You may, of course, take any family heirlooms."

Knowing the veil concealed her wide-eyed astonishment, Alpin strained to keep her voice calm. She'd cut cane to earn her keep before she'd depend on a man again. "And what of Paradise Plantation?" She held her breath. If Charles had gambled it away or mortgaged it . . .

Codrington batted the fly again. "I am at liberty to say only that five years ago he transferred ownership of all his worldly possessions."

Fear buzzed in her ears, obliterating the pounding of her heart and scattering her thoughts. Paradise gone. Impossible. This was her home. Where would she go? She could challenge Codrington. But to what end? She would expose her bitterness. Jeopardize any chance of righting this wrong. Right it! Keep your wits. There's time aplenty to learn the facts and think out a plan. She took a deep breath and put on a cheery face. "To whom did Charles transfer ownership?"

In a protective gesture, he closed the flap on the satchel and folded his hands over it. "The transfer was a private concern between gentlemen. I'm sworn to secrecy." He handed her the will. "Have you mastered reading, Lady Alpin?"

In four languages. But the slimy toad needn't know that. Let him think her ignorant; his own superiority might loosen his tongue. "The art of deciphering words can be difficult."

Benevolence lent him a pitying air. "I understand. And I suppose I can tell you that Charles, by transferring his estate to another party, repaid an old debt of gratitude."

Gratitude? To whom? How could Charles have been so cruel to leave her with only a paltry allowance? She had forgone marriage to shoulder his responsibilities. And for what? To care for a man who nursed a broken heart from a bottle and passed on his wealth to someone else? Her sacrifice had been for nothing. Someone else owned Paradise. Her stomach roiled. Who?

The answer lay in that satchel. Why else would Codrington guard it so fiercely? A name. She needed a name. Hatred filled her. If she could examine those papers she'd have a target for her ire. She knew the way. Once she had Codrington away from the house, she'd excuse herself for a female necessity. First she had to get his attention. She swept off the veil. He stared, gape-mouthed.

"Is something wrong, sir?"

He fumbled with the satchel. "I ah—you uh . . . It's just that Charles told me—"

"Told you what?"

"He told me that you were unmarriageable, more . . . mature. I expected—" His gaze fell to her breasts. "May I say you have preserved yourself admirably."

The clumsy comment, delivered with a lustful leer, disgusted Alpin. Because she was small, people always thought her younger than her age. As a girl she had hated being mistaken for a child. Now she could use a youthful appearance to her advantage.

"How very thoughtful of you, Mr. Codrington. Would you like to see the mill and the contraption?"

He jumped up so fast, the satchel fell to the floor, forgotten.

Twenty minutes later, her fingers trembling, she opened

the pouch and scanned the legal documents. At the sight of the name on the transfer papers she tossed back her head and groaned through clenched teeth. Her childhood rose up to haunt her.

By the time she replaced the papers and returned to the mill and her guest, Alpin had made her plans. She breathed deeply of the beloved smells of Barbados, but her thoughts had already turned to Scotland and Kildalton Castle. She must mount the next siege in the years-old war with the scoundrel who now controlled her destiny.

Kildalton Castle
May 1735

"And if I refuse?"

His neck craned, the soldier squinted into the dim interior of the falcon mews. "She was prepared for a refusal, my lord, and up to her old tricks, I trow."

Malcolm's hand stilled, his fingers holding a scrap of meat above the open mouth of a hungry owlet. The wounded mother owl looked on. "How is that, Alexander?"

"Lady Alpin said if you doona come and greet her personally, she'll carve out your eyes and feed them to the badgers."

Malcolm dropped the meat into the hungry maw. Childhood memories flashed in his mind: Alpin splintering his toy sword and throwing it down the privy shaft; Alpin howling with laughter as she locked him in the pantry; Alpin hiding in the tower room and crying herself to sleep; Alpin coming after him with a jar of buzzing hornets.

A shudder coursed through him. Years ago she had played havoc with the life of a gullible lad. Now the world-wise man would play havoc with hers. "I wonder what she'll do if I call her bluff?"

Alexander Lindsay moved cautiously down the aisle between roosting falcons, agitated kestrels, and a trio of golden eagles. The predators paced on their perches, wings stirring the air. When he reached Malcolm, Alexander doffed his bonnet and revealed a pate as barren as the pinnacles of Storr. "I only brought the message, my lord. 'Twas not my place to interrogate your guest."

"Guest?" Malcolm laughed. The wide-eyed and downy owlet peeped for more food. Smiling, Malcolm tore another piece of meat from the carcass and fed it to the eager bird. "Tell the Lady Alpin I'm busy."

Alexander eyed the owl with wary curiosity. "The Lady Alpin—she also said if you wilna come, she'll change her mind about forgiving you for what you did to her in the tower room."

"*She* forgive *me?* Blessed Saint Ninian, she's twisted the events of the past. Send her to her kin in Sinclair."

"Aye, sir. England's the place for her kind." Alexander strolled out the door and closed it behind him.

Sinclair Manor. A short hour's ride away, south of Malcolm's Scottish holdings, and past Hadrian's Wall. England. Alpin would hate it there. She always had. Only now she couldn't don the clothing of a boot boy and seek sanctuary in Malcolm's Border fortress. As a lad he'd borne the brunt of her wrath. He'd been seven years old and she six when she'd been justly deemed uncontrollable and exiled to Barbados. Years of separation had dulled the enmity Malcolm felt toward her. But five years ago, when he'd learned of her treachery to her island guardian, he had put in motion the wheels of revenge.

A grinding ache, bone deep and soul scouring, held Malcolm immobile. Sensitive to his moods, the birds grew restless, their deadly sharp talons clicking on perches of rough-hewn oak. Malcolm felt cheated, self-betrayed, for he made a practice of leaving his cares outside the door of this darkened sanctuary. Today he'd brought them inside with them.

He'd also maneuvered Alpin MacKay into a corner. In a week or so he'd pay a call on her at the home of his English neighbor. Then he'd watch Alpin squirm like a mouse in a claw. Darkly pleased, he forced away the old pain and spoke reassuringly to the distressed owl.

The door swung open. Sunlight flooded the room. The owlet pecked Malcolm's finger. He drew back his hand, his senses fixed on the figure of a woman standing in the doorway.

"Hello, Malcolm." Her panniered skirt almost filling the opening, her features obscured by the brightness of the light, Alpin MacKay stepped into Malcolm's private haven.

Darkness settled over the mews again. Malcolm watched her blink, trying to focus her eyes. Alpin's expertise lay in deceit and avarice. Which, he wondered, would she practice first?

Although his thoughts hinged on past injustices, Malcolm couldn't help but admire the pleasant changes that had occurred in his childhood nemesis.

He remembered a scrawny hoyden with a grudge against the world, her matted hair trailing to her waist, and freckles dotting her nose and cheeks. Yet Alpin MacKay had matured into a vision of petite femininity. No taller than his chest, she looked small enough for him to carry on his hip, her neck slender enough for him to circle with one hand.

She wore a gown of sunny yellow satin, the bodice cut square across the top and dropping to a point below her narrow waist. Her dress was modest, but not even a monk's robe could hide the bountiful charms of Alpin MacKay.

"Where are you, Malcolm? I can't see." Her alluring violet eyes surveyed the mews. "Say something so I can find you."

The rich, husky quality of her voice also seemed at odds with the caviling shrew he'd been certain she'd become. But he'd changed, too, as she'd soon discover.

He tossed the rabbit carcass to the watchful mother owl, then walked to the door. "I'm here, Alpin."

She jumped back, her skirts tipping over an empty bucket. "Oh!" Delicate fingers curled around his forearm. "Please don't let me fall."

As a child she had always smelled of the food she filched and the animals she rescued. As a woman she smelled of sweet, exotic flowers blossoming in a tropical sun. The idea that anything about Alpin MacKay would please him shocked Malcolm more than her presence in his sanctuary. She should have gone to Sinclair Manor. Events of late had left her nowhere else to go. Malcolm had planned it that way.

"I doubt you would fall," he said. "You were always nimble on your feet."

She laughed, tipped back her head and squinted up at him. "That was before stays, skirts as big as hayricks, and modern shoes. Are you standing on a box?"

"A box?"

Her expression softened, but her eyes were still adjusting to the darkness. "Either that or you've grown tall as an oak."

He stared at the crown of her head and the thick coil of braids she'd made of her hair. Mahogany hued ringlets the size of his little finger framed her face. "You don't seem to have grown at all."

She pursed her lips. "I expected a more original observation from you, Malcolm Kerr. A kinder one, too."

She could expect whatever the hell she wanted, but James III would sit on the throne of the British Isles before she'd get kindness from Malcolm Kerr. "Why, I wonder," he mused, "for kindness was never the way between us."

"Because . . . because we've known each other for so long."

"A circumstance," he murmured, "that brought me great heartache and other assorted pains as a lad."

"Oh, come now." She leaned into him, her shoulder pressing against his ribs. "Surely after twenty years you've outgrown hating me. I've certainly outgrown playing tricks on you."

Tricks? She had a gift for understatement. "But you haven't outgrown threats, unless carving out my eyes and feeding them to badgers is your way of greeting an old acquaintance."

She quivered with indignation, a trait she'd mastered before she'd lost her milk teeth. "You are *not* an acquaintance. You're my oldest friend. And I was only jesting."

"I'm relieved, then," he mocked and threw open the door. Shielding his eyes from the sunlight, he stepped outside. Alpin's closed carriage stood across the castle yard. Releasing her, Malcolm turned, plunged his arms into a barrel of rainwater and began scrubbing his hands. "It's nice of you to visit. You had a pleasant voyage?"

"Visit?" Lifting her chin, she cupped her hands over her

brow to shield her eyes from the sun. "I've come all the way from Barbados to see you, and all you have to say is some insipid nicety before sending me off?" A sheen of tears glistened in her eyes. "I'm wounded, Malcolm. And perplexed."

Guilt pricked his conscience. He hadn't witnessed the trouble she'd caused in Barbados. He believed it, though, for Alpin MacKay could turn a May Fair into a bloody feud. "I had no intention of wounding you."

She smiled and rubbed her eyes. "I'm relieved," she said in a rush. "I have a million questions to ask you, and that many stories of my own to bore you with. You can't believe how different Barbados is—" She stopped, her eyes wide in surprise.

"What's amiss?" he said, thinking he'd never seen a woman with lashes so long and skin so sweetly kissed by the sun. He knew her age to be twenty-seven. She looked nineteen.

"My God," she breathed, her gaze scouring his face. "You're the image of my Night Angel."

Admiration turned to puzzlement. "Night Angel?"

She stared at the old tiltyard, concentration creasing her forehead. At length she shook her head as if clearing her thoughts. "'Tis nothing but my memory deceiving me. Your hair's so dark, and yet you favor Lord Duncan."

At the mention of his father, Malcolm thought again about the misery this selfish woman had visited on everyone who had ever befriended her. But now was not the time to reveal his feelings or his plans for Alpin MacKay. Now was the time to bait her with friendship and go fishing for her trust. "Mother would certainly agree that I favor Papa."

"You mean Lady Miriam. How is she?"

Honestly he said, "My stepmother is still the fairest of women."

Alpin turned to the castle entrance, excitement dancing in her unusual eyes. "Is she here?"

"Nay. She and Papa are in Constantinople."

"I'm disappointed. She was always kind to me. I did so want to see her. Is she still a diplomat?"

Pride and affection warmed him. "Aye. Sultan Mahmud

wants a peace with Persia. He asked King George to send her."

A sigh lifted Alpin's shoulders and drew his attention to the symmetrical planes of her collarbone and the thin gold chain that disappeared into her cleavage. "Must be grand to be so valued," she said. "Imagine the king asking favors."

The soldiers on the wall had turned to stare. The fletcher stood in the door of his shop conversing with Alexander Lindsay. Passersby slowed, their curious gazes darting from their laird to his lovely visitor. Malcolm reached for a towel. "I think she would prefer a sojourn in Bath to a summer in Byzantium."

"I prefer the Borders. It's grand to be home." Alpin scanned the battlements, then the castle towers. "Have you brothers and sisters?"

Home? He considered challenging her absurd declaration, but decided to cast out another line of cordiality. "Aye, I've three sisters."

A dimple dented her cheek. "Oh, how wonderful for you. Are they here?"

He almost laughed and revealed how peaceful his home had become without his gregarious siblings. He had no business speaking so casually to Alpin MacKay. He had business with her all right. The very gratifying business of retribution. He tossed the towel aside. "Nay. The eldest married last fall. The other two are with Mama and Papa."

Alpin threaded her arm through his and strolled toward the carriage, pulling him along. "I can't imagine why they'd want to leave this place."

Looking down he could see the mounds of her breasts and a familiar Roman coin at the end of a chain. His mind fogged with hazy images of a skinny ass and stick-thin legs shinnying up the drainpipe on the castle tower. Lord, she'd changed. "You always hated Kildalton Castle."

"Oh, Malcolm. I was such an angry child." Her guileless expression softened his heart. Her lush assets had an opposite and unwelcome effect. "I had nothing, no one, back then. I always felt safe and protected here. Don't you?"

"Well, aye," he found himself saying. "Kildalton Castle has a way of capturing your soul."

"See?" She hugged his arm. "You're a romantic at heart."

She'd been a solitary child. Before his death her guardian in Barbados had lamented in his letters to Malcolm that he feared she'd never find a kindred spirit. Now she was destitute. What farce did she play? "You've had quite a change of heart," he said.

"Of course." Her hand touched his. "I'm a woman now."

He didn't need his father's fake spectacles to see that. "You used to call me a sniveling cur."

She looked at his arms, his chest, his neck. An artless, feminine smile again revealed that dimple. "Don't expect me to call you names now. You're a formidable presence, Malcolm Kerr."

If he didn't know better he'd think she was flirting. The prospect both baffled and inspired him. He stared at the ancient coin. "You're an interesting surprise, Alpin MacKay."

"Oh! Do you truly think so?" She squeezed his hand and turned her attention to the row of new barracks against the castle wall. "Wasn't the butcher's shop there?"

Memory stirred his ire. "The butcher *used* to be there. You tossed his knives into the blacksmith's forge and set fire to his chopping block."

"You remember?" She shook her head, jostling the heavy coil of braids. "I was so selfish."

"Except to strays or injured beasts."

"You remember that too." A wistful smile enhanced her youthful appearance. "I couldn't bear to see any animal hurt. What ever happened to Hattie?"

"Your three-legged rabbit." Years ago, in an attempt to win the favor of Malcolm's father, her uncle had forced her to give up her pet to Malcolm. Alpin had been forlorn. An hour later she had rallied and in a wicked move she had wrecked Malcolm's future. Even now the wound smarted. "Hattie turned out to be an exceptional breeder." The irony of the subject made him grin. "Sweeper's Heath is overrun with brown rabbits."

"I knew you'd care for her. Will you take me to Sweeper's Heath? I'd love to see Hattie's offspring."

Like a blow from a well-trained opponent, reality struck him. Her guardians were dead. The plantation in Barbados she had called home now belonged to Malcolm. But she couldn't know that. The transaction had been a private affair.

"Will you, Malcolm?"

"That depends. Why are you here now?"

New tears filled her eyes. "You mean why am I here *at last*. Oh, Malcolm. For years I begged Charles to send me home. There was never enough money, he said. Then after dear Adrienne died he hardly spoke at all. The rum finally killed him, you know. He did leave me a stipend. So I dashed out straightaway and bought passage on the first packet home."

"Come now, Alpin," he scoffed. "You hated the Borders."

"I hated everything and almost everyone then, or have you forgotten?" As if brushing away a pesky insect, she waved her hand. "Enough about me. I've a surprise in the carriage."

Malcolm shortened his long stride to match her quick, determined steps. He wondered what sort of wounded creature she'd brought. As they approached the carriage he noticed the trunks and hat boxes fastened to the boot. "You haven't been to see your uncle?"

She sent him a puzzled frown. "I thought only of coming to you."

He'd schemed to get her home and under the control of the uncle she hated. If she thought to avoid her fate, she'd be disappointed—another prospect Malcolm relished. He lifted an eyebrow. "What would your uncle say?"

"Oh! I've been too bold." She ducked her head, but not before he saw a flush stain her cheeks. "Island life loosens the manners and the tongue, or so the visitors say. It's just that you and I were so close."

"We were close all right, especially when you held a dirk to my throat and tied me to a tree." He shuddered at the thought of what had come after.

She reached for the carriage door. "Let's not squabble. I'm harmless now, I assure you."

Oh, aye, he thought, as harmless as Eve with a bushel of quinces. But he was no naive Adam, languishing in Eden and yearning for forbidden fruit. He *was* a lord of the Border, perilously trapped between Jacobite clan chiefs to the north and loyal English subjects to the south. He needed a pretty diversion. He wanted retribution. So he'd meddled in her future and reduced her alternatives to none.

"Perhaps," he said, watching her fondle the brass handle, "you would join me for supper before you continue on your way."

Her hand stilled. "Continue on my way?" She again craned her neck to look at him. "I thought you'd want to see me."

He did, but their meetings would be at his convenience and in her uncle's English manor house. "You can't expect to stay here at Kildalton. 'Tis unseemly. After we've eaten, I'll have Alexander escort you across the border to Sinclair."

"My staying here is unseemly?" She chuckled. "Thank you for attempting to flatter me and guard my reputation, but I've been on the shelf for so many years, I'm dusty. Unless you were concerned about *your* reputation. Are you a rogue?"

He braced his hands on his hips and laughed so hard the tassels on his sporran quivered. "If I am, Alpin, you can rest assured I'll keep my lusty proclivities on a short leash."

Her mouth dropped open, and she slapped her hand against her cheek. "It's your wife, isn't it?"

Humor vanished. The old enmity returned in full force. Because of her, he'd never marry. She couldn't know that, but surely the gossips in Whitley Bay told her Malcolm had no wife.

Unable to meet her inquisitive gaze, he stared at the soldiers on the battlement. "I have yet to wed." *Thanks to you.*

"And you're so blasé about your bachelorhood. Unless . . ." Devilry twinkled in her eyes. "You can't be waiting for me to fulfill that childish bargain we made years ago."

Memory failed him. "Which bargain?"

"Since your father wouldn't beget you a baby brother, you made me promise to give you a child. Being only six, I thought 'twas a matter of spending the night alone at the inn in Bothly Green."

"I assume you now know it takes more."

Tucking her chin to her shoulder, she said, "In exchange, you agreed not to tell your father or my uncle that I was hiding in the tower room. You reneged. They found me and packed me off to Barbados."

Bitterness engulfed him. "I did not tell my father that you'd run away from Sinclair Manor. Nor did I tell your uncle you were here."

The intensity of her gaze captured him. "Truly?" she asked, disbelief in her husky tone.

"Truly. So you shouldn't despair at falling under the baron's protection again. He's eager to look after you."

Her confident stare and winsome smile unnerved Malcolm. "I couldn't possibly go to him," she said. "Charles left you his plantation and all his possessions." With a flick of her wrist, she opened the door.

"As one of his possessions, I now belong to you."

Look for *Border Bride* in Fall 1993
Wherever Paperback Books Are Sold